READERS ❧ W9-AAS-432
THE CABINET OF CURIOSITIES

more . . .

THE CABINET of CURIOSITIES

PRESTON & CHILD

THE CABINET of CURIOSITIES

GC

GRAND CENTRAL
PUBLISHING

NEW YORK   BOSTON

Copyright © 2002 by Splendide Mendax, Inc. and Lincoln Child
Excerpt from *Still Life with Crows* copyright © 2003 by Splendide Mendax, Inc. and Lincoln Child

Cover design by Flag
Cover art by Tony Greco
Handlettering by Charles Nix

Grand Central Publishing
Hachette Book Group
237 Park Avenue
New York, NY 10017
www.HachetteBookGroup.com

Grand Central Publishing is a division of Hachette Book Group, Inc. The Grand Central Publishing name and logo is a trademark of Hachette Book Group, Inc.

The Hachette Speakers Bureau provides a wide range of authors for speaking events. To find out more, go to www.hachettespeakersbureau.com or call (866) 376-6591.

The publisher is not responsible for websites (or their content) that are not owned by the publisher.

Printed in the United States of America

Originally published in hardcover by Hachette Book Group
First mass market edition: June 2003
Reissued: April 2010
First one-time-only edition: November 2012

10 9 8 7 6 5 4 3 2 1
OPM

Douglas Preston and Lincoln Child dedicate this book to the teachers, professors, and librarians of America, most especially those who have made a difference in our own lives.

ACKNOWLEDGMENTS

Lincoln Child would like to thank Lee Suckno, M.D.; Bry Benjamin, M.D.; Anthony Cifelli, M.D.; and Traian Parvulescu, M.D., for their assistance. Thanks also to my family, nuclear and extended, for their love and support. Special thanks to Nancy Child, my mother, for operatic advice.

Douglas Preston expresses his great appreciation to Christine and Selene for their invaluable advice on the manuscript, and, as always, would like to give his thanks to Aletheia and Isaac. He would also like to thank James Mortimer Gibbons, Jr., M.D., for his very helpful medical expertise.

We'd like to thank Jon Couch for his tireless and painstaking work on the firearms details of the book. Thanks also to Jill Nowak for her careful reading of the manuscript. And we owe a particularly great debt to Norman San Agustin, M.D., surgeon extraordinaire, for his extensive assistance on surgical technique and his review of the manuscript. And, as always, our deep appreciation to those who make the Preston-Child novels possible, in particular Betsy Mitchell, Jaime Levine, Eric Simonoff, and Matthew Snyder.

Boneyard

ONE

PEE-WEE BOXER SURVEYED THE JOBSITE WITH DISGUST. The foreman was a scumbag. The crew were a bunch of losers. Worst of all, the guy handling the Cat didn't know jack about hydraulic excavators. Maybe it was a union thing; maybe he was friends with somebody; either way, he was jerking the machine around like it was his first day at Queens Vo-Tech. Boxer stood there, beefy arms folded, watching as the big bucket bit into the brick rubble of the old tenement block. The bucket flexed, stopped suddenly with a squeal of hydraulics, then started again, swinging this way and that. Christ, where did they get these jokers?

He heard a crunch of footsteps behind him and turned to see the foreman approaching, face caked in dust and sweat. "Boxer! You buy tickets to this show, or what?"

Boxer flexed the muscles of his massive arms, pretending not to hear. He was the only one on the site who knew construction, and the crews resented him for it. Boxer didn't care; he liked keeping to himself.

He heard the excavator rattle as it carved into the solid wall of old fill. The lower strata of older buildings lay open to the sun, exposed like a fresh wound: above, asphalt and cement; below, brick, rubble, then more brick. And below that, dirt. To sink the footings for the glass apartment tower well into bedrock, they had to go deep.

He glanced out beyond the worksite. Beyond, a row of Lower East Side brownstones stood starkly in the brilliant afternoon light. Some had just been renovated. The rest would soon follow. Gentrification.

"Yo! Boxer! You deaf?"

Boxer flexed again, fantasizing briefly about sinking his fist into the guy's red face.

"Come on, get your ass in gear. This isn't a peepshow."

The foreman jerked his head toward Boxer's work detail. Not coming any closer, though. So much the better for him. Boxer looked around for his shift crew. They were busy piling bricks into a Dumpster, no doubt for sale to some pioneering yuppie around the corner who liked crappy-looking old bricks at five dollars each. He began walking, just slowly enough to let the foreman know he wasn't in any hurry.

There was a shout. The grinding of the excavator ceased suddenly. The Cat had bit into a brick foundation wall, exposing a dark, ragged hole behind it. The operator swung down from the idling rig. Frowning, the foreman walked over, and the two men started talking animatedly.

"Boxer!" came the foreman's voice. "Since you ain't doing squat, I got another job for you."

Boxer altered his course subtly, as if that was the way he'd already been going, not looking up to acknowledge he had heard, letting his attitude convey the contempt he felt for the scrawny foreman. He stopped in front of the guy, staring at the man's dusty little workboots. Small feet, small dick.

Slowly, he glanced up.

"Welcome to the world, Pee-Wee. Take a look at this."

Boxer gave the hole the merest glance.

"Let's see your light."

Boxer slipped the ribbed yellow flashlight out of a loop in his pants and handed it to the foreman.

The foreman switched it on. "Hey, it works," he said, shaking his head at the miracle. He leaned into the hole. The guy looked like an idiot, standing daintily on tiptoe atop a fallen pile of brick, his head and torso invisible within the ragged hole. He said something but it was too muffled to make out. He withdrew.

"Looks like a tunnel." He wiped his face, smearing the dust into a long black line. "Whew, stinks in there."

"See King Tut?" someone asked.

Everyone but Boxer laughed. Who the hell was King Tut?

"I sure as shit hope this isn't some kind of archaeological deal." He turned to Boxer. "Pee-Wee, you're a big, strong fella. I want you to check it out."

Boxer took the flashlight and, without a glance at the weenies around him, hoisted himself up the collapsed pile of bricks and into the hole the excavator had cut into the wall. He knelt atop the broken bricks, shining his light into the cavity. Below was a long, low tunnel. Cracks doglegged up through the walls and across the ceiling. It looked just about ready to collapse. He hesitated.

"You going in, or what?" came the voice of the foreman.

He heard another voice, a whiny imitation. "But it's not in my *union contract*." There were guffaws.

He went in.

Bricks had spilled down in a talus to the floor of the tunnel. Boxer half scrambled, half slid in, raising clouds of dust. He found his feet and stood up, shining the light ahead. It lanced through the dust, not getting far. From inside, the place seemed even darker. He waited for his eyes to adjust and the dust to settle. He heard conversation and laughter from above, but faintly, as if from a great distance.

He took a few steps forward, shining the beam back and forth. Thread-like stalactites hung from the ceiling, and a draft of foul-smelling air licked his face. Dead rats, probably.

The tunnel appeared to be empty, except for a few pieces of coal. Along both sides were a long series of arched niches, about three feet across and five high, each crudely bricked up. Water glistened on the walls, and he heard a chorus of faint dripping sounds. It seemed very quiet now, the tunnel blocking all noise from the outside world.

He took another step, angling the flashlight beam along the walls and ceiling. The network of cracks seemed to grow even more extensive, and pieces of stone jutted from the arched ceiling. Cautiously, he backed up, his eye straying once again to the bricked-up niches along both walls.

He approached the closest one. A brick had recently fallen out, and the others looked loose. He wondered what might be inside the niches. Another tunnel? Something deliberately hidden?

He shined the light into the brick-hole, but it could not penetrate the blackness beyond. He put his hand in, grasped the lower brick, and wiggled it. Just as he thought: it, too, was loose. He jerked it out with a shower of lime dust. Then he pulled out another, and another. The foul odor, much stronger now, drifted out to him.

He shined the light in again. Another brick wall, maybe three feet back. He angled the light toward the bottom of the arch, peering downward. There was something there, like a dish. Porcelain. He shuffled back a step, his eyes watering in the fetid air. Curiosity struggled with a vague sense of alarm. Something was definitely inside there. It might be old and valuable. Why else would it be bricked up like that?

He remembered a guy who once found a bag of silver dollars while demolishing a brownstone. Rare, worth a couple thousand. Bought himself a slick new Kubota riding mower. If it was valuable, screw them, he was going to pocket it.

He plucked at his collar buttons, pulled his T-shirt over his nose, reached into the hole with his flashlight arm, then resolutely ducked his head and shoulders in after it and got a good look.

For a moment he remained still, frozen in place. Then his head jerked back involuntarily, slamming against the upper course of bricks. He dropped the light into the hole and staggered away, scraping his forehead this time, lurching back into the dark, his feet backing into bricks. He fell to the floor with an involuntary cry.

For a moment, all was silent. The dust swirled upward, and far above there was a feeble glow of light from the outside world. The stench swept over him. With a gasp he staggered to his feet, heading for the light, scrambling up the slide of bricks, falling, his face in the dirt, then up again and scrabbling with both hands. Suddenly he was out in the clear light, tumbling headfirst down the other side of the brick pile, landing facedown with a stunning blow. He vaguely heard laughter, which ceased as soon as he rolled over. And then there was a rush to his side, hands picking him up, voices talking all at once.

"Jesus Christ, what happened to you?"

"He's hurt," came a voice. "He's all bloody."

"Step back," said another.

Boxer tried to catch his breath, tried to control the hammering of his heart.

"Don't move him. Call an ambulance."

"Was it a cave-in?"

The yammering went on and on. He finally coughed and sat up, to a sudden hush.

"Bones," he managed to say.

"Bones? Whaddya mean, bones?"

"He's not making any sense."

Boxer felt his head begin to clear. He looked around, feeling the hot blood running down his face. "Skulls, bones. Piled up. Dozens of them."

Then he felt faint and lay down again, in the bright sunlight.

TWO

NORA KELLY LOOKED OUT FROM THE WINDOW OF HER fourth-floor office over the copper rooftops of the New York Museum of Natural History, past the cupolas and minarets and gargoyle-haunted towers, across the leafy expanse of Central Park. Her eye came to rest at last on the distant buildings along Fifth Avenue: a single wall, unbroken and monolithic, like the bailey of some limitless castle, yellow in the autumn light. The beautiful vista gave her no pleasure.

Almost time for the meeting. She began to check a sudden swell of anger, then reconsidered. She would need that anger. For the last eighteen months, her scientific budget had been frozen. During that time, she had watched the number of museum vice presidents swell from three to twelve, each pulling down two hundred grand. She had watched the Public Relations Department turn from a sleepy little office of genial old ex-newspaper reporters to a suite of young, smartly dressed flacks who knew nothing about archaeology, or science. She had seen the upper echelons at the Museum, once populated by scientists and educators, taken over by lawyers and fund-raisers. Every ninety-degree angle in the Museum had been converted into the corner office of some functionary. All the money went to putting on big fund-raisers that raised more money for yet more fund-raisers, in an endless cycle of onanistic vigor.

And yet, she told herself, it was still *the* New York Museum: the greatest natural history museum in the world. She was lucky to have this job. After the failure of her most recent efforts—the strange archaeological expedition she'd led to Utah, and the abrupt termination of the planned Lloyd Museum—she needed this job to work out. This time, she told herself, she would play it cool, work within the system.

She turned away from the window and glanced around the office. System or no system, there was no way she could complete her research on the Anasazi-Aztec connection without more money. Most importantly, she needed a careful series of accelerator mass spectrometer C-14 dates on the sixty-six organics she had brought back from last summer's survey of southern Utah. It would cost $18,000, but she had to have those damn dates if she was ever going to complete her work. She would ask for that money now, let the other stuff wait.

It was time. She rose and headed out the door, up a narrow staircase, and into the plush trappings of the Museum's fifth floor. She paused outside the first vice president's office to adjust her gray suit. That was what these people understood best: tailored clothing and a smart look. She arranged her face into a pleasantly neutral expression and poked her head in the door.

The secretary had gone out to lunch. Boldly, Nora walked through and paused at the door to the inner office, heart pounding. She *had* to get the money: there was no way she could leave this office without it. She steeled herself, smiled, and knocked. The trick was to be nice but firm.

"Come in," said a brisk voice.

The corner office beyond was flooded with morning light. First Vice President Roger Brisbane III was sitting behind a gleaming Bauhaus desk. Nora had seen pictures of this space back when it belonged to the mysterious Dr. Frock. Then it had been a real curator's office, dusty and messy, filled with fossils and books, old Victorian wing chairs, Masai spears, and a stuffed dugong. Now, the place looked like the waiting room of an oral surgeon. The only sign that it might be a museum office was a locked glass case sitting on Brisbane's desk, inside of which reposed a number of spectacular gemstones— cut and uncut—winking and glimmering in little nests of velvet. Museum scuttlebutt held that Brisbane had intended to be a gemologist, but was forced into law school by a pragmatic father. Nora hoped it was true: at least then he might have some understanding of science.

She tried to make her smile as sincere as possible. Brisbane looked sleek and self-assured. His face was as cool, smooth, and pink as the inside of a conch—exquisitely shaved, patted, groomed, and eau-de-cologned. His wavy brown hair, thick and glossy with health, was worn slightly long.

"Dr. Kelly," said Brisbane, exposing a rack of perfect orthodontry. "Make yourself at home."

Nora dropped gingerly into a construction of chrome, leather, and wood that purported to be a chair. It was hideously uncomfortable and squeaked with every movement.

The young VP threw himself back in his chair with a rustle of worsted and put his hands behind his head. His shirtsleeves were rolled back in perfect creases, and the knot of his English silk tie formed an impeccably dimpled triangle. *Was that,* Nora thought, *a bit of makeup on his face, under and around his eyes, hiding a few wrinkles? Good*

God, it was. She looked away, realizing she was staring too hard.

"How go things in the rag and bone shop?" Brisbane asked.

"Great. Fine. There's just one small thing I wanted to talk to you about."

"Good, good. I needed to talk to you, too."

"Mr. Brisbane," Nora began quickly, "I—"

But Brisbane stopped her with a raised hand. "Nora, I know why you're here. You need money."

"That's right."

Brisbane nodded, sympathetically. "You can't complete your research with a frozen budget."

"That's right," repeated Nora, surprised but wary. "It was a tremendous coup to get the Murchison Grant to do the Utah Anasazi survey, but there's no way I can finish the work without a really good series of carbon-14 dates. Good dates are the foundation for everything else." She tried to keep her voice pleasantly obedient, as if eager to play the ingenue.

Brisbane nodded again, his eyes half closed, swiveling slightly in his chair. Despite herself, Nora began to feel encouraged. She hadn't expected as sympathetic a reaction. It seemed to be working.

"How much are we talking about?" Brisbane asked.

"With eighteen thousand dollars, I could get all sixty-six samples dated at the University of Michigan, which has the best mass spectrometer laboratory for carbon-14 dating in the world."

"Eighteen thousand dollars. Sixty-six samples."

"That's right. I'm not asking for a permanent budget increase, just a one-time grant."

"Eighteen thousand dollars," Brisbane repeated slowly as

if considering. "When you really think about it, Dr. Kelly, it doesn't seem like much, does it?"

"No."

"It's very little money, actually."

"Not compared to the scientific results it would bring."

"Eighteen thousand. What a coincidence."

"Coincidence?" Nora suddenly felt uneasy.

"It just happens to be exactly what you are going to need to cut *out* of your budget next year."

"You're *cutting* my budget?"

Brisbane nodded. "Ten percent cuts across the board. All scientific departments."

Nora felt herself begin to tremble, and she gripped the chrome arms of the chair. She was about to say something, but, remembering her vow, turned it into a swallow.

"The cost of the new dinosaur halls turned out to be more than anticipated. That's why I was glad to hear you say it wasn't much money."

Nora found her breath, modulated her voice. "Mr. Brisbane, I can't complete the survey with a cut like that."

"You're going to *have* to. Scientific research is only a small part of the Museum, Dr. Kelly. We've an obligation to put on exhibitions, build new halls, and entertain the public."

Nora spoke hotly. "But basic scientific research is the lifeblood of this Museum. Without science, all this is just empty show."

Brisbane rose from his chair, strolled around his desk, and stood before the glass case. He punched a keypad, inserted a key. "Have you ever seen the Tev Mirabi emerald?"

"The what?"

Brisbane opened the case and stretched a slender hand toward a cabochon emerald the size of a robin's egg. He plucked it from its velvet cradle and held it up between thumb and forefinger. "The Tev Mirabi emerald. It's flawless. As a gemologist by avocation, I can tell you that emeralds of this size are *never* flawless. Except this one."

He placed it before his eye, which popped into housefly-like magnification. He blinked once, then lowered the gem.

"Take a look."

Nora again forced herself to swallow a rejoinder. She took the emerald.

"Careful. You wouldn't want to drop it. Emeralds are brittle."

Nora held it gingerly, turned it in her fingers.

"Go ahead. The world looks different through an emerald."

She peered into its depths and saw a distorted world peering back, in which moved a bloated creature like a green jellyfish: Brisbane.

"Very interesting. But Mr. Brisbane—"

"Flawless."

"No doubt. But we were talking about something else."

"What do you think it's worth? A million? Five? Ten? It's unique. If we sold it, all our money worries would be over." He chuckled, then placed it to his own eye again. The eye swiveled about behind the emerald, black, magnified, wet-looking. "But we can't, of course."

"I'm sorry, but I don't get your point."

Brisbane smiled thinly. "You and the rest of the scientific staff. You all forget one thing: it *is* about show. Take this emerald. Scientifically, there's nothing in it that you couldn't find in an emerald a hundredth its size. But people don't want to see *any* old emerald: they want to see the *biggest* emerald. *Show,* Dr. Kelly, is the lifeblood of this Museum. How long do you think your precious scientific research would last if people stopped coming, stopped being interested, stopped giving money? You need *collections:* dazzling exhibitions, colossal meteorites, dinosaurs, planetariums, gold, dodo birds, and giant emeralds to keep people's attention. Your work just doesn't fall into that category."

"But my work *is* interesting."

Brisbane spread his hands. "My dear, everyone here thinks their research is the most interesting."

It was the "my dear" that did it. Nora rose from her chair, white-lipped with anger. "I shouldn't have to sit here justifying my work to you. The Utah survey will establish exactly when the Aztec influence came into the Southwest and transformed Anasazi culture. It will tell us—"

"If you were digging up dinosaurs, it would be different. That's where the action is. And it happens that's also where the *money* is. The fact is, Dr. Kelly, nobody seems terribly concerned with your little piles of potsherds except yourself."

"The fact is," said Nora hotly, "that you're a miscarried scientist yourself. You're only playing at being a bureaucrat, and, frankly, you're overdoing the role."

As soon as Nora spoke she realized she had said too much. Brisbane's face seemed to freeze for a moment. Then he recovered, gave her a cool smile, and twitched his handkerchief out of his breast pocket. He began polishing the emerald, slowly and repetitively. Then he placed it back in the case, locked it, and then began polishing the case itself, first the top and then the sides, with deliberation. Finally he spoke.

"Do not excite yourself. It hardens the arteries and is altogether bad for your health."

"I didn't mean to say that, and I'm sorry, but I won't stand for these cuts."

Brisbane spoke pleasantly. "I've said what I have to say. For those curators who are unable or unwilling to find the cuts, there's no problem—I will be happy to find the cuts for them." When he said this, he did not smile.

Nora closed the door to the outer office and stood in the hallway, her mind in turmoil. She had sworn to herself not to leave without the extra money, and here she was, worse off than before she went in. Should she go to Collopy, the Museum's director? But he was severe and unapproachable, and that would surely piss off Brisbane. She'd already shot her mouth off once. Going over Brisbane's head might get her fired. And whatever else she did, she *couldn't* lose this job. If that happened, she might as well find another line of work. Maybe she could find the money somewhere else, rustle up another grant somewhere. And there was another budget review in six months. One could always hope . . .

Slowly, she descended the staircase to the fourth floor. In the corridor she paused, surprised to see the door to her office wide open. She looked inside. In the place she had been standing not fifteen minutes before, a very odd-looking man was now framed by the window, leafing through a monograph. He was wearing a dead black suit, severely cut, giving him a distinctly funereal air. His skin was very pale, whiter than she had ever seen on a living body. His blond hair, too, was almost white, and he turned the pages of the monograph with astonishingly long, slender, ivory fingers.

"Excuse me, but what are you doing in my office?" Nora asked.

"Interesting," the man murmured, turning.

"I'm sorry?"

He held up a monograph, *The Geochronology of Sandia*

Cave. "Odd that only whole Folsom points were found above the Sandia level. Highly suggestive, don't you think?" He spoke with a soft, upper-class southern accent that flowed like honey.

Nora felt her surprise turning to anger at this casual invasion of her office.

He moved toward a bookcase, slid the monograph back into its place on the shelf, and began perusing the other volumes, his finger tapping the spines with small, precise movements. "Ah," he said, slipping out another monograph. "I see the Monte Verde results have been challenged."

Nora stepped forward, jerked the monograph out of his hand, and shoved it back onto the shelf. "I'm busy at the moment. If you want an appointment, you can call. Please close the door on your way out." She turned her back, waiting for him to leave. *Ten percent.* She shook her head in weary disbelief. How could she possibly manage it?

But the man didn't leave. Instead, she heard his mellifluous plantation voice again. "I'd just as soon speak now, if it's all the same to you. Dr. Kelly, may I be so bold as to trouble you with a vexatious little problem?"

She turned. He had extended his hand. Nestled within it was a small, brown skull.

THREE

NORA GLANCED FROM THE SKULL BACK TO THE VISITOR'S face. "Who are you?" Regarding him more carefully now, she noticed just how pale his blue eyes were, how fine his features. With his white skin and the classical planes of his face, he looked as if he'd been sculpted of marble.

He made a decorous gesture somewhere between a nod and a bow. "Special Agent Pendergast, Federal Bureau of Investigation."

Nora's heart sank. Was this more spillover from the trouble-plagued Utah expedition? Just what she needed. "Do you have a badge?" she asked wearily. "Some kind of ID?"

The man smiled indulgently, and slipped a wallet out of his suit pocket, allowing it to fall open. Nora bent down to scrutinize the badge. It certainly looked real—and she had seen enough of them over the last eighteen months.

"All right, all right, I believe you. Special Agent—" She hesitated. What the hell was his name? She glanced down but the shield was already on its way back into the folds of his suit.

"Pendergast," he finished for her. Then he added, almost as if he had read her thoughts: "This has nothing to do with what happened in Utah, by the way. This is an entirely different case."

She looked at him again. This dapper study in black and white hardly looked like the G-men she had met out west. He seemed unusual, even eccentric. There was something almost appealing in the impassive face. Then she glanced back down at the skull. "I'm not a physical anthropologist," she said quickly. "Bones aren't my field."

Pendergast's only reply was to offer her the skull.

She reached for it, curious despite herself, turning it over carefully in her hands.

"Surely the FBI has forensic experts to help them with this sort of thing?"

The FBI agent merely smiled and walked to the door, closing and locking it. Gliding toward her desk, he plucked the phone from its cradle and laid it gently to one side. "May we speak undisturbed?"

"Sure. Whatever." Nora knew she must sound flustered, and was angry at herself for it. She had never met someone quite so self-assured.

The man settled himself into a wooden chair opposite her desk, throwing one slender leg over the other. "Regardless of your discipline, I'd like to hear your thoughts on this skull."

She sighed. Should she be talking to this man? What would the Museum think? Surely they would be pleased that one of their own had been consulted by the FBI. Maybe this was just the kind of "publicity" Brisbane wanted.

She examined the skull once again. "Well, to start with, I'd say this child had a pretty sad life."

Pendergast made a tent of his fingers, raising one eyebrow in mute query.

"The lack of sutural closing indicates a young teenager.

The second molar is only just erupted. That would put him or her at around thirteen, give or take a few years. I would guess female, by the gracile brow ridges. *Very* bad teeth, by the way, with no orthodontry. That suggests neglect, at least. And these two rings in the enamel indicate arrested growth, probably caused by two episodes of starvation or serious illness. The skull is clearly old, although the condition of the teeth suggests a historic, as opposed to prehistoric, dating. You wouldn't see this kind of tooth decay in a prehistoric specimen, and anyway it looks Caucasoid, not Native American. I would say it's at least seventy-five to a hundred years old. Of course, this is all speculation. Everything depends on where it was found, and under what conditions. A carbon-14 date might be worth considering." At this unpleasant reminder of her recent meeting, she paused involuntarily.

Pendergast waited. Nora had the distinct feeling that he expected more. Feeling her annoyance returning, she moved toward the window to examine the skull in the bright morning light. And then, as she stared, she felt a sudden sick feeling wash over her.

"What is it?" Pendergast asked sharply, instantly aware of the change, his wiry frame rising from the chair with the intensity of a spring.

"These faint scratches at the very base of the occipital bone . . ." She reached for the loup that always hung around her neck and fitted it to her eye. Turning the skull upside down, she examined it more closely.

"Go on."

"They were made by a knife. It's as if someone were removing tissue."

"What kind of tissue?"

She felt a flood of relief as she realized what it was.

"These are the kind of marks you would expect to see caused by a scalpel, during a postmortem. This child was autopsied. The marks were made while exposing the upper part of the spinal cord, or perhaps the medulla oblongata."

She placed the skull on the table. "But I'm an archae-ologist, Mr. Pendergast. You'd do better to use the expertise of someone else. We have a physical anthropologist on staff, Dr. Weidenreich."

Pendergast picked the skull up, sealing it in a Ziploc bag. It disappeared into the folds of his suit without a trace, like a magician's trick. "It is precisely your *archaeological* expertise I need. And now," he continued briskly, replacing the telephone and unlocking the door in swift economical movements, "I need you to accompany me downtown."

"Downtown? You mean, like headquarters?"

Pendergast shook his head.

Nora hesitated. "I can't just leave the Museum. I've got work to do."

"We won't be long, Dr. Kelly. Time is of the essence."

"What's this all about?"

But he was already out of her office, striding on swift silent feet down the long corridor. She followed, unable to think of what else to do, as the agent led the tortuous back way down a series of staircases, through Birds of the World, Africa, and Pleistocene Mammals, arriving at last in the echoing Great Rotunda.

"You know the Museum pretty well," she said as she struggled to keep up.

"Yes."

Then they were out the bronze doors and descending the vast sweep of marble stairs to Museum Drive. Agent Pendergast stopped at the base and turned in the bright fall light. His eyes were now white, with only a hint of color. As he moved, she suddenly had the impression of great physical power beneath the narrow suit. "Are you familiar with the New York Archaeological and Historic Preservation Act?" he asked.

"Of course." It was the law that stopped digging or construction in the city if anything of archaeological value was uncovered, until it could be excavated and documented.

"A rather interesting site was uncovered in lower Manhattan. You'll be the supervising archaeologist."

"Me? I don't have the experience or authority—"

"Fear not, Dr. Kelly. I'm afraid we'll find your tenure all too brief."

She shook her head. "But why me?"

"You've had some experience in this, ah, *particular* kind of site."

"And just what kind of site is that?"

"A charnel."

She stared.

"And now," he said, gesturing toward a '59 Silver Wraith idling at the curb, "we must be on our way. After you, please."

FOUR

NORA STEPPED OUT OF THE ROLLS-ROYCE, FEELING uncomfortably conspicuous. Pendergast closed the door behind her, looking serenely indifferent to the incongruity of the elegant vehicle parked amid the dust and noise of a large construction site.

They crossed the street, pausing at a high chain-link fence. Beyond, the rich afternoon light illuminated the skeletal foundations of a row of old buildings. Several large Dumpsters full of bricks lined the perimeter. Two police cars were parked along the curb and Nora could see uniformed cops standing before a hole in a brick retaining wall. Nearby stood a knot of businessmen in suits. The construction site was framed by forlorn tenements that winked back at them through empty windows.

"The Moegen-Fairhaven Group are building a sixty-five-story residential tower on this site," said Pendergast. "Yesterday, about four o'clock, they broke through that brick wall, there. A worker found the skull I showed you in a barrow inside. Along with many, many more bones."

Nora glanced in the indicated direction. "What was on the site before?"

"A block of tenements built in the late 1890s. The tunnel, however, appears to predate them."

Nora could see that the excavator had exposed a clear profile. The old retaining wall lay beneath the nineteenth-century footings, and the hole near its base was clearly part of an earlier structure. Some ancient timbers, burned and rotten, had been piled to one side.

As they walked along the fence, Pendergast leaned toward her. "I'm afraid our visit may be problematic, and we have very little time. The site has changed alarmingly in just the last few hours. Moegen-Fairhaven is one of the most energetic developers in the city. And they have a remarkable amount of, ah, pull. Notice there are no members of the press on hand? The police were called very quietly to the scene." He steered her toward a chained gate in the fence, manned by a cop from whose belt dangled cuffs, radio, nightstick, gun, and ammunition. The combined weight of the accoutrements pulled the belt down, allowing a blue-shirted belly to hang comfortably out.

Pendergast stopped at the gate.

"Move on," said the cop. "Nothing to see here, pal."

"On the contrary." Pendergast smiled and displayed his identification. The cop leaned over, scowling. He looked back up into the agent's face, then back down, several times.

"FBI?" He hiked up his belt with a metallic jangle.

"Those are the three letters, yes." And Pendergast placed the wallet back in his suit.

"And who's your companion?"

"An archaeologist. She's been assigned to investigate the site."

"Archaeologist? Hold on."

The cop ambled across the lot, stopping at the knot of policemen. A few words were exchanged, then one of the cops broke away from the group. A brown-suited man followed at a trot. He was short and heavyset, and his pulpy neck bulged over a tight collar. He took steps that were too big for his stubby legs, giving his walk an exaggerated bounce.

"What the hell's this?" he panted as he approached the gate, turning to the newly arrived cop. "You didn't say anything about the FBI."

Nora noticed that the new cop had gold captain's bars on his shoulders. He had thinning hair, a sallow complexion, and narrow black eyes. He was almost as fat as the man in the brown suit.

The captain looked at Pendergast. "May I see your identification?" His voice was small and tight and high.

Pendergast once again removed his wallet. The captain took it, examined it, and handed it back through the gate.

"I'm sorry, Mr. Pendergast, the FBI has no jurisdiction here, particularly the *New Orleans* office. You know the procedure."

"Captain—?"

"Custer."

"Captain Custer, I am here with Dr. Nora Kelly, of the New York Museum of Natural History, who has been placed in charge of the archaeological survey. Now, if you'll let us in—"

"This is a construction site," broke in the brown-suited man. "We're trying to build a building here, in case you hadn't noticed. They've already got a man looking at the bones. Christ Almighty, we're losing forty thousand dollars a day here, and now the FBI?"

"And who might you be?" Pendergast asked the man, in a pleasant voice.

His eyes flickered from side to side. "Ed Shenk."

"Ah, Mr. *Shenk.*" In Pendergast's mouth, the name sounded like some kind of crude implement. "And your position with Moegen-Fairhaven?"

"Construction manager."

Pendergast nodded. "Of course you are. Pleased to meet you, Mr. Shenk." Immediately, he turned back to the captain, ignoring Shenk completely.

"Now, Captain Custer," he continued in the same mild voice, "am I to understand that you will not open the gate and allow us to proceed with our work?"

"This is a very important project for the Moegen-Fairhaven Group, and for this community. Progress has been slower than it should be, and there's concern at the very highest levels. Mr. Fairhaven visited the site himself yesterday evening. The last thing they want is more delays. I've had no word about FBI involvement, and I don't know anything about any archaeological business—" He stopped. Pendergast had taken out his cell phone.

"Who're you calling?" Custer demanded.

Pendergast said nothing, the smile still on his face. His fingers flew over the tiny buttons with amazing speed.

The captain's eyes darted toward Shenk, then away again.

"Sally?" Pendergast spoke into the phone. "Agent Pendergast here. May I speak with Commissioner Rocker?"

"Now, look—" began the captain.

"Yes, please, Sally. You're a treasure."

"Perhaps we could discuss this inside." There was a rattling of keys. Captain Custer began to unlock the gate.

"If you could kindly interrupt him for me, I'd be so grateful."

"Mr. Pendergast, there's no need for this," said Custer. The gate swung open.

"Sally? I'll call back," said Pendergast, snapping the phone shut.

He stepped past the gate, Nora at his side. Without pausing or speaking, the FBI agent took off across the rubbled ground, trotting directly toward the hole in the brick wall. The others, taken by surprise, began to follow. "Mr. Pendergast, you have to understand—" the captain said as he struggled to keep up. Shenk followed angrily, like a bull. He stumbled, cursed, kept coming.

As they approached the hole, Nora could see a faint glow within, and a flash of light. A pause, another flash. Someone was taking pictures.

"Mr. Pendergast—" Captain Custer called.

But the lithe FBI agent was bounding up the pile of rubble. The others halted at the base, breathing heavily. Nora followed Pendergast, who had already vanished into the dark hole. She paused on the broken wall and peered down.

"Do come in," said Pendergast, in his most inviting southern voice.

She scrambled down the fallen bricks, coming to a stop on the damp floor. There was another flash of light. A man in a white labcoat was bent over, examining something in a small arched niche. A photographer stood at another niche with a four-by-five camera, bracketed by two slave flash units.

The man in the white coat straightened up, peering at them through the dust. He had a thick shock of gray hair that, combined with his round black-framed glasses, made him look faintly like an old Bolshevik revolutionary.

"Who the devil are you, barging in like this?" he cried, his voice echoing down the barrow. "I was not to be disturbed!"

"FBI," rapped out Pendergast. His voice was now totally

different: sharp, stern, officious. With a snap of leather, he shoved his badge toward the man's face.

"Oh," the man said, faltering. "I see."

Nora looked from one to the other, surprised at Pendergast's apparent ability to read people instantly, then manipulate them accordingly.

"May I ask you to please vacate the site while my colleague, Dr. Kelly, and I make an examination?"

"Look here, I'm in the middle of my work."

"Have you touched anything?" It came out as a threat.

"No . . . not really. Of course, I've handled some of the bones—"

"You handled some of the bones?"

"Consistent with my responsibility to determine cause of death—"

"You *handled* some of the *bones?*" Pendergast pulled a thin pad and a gold pen from his jacket pocket and made a note, shaking his head in disgust. "Your name, Doctor?"

"Van Bronck."

"I'll make a note of it for the hearing. And now, Dr. Van Bronck, if you'll kindly let us proceed."

"Yes, sir."

Pendergast watched as the ME and the photographer climbed laboriously out of the tunnel. Then he turned to Nora and spoke in a low, rapid voice. "It's your site now. I've bought us an hour, maybe less, so make the best of it."

"The best of what?" Nora asked in a panic. "Just what am I supposed to be doing? I've never—"

"You're trained in ways that I'm not. Survey the site. I want to know *what happened here*. Help me understand it."

"In an hour? I don't have any tools, anything to store samples—"

"We're almost too late as it is. Did you notice they had the precinct captain on the site? As I said, Moegen-Fairhaven pulls an enormous amount of weight. This will be our only chance. I need the maximum amount of information in the minimum amount of time. It's extremely important." He handed her the pen and pad, then withdrew two slender penlights from his coat and passed one to her.

Nora switched it on. For its size, the penlight was very powerful. She looked around, taking note of her surroundings for the first time. It was cool and silent. Motes drifted in the single banner of light streaming through the broken hole. The air smelled corrupt, a mixture of fungus, old meat, and mold. She breathed it in deeply nevertheless, trying to focus. Archaeology was a slow, methodical business. Here, faced with a ticking clock, she barely knew where to begin.

She hesitated another moment. Then she began to sketch the tunnel. It was about eighty feet long, ten feet high at the arch, bricked up at the ends. The ceiling was filmed with cracks. The dust covering the floor had been recently disturbed, more so than could be explained by the presence of a single medical examiner: Nora wondered how many construction workers and policemen had already wandered through here.

Half a dozen niches ran along both walls. She walked along the wet floor of the tunnel, sketching, trying to get an overall sense of the space. The niches, too, had once been bricked up, but now the bricks had been removed and were stacked beside each alcove. As she turned the flashlight into each niche, she saw essentially the same thing: a jumble of skulls and bones, shreds of clothing, bits of old flesh, gristle, and hair.

She glanced over her shoulder. At the far end, Pendergast was making his own examination, profile sharp in the shaft of light, quick eyes darting everywhere. Suddenly he knelt, peering intently not at the bones, but at the floor, plucking something out of the dust.

Completing her circuit, Nora turned to examine the first niche more closely. She knelt in front of the alcove and scanned it quickly, trying to make sense of the charnel heap, doing her best to ignore the smell.

There were three skulls in this niche. The skulls were not connected to the backbones—they had been decapitated—but the rib cages were complete, and the leg bones, some flexed, were also articulated. Several vertebrae seemed to have been damaged in an unusual way, cut open as if to expose the spinal cord. A snarled clump of hair lay nearby. Short. A boy's. Clearly, the corpses had been cut into pieces and piled in the niche, which made sense, considering the dimensions of the alcove. It would have been inconvenient to fit a whole body in the cramped space, but one severed into parts . . .

Swallowing hard, she glanced at the clothing. It appeared to have been thrown in separately from the body parts. She reached out a hand, paused with an archaeologist's habitual restraint, then remembered what Pendergast had said. Carefully, she began lifting out the clothing and bones, making a mental list as she did so. Three skulls, three pairs of shoes, three articulated rib cages, numerous vertebrae, and assorted small bones. Only one of the skulls showed marks similar to the skull Pendergast had originally shown her. But many of the vertebrae had been cut open in the same way, from the first lumbar vertebra all the way to the sacrum. She kept sorting. Three pairs of pants; buttons, a comb, bits of gristle and desiccated flesh; six sets of leg bones, feet out of their shoes. The shoes had been tossed in separately. *If only I had sample bags,* she thought. She pulled some hair out of a clump—part of the scalp still attached—and shoved it in her pocket. This was crazy: she hated working without proper equipment. All her professional instincts rebelled against such hasty, careless work.

She turned her attention to the clothing itself. It was poor and rough, and very dirty. It had rotted, but, like the bones, showed no signs of rodent gnawing. She felt for her loup, fitted it to her eye, and looked more closely at a piece of clothing. Lots of lice; dead, of course. There were holes that seemed to be the result of excessive wear, and the clothing was heavily patched. The shoes were battered, some with hobnails worn completely off. She felt in the pockets of one pair of pants: a comb, a piece of string. She went through another set of pockets: nothing. A third set yielded a coin. She pulled it out, the fabric crumbling as she did so. It was an Indian head cent, dated 1877. She slipped everything hastily into her own pockets.

She moved to another alcove and again sorted and inventoried the remains as fast as she could. It was similar: three skulls and three dismembered bodies, along with three sets of clothing. She felt in the pockets of the pants: a bent pin and two more pennies, 1880 and 1872. Her eyes returned to the bones: once again, those strange marks on the vertebrae. She looked more closely. The lumbar vertebrae, always the lumbar, opened carefully—almost surgically—and pried apart. She slipped one of them into her pocket.

She went down the tunnel, examining each niche in turn, scribbling her observations in Pendergast's notebook. Each niche held exactly three corpses. All had been dismembered in the same fashion, at the neck, shoulders, and hips. A few of the skulls had the same dissection marks she'd noticed on the specimen Pendergast first showed her. All of the skeletons displayed severe trauma to the lower spinal column. From her cursory examination of skull morphology, they seemed to fit within the same age bracket—thirteen to twenty or so—and were a mixture of male and female, with male predominating. She wondered what the forensic examiner had discovered. There would be time to find that out later.

Twelve niches, three bodies to a niche . . . All very neat, very precise. At the next to the last niche, she stopped. Then she stepped back into the middle of the tunnel, trying hard not to think about the implications of what she was seeing, keeping her mind strictly on the facts. At any archaeological site, it was important to take a moment to stand still, to be quiet, to quell the intellect and simply absorb the feel of the place. She gazed around, trying to forget about the ticking clock, to blot out her preconceptions. A basement tunnel, pre-1890, carefully walled-up niches, bodies and clothes of some thirty-six young men and women. What was it built for? She glanced over at Pendergast. He was still at the far end, examining the bricked-up wall, prying out a bit of mortar with a knife.

She returned to the alcove, carefully noting the position of each bone, each article of clothing. Two sets of britches, with nothing in the pockets. A dress: filthy, torn, pathetic. She looked at it more closely. A girl's dress, small, slender. She picked up the brown skull nearby. A young female, a teenager, perhaps sixteen or seventeen. She felt a wave of horror: just underneath it was her mass of hair, long golden tresses, still tied in a pink lace ribbon. She examined the skull: same poor dental hygiene. Sixteen, and already her teeth were rotting. The ribbon was of silk and a much finer quality than the dress; it must have been her prized possession. This glimmering of humanity stopped her dead for a moment.

As she felt for a pocket, something crackled under her fingers. Paper. She fingered the dress, realizing that the piece of paper wasn't in a pocket at all, but sewn into the lining. She began to pull it from the alcove.

"Anything of interest, Dr. Kelly?"

She started at the medical examiner's voice. Van Bronck. His tone had changed: now he sounded arrogant. He stood over her.

She glanced around. In her absorption, she had not heard him return. Pendergast was by the entrance to the barrow, in urgent discussion with some uniformed figures peering down from above.

"If you call this sort of thing interesting," she said.

"I know you're not with the ME's office, so that must make you an FBI forensics expert."

Nora colored. "I'm not a medical doctor. I'm an archaeologist."

Dr. Van Bronck's eyebrows shot up and a sardonic smile spread over his face. He had a perfectly formed little mouth that looked as if it had been painted on by a Renaissance artist. It glistened as it articulated the precise words. "Ah. *Not* a medical doctor. I believe I misunderstood your colleague. Archaeology. How nice."

She had not had an hour; she had not even had half an hour.

She slid the dress back into the alcove, shoving it into a dusty crevice in the back. "And have you found anything of interest, *Doctor?*" she asked as casually as she could.

"I'd send you my report," he said. "But then, I could hardly expect you to understand it. All that professional jargon, you know." He smiled, and now the smile did not look friendly at all.

"I'm not finished here," she said. "When I am, I'd be glad to chat further." She began to move toward the last alcove.

"You can continue your studies after I remove the human remains."

"You're not moving anything until I've had a chance to examine it."

"Tell that to them." He nodded over her shoulder. "I don't know where you got the impression this was an *archaeological* site. Fortunately, that's all been straightened out."

Nora saw a group of policemen sliding into the barrow, heavy evidence lockers in their hands. The space was soon filled with a cacophony of curses, grunts, and loud voices. Pendergast was nowhere to be seen.

Last to enter were Ed Shenk and Captain Custer. Custer saw her and came forward, picking his way gingerly across the bricks, followed by a brace of lieutenants.

"Dr. Kelly, we've gotten orders from headquarters," he said, his voice quick and high-pitched. "You can tell your boss he's sadly confused. This is an unusual crime scene, but of no importance to present-day law enforcement, particularly the FBI. It's over a hundred years old."

And there's a building that needs to be built, Nora thought, glancing at Shenk.

"I don't know who hired you, but your assignment's over. We're taking the human remains down to the ME's office. What little else is here will be bagged and tagged."

The cops were dropping the evidence lockers onto the damp floor, and the chamber resounded with hollow thuds. The ME began removing bones from the alcoves with rubber-gloved hands and placing them into the lockers, tossing the clothing and other personal effects aside. Voices mingled with the rising dust. Flashlight beams stabbed through the murk. The site was being ruined before her eyes.

"Can my men escort you out, miss?" said Captain Custer, with exaggerated courtesy.

"I can find my own way," Nora replied.

The sunlight temporarily blinded her. She coughed, breathed in the fresh air, and looked around. The Rolls was still parked at the street. And there was Pendergast, leaning against it, waiting.

She marched out the gate. His head was tilted away from the sun, his eyes half closed. In the bright afternoon light, his skin looked as pale and translucent as alabaster.

"That police captain was right, wasn't he?" she said. "You've got no jurisdiction here."

He slowly lowered his head, a troubled look on his face. She found her anger evaporating. He removed a silk handkerchief from his pocket and dabbed at his forehead. Almost as she watched, his face reassumed its habitual opaque expression, and he spoke. "Sometimes, there's no time to go through proper channels. If we'd waited until tomorrow, the site would have been gone. You see how quickly Moegen-Fairhaven works. If this site *were* declared of archaeological value, it would shut them down for weeks. Which of course they could not allow to happen."

"But it *is* of archaeological value!"

Pendergast nodded. "Of course it is. But the battle is already lost, Dr. Kelly. As I knew it would be."

As if in response, a large yellow excavator fired up, its motor coughing and snarling. Construction workers began to appear, emerging from trailers and truck cabs. Already the blue lockers were coming out of the hole and being loaded into an ambulance. The excavator lurched and made a lumbering move toward the hole, its bucket rising, iron teeth dribbling dirt.

"What did you find?" Pendergast asked.

She paused. Should she tell him about the paper in the dress? It was probably nothing, and besides, it was gone.

She tore the hastily scribbled pages from the pad and returned it to him. "I'll write up my general observations for you this evening," she said. "The lumbar vertebrae of the victims seem to have been deliberately opened. I slipped one into my pocket."

Pendergast nodded. "There were numerous shards of glass embedded in the dust. I took a few for analysis."

"Other than the skeletons, there were some pennies in the alcoves, dated 1872, 1877, and 1880. A few articles in the pockets."

"The tenements here were erected in 1897," murmured Pendergast, almost to himself, his voice grave. "There's our *terminus ante quem*. The murders took place before 1897 and were probably clustered around the dates of the coins—that is, the 1870s."

A black stretch limousine slid up behind them, its tinted windows flaring in the sun. A tall man in an elegant charcoal suit got out, followed by several others. The man glanced around the site, his gaze quickly zeroing in on Pendergast. He had a long, narrow face, eyes spaced wide apart, black hair, and cheekbones so high and angular they could have been fashioned with a hatchet.

"And there's Mr. Fairhaven himself, to ensure there are no more untoward delays," Pendergast said. "I think this is our cue to leave."

He opened the car door for her, then climbed in himself. "Thank you, Dr. Kelly," he said, indicating to his driver to start the car. "Tomorrow we will meet again. In a more official capacity, I trust."

As they eased out into the Lower East Side traffic, Nora

looked at him. "How did you learn about this site, anyway? It was just uncovered yesterday."

"I have contacts. Most helpful in my line of work."

"I'll bet. Well, speaking of contacts, why didn't you just try your friend the police commissioner again? Surely he could have backed you up."

The Rolls turned smoothly onto East River Drive, its powerful engine purring. "Commissioner?" Pendergast blinked over at her. "I don't have the pleasure of his acquaintance."

"Then who were you calling back there, then?"

"My apartment." And he smiled ever so slightly.

FIVE

WILLIAM SMITHBACK JR. STOOD, QUITE SELF-CONSCIOUSLY, in the doorway of Café des Artistes. His new suit of dark blue Italian silk rustled as he scanned the dimly lit room. He tried to keep his normal slouch in check, his back ramrod straight, his bearing dignified, aristocratic. The Armani suit had cost him a small fortune, but as he stood in the entryway he knew it had been worth every penny. He felt sophisticated, urbane, a bit like Tom Wolfe—though of course he didn't dare try the full rig, white hat and all. The paisley silk handkerchief poking out of his pocket was a nice touch, though perhaps a bit flamboyant, but then again he was a famous writer—almost famous anyway, if only his last damn book had inched up two more slots it would have made the list—and he could get away with such touches. He turned with what he hoped was casual elegance and arched an eyebrow in the direction of the maître d', who immediately strode over with a smile.

Smithback loved this restaurant more than any other in New York City. It was decidedly untrendy, old-fashioned, with superb food. You didn't get the Bridge and Tunnel crowd in here like you did at Le Cirque 2000. And the

Howard Chandler Christie mural added just the right touch of kitsch.

"Mr. Smithback, how nice to see you this evening. Your party just arrived."

Smithback nodded gravely. Being recognized by the maître d' of a first-class restaurant, although he would be loath to admit it, meant a great deal to him. It had taken several visits, several well-dropped twenties. What clinched it was the casual reference to his position at the *New York Times.*

Nora Kelly sat at a corner table, waiting for him. As usual, just seeing her sent a little electric current of pleasure through Smithback. Even though she'd been in New York well over a year, she still retained a fresh, out-of-place look that delighted him. And she never seemed to have lost her Santa Fe tan. Funny, how they'd met under the worst possible of circumstances: an archaeological expedition to Utah in which they'd both almost lost their lives. Back then, she'd made it clear she thought him arrogant and obnoxious. And here they were, two years later, about to move in together. And Smithback couldn't imagine ever spending a day apart from her.

He slid into the banquette with a smile. She looked great, as always: her copper-colored hair spilling over her shoulders, deep green-brown eyes sparkling in the candle-light, the sprinkling of freckles on her nose adding a perfect touch of boyishness. Then his gaze dropped to her clothes. Now, those left something to be desired. God, she was actually *dirty.*

"You won't believe the day I had," she said.

"Hum." Smithback adjusted his tie and turned ever so slightly, allowing the light to catch the elegantly cut shoulder of his suit.

"I swear, Bill, you aren't going to believe it. But remember, this is off the record."

Now Smithback felt slightly hurt. Not only had she failed to notice the suit, but this business about their conversation being off the record was unnecessary. "Nora, *everything* between us is off the record—"

She didn't wait for him to finish. "First, that scumbag Brisbane cut my budget ten percent."

Smithback made a sympathetic noise. The Museum was perpetually short of money.

"And then I found this really weird man in my office."

Smithback made another noise, slyly moving his elbow into position beside his water glass. Surely she'd notice the dark silk against the white nap of the tablecloth.

"He was reading my books, acting like he owned the place. He looked just like an undertaker, dressed in a black suit, with really white skin. Not albino, just *white*."

An uncomfortable feeling of déjà vu began to well up in Smithback's mind. He dismissed it.

"He said he was from the FBI, and he dragged me downtown, to a building site where they'd uncovered—"

Abruptly, the feeling returned. "Did you say *FBI?*" No way. Not him. It couldn't be.

"Yes, the FBI. Special Agent—"

"Pendergast," Smithback finished for her.

Now it was Nora's turn to look astonished. "You know him?"

"Know him? He was in my book on the Museum murders. That book of mine you *said* you read."

"Oh yeah, right. Right."

Smithback nodded, too preoccupied to be indignant. Pendergast was not back in Manhattan on a social visit. The man showed up only when there was trouble. Or maybe he just seemed to always bring trouble with him. Either way, Smithback hoped to God it wasn't trouble like the last time.

The waiter appeared and took their orders. Smithback, who'd been anticipating a small dry sherry, ordered a martini instead. *Pendergast. Oh, God.* As much as he'd admired the man, he hadn't been sorry to see him and his black suit heading back to New Orleans.

"So tell me about him," Nora said, leaning back in her chair.

"He's . . ." Smithback paused, feeling uncharacteristically at a loss for words. "He's unorthodox. Charming, a southern aristocrat, lots of dough, old family money, pharmaceuticals or something. I really don't know what his relationship is with the FBI. He seems to have free rein to poke into anything he likes. He works alone and he's very, very good. He knows a lot of important people. As far as the man personally, I don't know anything about him. He's a cipher. You never know what he's really thinking. Christ, I don't even know his first name."

"He can't be that powerful. He got trumped today."

Smithback arched his eyebrows. "What happened? What did he want?"

Nora told him about their hasty visit to the charnel pit at the construction site. She finished just as their morel and black truffle *quenelles* arrived.

"Moegen-Fairhaven," said Smithback, digging a fork into the mousse, releasing a heavenly aroma of musk and the deep forest. "Weren't those the guys that got in trouble for ripping down that SRO without a permit—when there were still people living there?"

"The single-room occupancy on East First? I think so."

"Nasty bunch."

"Fairhaven was arriving in a stretch limo just as we left."

"Yeah. And in a Rolls, you said?" Smithback had to laugh. When he'd been investigating the Museum murders, Pendergast went around in a Buick. The conspicuousness of a Rolls had to mean something—everything Pendergast did served a purpose. "Well, you rode in style, anyway. But this really doesn't sound like something Pendergast would be interested in."

"Why not?"

"It's an incredible site, but it *is* over a hundred years old. Why would the FBI, or any law enforcement agency, be interested in a crime scene that's ancient history?"

"It isn't an ordinary crime scene. Three dozen young people, murdered, dismembered, and walled up in a subterranean crawlspace. That's one of the biggest serial killings in U.S. history."

Their waiter returned, sliding a dish in front of Smithback: steak *au poivre,* cooked rare. "Nora, come on," he said, lifting his knife eagerly. "The murderer is long dead. It's a historical curiosity. It'll make a great story in the paper—come to think of it—but I still can't see why the FBI would take an interest."

He felt Nora glowering at him. "Bill, this is off the record. Remember?"

"It's almost prehistoric, Nora, and it would make a sensational story. How could it possibly hurt—?"

"*Off* the *record.*"

Smithback sighed. "Just give me first shot, Nora, when the time comes."

Nora smirked. "You always get first shot, Bill. You know that."

Smithback chuckled and sliced a tender corner off his steak. "So what did you find down there?"

"Not much. A bunch of stuff in the pockets—some old coins, a comb, pins, string, buttons. These people were *poor.*

I took a vertebra, a hair sample, and . . ." She hesitated.
"There was something else."

"Out with it."

"There was a piece of paper sewed into the lining of one
girl's dress. It felt like a letter. I can't stop thinking about it."

Smithback leaned forward. "What'd it say?"

"I had to put the dress back before I could take a closer
look."

"You mean it's still there?"

Nora nodded.

"What are they going to do with the stuff?"

"The ME took away the bones, but they said they were
going to bag the rest. I got the sense they were eager to lose
track of the stuff in some warehouse. The quicker they can
get rid of it, the less chance it'll be declared an archaeological
site. I've seen developers tear up a site just to make sure that
when the archaeologists arrive there's nothing left to
examine."

"That's illegal, isn't it? Aren't they supposed to stop if
it's important?"

"If the site's gone, how can you prove it was important?
Developers destroy dozens of archaeological sites in America
in just this way, every single day."

Smithback mumbled his righteous indignation as he made
headway into the steak. He was famished. Nobody did steak
like Café des Artistes. And the helpings were decent, man-
sized, none of this nouvelle cuisine crap, the tippy little
structure of food in the middle of a giant white plate splashed
with Jackson Pollock–like dribbles of sauce . . .

"Why would the girl sew the letter into her dress?"

Smithback looked up, took a swig of red wine, another
bite of steak. "Love letter, perhaps?"

"The more I think about it, the more I think it could be

important. It would at least be a clue to who these people were. Otherwise, we may never find out, with their clothes gone and the tunnel destroyed." She was looking at him earnestly, her entrée untouched. "Damn it, Bill, that *was* an archaeological site."

"Probably torn up by now, like you said."

"It was late in the day. I stowed the dress back in the alcove."

"They probably removed it with the rest of the stuff, then."

"I don't think so. I stuffed it into a crevice in the rear of the alcove. They were rushing. They could easily have missed it."

Smithback saw the gleam in Nora's hazel eyes. He'd seen that look before.

"No way, Nora," he said quickly. "They must have security at the site. It's probably lit up brighter than a stage. Don't even think about it." Next thing, she would insist on his coming along.

"You've got to come with me. Tonight. I need that letter."

"You don't even know if it is a letter. It might be a laundry slip."

"Bill, even a *laundry* slip would be an important clue."

"We could be arrested."

"No, you won't."

"What's this *you* shit?"

"I'll distract the guard while you go over the fence. You can make yourself inconspicuous." As she spoke, Nora's eyes grew brighter. "Yes. You can be dressed like a homeless bum, say, just poking through the garbage. If they catch you, the worst they'll do is make you move on."

Smithback was aghast. "Me? A bum? No way. *You* be the bum."

"No, Bill, that won't work. I have to be the hooker."

The last forkful of steak froze halfway to Smithback's mouth.

Nora smiled at him. Then she spoke. "You just spilled brandy sauce all down the front of your nice new Italian suit."

SIX

NORA PEERED AROUND THE CORNER OF HENRY STREET,
shivering slightly. It was a chilly night, and her scant black
mini-dress and silver spandex top provided little warmth.
Only the heavy makeup, she thought, added any R-factor to
her person. In the distance, traffic droned through Chatham
Square, and the vast black bulk of the Manhattan Bridge
loomed ominously nearby. It was almost three o'clock in the
morning, and the streets of the Lower East Side were
deserted.

"What can you see?" Smithback asked from behind her.

"The site's pretty well lit. I can only see one guard,
though."

"What's he doing?"

"Sitting in a chair, smoking and reading a paperback."

Smithback scowled. It had been depressingly easy to
transform him to bumhood. His rangy frame was draped in
a shiny black raincoat over a checked shirt, a dirty pair of
jeans, and tattered Keds. There had been no shortage of
cheesy old clothing in Smithback's closet to choose from.
A bit of charcoal on the face, olive oil rubbed into the hair,

and a tote consisting of five nested plastic bags with unwashed clothes at the bottom completed the disguise.

"What's he look like?" Smithback asked.

"Big and mean."

"Cut it out." Smithback was in no mood for humor. Dressed as they were, they had been unable to flag down a cab in the Upper West Side, and had been forced to take the subway. Nobody had actually propositioned her, but she had gotten plenty of stares, with follow-up glances at Smithback that clearly read, *What's a high-priced call girl doing with that bum?* The long ride, with two transfers, had not improved Smithback's mood.

"This plan of yours is pretty weak," Smithback said. "Are you sure you can handle yourself?" He was a mask of irritation.

"We both have our cell phones. If anything happens, I'll scream bloody murder and you call 911. But don't worry—he's not going to make trouble."

"He's going to be too busy looking at your tits," said Smithback unhappily. "With that top, you might as well not be wearing anything."

"Trust me, I can take care of myself. Remember, the dress is in the second to last niche on the right. Feel along the rear wall for the crevice. Once you're safely out, call me. Now, here goes."

She stepped out into the streetlight and began walking down the sidewalk toward the construction entrance, her pumps making a sharp clicking noise on the pavement, her breasts bouncing. As she got close, she stopped, fished in her little gold handbag, and made an exaggerated little *moue*. She could already feel the guard's eyes on her. She dropped a lipstick, bent down to pick it up—making sure he got a good look up her dress in the process—and touched up her lips. Then she fished in the bag again, cursed, and looked around. She let her eyes fall on the guard. He was staring back, the book lying unheeded in his lap.

"Shit. Left my cigarettes back at the bar." She flashed him a smile.

"Here," he said, rising hastily. "Take one of mine."

She sidled over and accepted the cigarette through the gap in the chain-link gate, positioning herself to ensure his back would be turned to the construction site. She hoped to God Smithback would work fast.

The guard withdrew a lighter, tried to stick it through the gate, failed. "Just a minute, let me unlock this."

She waited, cigarette in hand.

The gate swung open and he flicked the lighter. She approached and bent over the flame, drawing the smoke in, hoping she wouldn't cough. "Thanks."

"Sure," said the guard. He was young, sandy-haired, neither fat nor thin, a little dopey-looking, not terribly strong, clearly flustered by her presence. Good.

She stood there, taking another drag. "Nice night," she said.

"You must be cold."

"A little."

"Here, take this." With a gallant flourish he took off his coat and draped it over her shoulders.

"Thanks." The guard looked as if he could hardly believe his good fortune. Nora knew she was attractive; knew that her body, with all her years spent backpacking in the remote desert, wasn't too bad, either. The heavy makeup gave her a sense of security. Never in a million years would he later be able to identify the archaeologist from the New York Museum of Natural History. In an odd way the outfit made her feel sassy, bold, a little sexy.

She heard a distant rattle; Smithback must be climbing over the chain-link fence. "You work here every night?" she said hastily.

"Five nights a week," the guard said, his Adam's apple bobbing. "Now that construction's begun. You, er, live around here?"

She nodded vaguely toward the river. "And you?"

"Queens."

"Married?"

She saw his left hand, where she had previously noted a wedding band, slide behind his gun holster. "Not me."

She nodded, took another drag. It made her dizzy. How could people smoke these things? She wished Smithback would hurry up.

She smiled and dropped the butt, grinding it under her toe.

Instantly the pack was out. "Another?"

"No," she said, "trying to cut back."

She could see him eyeing her spandex top, trying to be subtle. "You work in a bar?" he asked, then colored. Awkward question. Nora heard another sound, a few falling bricks.

"Sort of," she said, pulling the jacket tighter around her shoulders.

He nodded. He was looking a little bolder now. "I think you're very attractive," he said, hastily, blurting it out.

"Thanks," she said. God, it was a thirty-second job. What was taking Smithback so long?

"Are you, ah, free later?"

Deliberately, she looked him up and down. "You want a date?"

"Yeah. Yeah, sure."

There was another, louder sound: the rattling of a chain-link fence. Smithback climbing out? The guard turned toward it.

"What kind of date?" Nora asked.

He looked back at her, no longer trying to hide the roaming of his lascivious eyes. Nora felt naked beneath his gaze. There was another rattle. The guard turned again and this time saw Smithback. He was pretty hard to miss: clinging to the top of the fence, trying to unsnag his filthy raincoat.

"Hey!" the guard yelled.

"Forget him," said Nora hastily. "He's just some bum."

Smithback struggled. Now he was trying to slip out of his raincoat, but had only succeeded in becoming more tangled.

"He's not supposed to be in there!" the guard said.

This, unfortunately, was a guy who took his job seriously.

The man clapped his hand to his gun. "Hey you!" he yelled louder. "Hey!" He took a step toward the writer.

Smithback struggled frantically with the raincoat.

"Sometimes I do it for free," Nora said.

The guard swiveled back to her, eyes wide, the bum on the fence instantly forgotten. "You do?"

"Sure. Why not? Cute guy like you . . ."

He grinned like an idiot. Now she noticed his ears stuck out. What a weenie, so eager to cheat on his wife. Cheap, too.

"Right now?" he asked.

"Too cold. Tomorrow." She heard a ripping sound, a thud, a muffled curse.

"Tomorrow?" He looked devastated. "Why not now? At your place."

She took off the coat and gave it back to him. "Never at my place."

He took a step toward her. "There's a hotel around the corner." He reached over, trying to snake an arm around her waist.

She skipped back lightly with another smile as her cell phone rang. Flooded with relief, she flipped it open.

"Mission accomplished," came Smithback's voice. "You can get away from that creep."

"Sure, Mr. McNally, I'd love to," she said warmly. "That sounds nice. See you there." She made a smacking kiss into the phone and snapped it shut.

She turned to the guard. "Sorry. Business." She took another step back.

"Wait. Come on. You said—" There was a note of desperation in the guard's voice.

She took a few more steps back and shut the chain-link gate in his face. "Tomorrow. I promise."

"No, wait!"

She turned and began walking quickly down the sidewalk.

"Hey, come on! Wait! Lady, please!" His desperate pleas echoed among the tenements.

She ducked around the corner. Smithback was waiting, and he hugged her briefly. "Is that creep following?"

"Just keep going."

They began running down the sidewalk, Nora wobbling on her high heels. They turned the far corner and crossed the street, then paused, panting and listening. The guard was not following.

"Christ," said Smithback, sinking against a wall. "I think I broke my arm falling off that goddamn fence." He held up his arm. His raincoat and shirt had been torn and his bleeding elbow stuck out of the hole.

Nora examined it. "You're fine. Did you get the dress?"

Smithback patted his grimy bag.

"Great."

Smithback looked around. "We're never going to find a cab down here," he said with a groan.

"A cab wouldn't stop anyway. Remember? Give me your raincoat. I'm freezing."

Smithback wrapped it around her. He paused, grinning. "You look kind of . . . sexy."

"Stow it." She began walking toward the subway.

Smithback skipped after her. At the entrance to the subway, he stopped. "How about a date, lady?" he leered. "Hey lady, please!" He imitated the guard's last, despairing entreaties.

She looked at him. His hair was sticking out in all directions, his face had become even filthier, and he smelled of mold and dust. He couldn't have looked more ridiculous.

She had to smile. "It's going to cost you big-time. I'm high-class."

He grinned. "Diamonds. Pearls. Greenbacks. Nights dancing in the desert under the coyote moon. Anything you want, baby."

She took his hand. "Now, that's my kind of john."

SEVEN

NORA LOCKED THE DOOR TO HER OFFICE, PLACED THE packet on a chair, and cleared her desk of papers and tottering stacks of publications. It was just past eight in the morning, and the Museum seemed to be still asleep. Nevertheless, she glanced at the window set into her office door, and then—with a guilty impulse she did not quite understand—walked over to it and pulled down the blind. Then she carefully covered the desktop with white acid-free paper, taped it to the corners, laid another sheet on top, and placed a series of sample bags, stoppered test tubes, tweezers, and picks along one edge. Unlocking a drawer of her desk, she laid out the articles she had taken from the site: coins, comb, hair, string, vertebra. Lastly, she laid the dress atop the paper. She handled it gently, almost gingerly, as if to make up for the abuse it had endured over the last twenty-four hours.

Smithback had been beside himself with frustration the night before, when she had refused to slit open the dress immediately and see what, if anything, was written on the paper hidden inside. She could see him in her mind's eye: still in his hobo outfit, drawn up to a height of indignation only a journalist with a need to know could feel. But she'd been unmoved. With the site destroyed, she was determined to squeeze every bit of information out of the dress that she could. And she was going to do it right.

She took a step back from the desk. In the bright light of the office, she could examine the dress in great detail. It was long, quite simple, made of coarse green wool. It looked nineteenth-century, with a high collaret-style neckline; a trim bodice, falling in long pleats. The bodice and pleats were lined with white cotton, now yellowed.

Nora slid her hand down the pleats and, right below the waistline, felt the crinkle of paper. *Not yet,* she told herself as she sat down at the desk. *One step at a time.*

The dress was heavily stained. It was impossible to tell, without a chemical analysis, what the stains were—some looked like blood and body fluids, while others could be grease, coal dust, perhaps wax. The hemline was rubbed and torn, and there were some tears in the fabric itself, the larger ones carefully sewn up. She examined the stains and tears with her loup. The repairs had been done with several colored threads, none green. A poor girl's effort, using whatever was at hand.

There was no sign of insect or rodent damage; the dress had been securely walled up in its alcove. She switched lenses on the loup and looked more closely. She could see a significant amount of dirt, including black grains that looked like coal dust. She took a few of these and placed them in a small glassine envelope with the tweezers. She removed other particles of grit, dirt, hair, and threads, and placed them in additional bags. There were other specs, even smaller than the grit; she lugged over a portable stereozoom microscope, laid it on the table, and brought it into focus.

Immediately, dozens of lice leapt into view, dead and dry, clinging to the crudely woven fabric, intermingled with smaller mites and several giant fleas. She jerked her head back involuntarily. Then, smiling at herself, she took a closer, more studied look. The dress was a rich landscape of foreign biology, along with an array of substances that could occupy a forensic chemist for weeks. She wondered how useful such an analysis would be, considered the cost, and temporarily shelved the idea. She brought the forceps forward to take more samples.

Suddenly, the silence in her office seemed all too absolute; there was a crawling sensation at the base of her neck. She swiveled, gasped; Special Agent Pendergast was standing behind her, hands behind his back.

"Jesus!" she said, leaping out of the chair. "You scared the hell out of me!"

Pendergast bowed slightly. "My apologies."

"I thought I locked that door."

"You did."

"Are you a magician, Agent Pendergast? Or did you simply pick my lock?"

"A little of both, perhaps. But these old Museum locks are so crude, one can hardly call it 'picking.' I am well known here, which requires me to be discreet."

"Do you think you could call ahead next time?"

He turned to the dress. "You didn't have this yesterday afternoon."

"No. I didn't."

He nodded. "Very resourceful of you, Dr. Kelly."

"I went back last night—"

"No details of any questionable activities, please. However, my congratulations."

She could see he was pleased.

He held out his hand. "Proceed."

Nora turned back to her work. After a while, Pendergast spoke. "There were many articles of clothing in the tunnel. Why this dress?"

Without a word, Nora carefully turned up the pleats of the dress, exposing a crudely sewn patch in the cotton lining. Immediately, Pendergast moved closer.

"There's a piece of paper sewn inside," she said. "I came upon it just before they shut down the site."

"May I borrow your loup?"

Nora lifted it over her head and handed it to him. Bending over the dress, he examined it with a thorough professionalism that surprised and impressed Nora. At last he straightened up.

"Very hasty work," he said. "You'll note that all the other stitching and mending was done carefully, almost lovingly. This dress was some girl's prize garment. But this one stitch was made with thread pulled from the dress itself, and the holes are ragged—I would guess they were made with a splinter of wood. This was done by someone with little time, and with no access to even a needle."

Nora moved the microscope over the patch, using its camera to take a series of photographs at various magnifications. Then she fixed a macro lens and took another series. She worked efficiently, aware that Pendergast's eyes were upon her.

She put the microscope aside and picked up the tweezers. "Let's open it up."

With great care, she teased the end of the thread out and began to undo the patch. A few minutes of painstaking work and it lay loose. She placed the thread in a sample tube and lifted the material.

Underneath was a piece of paper, torn from the page of a book. It had been folded twice.

Nora put the patch into yet another Ziploc bag. Then, using two pairs of rubber-tipped tweezers, she unfolded the paper. Inside was a message, scratched in crude brown letters. Parts of it were stained and faded, but it read unmistakably:

i aM MarY GreeNe agt 19 Years No. 16 WaTTer sTreeT

Nora moved the paper to the stage of the stereozoom and looked at it under low power. After a moment she stepped back, and Pendergast eagerly took her place at the eyepieces. Minutes went by as he stared. Finally he stepped away.

"Written with the same splinter, perhaps," he said.

Nora nodded. The letters had been formed with little scratches and scrapes.

"May I perform a test?" Pendergast asked.

"What kind?"

Pendergast slipped out a small stoppered test tube. "It will involve removing a tiny sample of the ink on this note with a solvent."

"What is that stuff?"

"Antihuman rabbit serum."

"Be my guest." Strange that Pendergast carried forensic chemicals around in his pockets. What did the agent not have hidden inside that bottomless black suit of his?

Pendergast unstoppered the test tube, revealing a tiny swab. Using the stereozoom, he applied it to a corner of a letter, then placed it back in its tube. He gave it a little shake and held it to the window. After a moment, the liquid turned blue. He turned to face her.

"So?" she asked, but she had already read the results in his face.

"The note, Dr. Kelly, was written in human blood. No doubt the very blood of the young woman herself."

EIGHT

SILENCE DESCENDED IN THE MUSEUM OFFICE. NORA FOUND she had to sit down. For some time nothing was said; Nora could vaguely hear traffic sounds from below, the distant ringing of a phone, footsteps in the hall. The full dimension of the discovery began to sink in: the tunnel, the thirty-six dismembered bodies, the ghastly note from a century ago.

"What do you think it means?" she asked.

"There can be only one explanation. The girl must have known she would never leave that basement alive. She didn't want to die an unknown. Hence she deliberately wrote down her name, age, and home address, and then concealed it. A self-chosen epitaph. The only one available to her."

Nora shuddered. "How horrible."

Pendergast moved slowly toward her bookshelf. She followed him with her eyes.

"What are we dealing with?" she asked. "A serial killer?"

Pendergast did not answer. The same troubled look that had come over him at the digsite had returned to his face. He continued to stand in front of the bookshelf.

"May I ask you a question?"

Pendergast nodded again.

"Why are you involved in this? Hundred-and-thirty-year-old serial killings are not exactly within the purview of the FBI."

Pendergast plucked a small Anasazi bowl from the shelf and examined it. "Lovely Kayenta black-on-white." He looked up. "How is your research on the Utah Anasazi survey going?"

"Not well. The Museum won't give me money for the carbon-14 dates I need. What does that have to—"

"Good."

"Good?"

"Dr. Kelly, are you familiar with the term, 'cabinet of curiosities'?"

Nora wondered at the man's ability to pile on non sequiturs. "Wasn't it a kind of natural history collection?"

"Precisely. It was the precursor to the natural history museum. Many educated gentlemen of the eighteenth and nineteenth centuries collected strange artifacts while roaming the globe—fossils, bones, shrunken heads, stuffed birds, that sort of thing. Originally, they simply displayed these artifacts in cabinets, for the amusement of their friends. Later—when it became clear people would pay money to visit them— some of these cabinets of curiosities grew into commercial enterprises. They still called them 'cabinets of curiosities' even though the collections filled many rooms."

"What does this have to do with the murders?"

"In 1848, a wealthy young gentleman from New York, Alexander Marysas, went on a hunting and collecting expedition around the world, from the South Pacific to Tierra del Fuego. He died in Madagascar, but his collections—most extraordinary collections they were—came back in the hold of his ship. They were purchased by an entrepreneur, John

Canaday Shottum, who opened J. C. Shottum's Cabinet of Natural Productions and Curiosities in 1852."

"So?"

"Shottum's Cabinet was the building that once stood above the tunnel where the skeletons were found."

"How did you find all this out?"

"Half an hour with a good friend of mine who works in the New York Public Library. The tunnel you explored was, in fact, the coal tunnel that serviced the building's original boiler. It was a three-story brick building in the Gothic Revival style popular in the 1850s. The first floor held the cabinet and something called a 'Cyclorama,' the second floor was Shottum's office, and the third floor was rented out. The cabinet seems to have been quite successful, though the Five Points neighborhood around it was at the time one of Manhattan's worst slums. The building burned in 1881. Shottum died in the fire. The police report suspected arson, but no perpetrator was ever found. It remained a vacant lot until the row of tenements was built in 1897."

"What was on the site before Shottum's Cabinet?"

"A small hog farm."

"So all those people must have been murdered while the building was Shottum's Cabinet."

"Exactly."

"Do you think Shottum did it?"

"Impossible to know as of yet. Those glass fragments I found in the tunnel were mostly broken test tubes and distillation apparatus. On them, I found traces of a variety of chemicals that I have yet to analyze. We need to learn a great deal more about J. C. Shottum and his cabinet of curiosities. I wonder if you would be so kind as to accompany me?"

He obligingly opened the door to her office, and Nora

automatically followed him into the hallway. He continued talking as they walked down the hall and took an elevator to the fifth floor. As the elevator doors hissed open, Nora suddenly came to her senses.

"Wait a minute. Where are we going? I've got work to do."

"As I said, I need your help."

Nora felt a short jolt of irritation: Pendergast spoke so confidently, as if he already owned her time. "I'm sorry, but I'm an archaeologist, not a detective."

He raised his eyebrows. "Is there a difference?"

"What makes you think I'd be interested?"

"You already are interested."

Nora fumed at the man's presumption, although what he said was perfectly true. "And just how will I explain this to the Museum?"

"That, Dr. Kelly, is the nature of our appointment."

He pointed to a door at the end of the hall, with the name of the occupant in gold lettering on a wooden plaque.

"Oh, no," groaned Nora. "No."

They found Roger Brisbane ensconced in his Bauhaus chair, crisp Turnbull & Asser shirt rolled up at the cuffs, looking every inch the lawyer. His prized gems still nestled in their glass box, the only touch of warmth in the cold immaculate office. He nodded toward two chairs opposite his desk. It did not look like Brisbane was in a good mood.

"Special Agent Pendergast," Brisbane said, glancing from his appointment book up to Pendergast without acknowledging Nora. "Now, why is that name familiar?"

"I've done work in the Museum before," said Pendergast, in his creamiest drawl.

"Who did you work for?"

"You misapprehend. I said I did work *in* the Museum, not *for* it."

Brisbane waved his hand. "Whatever. Mr. Pendergast, I enjoy my quiet mornings at home. I fail to see what the emergency was that required my presence in the office at such an hour."

"Crime never sleeps, Mr. Brisbane." Nora thought she detected a note of dry humor in Pendergast's voice.

Brisbane's eyes veered toward Nora, then away again. "Dr. Kelly's responsibilities are here. I thought I made that clear on the telephone. Normally the Museum would be delighted to help the FBI, but I just don't see how we can in this particular case."

Instead of answering, Pendergast's gaze lingered on the gems. "I didn't know the famous Mogul Star Sapphire had been taken off public display. That *is* the Mogul Star, is it not?"

Brisbane shifted in his chair. "We periodically rotate the exhibits, to give visitors a chance to see things that are in storage."

"And you keep the, ah, excess inventory here."

"Mr. Pendergast, as I said, I fail to see how we can help you."

"This was a unique crime. You have unique resources. I need to make use of those resources."

"Did the crime you mention take place in the Museum?"

"No."

"On Museum property?"

Pendergast shook his head.

"Then I'm afraid the answer is no."

"Is that your final word on the subject?"

"Absolutely. We don't want the Museum mixed up in any way with police work. Being involved in investigations, lawsuits, sordidness, is a sure way to draw the Museum into unwelcome controversy. As you well know, Mr. Pendergast."

Pendergast removed a piece of paper from his vest pocket and laid it in front of Brisbane.

"What's this?" Brisbane said, without looking at it.

"The Museum's charter with the City of New York."

"What relevance is that?"

"It states that one of the responsibilities of Museum employees is to perform pro bono public service to the City of New York."

"We do that every day by running the Museum."

"Ah, but that is precisely the problem. Up until fairly recently, the Museum's Anthropology Department regularly assisted the police in forensic matters. It was part of their duties, as a matter of fact. You remember, of course, the infamous Ashcan Murder of November 7, 1939?"

"Pity, I must have missed that particular piece in the *Times* that day."

"A curator here was instrumental in solving that case. He found the burned rim of an orbit in an ashcan, which he was able to identify as positively human—"

"Mr. Pendergast, I am not here for a history lesson." Brisbane rose out of his chair and flicked on his jacket. "The answer is no. I have business to attend to. Dr. Kelly, please return to your office."

"I am sorry to hear that. There will be adverse publicity, of course."

At these two words, Brisbane paused, then a cold smile crept onto his face. "That sounded remarkably like a threat."

Pendergast continued in his genial, southern fashion. "The truth is, the charter clearly calls for service to the City *outside* of regular curatorial duties. The Museum has not been keeping its contract with the City of New York now for close to a decade, despite the fact that it receives millions in tax dollars *from* the citizens of New York. Far from providing public service, you have now closed your library to all but Ph.D.'s; you have closed your collections to everyone except so-called accredited academics; and you charge fees for everything, all in the name of intellectual property rights. You have even begun suggesting an admission fee, despite the fact that this is clearly barred by your charter. It says right here: . . . *for the Creation of a Museum of Natural History for the City of New York, to be Open and Free to all Members of the Public, without Restriction . . .*"

"Let me see that."

Brisbane read it, his smooth brow contracting into the faintest wrinkle.

"Old documents can be so inconvenient, don't you think, Mr. Brisbane? Like the Constitution. Always there when you least want it."

Brisbane let it drop to the desk, his face reddening for a moment before returning to its usual healthy pink. "I'll have to take this up with the board."

Pendergast smiled slightly. "An excellent start. I think perhaps the Museum can be left to work this little problem out on its own—what do you think, Mr. Brisbane?— provided I am given what little help I need from Dr. Kelly."

There was a silence. Then Brisbane looked up, a new look in his eyes. "I see."

"And I assure you I will not take up an undue amount of Dr. Kelly's time."

"Of course you won't," said Brisbane.

"Most of the work will be archival in nature. She'll be on the premises and available, should you need her."

Brisbane nodded.

"We will do all we can to avoid unpleasant publicity. Naturally, all this would be kept confidential."

"Naturally. It is always best that way."

"I just want to add that Dr. Kelly did not seek me out. I have imposed this duty on her. She has already informed me she would rather be working on her potsherds."

"Of course."

An opaque veil had dropped over Brisbane's face. It was hard for Nora to tell what he was thinking. She wondered if this little hardball play of Pendergast's was going to damage her prospects at the Museum. It probably would. She darted a reproachful glance toward Pendergast.

"Where did you say you were from?" Brisbane asked.

"I didn't. New Orleans."

Brisbane immediately pushed himself back in his chair, and with a smile said: "New Orleans. Of course. I should have known from the accent. You're a rather long way from home, Mr. Pendergast."

Pendergast bowed, holding the door open for Nora. She stepped through it, feeling shocked. Down the hall, she halted and spoke to Pendergast. "You totally blindsided me back there. I had no idea what you were up to until we were in Brisbane's office. I don't appreciate it."

Pendergast turned his pale eyes on her. "My methods are unorthodox, but they have one advantage."

"And what is that?"

"They work."

"Yeah, but what about my career?"

Pendergast smiled. "May I offer a prediction?"

"For what it's worth, why not?"

"When this is over, you will have been promoted."

Nora snorted. "Right. After you blackmailed and humiliated my boss, he's going to promote me."

"I'm afraid I don't suffer petty bureaucrats gladly. A very bad habit, but one I find hard to break. Nevertheless, you will find, Dr. Kelly, that humiliation and blackmail, when used judiciously, can be marvelously effective."

At the stairwell, Nora paused once again.

"You never answered my question. Why is the FBI concerned with killings that are over a century old?"

"All in good time, Dr. Kelly. For now, let it suffice to say that, on a purely personal level, I find these killings rather— ah—interesting."

Something in the way Pendergast said "interesting" sent the faintest of shudders through Nora.

Men of Science

ONE

THE MUSEUM'S VAST CENTRAL ARCHIVES LAY DEEP IN THE basement, reachable only through several sets of elevators, winding corridors, stairs, and passageways. Nora had never been to the Archives before—she did not, in fact, know anybody who ever had—and as she descended deeper and deeper into the bowels of the Museum, she wondered if perhaps she had made a wrong turn somewhere.

Before accepting the job at the Museum, she had taken one of the tours that threaded their way through its endless galleries. She had heard all the statistics: it was physically the largest museum in the world, consisting of two dozen interconnected buildings built in the nineteenth century, forming a bizarre maze of more than three thousand rooms and almost two hundred miles of passageways. But mere numbers could not capture the claustrophobic feeling of the endless, deserted corridors. *It was enough,* she thought, *to give the Minotaur a nervous breakdown.*

She stopped, consulted her map, and sighed. A long brick passageway ran straight ahead, illuminated by a string of light bulbs in cages; another ran off from it at right angles. Everything smelled of dust. She needed a landmark, a fixed point to get her bearings. She looked around. A padlocked metal door nearby had a weathered sign: *Titanotheres.* A door across the hall from it read: *Chalicotheres and Tapiroids.* She checked the oversized map, finally locating her position with difficulty. She wasn't lost, after all: it was just ahead and around the corner. *Famous last words,* she thought, walking forward, hearing the echoing rap of her heels against the concrete floor.

She stopped at a massive set of oaken doors, ancient and scarred, marked *Central Archives.* She knocked, listening to the rap resound cavernously on the far side. There came a sudden rattle of papers, the sound of a dropped book, a great clearing of phlegm. A high-pitched voice called out, "Just a moment, please!"

There was a slow shuffling, then the sound of numerous locks being unfastened. The door opened, revealing a short, round, elderly man. He had a vastly hooked red nose, and a fringe of long white hair descended from the gleaming dome above it. As he looked up at her, a smile of greeting broke out, dispelling the air of melancholy on his veined face.

"Ah, come in, do come in," he said. "Don't let all these locks frighten you. I'm an old man, but I don't bite. *Fortunate senex!*"

Nora took a step forward. Dust lay everywhere, even on the worn lapels of the man's jacket. A lamp with a green shade cast a small pool of light on the old desk, piled high with papers. On one side sat an elderly Royal typewriter, perhaps the only thing in the room not covered in dust. Beyond the desk, Nora could see cast-iron shelves laden with books and boxes stretching back into a gloom as deep as the ocean. In the dimness, it was impossible to judge how far the room extended.

"Are you Reinhart Puck?" Nora asked.

The man set up a vigorous nodding, his cheeks and bow tie flapping in response. "At your service." He bowed, and for an alarmed moment Nora thought he might reach out to kiss her hand. Instead, there was another loud sound of phlegm being forced against its will somewhere within his windpipes.

"I'm looking for information on—on cabinets of curiosities," Nora continued, wondering if that was the correct pluralization.

The man, busy relocking the door, glanced over, his rheumy eyes lighting up. "Ah! You've come to the right place. The Museum absorbed most of the old cabinets of early New York. We have all their collections, their papers. Where shall we begin?" He slammed the last bolt home, then rubbed his hands together, smiling, clearly happy to be of service to someone.

"There was a cabinet of curiosities in lower Manhattan known as Shottum's Cabinet."

He wrinkled his brow. "Shottum's . . . Ah, yes. Yes, indeed. Quite popular these days, Shottum's. But first things first. Please sign the register, and then we can get started." He motioned her to follow him around the desk, where he produced a leather-bound ledger, so old and rubbed that Nora was tempted to ask for a quill pen. She took the proffered ballpoint, wrote in her name and department.

"Why all the locks and bolts?" she asked, handing back the pen. "I thought all the really valuable stuff, the gold and diamonds and the rest, was kept in the Secure Area."

"It's the new administration. Added all this red tape, after the unpleasantness a few years back. It's not as if we're all that busy, you know. Just researchers and doctoral candidates, or the occasional wealthy patron with an interest in the history of science." He returned the register, then shuffled over to a huge bank of old ivory light switches, big as clothes pegs, and snapped a few on. Deep in the vast space there was a flicker, then another, and a dim light appeared. Puck set off toward it at a slow hobble, his feet scraping on the stone floor. Nora followed, glancing up at the dark walls of shelving. She felt as if she were walking through a dark forest toward the distant glow of a welcoming cottage.

"Cabinets of curiosities, one of my favorite subjects. As you no doubt know, Delacourte's was the first cabinet, established in 1804." Puck's voice echoed back over his stooped shoulders. "It was a marvelous collection. A whale eyeball pickled in whiskey, a set of hippo teeth, a mastodon tusk found in a bog in New Jersey. And of course the last dodo egg, of a Rodrigues Solitaire to be exact. The egg was brought back live in a crate, but then after they put it on display it appeared to have hatched, and— Aha, here we are."

He stopped abruptly, reached up to drag a box down from a high shelf, and opened its lid. Instead of the Shottum's Cabinet material Nora hoped for, inside was a large eggshell, broken into three pieces. "There's no provenience on these things, so they didn't accession them into the main Museum collection. That's why we've got them here." He pointed reverently at the pieces of shell, licking his lips. "Delacourte's Cabinet of Natural History. They charged twenty-five cents admission, quite a sum at the time."

Replacing the box, he slid a thick three-ring binder off an adjoining shelf and began flipping through it. "What would you like to know about the Delacourte Cabinet?"

"It was actually Shottum's Cabinet of Natural Productions and Curiosities that I was interested in. John Canaday Shottum." Nora swallowed her impatience. It would clearly be useless to rush Mr. Puck.

"Yes, yes, Shottum's." He resumed his shuffling down the row of boxes, binders, and books.

"How did the Museum acquire these cabinets?" she asked.

"Once the Museum opened, with free admission, it put most of them out of business. Of course, a lot of the stuff the old cabinets displayed were fakes, you know. But some of it held real scientific value. As the cabinets went bankrupt, McFadden, an early curator here, bought them up for the Museum."

"Fakes, you said?"

Puck nodded portentously. "Sewing two heads onto a calf. Taking a whale bone and dying it brown, saying it came from a dinosaur. We have some of those."

As he moved on to the next row, Nora hastened to keep up, wondering how to guide this flood of information in the direction she wanted.

"Cabinets were all the rage. Even P. T. Barnum once owned a cabinet known as Scudder's American Museum. He added live exhibits. And that, young lady, was the beginning of his circus."

"Live exhibits?"

"He displayed Joice Heth, a wizened old black woman who Barnum claimed was George Washington's 161-year-old nurse. Exposed as a fraud by the father of our own Tinbury McFadden."

"Tinbury McFadden?" Nora was starting to panic. Would she ever get out of here?

"Tinbury McFadden. A curator here back in the late nineteenth century. He had a particular interest in cabinets of curiosities. Queer fellow. Just up and disappeared one day."

"I'm interested in Shottum's Cabinet. John Canaday *Shottum*."

"We're getting there, young lady," said Puck, with the slightest touch of irritation. "We don't have much from Shottum's. It burned in 1881."

"Most of the stuff was collected by a man named Marysas. Alexander Marysas," Nora said, hoping to keep his mind on the subject at hand.

"Now, *there* was an odd fellow. Marysas came from a rich New York family, died in Madagascar. I believe the chief made an umbrella out of his skin to protect his baby grandson from the sun . . ."

They followed a labyrinthine path between shelves groaning with papers, boxes, and bizarre artifacts. Puck snapped more ivory switches; more lights went on ahead of them, while others winked out behind, leaving them in an island of light surrounded by a vast ocean of darkness. They came to an open area in the shelves where some large specimens stood on oak platforms—a woolly mammoth, shriveled but still huge; a white elephant; a giraffe missing its head. Nora's heart sank when Puck stopped.

"Those old cabinets would do anything to draw the paying public. Take a look at this baby mammoth. Found freeze-dried in Alaska." He reached underneath it and pressed something; there was a soft click and a trapdoor flopped open in the belly.

"This was part of a sideshow routine. A label said the mammoth had been frozen for 100,000 years and that a scientist was going to thaw it out and try to revive it. Before the sideshow opened, a small man would climb in through that trapdoor. When the place had filled with spectators, another man posing as a scientist would come out and give a lecture and start warming the thing with a brazier. Then the man inside would start moving the trunk and making noises. Cleared the place out in seconds." Puck chuckled. "People were a lot more innocent back then, weren't they?" He reached under and carefully closed the trapdoor.

"Yes, yes," said Nora. "This is very interesting, Mr. Puck, and I appreciate the tour. But I'm pressed for time, and I really would like to see the *Shottum* material now."

"We're here." Puck rolled a metal ladder into place, climbed up into the gloom, and descended with a small box.

"*O terque quaterque beati!* Here's your Mr. Shottum. It wasn't the most interesting cabinet, I'm afraid. And since it burned, we don't have much from it—just these few papers." Puck opened the box, peered inside. "Great heavens, what a mess," he clucked disapprovingly. "I don't understand, considering . . . Ah, well, when you're done with these, I can show you the Delacourte papers. Much more comprehensive."

"I'm afraid there won't be time, at least not today."

Puck grunted with dissatisfaction. Nora glanced at him, felt a stab of pity for the lonely old man.

"Ah, here's a letter from Tinbury McFadden," Puck said, plucking a faded paper from the box. "Helped Shottum classify his mammals and birds. He advised a lot of the cabinet owners. Hired himself out." He rummaged some more. "He was a close friend of Shottum's."

Nora thought for a moment. "Can I check out this box?"

"Have to look at it in the Research Room. Can't let it leave the Archives."

"I see." Nora paused, thinking. "You said Tinbury McFadden was a close friend of Shottum's? Are his papers in here, too?"

"Are *they* here? Good heaven, we've got mountains of his papers. *And* his collections. He had quite a cabinet himself, only he never displayed it. Left it to the Museum, but none of the stuff had any provenience and was full of fakes, so they stuck it down here. For historical purposes. No scientific value, they said." Puck sniffed. "Not worthy of the main collection."

"May I see it?"

"Of course, of course!" And Puck was shuffling off again in a new direction. "Right around the corner."

They stopped at last before two shelves. The upper was full of more papers and boxes. On top of one box was a promissory note, with a faded inventory of items transferred from J. C. Shottum to T. F. McFadden, as payment for Services Rendered and Promised. The lower shelf was stuffed with a variety of curious objects. Glancing over them, Nora saw stuffed animals wrapped in wax paper and twine, dubious-looking fossils, a double-headed pig floating in a glass jeroboam, a dried anaconda curled into a giant five-foot knot, a stuffed chicken with six legs and four wings, and a bizarre box made out of an elephant's foot.

Puck blew his nose like a trumpet, wiped his eyes. "Poor Tinbury would turn over in his grave if he knew that his precious collection ended up down here. He thought it had priceless scientific value. Of course, that was at a time when many of the Museum's curators were amateurs with poor scientific credentials."

Nora pointed to the promissory note. "This seems to indicate Shottum gave McFadden specimens in exchange for his work."

"A standard practice."

"So some of these things came from Shottum's Cabinet?"

"Without a doubt."

"Could I examine these specimens, too?"

Puck beamed. "I'll move all of it to the Research Room and set it up on tables. When it's ready, I'll let you know."

"How long will that take?"

"A day." His face reddened with the pleasure of being of use.

"Don't you need help moving these things?"

"Oh, yes. My assistant, Oscar, will do it."

Nora looked around. "Oscar?"

"Oscar Gibbs. He usually works up in Osteology. We don't get many visitors down here. I call him down for special work like this."

"This is very kind of you, Mr. Puck."

"Kind? The pleasure's all mine, I assure you, my dear girl!"

"I'll be bringing a colleague."

An uncertain look clouded Puck's face. "A colleague? There are rules about that, what with the new security and all . . ." He hesitated, almost embarrassed.

"Rules?"

"Only Museum staff allowed. The Archives used to be open to everybody, but now we've been restricted to Museum staff. And trustees."

"Special Agent Pendergast is, ah, *connected* with the Museum."

"*Agent* Pendergast? Yes, the name's familiar . . . Pendergast. I remember him now. The southern gentleman. Oh, dear." A momentary look of distress crossed the man's face. "Well, well, as you wish. I'll expect you both tomorrow at nine o'clock."

TWO

PATRICK MURPHY O'SHAUGHNESSY SAT IN THE PRECINCT captain's office, waiting for him to get off the phone. He had been waiting five minutes, but so far Custer hadn't even looked in his direction. Which was just fine with him. O'Shaughnessy scanned the walls without interest, his eyes moving from commendation plaques to departmental shooting trophies, lighting at last upon the painting on the far wall. It showed a little cabin in a swamp, at night, under a full moon, its windows casting a yellow glow over the waters. It was a source of endless amusement to the 7th Precinct that their captain, with all his mannerisms and his pretensions to culture, had a velvet painting proudly displayed in his office. There had even been talk of getting an office pool together, soliciting donations for a less revolting replacement. O'Shaughnessy used to laugh along with them, but now he found it pathetic. It was all so pathetic.

The rattle of the phone in its cradle brought him out of his reverie. He looked up as Custer pressed his intercom button.

"Sergeant Noyes, come in here, please."

O'Shaughnessy looked away. This wasn't a good sign.

Herbert Noyes, recently transferred from Internal Affairs, was Custer's new personal assistant and numero uno ass-kisser. Something unpleasant was definitely up.

Almost instantly, Noyes entered the office, the usual unctuous smile breaking the smooth lines of his ferret-like head. He nodded politely to Custer, ignored O'Shaughnessy, and took the seat closest to the captain's desk, chewing gum, as usual. His skinny form barely made a dent in the burgundy-colored leather. He'd come in so fast it was almost as if he'd been hovering outside. O'Shaughnessy realized he probably had been.

And now, at last, Custer turned toward O'Shaughnessy. "Paddy!" he said in his high, thin voice. "How's the last Irish cop on the force doing these days?"

O'Shaughnessy waited just long enough to be insolent, and then answered: "It's Patrick, sir."

"Patrick, Patrick. I thought they called you Paddy," Custer went on, some of the hearty bluster gone.

"There are still plenty of Irish on the force, sir."

"Yeah, yeah, but how many are named Patrick Murphy O'Shaughnessy? I mean, is that Irish or what? That's like Chaim Moishe Finkelstein, or Vinnie Scarpetta Gotti della Gambino. Ethnic. Very ethnic. But hey, don't get me wrong. Ethnic's good."

"Very good," Noyes said.

"I'm always saying we need diversity on the force. Right?"

"Sure," O'Shaughnessy replied.

"Anyway, *Patrick,* we've got a little problem here. A few days ago, thirty-six skeletons were uncovered at a construction site here in the precinct. You may have heard of it. I supervised the investigation myself. It's a Moegen-Fairhaven development. You know them?"

"Sure I do." O'Shaughnessy glanced pointedly at the oversized Montblanc fountain pen in Custer's shirt pocket. Mr. Fairhaven had given them as Christmas presents to all the precinct captains in Manhattan the year before.

"Big outfit. Lots of money, lots of friends. Good people. Now these skeletons, Patrick, are well over a century old. It's our understanding that some maniac back in the eighteen hundreds murdered these people and hid them in a basement. With me so far?"

O'Shaughnessy nodded.

"Have you ever had any experience with the FBI?"

"No, sir."

"They tend to think working cops are stupid. They like to keep us in the dark. It's fun for them."

"It's a little game they play," said Noyes, with a small bob of his shiny head. It was hard to make a crew cut look oily, but somehow Noyes managed.

"That's exactly right," Custer said. "You know what we're saying, Patrick?"

"Sure." They were saying he was about to get some shit-stink assignment involving the FBI: that's what he knew.

"Good. For some reason, we've got an FBI agent poking around the site. He won't say why he's interested. He's not even local, from New Orleans, believe it or not. But the guy's got pull. I'm still looking into it. The boys in the New York office don't like him any more than we do. They told me some stories about him, and I didn't like what I heard. Wherever this guy goes, trouble follows. You with me?"

"Yes, sir."

"This guy's been calling all over the place. Wants to see the bones. Wants to see the pathologist's report. Wants everything under the sun. He doesn't seem to get that the crime's ancient history. So now, Mr. Fairhaven is concerned.

He doesn't want this getting blown out of proportion, you know? He's gonna have to rent those apartments. You get my drift? And when Mr. Fairhaven gets concerned, he calls the mayor. The mayor calls Commissioner Rocker. The commissioner calls the commander. And the commander calls me. Which means that now *I'm* concerned."

O'Shaughnessy nodded. *Which means now I'm supposed to be concerned, which I'm not.*

"Very concerned," said Noyes.

O'Shaughnessy allowed his face to relax into the most unconcerned of looks.

"So here's what's going to happen. I'm going to assign you to be this guy's NYPD liaison. You stick to him like a fly to, er, honey. I want to know what he's doing, where he goes, and especially what he's up to. But don't get too friendly with the guy."

"No, sir."

"His name is Pendergast. Special Agent Pendergast." Custer turned over a piece of paper. "Christ, they didn't even give me his first name here. No matter. I've set up a meeting with you and him tomorrow, two P.M. After that, you stay with him. You're there to *help* him, that's the official line. But don't be *too* helpful. This guy's ticked off a lot of people. Here, read for yourself."

O'Shaughnessy took the proffered file. "Do you want me to remain in uniform, sir?"

"Hell, that's just the point! Having a uniformed cop sticking to him like a limpet is going to cramp his style. You get me?"

"Yes, sir."

The captain sat back in his chair, looking at him skeptically. "Think you can do this, Patrick?"

O'Shaughnessy stood up. "Sure."

"Because I've been noticing your *attitude* recently." Custer put a finger to the side of his nose. "A friendly word of advice. Save it for Agent Pendergast. Last thing you, of all people, need is more attitude."

"No attitude, sir. I'm just here to protect and serve." He pronounced *sairve* in his best Irish brogue. "Top of the mornin' to you, Captain."

As O'Shaughnessy turned and left the office, he heard Custer mutter "wise ass" to Noyes.

THREE

"A PERFECT AFTERNOON TO TAKE IN A MUSEUM," SAID Pendergast, looking up at a lowering sky.

Patrick Murphy O'Shaughnessy wondered if it was some kind of joke. He stood on the steps of the Elizabeth Street precinct house, staring off into nowhere. The whole thing was a joke. The FBI agent looked more like an undertaker than a cop, with his black suit, blond-white hair, and movie-cliché accent. He wondered how such a piece of work ever got his ass through Quantico.

"The Metropolitan Museum of Art is a cultural paradigm, Sergeant. One of the great art museums of the world. But of course you knew that. Shall we go?"

O'Shaughnessy shrugged. Museums, whatever, he was supposed to stay with this guy. What a crappy assignment.

As they descended the steps, a long gray car came gliding up from where it had been idling at the corner. For a second O'Shaughnessy could hardly believe it. A Rolls. Pendergast opened the door.

"Drug seizure?" O'Shaughnessy asked.

"No. Personal vehicle."

Figures. New Orleans. They were all on the take down

there. Now he had the guy pegged. Probably up here on some kind of drug business. Maybe Custer wanted in. That's why he put him, of all the cops in the precinct, on this guy's ass. This was looking worse by the minute.

Pendergast continued holding the door. "After you."

O'Shaughnessy slid in the back, sinking immediately into creamy white leather.

Pendergast ducked in beside him. "To the Metropolitan Museum," he told the driver. As the Rolls pulled away from the curb, O'Shaughnessy caught a glimpse of Captain Custer standing on the steps, staring after them. He resisted the impulse to flip him the bird.

O'Shaughnessy turned to Pendergast and gave him a good look. "Here's to success, Mister FBI Agent."

He turned away to look out the window. There was a silence on the other side.

"The name is Pendergast," came the soft voice, finally.

"Whatever."

O'Shaughnessy continued to look out the window. He allowed a minute to pass, and then he said: "So what's at the museum? Some dead mummies?"

"I have yet to meet a live mummy, Sergeant. However, it is not the Egyptian Department we are going to."

A wise guy. He wondered how many more assignments he'd have like this. Just because he made a mistake five years ago, they all thought he was Mister Expendable. Any time there was something funny coming down the pike, it was always: *We've got a little problem here, O'Shaughnessy, and you're just the man to take care of it.* But it was usually just penny-ante stuff. This guy in the Rolls, he looked big-time. This was different. This looked illegal. O'Shaughnessy thought of his long-gone father and felt a stab of shame. Thank God the man wasn't around to see him now. Five generations of O'Shaughnessys in the force, and now everything gone to shit. He wondered if he could hack the eleven more years required before an early severance package became available.

"So what's the game?" O'Shaughnessy asked. No more sucker work: he was going to keep his eyes open and his head up on this one. He didn't want any stray shit to fall when he wasn't looking up.

"Sergeant?"

"What."

"There is no game."

"Of course not." O'Shaughnessy let out a little snort. "There never is." He realized the FBI agent was looking at him intently. He continued looking away.

"I can see that you're under a misapprehension here, Sergeant," came the drawl. "We should rectify that at once. You see, I can understand why you'd jump to that conclusion. Five years ago, you were caught on a surveillance tape taking two hundred dollars from a prostitute in exchange for releasing her. I believe they call it a 'shakedown.' Have I got that right?"

O'Shaughnessy felt a sudden numbness, followed by a slow anger. Here it was again. He said nothing. What was there to say? It would have been better if they'd cashiered him.

"The tape got sent to Internal Affairs. Internal Affairs paid you a visit. But there were differing accounts of what happened, nothing was proven. Unfortunately, the damage was done, and since that time you've seen your career—how should I put it?—remain in stasis."

O'Shaughnessy continued looking out the window, at the rush of buildings. *Remain in stasis. You mean, go nowhere.*

"And you've caught nothing since but a series of

questionable assignments and gray-area errands. Of which you no doubt consider this one more."

O'Shaughnessy spoke to the window, his voice deliberately tired. "Pendergast, I don't know what your game is, but I don't need to listen to this. I really don't."

"I saw that tape," said Pendergast.

"Good for you."

"I heard, for example, the prostitute pleading with you to let her go, saying that her pimp would beat her up if you didn't. Then I heard her insisting you take the two hundred dollars, because if you didn't, her pimp would assume she had betrayed him. But if you *took* the money, he would only think she'd bribed her way out of custody and spare her. Am I right? So you took the money."

O'Shaughnessy had been through this in his own mind a thousand times. What difference did it make? He didn't have to take the money. He hadn't given it to charity, either. Pimps were beating up prostitutes every day. He should've left her to her fate.

"So now you're cynical, you're tired, you've come to realize that the whole idea of *protect and serve* is farcical, especially out there on the streets, where there doesn't even seem to be right or wrong, nobody worth protecting, and nobody worth serving."

There was a silence.

"Are we through with the character analysis?" O'Shaughnessy asked.

"For the moment. Except to say that, yes, this is a questionable assignment. But not in the way you're thinking."

The next silence stretched into minutes.

They stopped at a light, and O'Shaughnessy took an opportunity to cast a covert glance toward Pendergast. The man, as if knowing the glance was coming, caught his eye and pinned it. O'Shaughnessy almost jumped, he looked away so fast.

"Did you, by any chance, catch the show last year, *Costuming History*?" Pendergast asked, his voice now light and pleasant.

"What?"

"I'll take that as a no. You missed a splendid exhibition. The Met has a fine collection of historical clothing dating back to the early Middle Ages. Most of it was in storage. But last year, they mounted an exhibition showing how clothing evolved over the last six centuries. Absolutely fascinating. Did you know that all ladies at Louis XIV's court at Versailles were required to have a thirteen-inch waist or less? And that their dresses weighed between thirty and forty pounds?"

O'Shaughnessy realized he didn't know how to answer. The conversation had taken such a strange and sudden tack that he found himself momentarily stunned.

"I was also interested to learn that in the fifteenth century, a man's codpiece—"

This tidbit was mercifully interrupted by a screech of brakes as the Rolls swerved to avoid a cab cutting across three lanes of traffic.

"Yankee barbarians," said Pendergast mildly. "Now, where was I? Ah yes, the codpiece . . ."

The Rolls was caught in Midtown traffic now, and O'Shaughnessy began to wonder just how much longer this ride was going to take.

The Great Hall of the Metropolitan Museum was sheeted in Beaux Arts marble, decorated with vast sprays of flowers, and almost unbearably crowded. O'Shaughnessy hung back while the strange FBI agent talked to one of the harried volunteers at the information desk. She picked up a phone, called someone, then put it down again, looking highly irritated. O'Shaughnessy began to wonder what this Pendergast was up to. Throughout the extended trip uptown he'd said nothing about his intended plan of action.

He glanced around. It was an Upper East Side crowd, for sure: ladies dressed to the nines clicking here and there in high heels, uniformed schoolchildren lined up and well behaved, a few tweedy-looking academics wandering about with thoughtful faces. Several people were staring at him disapprovingly, as if it was in bad taste to be in the Met wearing a police officer's uniform. He felt a rush of misanthropy. Hypocrites.

Pendergast motioned him over, and they passed into the museum, running a gauntlet of ticket takers in the process, past a case full of Roman gold, plunging at last into a confusing sequence of rooms crowded with statues, vases, paintings, mummies, and all manner of art. Pendergast talked the whole time, but the crowds were so dense and the noise so deafening, O'Shaughnessy caught only a few words.

They passed through a quieter suite of rooms full of Asian art, finally arriving in front of a door of shiny gray metal. Pendergast opened it without knocking, revealing a small reception area. A strikingly good-looking receptionist sat behind a desk of blond wood. Her eyes widened slightly at the sight of his uniform. O'Shaughnessy gave her a menacing look.

"May I help you?" She addressed Pendergast, but her eyes continued to flicker anxiously toward O'Shaughnessy.

"Sergeant O'Shaughnessy and Special Agent Pendergast are here to see Dr. Wellesley."

"Do you have an appointment?"

"Alas, no."

The receptionist hesitated. "I'm sorry. Special Agent—?"

"Pendergast. Federal Bureau of Investigation."

At this she flushed deeply. "Just a moment." She picked up her phone. O'Shaughnessy could hear it ringing in an office just off the reception area.

"Dr. Wellesley," the secretary said, "there is a Special Agent Pendergast from the FBI and a police officer here to see you."

The voice that echoed out of the office was easily heard by all. It was a crisp, no-nonsense voice, feminine, yet cold as ice, and so unrelievedly English it made O'Shaughnessy bristle.

"Unless they are here to arrest me, Heather, the gentlemen can make an appointment like everyone else. I am engaged."

The crash of her telephone hitting the cradle was equally unmistakable.

The receptionist looked up at them with high nervousness. "Dr. Wellesley—"

But Pendergast was already moving toward the office from which the voice had issued. *This is more like it,* O'Shaughnessy thought, as Pendergast swung open the door, placing himself squarely in the doorway. At least the guy, for all his pretensions, was no pushover. He knew how to cut through the bullshit.

The unseen voice, laden with sarcasm, cut the air. "Ah, the proverbial copper with his foot in the door. Pity it wasn't locked so you could batter it down with your truncheon."

It was as if Pendergast had not heard. His fluid, honeyed voice filled the office with warmth and charm. "Dr. Wellesley, I have come to you because you are the world's foremost authority on the history of dress. And I hope you'll permit me to say your identification of the Greek peplos of

Vergina was most thrilling to me personally. I have long had an interest in the subject."

There was a brief silence. "Flattery, Mr. Pendergast, will at least get you inside."

O'Shaughnessy followed the agent into a small but very well-appointed office. The furniture looked like it had come directly from the museum's collection, and the walls were hung with a series of eighteenth-century watercolors of opera costumes. O'Shaughnessy thought they might be the characters of Figaro, Rosina, and Count Almaviva from *The Barber of Seville*. Opera was his sole, and his secret, indulgence.

He seated himself, crossing and then uncrossing his legs, shifting in the impossibly uncomfortable chair. No matter what he did, he still seemed to take up too much space. The blue of his uniform seemed unbearably gauche amid the elegant furnishings. He glanced back up at the watercolors, allowing the bars of an aria to go through his head.

Wellesley was an attractive woman in her mid-forties, beautifully dressed. "I see you admire my pictures," she said to O'Shaughnessy, eyeing him shrewdly.

"Sure," said O'Shaughnessy. "If you like dancing in a wig, pumps, and straitjacket."

Wellesley turned to Pendergast. "Your associate has a rather queer sense of humor."

"Indeed."

"Now what can I do for you gentlemen?"

Pendergast removed a bundle from under his suit, loosely wrapped in paper. "I would like you to examine this dress," he said, unrolling the bundle across the curator's desk. She backed up slightly in horror as the true dimensions of its filth were exposed to view.

O'Shaughnessy thought he detected a peculiar smell. Very

peculiar. It occurred to him that maybe, just maybe, Pendergast wasn't on the take—that this was for real.

"Good lord. Please," she said, stepping farther back and putting a hand before her face. "I do not do police work. Take this revolting thing away."

"This revolting thing, Dr. Wellesley, belonged to a nineteen-year-old girl who was murdered over a hundred years ago, dissected, dismembered, and walled up in a tunnel in lower Manhattan. Sewn up into the dress was a note, which the girl wrote in her own blood. It gave her name, age, and address. Nothing else—ink of that sort does not encourage prolixity. It was the note of a girl who knew she was about to die. She knew that no one would help her, no one would save her. Her only wish was that her body be identified—that she not be forgotten. I could not help her then, but I am trying to now. That is why I am here." The dress seemed to quiver slightly, and O'Shaughnessy realized with a start that the FBI agent's hand was trembling with emotion. At least, that's how it looked to him. That a law officer would actually *care* about something like this was a revelation.

The silence that followed Pendergast's statement was profound.

Without a word, Wellesley bent down over the dress, fingered it, turned up its lining, gently stretched the material in several directions. Reaching into a drawer of her desk, she pulled out a large magnifying glass and began examining the stitching and fabric. Several minutes passed. Then she sighed and sat down in her chair.

"This is a typical workhouse garment," she said. "Standard issue in the latter part of the nineteenth century. Cheap woolen fabric for the exterior, scratchy and coarse but actually quite warm, lined with undyed cotton. You can see from the pattern cuts and stitching that it was probably made by the girl herself, using fabric issued to her by the workhouse. The fabrics came in several basic colors—green, blue, gray, and black."

"Any idea which workhouse?"

"Impossible to say. Nineteenth-century Manhattan had quite a few of them. They were called 'houses of industry.' They took in abandoned children, orphans, and runaways. Harsh, cruel places, run by the so-called religious."

"Can you give me a more precise date on the dress?"

"Not with any accuracy. It seems to be a rather pathetic imitation of a style popular in the early eighteen eighties, called a Maude Makin. Workhouse girls usually tried to copy dresses they liked out of popular magazines and penny press advertisements." Dr. Wellesley sighed, shrugged. "That's it, I'm afraid."

"If anything else comes to mind, I can be contacted through Sergeant O'Shaughnessy here."

Dr. Wellesley glanced up at O'Shaughnessy's name tag, then nodded.

"Thank you for your time." The FBI agent began rolling up the dress. "That was a lovely exhibition you curated last year, by the way."

Dr. Wellesley nodded again.

"Unlike most museum exhibitions, it had wit. Take the houppelande section. I found it delightfully amusing."

Concealed in its wrapper, the dress lost its power to horrify. The feeling of gloom that had settled over the office began to lift. O'Shaughnessy found himself echoing Custer: what was an FBI agent doing messing around with a case 120 years old?

"Thank you for noticing what none of the critics did," the woman replied. "Yes, I meant it to be fun. When you finally understand it, human dress—beyond what is necessary for warmth and modesty—can be marvelously absurd."

Pendergast stood. "Dr. Wellesley, your expertise has been most valuable."

Dr. Wellesley rose as well. "Please call me Sophia." O'Shaughnessy noticed her looking at Pendergast with new interest.

Pendergast bowed and smiled. Then he turned to go. The curator came around her desk to see him through the waiting room. At the outer door, Sophia Wellesley paused, blushed, and said, "I hope to see you again, Mr. Pendergast. Perhaps soon. Perhaps for dinner."

There was a brief silence. Pendergast said nothing.

"Well," said the curator crisply, "you know where to reach me."

They walked back through the thronged, treasure-laden halls, past the Khmer devatars, past the reliquaries encrusted with gems, past the Greek statues and the Red Attic vases, down the great crowded steps to Fifth Avenue. O'Shaughnessy whistled an astringent little chorus of Sade's "Smooth Operator." If Pendergast heard, he gave no sign.

Moments later, O'Shaughnessy was sliding into the white leather cocoon of the Rolls. When the door shut with a solid, reassuring *thunk,* blessed silence returned. He still couldn't figure out what to make of Pendergast—maybe the guy, for all his expensive tastes, was on the up-and-up. He sure as hell knew this: he was going to keep his eyes and ears open.

"Across the park to the New York Museum of Natural History, please," Pendergast told the driver. As the car accelerated into traffic, the agent turned to O'Shaughnessy.

"How is it that an Irish policeman came to love Italian opera?"

O'Shaughnessy gave a start. When had he mentioned opera?

"You disguise your thoughts poorly, Sergeant. While you were looking at the drawings from *The Barber of Seville,* I saw your right index finger unconsciously tapping the rhythm to Rosina's aria, *'Una voce poco fa.'*"

O'Shaughnessy stared at Pendergast. "I bet you think you're a real Sherlock Holmes."

"One does not often find a policeman with a love of opera."

"What about you? You like opera?" O'Shaughnessy threw the question back at him.

"I loathe it. Opera was the television of the nineteenth century: loud, vulgar, and garish, with plots that could only be called infantile."

For the first time, O'Shaughnessy smiled. He shook his head. "Pendergast, all I can say is, your powers of observation aren't nearly as formidable as you seem to think. Jesus, what a philistine."

His smile widened as he saw a look of irritation cloud the FBI agent's face for no more than an instant. He had finally gotten to him.

FOUR

NORA USHERED PENDERGAST AND THE DOUR-LOOKING little policeman through the doorway of Central Archives, a little relieved she'd had no trouble finding her way this time.

Pendergast paused inside the door, inhaling deeply. "Ahhh. The smell of history. Drink it in, Sergeant." He put out his hands, fingers extended, as if to warm them on the documents within.

Reinhart Puck advanced toward Pendergast, head wagging. He wiped his shining pate with a handkerchief, then stuffed the cloth into a pocket with awkward fingers. The sight of the FBI agent seemed to both please and alarm him. "Dr. Pendergast," he said. "A pleasure. I don't think we've met since, let's see, the Troubles of '95. Did you take that trip to Tasmania?"

"I did indeed, thank you for remembering. And my knowledge of Australian flora has increased proportionately."

"And how's the, er, your department?"

"Splendid," said Pendergast. "Allow me to introduce Sergeant O'Shaughnessy."

The policeman stepped out from behind Pendergast, and

Puck's face fell. "Oh, dear. There is a rule, you see. Non-Museum employees—"

"I can vouch for him," said Pendergast, a note of finality in his voice. "He is an outstanding member of the *police* force of our city."

"I see, I see," Puck said unhappily, as he worked the locks. "Well, you'll all have to sign in, you know." He turned away from the door. "And this is Mr. Gibbs."

Oscar Gibbs nodded curtly. He was small, compact, and African-American, with hairless arms and a closely shaven head. For his size, his build was so solid he seemed fashioned out of butcher-block. He was covered with dust and looked distinctly unhappy to be there.

"Mr. Gibbs has kindly set up everything for you in the Research Room," said Puck. "We'll go through the formalities, and then if you'll be so good as to follow me?"

They signed the book, then advanced into the gloom, Puck lighting the way, as before, by the banks of ivory switches. After what seemed an interminable journey, they arrived at a door set into the plastered rear wall of the Archives, with a small window of glass and metal meshing. With a heavy jangle of keys, Puck laboriously unlocked it, then held it open for Nora. She stepped inside. The lights came up and she almost gasped in astonishment.

Polished oak paneling rose from a marble floor to an ornate, plastered and gilded ceiling of rococo splendor. Massive oaken tables with claw feet dominated the center of the room, surrounded by oak chairs with red leather seats and backs. On each table sat small leather-sided boxes, containing special pencils and paper for note-taking. Heavy chandeliers of worked copper and crystal hung suspended above each table. Two of the tables were covered by a variety of objects, and a third had been laid out with boxes, books, and papers. A massive, bricked-up fireplace, surrounded by pink marble, stood at the far end of the room. Everything was hoary with the accumulated patina of years.

"This is incredible," said Nora.

"Yes, indeed," said Puck. "One of the finest rooms in the Museum. Historical research used to be very important." He sighed. "Times have changed. *O tempo, O mores,* and all that. Please remove all writing instruments from your pockets, and put on those linen gloves before handling any of the objects. I will need to take your briefcase, Doctor." He glanced disapprovingly at the gun and handcuffs dangling from O'Shaughnessy's service belt, but said nothing.

They laid their pens and pencils into a proffered tray. Nora and the others slid on pairs of spotless gloves.

"I will withdraw. When you are ready to leave, call me on that telephone. Extension 4240. If you want photocopies of anything, fill out one of these sheets."

The door eased shut. There was the sound of a key turning in a lock.

"Did he just lock us in?" O'Shaughnessy asked.

Pendergast nodded. "Standard procedure."

O'Shaughnessy stepped back into the gloom. *He was an odd man,* Nora thought; *quiet, inscrutable, handsome in a Black Irish kind of way.* Pendergast seemed to like him. O'Shaughnessy, on the other hand, looked as if he didn't like anybody.

The agent clasped his hands behind his back and made a slow circuit of the first table, peering at each object in turn. He did the same with the second table, then moved to the third table, laden with its assorted papers.

"Let's see this inventory you mentioned," he said to Nora.

Nora pointed out the promissory note with the inventory she had found the day before. Pendergast looked it over, and then, paper in hand, made another circuit. He nodded at a stuffed okapi. "That came from Shottum's," he said. "And that." He nodded to the elephant's-foot box. "Those three penis sheaths and the right whale baculum. The Jivaro shrunken head. All from Shottum's, payment to McFadden for his work." He bent down to examine the shrunken head. "A fraud. Monkey, not human." He glanced up at her. "Dr. Kelly, would you mind looking through the papers while I examine these objects?"

Nora sat down at the third table. There was the small box of Shottum's correspondence, along with another, much larger, box and two binders—McFadden's papers, apparently. Nora opened the Shottum box first. As Puck had noted, the contents were in a remarkable state of disarray. What few letters were here were all in the same vein: questions about classifications and identifications, tiffs with other scientists over various arcane subjects. It illuminated a curious corner of nineteenth-century natural history, but shed no light on a heinous nineteenth-century crime. As she read through the brief correspondence, a picture of J. C. Shottum began to form in her mind. It was not the image of a serial killer. He seemed a harmless enough man, fussy, narrow, a little querulous perhaps, bristling with academic rivalries. The man's interests seemed exclusively related to natural history. *Of course, you can never tell,* she thought, turning over the musty pages.

Finding nothing of particular interest, Nora turned to the much larger—and neater—boxes of Tinbury McFadden's correspondence. They were mostly notes from the long-dead curator on various odd subjects, written in a fanatically small hand: lists of classifications of plants and animals, drawings of various flowers, some quite good. At the bottom was a thick packet of correspondence to and from various men of science and collectors, held together by an ancient string that flew apart when she touched it. She riffled through them, arriving finally at a packet of letters from Shottum to McFadden. The first began, "My Esteemed Colleague."

> *I herewith transmit to you a Curious Relic said to be from the Isle of Kut, off the coast of Indochine, depicting a simian in coito with a Hindoo goddess, carved from walrus ivory. Would you be so kind as to identify the species of simian?*
>   *Your colleague, J. C. Shottum*

She slid out the next letter:

> *My Dear Colleague,*
>   *At the last meeting at the Lyceum, Professor Blackwood presented a fossil which he claimed was a Devonian Age crinoid from the Montmorency Dolomites. The Professor is sadly mistaken. LaFleuve himself identified the Montmorency Dolomites as Permian, and needs make a corrective note of it in the next Lyceum Bulletin . . .*

She flipped through the rest. There were letters to others as well, a small circle of like-minded scientists, including Shottum. They were all obviously well acquainted with one another. Perhaps the killer might be found in that circle. It seemed likely, since the person must have had easy access to Shottum's Cabinet—if it wasn't Shottum himself.

She began to make a list of correspondents and the nature of their work. Of course, it was always possible this was a waste of time, that the killer might have been the building's janitor or coal man—but then she remembered the crisp, professional scalpel marks on the bones, the almost surgical dismemberments. No, it was a man of science—that was certain.

Taking out her notebook, she began jotting notes.

Letters to/from Tinbury McFadden:

CORRESPONDENT	SUBJECTS OF CORRESPONDENCE	POSITION	DATES OF CORRESPONDENCE
J. C. Shottum	Natural history, anthropology, the Lyceum	Owner, Shottum's Cabinet of Natural Productions and Curiosities New York	1869–1881
Prof. Albert Blackwood	The Lyceum, the Museum	Founder, New York Museum of Natural History	1865–1878
Dr. Asa Stone Gilcrease	Birds	Ornithologist New York	1875–1887
Col. Sir Henry C. Throckmorton, Bart., F.R.S.	African mammals (big game)	Collector, explorer sportsman London	1879–1891
Prof. Enoch Leng	Classification	Taxonomist, chemist New York	1872–1881
Miss Guenevere LaRue	Christian missions for Borrioboola-Gha, in the African Congo	Philanthropist New York	1870–1872

CORRESPONDENT	SUBJECTS OF CORRESPONDENCE	POSITION	DATES OF CORRESPONDENCE
Dumont Burleigh	Dinosaur fossils, the Lyceum	Oilman, collector Cold Spring, New York	1875–1881
Dr. Ferdinand Huntt	Anthropology, archaeology	Surgeon, collector Oyster Bay, Long Island	1869–1879
Prof. Hiram Howlett	Reptiles and amphibians	Herpetologist Stormhaven, Maine	1871–1873

The penultimate name gave her pause. A surgeon. Who was Dr. Ferdinand Huntt? There were quite a few letters from him, written in a large scrawl on heavy paper with a beautifully engraved crest. She flipped through them.

> *My Dear Tinbury,*
> *With regard to the Odinga Natives, the barbaric custom of Male Partum is still quite prevalent. When I was in the Volta I had the dubious privilege of witnessing childbirth. I was not allowed to assist, of course, but I could hear the shrieks of the husband quite clearly as the wife jerked on the rope affixed to his genitalia with every contraction she experienced. I treated the poor man's injuries—severe lacerations—following the birth . . .*

> *My Dear Tinbury,*
> *The Olmec Jade phallus I herewith enclose from La Venta, Mexico, is for the Museum, as I understand you have nothing from that extremely curious Mexican culture . . .*

She sorted through the packet of correspondence, but it was again all in the same vein: Dr. Huntt describing various bizarre medical customs he had witnessed in his travels across Central America and Africa, along with notes that had apparently accompanied artifacts sent back to the Museum. He seemed to have an unhealthy interest in native sexual practices; it made him a prime candidate in Nora's mind.

She felt a presence behind her and turned abruptly. Pendergast stood, arms clasped behind his back. He was staring down at her notes, and there was a sudden look on his face that was so grim, so dark, that Nora felt her flesh crawl.

"You're always sneaking up on me," she said weakly.

"Anything interesting?" The question seemed almost pro forma. Nora felt sure he had already discovered something important, something dreadful, on the list—and yet he did not seem inclined to share it.

"Nothing obvious. Have you ever heard of this Dr. Ferdinand Huntt?"

Pendergast gave the name a cursory glance, without interest. Nora became aware of the man's conspicuous lack of any scent whatsoever: no smell of tobacco, no smell of cologne, nothing.

"Huntt," he said finally. "Yes. A prominent North Shore family. One of the early patrons of the Museum." He straightened up. "I've examined everything save the elephant's-foot box. Would you care to assist me?"

She followed him over to the table laid out with Tinbury McFadden's old collections, a decidedly motley assortment. Pendergast's face had once again recovered its poise. Now Officer O'Shaughnessy, looking skeptical, emerged from the shadows. Nora wondered what, exactly, the policeman had to do with Pendergast.

They stood before the large, grotesque elephant's foot, replete with brass fittings.

"So it's an elephant's foot," O'Shaughnessy said. "So?"

"Not just a foot, Sergeant," Pendergast replied. "A box, made from an elephant's foot. Quite common among big-game hunters and collectors in the last century. Rather a nice specimen, too, if a little worn." He turned to Nora. "Shall we look inside?"

Nora unclasped the fittings and lifted the top of the box. The grayish skin felt rough and nubbled beneath her gloved fingers. An unpleasant smell rose up. The box was empty.

She glanced over at Pendergast. If the agent was disappointed, he showed no sign.

For a moment, the little group was still. Then Pendergast himself bent over the open box. He examined it a moment, his body immobile save for the pale blue eyes. Then his fingers shot forward and began moving over the surface of the box, pressing here and there, alighting at one spot for a moment, then scuttling on. Suddenly there was a click, and a narrow drawer shot out from below, raising a cloud of dust. Nora jumped at the sound.

"Rather clever," said Pendergast, removing a large envelope, faded and slightly foxed, from the drawer. He turned it over once or twice, speculatively. Then he ran a gloved finger beneath the seam, easing it open and withdrawing several sheets of cream-laid paper. He unfolded them carefully, passed his hand across the topmost sheet.

And then he began to read.

FIVE

To My Colleague, Tinbury McFadden

July 12, 1881

Esteemed Colleague,

I write these lines in earnest hope that you will never have need to read them; that I will be able to tear them up and dash them into the coal scuttle, products of an overworked brain and fevered imagination. And yet in my soul I know my worst fears have already been proven true. Everything I have uncovered points incontrovertibly to such a fact. I have always been eager to think the best of my fellow man—after all, are we not all moulded from the same clay? The ancients believed life to have generated spontaneously within the rich mud of the Nile; and who am I to question the symbolism, if not the scientific fact, of such belief? And yet there have been Events, McFadden; dreadful events that can support no innocent explanation.

It is quite possible that the details I relate herein may

cause you to doubt the quality of my mind. Before I proceed, let me assure you that I am in full command of my faculties. I offer this document as evidence, both to my dreadful theorem and to the proofs I have undertaken in its defense.

I have spoken before of my growing doubts over this business of Leng. You know, of course, the reasons I allowed him to take rooms on the third floor of the Cabinet. His talks at the Lyceum proved the depth of his scientific and medical knowledge. In taxonomy and chemistry he has few, if any, peers. The notion that enlightening, perhaps even forward-reaching, experiments would be taking place beneath my own roof was a pleasant one. And, on a practical note, the additional hard currency offered by his rent was not unwelcome.

At first, my trust in the man seemed fully justified. His curatorial work at the Cabinet proved excellent. Although he kept highly irregular hours, he was unfailingly polite, if a little reserved. He paid his rent money promptly, and even offered medical advice during the bouts of grippe that plagued me throughout the winters of '73 and '74.

It is hard to date with any precision my first glimmerings of suspicion. Perhaps it began with what, in my perception, was a growing sense of secretiveness about the man's affairs. Although he had promised early on to share the formal results of his experiments, except for an initial joint inspection when the lease was signed I was never invited to see his chambers. As the years passed, he seemed to grow more and more absorbed in his own studies, and I was forced to take on much of the curatorial duties for the Cabinet myself.

I had always believed Leng to be rather sensitive about his work. You will no doubt recall the early and somewhat eccentric talk on Bodily Humours he presented to the Lyceum. It was not well received—some members even had the ill breeding to titter on one or two occasions during the lecture—and henceforth Leng never returned to the subject. His future talks were all models of traditional scholarship. So at first, I ascribed his hesitancy to discuss personal work to this same innate circumspection. However, as time went on, I began to realize that what I had thought to be professional shyness was, in fact, active *concealment.*

One spring evening earlier this year, I had occasion to stay on very late at the Cabinet, finishing work on an accumulation of documents and preparing the exhibition space for my latest acquisition, the double-brained child, of which we have previously spoken. This latter task proved far more engrossing than the tiresome paperwork, and I was rather surprised to hear the city bell toll midnight.

It was in the moments following, as I stood, listening to the echoes of the bell die away, that I became aware of another sound. It came from over my head: a kind of heavy shuffling, as if of a man bearing some heavy burden. I cannot tell you why precisely, McFadden, but there was something in that sound that sent a thrill of dread coursing through me. I listened more intently. The sound died away slowly, the footsteps retreating into a more distant room.

Of course there was nothing for me to do. In the morning, as I reflected on the event, I realized the culprit was undoubtedly my own tired nerves. Unless some more sinister meaning should prove to be attached to the footsteps—which seemed a remote possibility—there was no cause for approaching Leng on the matter. I ascribed my alarm to my own perverse state of mind at the time. I had succeeded in creating a rather sensational backdrop for displaying the double-brained child, and no doubt this, along with the late hour, had roused the more morbid aspects of my imagination. I resolved to put the matter behind me.

It chanced that some few weeks later—the fifth of July, last week, to be precise—another event took place to which I most earnestly commend your attention. The circumstances were similar: I remained late at the Cabinet, preparing my upcoming paper for the Lyceum journal. As you know, writing for learned bodies such as the Lyceum is difficult for me, and I have fallen into certain routines which ease the process somewhat. My old teakwood writing desk, the fine vellum paper upon which this note is now being written, the fuchsia-colored ink made by M. Dupin in Paris—these are the petty niceties which make composition less onerous. This evening, inspiration came rather more easily than usual, however, and around half past ten I found it necessary to sharpen some new pens before work could continue. I turned away from my desk briefly to effect this. When I returned I found, to my utmost astonishment, that the page on which I had been at work had been soiled with some small number of inkstains.

I am most fastidious with a pen, and was at a loss to explain how this came about. It was only when I took up my blotter to clear away the stains that I realized they differed slightly in color from the fuchsia of my pen, being a somewhat lighter shade. And when I blotted them aside, I realized they were of a thicker, more viscous, consistency than my French ink.

Imagine my horror, then, when a *fresh* drop landed upon my wrist as I was in the act of lifting the blotter from the paper.

Immediately, I lifted my eyes to the ceiling above my head. What devilment was this? A small but widening crimson stain was leaching between the floorboards of Leng's chambers overhead.

It was the work of a moment to mount the stairs and pound upon his door. I cannot describe precisely the sequence of thoughts that ran through my mind—foremost among them, however, was fear that the Doctor had fallen victim to foul play. There had been rumors circulating through the neighborhood of a certain vicious and predatory murderer, but one pays little heed to the gossip of the lower classes, and alas, death is a frequent visitor to the Five Points.

Leng answered my frantic summons in due course, sounding a trifle winded. An accident, he said through the door: he had cut his arm rather severely during an experimental procedure. He declined my offers of assistance, and said he had already done the necessary suturing himself. He regretted the incident, but refused to open the door. At last I went away, riven by perplexity and doubt.

The morning following, Leng appeared at my doorstep. He had never called on me at my residence before, and I was surprised to see him. I observed that one arm had been bandaged. He apologized profusely for the inconvenience of the previous night. I invited him inside, but he would not stay. With another apology, he took his leave.

I watched with unsettled heart as he descended the walk and stepped into an omnibus. I pray you will do the honor of understanding me when I say that Leng's visit, coming upon the heels of such strange events at the Cabinet, had precisely the opposite effect to which he had intended. I felt now more sure than ever that, whatever it was he was about, it would not stand up to scrutiny in the honest light of day.

I fear I can write no more this evening. I will hide this letter inside the elephant's-foot box that, along with a group of curiosities, is being forwarded to you at the Museum in two days' time. God willing, I will find the fortitude to return to this and conclude it on the morrow.

July 13, 1881

I must now summon the strength of will to complete my narrative.

In the aftermath of Leng's visit, I found myself in the grip of a terrific internal struggle. A sense of scientific idealism, coupled perhaps with prudence, argued that I should take the man's explanation at its face value. Yet another inner voice argued that it was beholden on me, as a gentleman and a man of honor, to learn the truth for myself.

At last I resolved to discover the nature of the man's experiments. If they proved benign, I could be accused of inquisitiveness—nothing more.

Perhaps you will consider me the victim of unmanly feelings in this matter. I can only say that those vile crimson drops now seemed as imprinted upon my brain as they had been upon my wrist and my writing-paper. There was something about Leng—about the manner in which he had looked at me, there upon my doorstep—that made me feel almost a stranger in my own home. There was some manner of chill speculativeness behind those indifferent-looking eyes that froze my blood. I could no longer tolerate having the man under my roof without knowing the full breadth of his work.

By some personal caprice unfathomable to me, Leng had recently begun donating his medical services to a few local Houses of Industry. As a result, he was invariably absent from his chambers during the latter part of the afternoon. It was on Monday last, July 11, that I saw him through the front windows of the Cabinet. He was crossing the avenue, clearly on his way to the workhouses.

I knew this was no accident: fate had afforded me this opportunity.

It was with some trepidation that I ascended to the third floor. Leng had changed the lock on the door leading into his room, but I retained a skeleton key which turned the wards and unshot the bolt. I let the door fall open before me, then stepped inside.

Leng had decorated the front room into the semblance of a parlor. I was struck by his choice of decoration: gaudy sporting prints were on the walls, and the tables were aclutter with tabloids and penny-dreadfuls. Leng had always struck me as a man of elegance and refinement; yet this room seemed to reflect the tastes of uncultured youth. It was the sort of dive a pool-room tramp or a girl of low breeding would find inviting. There was a pall of dust over everything, as if Leng had spent little time in the parlor of late.

A heavy brocade curtain had been hung over the doorway leading into the rear rooms. I lifted it aside with the end of my walking stick. I thought I had been prepared for almost anything, but what I found was, perhaps, what I least expected.

The rooms were almost entirely empty. There were at

least half a dozen large tables, here and there, whose scarred surfaces bore mute testimony to hours of experimental labor. But they were devoid of furnishing. There was a strong ammoniac smell in the air of these rooms that almost choked me. In one drawer I found several blunt scalpels. All the other drawers I examined were empty, save for dust mites and spiders.

After much searching, I located the spot in the floorboards through which the blood had seeped a few nights before. It seemed to have been etched clean with acid; aqua regia, judging by the odor. I glanced around at the walls then, and noticed other patches, some large, others small, that also seemed to indicate recent cleaning.

I must confess to feeling rather a fool at that moment. There was nothing here to excite alarm; nothing that would rouse the faintest trace of suspicion in even the most perspicacious policeman. And yet the sense of dread refused to wholly leave me. There was something about the oddly decorated parlor, the smell of chemicals, the meticulously cleaned walls and floor, that troubled one. Why were these hidden back rooms clean, while the parlor had been allowed to gather dust?

It was at that moment I remembered the basement.

Years before, Leng had asked, in an offhand way, if he could use the old coal tunnel in the basement for storing excess laboratory equipment. The tunnel had fallen into disuse a few years earlier, with the installation of a new boiler, and I had no need of it myself. I had given him the key and promptly forgotten the matter.

My feelings on descending the cellar stairway behind the Cabinet can scarcely be described. On one occasion I halted, wondering if I should summon an escort. But once again, sane reasoning prevailed. There was no sign of foul play. No—the only thing for it was to proceed myself.

Leng had affixed a padlock to the coal cellar door. Seeing this, I was momentarily overcome by a sense of relief. I had done my utmost; there was nothing else but mount the stairs. I even went so far as to turn around and take the first step. Then I stopped. The same impulse that had brought me this far would not let me leave until I had seen this bad business through.

I raised my foot to kick in the door. Then I hesitated. If I could contrive to remove the lock with a pair of bolt cutters, I reasoned, Leng would think it the work of a sneak-thief.

It was the work of five minutes to retrieve the necessary implement and cut through the hasp of the lock. I dropped it to the ground, then pushed the door wide, allowing the afternoon light to stream down the stairway behind me.

Immediately upon entering, I was overwhelmed with far different sensations than those that had gripped me on the third floor. Whatever work had ceased in Leng's chambers was, clearly, still active here.

Once again, it was the odor I noticed first. As before, there was a smell of caustic reagents, perhaps mixed with formaldehyde or ether. But these were masked by something much richer and more powerful. It was a scent I recognized from passing the hog butcheries on Pearl and Water Streets: it was the smell of a slaughterhouse.

The light filtering down the rear stairs made it unnecessary for me to ignite the gas lamps. Here, too, were numerous tables: but these tables were covered with a complicated sprawl of medical instruments, surgical apparatus, beakers, and retorts. One table contained perhaps three score small vials of light amber liquid, carefully numbered and tagged. A vast array of chemicals were arranged in cabinets against the walls. Sawdust had been scattered across the floor. It was damp in places; scuffing it with the toe of my boot, I discovered that it had been thrown down to absorb a rather large quantity of blood.

I knew now that my apprehensions were not entirely without merit. And yet, I told myself, there was still nothing to raise alarm here: dissections were, after all, a cornerstone of science.

On the closest table was a thick sheaf of carefully jotted notes, gathered into a leather-bound journal. They were penned in Leng's distinctive hand. I turned to these with relief. At last, I would learn what it was Leng had been working towards. Surely some noble scientific purpose would emerge from these pages, to give the lie to my fears.

The journal did no such thing.

You know, old friend, that I am a man of science. I have never been what you might call a God-fearing fellow. But I feared God that day—or rather, I feared his wrath, that such unholy deeds—deeds worthy of Moloch himself— had been committed beneath my roof.

Leng's journal spelt it out in unwavering, diabolical detail. It was perhaps the clearest, most methodical set of scientific notes it has been my eternal misfortune to come across. There is no kind of explanatory gloss I can place upon his experiments; nothing, in fact, I can do but spell it all out as plainly and succinctly as I can.

For the last eight years, Leng has been working to perfect a method of prolonging human life. His own life, by evidence of the notations and recordings in the journal.

But—before God, Tinbury—he was using *other human beings* as material. His victims seemed made up almost entirely of young adults. Again and again, his journal mentioned dissections of human craniums and spinal columns, the latter on which he seems to have focused his depraved attentions. The most recent entries centered particularly on the cauda equina, the ganglion of nerves at the base of the spine.

I read for ten, then twenty minutes, frozen with fascination and horror. Then I dropped the abhorrent document back onto the table and stepped away. Perhaps I *was* a little mad at that point, after all; because I still contrived to find logic in all of this. Body-snatching the recent dead from graveyards is an unfortunate but necessary practice in the medical climate of our day, I told myself. Cadavers for medical research remain in critically short supply, and there is no way to supply the need without resorting to grave-robbing. Even the most respectable surgeons need resort to it, I told myself. And even though Leng's attempts at artificially prolonging life were clearly beyond the pale, it was still possible he might unintentionally achieve other breakthroughs that would have beneficial effects . . .

It was at that point, I believe, that I first noticed the sound.

To my left, there was a table I had not taken note of before. A large oilcloth had been spread over it, covering something large and rather bulky. As I watched, the faint sound came again, from beneath the oilcloth: the sound of some animal dispossessed of tongue, palate, vocal cords.

I cannot explain where I found the strength to approach it, other than my own overpowering need to know. I stepped forward, and then—before my resolution could falter—I gripped the greasy cloth and drew it away.

The sight uncovered in that dim light will haunt me until my last day. It lay upon its stomach. A gaping hole lay where the base of the spine had once been. The sound I had heard was, it seemed to me, the escaping gases of decay.

You might have thought me incapable of registering fresh shock at this point. Yet I noticed, with a rising sense of unreality, that both the corpse and the wound appeared fresh.

I hesitated for perhaps five, perhaps ten seconds. Then I drew closer, my mind possessed by one thought, and one thought only. Could this be the body that had bled so profusely on Leng's floor? How, then, to explain the rawness of the wound? Was it possible—even conceivable—that Leng would make use of two corpses within the span of a single week?

I had come this far: I had to know all. I reached forward, gingerly, to turn the body and check its lividity.

The skin felt supple, the flesh warm in the humid summer cellar. As I turned the body over and the face was exposed, I saw to my transcendent horror that a blood-soaked rag had been knotted around the mouth. I snatched my hand away; the thing rolled back onto the table, face upwards.

I stepped back, reeling. In my shock, I did not immediately understand the terrible import of that blood-soaked rag. I think if I had, I would have turned and fled that place—and in so doing been spared the final horror.

For it was then, McFadden, that the eyes above the rag fluttered open. They had once been human, but pain and terror had riven all humanity from their expression.

As I stood, transfixed by fear, there came another low moan.

It was, I knew now, not gas escaping from a corpse. And this was not the work of a man who trafficked with body snatchers, with corpses stolen from graveyards. This poor creature on the table was still alive. Leng practiced his abominable work on those who *still lived*.

Even as I watched, the horrible, pitiable thing on the table moaned once more, then expired. Somehow, I had the presence of mind to replace the body as I had found it, cover it with the oilcloth, close the door, and climb up out of that charnel pit into the land of the living . . .

I have barely moved from my chambers within the Cabinet since. I have been trying to gather courage for what I know in my heart remains to be done. You must see now, dear colleague, that there can be no mistake, no other explanation, for what I found in the basement. Leng's journal was far too comprehensive, too diabolically detailed, for there to be any misapprehension. As further evidence, on the attached sheet I have reproduced, from memory, some of the scientific observations and procedures this monstrous man recorded within its pages. I would go to the police, except I feel that only I can—

But hark! I hear his footstep on the stair even now. I must return this letter to its hiding place and conclude tomorrow.

God give me the strength for what I must now do.

SIX

ROGER BRISBANE LEANED BACK IN HIS OFFICE CHAIR, HIS eyes roaming the glass expanse of desk that lay before him. It was a long, enjoyable perambulation: Brisbane liked order, purity, simplicity, and the desk shone with a mirror-like perfection. At last, his gaze came to the case of jewels. It was that time of day when a lance of sunlight shot through the case, turning its occupants into glittering spheres and ovals of entangled light and color. One could call an emerald "green" or a sapphire "blue," but the words did no justice to the actual colors. There were no adequate words for such colors in any human language.

Jewels. They lasted forever, so hard and cold and pure, so impervious to decay. Always beautiful, always perfect, always as fresh as the day they were born in unimaginable heat and pressure. So unlike human beings, with their opaque rubbery flesh and their odoriferous descent from birth to the grave—a story of drool, semen, and tears. He should have become a gemologist. He would have been much happier surrounded by these blooms of pure light. The law career his father had chosen for him was nothing more than a vile parade of human failure. And his job in the Museum brought him in contact with that failure, day in and day out, in stark illumination.

He turned to lean over a computer printout with a sigh. It was now clear the Museum should never have borrowed one hundred million for its new state-of-the-art planetarium. More cuts were needed. Heads would have to roll. Well, at least that shouldn't be too hard to accomplish. The Museum was full of useless, tweedy, overpaid curators and functionaries, always whining about budget cuts, never answering their phones, always off on some research trip spending the Museum's money or writing books that nobody ever read. Cushy jobs, sinecures, unable to be fired because of tenure—unless exceptional circumstances existed.

He put the printout through a nearby shredder, then opened a drawer and pulled out several tied packets of inter-office correspondence. The mail of a dozen likely candidates, intercepted thanks to a man in the mailroom who had been caught organizing a Super Bowl pool on Museum time. With any luck, he'd find plenty of exceptional circumstances inside. It was easier—and easier to justify—than scanning e-mail.

Brisbane shuffled the packets without interest. Then he stopped, glancing at one of them. Here was a case in point: this man Puck. He sat in the Archives all day long, doing what? Nothing, except causing trouble for the Museum.

He untied the packet, riffled through the envelopes within. On the front and back of each were dozens of lines for addresses. The envelopes had a little red tie string and could be reused until they fell apart, simply by adding a new name to the next blank line. And there, on the second-to-last line was Puck's name. And following it was Nora's name.

Brisbane's hand tightened around the envelope. What was

it that arrogant FBI agent, Pendergast, had said? *Most of the work will be archival in nature.*

He unwound the string and slid out a single piece of paper. A whiff of dust rose from the envelope and Brisbane hastily raised a protective tissue to his nose. Holding the paper at arm's length, he read:

> *Dear Dr. Kelly,*
> *I found another small box of papers on Shottum's Cabinet, which somehow had been recently misplaced. Not nearly as astonishing as what you have already uncovered, yet interesting in its own way. I will leave it for you in the Archives Reading Room.*
> *P.*

Color crept into Brisbane's face, then drained out again. It was just as he thought: she was still working for that arrogant FBI agent, and she was continuing to enlist Puck's help. This thing had to be stopped. And Puck had to go. *Just look at this note,* Brisbane thought: manually typed on what was clearly an ancient typewriter. The very inefficiency of it made Brisbane's blood boil. The Museum was not a welfare program for eccentrics. Puck was a fossilized anachronism who should have been put out to pasture long before. He would gather suitable evidence, then draw up a recommended termination list for the next Executive Committee meeting. Puck's name would be at the top.

But what about Nora? He remembered the words of the Museum director, Collopy, at their recent meeting. *Doucement, doucement,* the director had murmured.

And softly it would be. For now.

SEVEN

SMITHBACK STOOD ON THE SIDEWALK, MIDWAY BETWEEN Columbus and Amsterdam, gazing speculatively up at the red-brick facade before him. One hundred eight West Ninety-ninth Street was a broad, prewar apartment house, unembarrassed by any distinguishing architecture, bright in the noonday sun. The bland exterior didn't bother him. What mattered lay within: a rent-stabilized, two-bedroom apartment, near the Museum, for only eighteen hundred a month.

He stepped back toward the street, giving the neighborhood a once-over. It wasn't the most charming Upper West Side neighborhood he had seen, but it had possibilities. Two bums sat on a nearby stoop, drinking something out of a paper bag. He glanced at his watch. Nora would be arriving in five minutes. Christ, this was going to be an uphill battle anyway, if only those bums would take a walk around the corner. He fished into his pocket, found a five dollar bill, and sauntered over.

"Nice day if it don't rain," he said.

The bums eyed him suspiciously.

Smithback brandished the five. "Hey, guys, go buy yourself lunch, okay?"

One of them grinned, exposing a row of decaying teeth. "For five bucks? Man, you can't buy a cup of Starbucks for five bucks. And my legs hurt."

"Yeah," said the other, wiping his nose.

Smithback pulled out a twenty.

"Oh, my aching legs—"

"Take it or leave it."

The closest bum took the twenty and the pair rose to their feet with histrionic groans and sniffles. Soon they were shuffling toward the corner, heading no doubt to the nearby liquor store on Broadway. Smithback watched their retreating backs. At least they were harmless rummys, and not crackheads or worse. He glanced around and saw, right on schedule, a blade-thin woman in black come clicking down the block, a bright, fake lipstick smile on her face. The real estate broker.

"You must be Mr. Smithback," she said in a smoker's croak as she took his hand. "I'm Millie Locke. I have the key to the apartment. Is your, er, partner here?"

"There she is now." Nora had just rounded the corner, cotton trenchcoat billowing, knapsack thrown over her shoulder. She waved.

When Nora arrived the agent took her hand, saying, "How lovely."

They entered a dingy lobby, lined on the left with mailboxes and on the right with a large mirror: a feeble attempt to make the narrow hall look bigger than it actually was. They pressed the button for the elevator. There was a whir and a rattle somewhere overhead.

"It's a perfect location," said Smithback to Nora. "Twenty-minute walk to the Museum, close to the subway station, a block and a half from the park."

Nora did not respond. She was staring at the elevator door, and she did not look happy.

The elevator creaked open and they stepped in. Smithback waited out the excruciatingly long ride, silently willing the damn elevator to hurry up. He had the unpleasant feeling that he, not just the apartment, was undergoing an inspection.

At last they got out at the sixth floor, took a right in a dim hallway, and stopped in front of a brown metal door with an eyehole set into it. The real estate broker unlocked four separate locks and swung the door open.

Smithback was pleasantly surprised. The apartment faced the street, and it was cleaner than he expected. The floors were oak; a bit warped, but oak nevertheless. One wall was exposed brick, the others painted sheetrock.

"Hey, what do you think?" he said brightly. "Pretty nice, huh?"

Nora said nothing.

"It's the bargain of the century," said the broker. "Eighteen hundred dollars, rent-stabilized. A/C. Great location. Bright, quiet."

The kitchen had old appliances, but was clean. The bedrooms were sunny with south-facing windows, which gave the little rooms a feeling of space.

They stopped in the middle of the living room. "Well, Nora," Smithback asked, feeling uncharacteristically shy, "what do you think?"

Nora's face was dark, her brow furrowed. This did not look good. The real estate broker withdrew a few feet, to give them the pretense of privacy.

"It's nice," she said.

"Nice? Eighteen hundred bucks a month for an Upper

West Side two-bedroom? In a prewar building? It's *awesome*."

The real estate broker leaned back toward them. "You're the first to see it. I guarantee you it'll be gone before sunset." She fumbled in her purse, removed a cigarette and a lighter, flicked on the lighter, and then with both hands poised inches apart, asked, "May I?"

"Are you all right?" Smithback asked Nora.

Nora waved her hand, took a step toward the window. She appeared to be looking intently at something far away.

"You did talk to your landlord about moving out, didn't you?"

"No, not quite yet."

Smithback felt his heart sink a little. "You haven't *told* him?"

She shook her head.

The sinking feeling grew more pronounced. "Come on, Nora. I thought we'd decided on this."

She looked out a window. "This is a big move for me, Bill. I mean, living together . . ." Her voice trailed off.

Smithback glanced around at the apartment. The real estate broker caught his eye, quickly looked away. He lowered his voice. "Nora, you do love me, right?"

She continued looking out the window. "Of course. But . . . this is just a really bad day for me, okay?"

"It's no big deal. It's not like we're engaged."

"Let's not talk about it."

"Not talk about it? Nora, *this* is the apartment. We're never going to find a better one. Let's settle the broker's fee."

"Broker's fee?"

Smithback turned to the agent. "What did you say your fee was for this place?"

The agent exhaled a cloud of smoke, gave a little cough.

"I'm glad you asked. It's quite reasonable. Of course, you can't just *rent* an apartment like this. I'm doing you a special favor just showing it to you."

"So how much is this fee?" Nora asked.

"Eighteen."

"Eighteen what? Dollars?"

"Percent. Of the first year's rent, that is."

"But that's—" Nora frowned, did the calculation in her head. "That's close to four thousand dollars."

"It's cheap, considering what you're getting. And I promise you, if you don't go for it, the next person will." She glanced at her watch. "They'll be here in ten minutes. That's how much time you have to make your decision."

"What about it, Nora?" Smithback asked.

Nora sighed. "I have to think about this."

"We don't have time to think about it."

"We have all the time in the world. This isn't the only apartment in Manhattan."

There was a brief, frozen silence. The real estate broker glanced again at her watch.

Nora shook her head. "Bill, I told you. It's been a bad day."

"I can see that."

"You know the Shottum collection I told you about? Yesterday we found a letter, a terrible letter, hidden among that collection."

Smithback felt a feeling akin to panic creeping over him. "Can we talk about this later? I really think this is the apartment—"

She rounded on him, her face dark. "Didn't you hear what I said? We found a *letter*. We know who murdered those thirty-six people!"

There was another silence. Smithback glanced over at the real estate broker, who was pretending to examine a window frame. Her ears were practically twitching. "You do?" he asked.

"He's an extremely shadowy figure named Enoch Leng. He seems to have been a taxonomist and a chemist. The letter was written by a man named Shottum, who owned a kind of museum on the site, called Shottum's Cabinet. Leng rented rooms from Shottum and performed experiments in them. Shottum grew suspicious, took a look into Leng's lab when he was away. He discovered that Leng had been kidnapping people, killing them, and then dissecting out part of their central nervous system and processing it—apparently, for self-administered injections."

"Good God. What for?"

Nora shook her head. "You're not going to believe this. He was trying to extend his life span."

"That's incredible." This was a story—a *gigantic* story. Smithback glanced over at the real estate broker. She was now intently examining the door jambs, her next appointment seemingly forgotten.

"That's what I thought." Nora shuddered. "God, I just can't get that letter out of my head. All the details were there. And Pendergast—you should have seen how grim his face was while he was reading it. Looked as if he was reading his own obituary or something. And then this morning, when I went down to check on some more Shottum material that had turned up, I learn that orders had come down for some conservation work in the Archives. All the Shottum papers were included. And now, they're gone. You can't tell me that's coincidence. It was either Brisbane or Collopy, I'm sure of that, but of course I can't come right out and ask them."

"Did you get a photocopy?"

The dark look on Nora's face lifted slightly. "Pendergast asked me to make one after we first read the letter. I didn't understand his hurry then. I do now."

"Do you have it?"

She nodded toward her briefcase.

Smithback thought for a moment. Nora was right: the conservation orders, of course, were no coincidence. What was the Museum covering up? Who was this man Enoch Leng? Was he connected to the early Museum in some way? Or was it just the usual Museum paranoia, afraid to let out any information that wasn't buffed and polished by their PR people? Then of course there was Fairhaven, the developer, who also happened to be a big contributor to the Museum . . . This whole story was getting good. Very good.

"Can I see the letter?"

"I was going to give it to you for safekeeping—I don't dare bring it back into the Museum. But I want it back tonight."

Smithback nodded. She handed him a thick envelope, which he shoved into his briefcase.

There was a sudden buzz of the intercom.

"There's my next appointment," said the broker. "Should I tell them you're taking it, or what?"

"We're not," said Nora decisively.

She shrugged, went to the intercom, and buzzed them in.

"Nora," Smithback implored. He turned to the real estate agent. "We *are* taking it."

"I'm sorry, Bill, but I'm just not ready."

"But last week you said—"

"I know what I said. But I can't think about apartments at a time like this. Okay?"

"No, it's *not* okay."

The doorbell rang and the broker moved to open the door. Two men came in—one bald and short, one tall and bearded—gave the living room a quick look, swept through the kitchen and into the bedrooms.

"Nora, please," Smithback said. "Look, I know this move to New York, the job at the Museum, hasn't been as smooth as you hoped. I'm sorry about that. But that doesn't mean you should—"

There was a lengthy interval while the shower was being turned on, then off. And then the couple were back in the living room. The inspection had taken less than two minutes.

"It's perfect," said the bald one. "Eighteen percent broker's fee, right?"

"Right."

"Great." A checkbook appeared. "Who do I make it out to?"

"Cash. We'll take it to your bank."

"Now wait just a minute," Smithback said, "we were here first."

"I'm so sorry," said one of the men politely, turning in surprise.

"Don't mind them," said the broker harshly. "Those people are on their way out."

"Come on, Bill." Nora began urging him to the door.

"We were here first! I'll take it myself, if I have to!"

There was a snap as the man detached the check. The broker reached for it. "I've got the lease right here," she said, patting her bag. "We can sign it at the bank."

Nora dragged Smithback out the door and slammed it shut. The ride downstairs was silent and tense.

A moment later, they were standing on the street. "I've

got to get back to work," Nora said, looking away. "We can talk about this tonight."

"We certainly will."

Smithback watched her stride down Ninety-ninth Street in the slanting light, the trenchcoat curling away from her perfect little behind, her long copper hair swinging back and forth. He felt stricken. After all they had been through, she still didn't want to live with him. What had he done wrong? Sometimes he wondered if she blamed him for pressuring her to move east from Santa Fe. It wasn't his fault the job at the Lloyd Museum had fallen through and her boss here in Manhattan was a prize asshole. How could he change her mind? How could he prove to her that he really loved her?

An idea began to form in his mind. Nora didn't really appreciate the power of the press, particularly the *New York Times*. She didn't realize just how cowed, how docile and cooperative, the Museum could be when faced with bad publicity. *Yes,* he thought, *this would work.* She would get the collections back, and get her carbon-14 dating funded, and more. She would thank him in the end. If he worked fast, he could even make the early edition.

Smithback heard a hearty yell. "Hey, friend!"

He turned. There were the two bums, fiery-faced now, holding on to each other, staggering up the sidewalk. One of them lifted a paper bag. "Have a drink on us!"

Smithback took out another twenty and held it up in front of the bigger and dirtier of the two. "Tell you what. In a few minutes, you'll see a thin lady dressed in black come out of this building with two guys. Her name's Millie. Give her a really big hug and kiss for me, will you? The sloppier the better."

"You bet!" The man snatched the bill and stuffed it into his pocket.

Smithback went down the street toward Broadway, feeling marginally better.

EIGHT

ANTHONY FAIRHAVEN SETTLED HIS LEAN, MUSCULAR frame into the chair, spread a heavy linen napkin across his lap, and examined the breakfast that lay before him. It was minuscule, yet arrayed with excessive care on the crisp white damask: a china glass of tea, two water biscuits, royal jelly. He drained the tea in a single toss, nibbled absently at the cracker, then wiped his lips and signaled the maid for his papers with a curt motion.

The sun streamed in through the curved glass wall of his breakfast atrium. From his vantage point atop the Metropolitan Tower, all of Manhattan lay prostrate at his feet, glittering in the dawn light, windows winking pink and gold. His own personal New World, waiting for him to claim his Manifest Destiny. Far below, the dark rectangle of Central Park lay like a gravedigger's hole in the midst of the great city. The light was just clipping the tops of the trees, the shadows of the buildings along Fifth Avenue lying across the park like bars.

There was a rustle and the maid laid the two papers before him, the *New York Times* and the *Wall Street Journal*. Freshly ironed, as he insisted. He picked up the

Times and unfolded it, the warm scent of newsprint reaching his nostrils, the sheets crisp and dry. He gave the paper a little shake to loosen it, and turned to the front page. He scanned the headlines. Middle East peace talks, mayoral election debates, earthquake in Indonesia. He glanced below the fold.

Momentarily, he stopped breathing.

NEWLY DISCOVERED LETTER SHEDS LIGHT ON 19TH-CENTURY KILLINGS

BY WILLIAM SMITHBACK JR.

He blinked his eyes, took a long, deep breath, and began to read.

NEW YORK — October 8. A letter has been found in the archives of the New York Museum of Natural History that may help explain the grisly charnel discovered in lower Manhattan early last week.

In that discovery, workmen constructing a residential tower at the corner of Henry and Catherine streets unearthed a basement tunnel containing the remains of thirty-six young men and women. The remains had been walled up in a dozen alcoves in what was apparently an old coal tunnel dating from the middle of the nineteenth century. Preliminary forensic analysis showed that the victims had been dissected, or perhaps autopsied, and subsequently dismembered. Preliminary dating of the site by an archaeologist, Nora Kelly, of the New York Museum of Natural History, indicated that the killings had occurred between 1872 and 1881, when the corner was occupied by a three-story building housing a private museum known as "J. C. Shottum's Cabinet of Natural Productions and Curiosities." The cabinet burned in 1881, and Shottum died in the fire.

In subsequent research, Dr. Kelly discovered the letter, which was written by J. C. Shottum himself. Written shortly before Shottum's death, it describes his uncovering of the medical experiments of his lodger, a taxonomist and chemist by the name of Enoch Leng. In the letter, Shottum alleged that Leng was conducting surgical experiments on human subjects, in an attempt to prolong his own life. The experiments appear to have involved the surgical removal of the lower portion of the spinal cord from a living subject. Shottum appended to his letter several passages from Leng's own detailed journal of his experiments. A copy of the letter was obtained by the *New York Times*.

If the remains are indeed from murdered individuals, it would be the largest serial killing in the history of New York City and perhaps the largest in U.S. history. Jack the Ripper, England's most famous serial killer, murdered seven women in the Whitechapel district of London in 1888. Jeffrey Dahmer, America's notorious serial killer, is known to have killed at least 17 people.

The human remains were removed to the Medical Examiner's office and have been unavailable for examination. The basement tunnel was subsequently destroyed by Moegen-Fairhaven, Inc., the developer of the tower, during normal construction activities.

According to Mary Hill, a spokesperson for Mayor Edward Montefiori, the site did not fall under the New York Archaeological and Historic Preservation Act. "This is an old crime scene of little archaeological interest," Ms. Hill said. "It simply did not meet the criteria spelled out in the Act. We had no basis to stop construction." Representatives of the Landmarks Preservation Commission, however, have taken a different view, and are reportedly asking a state senator and the New York Investigator's office to assemble a task force to look into the matter.

One article of clothing was preserved from the site, a dress, which was brought to the Museum for examination by Dr. Kelly. Sewn into the dress, Dr. Kelly found a piece of paper, possibly a note of self-identification, written by a young woman who apparently believed she had only a short time to live: "I am Mary Greene, agt [sic] 19 years, No. 16 Watter [sic] Street." Tests indicated the note had been written in human blood.

The Federal Bureau of Investigation has taken an interest in the case. Special Agent Pendergast, from the New Orleans office, has been observed on the scene. Neither the New York nor the New Orleans FBI offices would comment. The exact nature of his involvement has not been made public, but Pendergast is known as one of the highest ranking special agents in the Southern Region. He has worked on several high-profile cases in New York before. The New York City Police Department, meanwhile, has shown little interest in a crime that occurred more than a century ago. Captain Sherwood Custer, in whose precinct the remains were found, says the case is primarily of historical interest. "The murderer is dead. Any accomplices must be dead. We'll leave this one to the historians and continue to devote our resources to crime prevention in the twenty-first century."

Following the discovery of the letter, the New York Museum removed the Shottum Cabinet collection from the museum archives. Roger Brisbane, First Vice President of the Museum, called the move "part of a long-scheduled, ongoing conservation process, a coincidence that has nothing to do with these reports." He referred all further questions to Harry Medoker in the Museum's Public Relations Department. Mr. Medoker did not return several telephone calls from the *Times*.

The story continued on an inside page, where the reporter described the details of the old murders with considerable relish. Fairhaven read the article to the end, then turned back and read the first page once again. The dry leaves of the *Times* made a faint rustling sound in his hands, echoed by the trembling of the dead leaves clinging to the potted trees on the balcony outside the atrium.

Fairhaven slowly laid down the paper and looked out once again over the city. He could see the New York Museum across the park, its granite towers and copper roofs catching the newly minted light. He flicked his finger and another cup of tea arrived. He stared at the cup without pleasure, tossed it down. Another flick of his finger brought him a phone.

Fairhaven knew a great deal about real estate development, public relations, and New York City politics. He knew this article was a potential disaster. It called for firm, prompt action.

He paused, thinking who should receive the first telephone call. A moment later he dialed the mayor's private number, which he knew by heart.

NINE

DOREEN HOLLANDER, OF 21 INDIAN FEATHER LANE, PINE Creek, Oklahoma, had left her husband twenty-six stories overhead, mumbling and snoring in their hotel room. Gazing across the broad expanse of Central Park West, she decided now was the perfect time to view Monet's water lilies at the Metropolitan Museum. She'd wanted to get a glimpse of the famous paintings ever since seeing a poster at her sister-in-law's house. Her husband, service technician for Oklahoma Cable, hadn't the faintest interest in art. Chances were, he'd still be asleep when she returned.

Consulting the visitor's map the hotel had so generously volunteered, she was pleased to discover the museum lay just across Central Park. A short walk, no need to call for an expensive taxi. Doreen Hollander liked walking, and this would be the perfect way to burn off those two croissants with butter and marmalade she had unwisely eaten for breakfast.

She started off, crossing into the park at the Alexander Humbolt gate, walking briskly. It was a beautiful fall day, and the big buildings on Fifth Avenue shone above the treetops. New York City. A wonderful place, as long as you didn't have to live here.

The path dropped down and soon she came to the side of a lovely pond. She gazed across. Would it be better to go around it to the right, or to the left? She consulted her map and decided the left-hand way would be shorter.

She set off again on her strong farmgirl legs, inhaling the air. *Surprisingly fresh,* she thought. Bicyclists and Roller-bladers whizzed past as the road curved alongside the pond. Soon, she found herself at another fork. The main path swerved northward, but there was a footpath that continued straight, in the direction she was going, through a wood. She consulted her map. It didn't show the footpath, but she knew a better route when she saw it. She continued on.

Quickly, the path branched, then branched again, wandering aimlessly up and down through hillocks and little rocky outcrops. Here and there through the trees, she could still make out the row of skyscrapers along Fifth Avenue, beckoning her on, showing her the way. The woods grew more dense. And then she began to see the people. It was odd. Here and there, young men stood idly, hands in pockets, in the woods, waiting. But waiting for what? They were nice-looking young men, well dressed, with good haircuts. Out beyond the trees a bright fall morning was in progress, and she didn't feel the slightest bit afraid.

She hurried on as the woods grew thicker. She stopped to consult her map, a little puzzled, and discovered that she was in a place called the Ramble. It was a well-chosen name, she decided. Twice she had found herself turned completely around. It was as if the person who had designed this little maze of paths *wanted* people to get lost.

Well, Doreen Hollander was not one to get lost. Not in a tiny patch of woods in a city park, when after all she had grown up in the country, roaming the fields and woods of eastern Oklahoma. This walk was turning into a little adventure, and Doreen Hollander liked little adventures. That was why she had dragged her husband to New York City to begin with: to have a little adventure. Doreen forced herself to smile.

If this didn't beat all—now she was turned around yet again. With a rueful laugh she consulted her map. But on the map, the Ramble was marked simply as a large mass of leafy green. She looked around. Perhaps one of the nice-looking men could help her with directions.

But here, the woods were darker, thicker. Nevertheless, through a screen of leaves, she saw two figures. She approached. What were they doing in there? She took another step forward, pulled a branch aside, and peered through. The peer turned into a stare, and the stare turned into a mask of frozen horror.

Then, abruptly, she backed away, turned, and began retracing her steps as quickly as she could. Now it was all clear. How perfectly disgusting. Her only thought was to get out of this terrible place as quickly as possible. All desire to see Monet's water lilies had flown from her head. She hadn't wanted to believe it, but it was all true. It was just as she'd heard tell on the *700 Club* on television, New York City as a modern Sodom and Gomorrah. She hurried along, her breath coming in short gasps, and she looked back only once.

When the swift footsteps came up behind her, she heard nothing and expected nothing. When the black hood came down hard and tight over her head, and the sudden wet stench of chloroform violated her nostrils, the last vision in her mind was of a twisted spire of salt glittering in the desolate light of an empty plain, a plume of bitter smoke rising in the distance.

TEN

THE EMINENT DR. FREDERICK WATSON COLLOPY SAT IN
state behind the great nineteenth-century leather-bound desk,
reflecting on the men and women who had preceded him in
this august position. In the Museum's glory years—the years,
say, when this vast desk was still new—the directors of the
Museum had been true visionaries, explorers and scientists
both. He lingered appreciatively over their names: Byrd,
Throckmorton, Andrews. Now, those were names worthy to
be cast in bronze. His appreciation waned somewhat as he
approached the more recent occupants of this grand corner
office—the unfortunate Winston Wright and his short-
tenured successor, Olivia Merriam. He felt no little
satisfaction in returning the office to its former state of
dignity and accomplishment. He ran a hand along his well-
trimmed beard, laid a finger across his lip in thoughtful
meditation.

And yet, here it was again: that persistent feeling of
melancholy.

He had been called upon to make certain sacrifices in
order to rescue the Museum. It distressed him that scientific
research was forced to take second place to galas, to glittering

new halls, to blockbuster exhibitions. Blockbuster—the word tasted repellent in the mouth. And yet, this was New York at the dawn of the twenty-first century, and those who did not play the game would not survive. Even his grandest forebears had their own crosses to bear. One bent with the winds of time. The Museum had survived—that was the important, that was the *only,* point.

He then reflected on his own distinguished scientific lineage: his great-grand-uncle Amasa Greenough, friend to Darwin and famed discoverer of the chitinous monkfish of the Indochine; his great-aunt Philomena Watson, who had done seminal work with the natives of Tierra del Fuego; his grandfather Gardner Collopy, the distinguished herpetologist. He thought of his own exciting work reclassifying the *Pongidae,* during the heady days of his youth. Perhaps, with luck and a goodly allowance of years, his tenure here at the Museum would rival the great directors of the past. Perhaps he, too, would have his name graven in bronze, enshrined in the Great Rotunda for all to see.

He still couldn't shake the feeling of melancholy that had settled around him. These reflections, normally so soothing, seemed not to help. He felt a man out of place, old-fashioned, superannuated. Even thoughts of his lovely young wife, with whom he had sported so delightfully that very morning before breakfast, failed to shake the feeling.

His eye took in the office—the pink marble fireplaces, the round tower windows looking out over Museum Drive, the oak paneling with its patina of centuries, the paintings by Audubon and De Clefisse. He regarded his own person: the somber suit with its old-fashioned, almost clerical cut, the starched white shirtfront, the silk bow tie worn as a sign of independence in thought and deed, the handmade shoes, and above all—as his eye fell on the mirror above the mantel—the handsome and even elegant face, if a touch severe, that wore its burden of years so gracefully.

He turned to his desk with a faint sigh. Perhaps it was the news of the day that made him gloomy. It sat on his desk, spread out in glaring newsprint: the damnable article, written by that same vile fellow who had caused so much trouble at the Museum back in '95. He had hoped the earlier removal of the offending materials from the Archives would have quieted things down. But now there was this letter to deal with. On every level, this had the potential to be a disaster. His own staff drawn in; an FBI agent running around; Fairhaven, one of their biggest supporters, under fire—Collopy's head reeled at the possibilities, all too hideous to contemplate. If this thing wasn't *handled,* it could very well cast a pall on his own tenure, or worse—

Do not go to that place, thought Frederick Watson Collopy. He would handle it. Even the worst disasters could be turned around with the right—what was the trendy word?—*spin.* Yes. That's what was needed here. A very delicate and artfully applied spin. *The Museum would not,* he thought, *react in its usual knee-jerk way.* The Museum would not decry the investigation; it would not protest the rifling of its archives; it would not denounce the unaccountable activities of this FBI agent; it would not deny responsibility, evade, or cover up. Nor would the Museum come to the aid of its biggest supporter, Fairhaven. At least, not on the surface. And yet, much could be done *in camera,* so to speak. A quiet word could be strategically placed here and there, reassurances given or taken away, money moved hither and yon. Gently. Very gently.

He depressed a button on his intercom, and spoke in a mild voice. "Mrs. Surd, would you be so good as to tell Mr. Brisbane I should like to see him at his convenience?"

"Yes, Dr. Collopy."

"Thank you most kindly, Mrs. Surd."

He released the button and settled back. Then he carefully folded up the *New York Times* and placed it out of sight, in the "To Be Filed" box at the corner of his desk. And, for the first time since leaving his bedroom that morning, he smiled.

ELEVEN

NORA KELLY KNEW WHAT THE CALL WAS ABOUT. SHE HAD seen the article in the morning paper, of course. It was the talk of the Museum, perhaps of all New York. She knew what kind of effect it would have on a man like Brisbane. She had been waiting all day for him to call her, and now, at ten minutes to five, the summons had finally come. He had waited until ten minutes to five. Letting her stew, no doubt. She wondered if that meant he would give her ten minutes to clear out of the Museum. It wouldn't surprise her.

The nameplate was missing from Brisbane's door. She knocked and the secretary called her in.

"Have a seat, please," said a haggard older woman who was clearly in a bad mood.

Nora sat. *Goddamned Bill,* she thought. What could he have been thinking? Admittedly, the guy was impulsive—he tended to act before engaging his cerebral cortex—but this was too much. She'd have his guts for garters, as her father used to say. She'd cut off his balls, fix them to a thong, and wear them around her waist like a bola. This job was *so* critical to her—yet here he was, practically typing out the pink slip himself. How *could* he have done this to her?

The secretary's phone buzzed. "You may go in," the older woman said.

Nora entered the inner office. Brisbane stood in front of a mirror placed at one side of his desk, tying a bow tie around his neck. He wore black pants with a satin stripe and a starched shirt with mother-of-pearl buttons. A tuxedo jacket was draped over his chair. Nora paused inside the door, waiting, but Brisbane said nothing nor in any way acknowledged her presence. She watched him deftly whip one end of the tie over the other, snug the end through.

Then he spoke: "Over the past few hours, I've learned a great deal about you, Dr. Kelly."

Nora remained silent.

"About a disastrous field expedition in the Southwestern desert, for example, in which your leadership and even scientific abilities were called into question. And about a certain William Smithback. I didn't know you were quite so *friendly* with this William Smithback of the *Times*."

There was another pause while he tugged on the ends of the tie. As he worked he craned his neck. It rose out of his collar, as pale and scrawny as a chicken's.

"I understand, Dr. Kelly, that you brought non-Museum personnel into the Archives, in direct violation of the rules of this Museum."

He tightened and adjusted. Nora said nothing.

"Furthermore, you've been doing outside work on Museum time, assisting this FBI agent. Again, a clear violation of the rules."

Nora knew it would be futile to remind Brisbane that he himself, however grudgingly, had authorized the work.

"Finally, it's a violation of Museum rules to have contact with the press, without clearing it through our public relations office first. There are good reasons for all these rules, Dr. Kelly. These are not mere bureaucratic regulations. They relate to the Museum's security, to the integrity of its collections and archives, and especially its reputation. Do you understand me?"

Nora looked at Brisbane, but could find no words.

"Your conduct has caused a great deal of anxiety here."

"Look," she said. "If you're going to fire me, get it over with."

Brisbane looked at her at last, his pink face forming an expression of mock surprise. "Who said anything about firing? Not only will we not fire you, but you are *forbidden* to resign."

Nora looked at him in surprise.

"Dr. Kelly, you will remain with the Museum. After all, you're the hero of the hour. Dr. Collopy and I are united on this. We wouldn't dream of letting you go—not after that self-serving, self-aggrandizing newspaper piece. You're bulletproof. For now."

Nora listened, her surprise slowly turning to anger.

Brisbane patted the bow tie, examined himself one last time in the mirror, and turned. "All your privileges are suspended. No access to the central collections or the Archives."

"Am I allowed to use the girls' room?"

"No contact with anyone on the outside involving Museum business. And especially no contact with that FBI agent or that journalist, Smithback."

No need to worry about Smithback, Nora thought, furious now.

"We know all about Smithback. There's a file on him downstairs that's a foot thick. As you probably know, he wrote a book about the Museum a few years back. That was before my time and I haven't read it, but I've heard it wasn't exactly Nobel Prize material. He's been persona non grata around here ever since."

He looked at her directly, his eyes cold and unwavering. "In the meantime, it's business as usual. Going to the new Primate Hall opening tonight?"

"I wasn't planning to."

"Start planning. After all, you're our employee of the week. People are going to want to see you up and about, looking chipper. In fact, the Museum will be issuing a press release about our own heroic Dr. Kelly, pointing out in the process how civic-minded the Museum is, how we have a long history of doing *pro bono* work for the city. Of course, you will deflect any further questions about this business by saying that *all* your work is *completely* confidential." Brisbane lifted the jacket from the chair and daintily shrugged himself into it, flicking a stray thread from his shoulders, touching his perfect hair. "I'm sure you can find a halfway decent dress among your things. Just be glad it isn't one of the fancy-dress balls the Museum's so fond of these days."

"What if I say no? What if I don't get with your little program?"

Brisbane shot his cuffs and turned to her again. Then his eyes flicked to the door, and Nora's gaze followed.

Standing in the doorway, hands folded before him, was Dr. Collopy himself. The director cut a fearsome, almost sinister figure as he silently walked the halls of the Museum, his thin frame dressed in formal severity, his profile that of an Anglican deacon's, his posture rigid and forbidding. Collopy, who came from a long background of gentleman scientists and inventors, had an enigmatic demeanor and a quiet voice that never seemed to be raised. To top it off, the man owned a brownstone on West End Avenue in which he lived with a gorgeous new wife, forty years his junior. Their relationship was the subject of endless comment and obscene speculation.

But today, Director Collopy was almost smiling. He took a step forward. The angular lines of his pale face looked much softer than usual, even animated. He actually took her hand between his own dry palms, eyes looking closely into hers, and Nora felt a faint and wholly unexpected tingle. She abruptly saw what that young wife must also have seen—a very vital man was hidden behind that normally impenetrable facade. Now, Collopy did smile—and when he did so, it was as if a heat lamp was switched on. Nora felt bathed in a radiance of charm and vigor.

"I know your work, Nora, and I've been following it with tremendous interest. To think that the great ruins of Chaco Canyon might have been influenced, if not built, by the Aztecs—it's important, even groundbreaking stuff."

"Then—"

He silenced her with a faint pressure to her hand. "I wasn't aware of the cuts in your department, Nora. We've all had to tighten our belts, but perhaps we've done so a little too indiscriminately."

Nora couldn't help glancing at Brisbane, but his face had shut down completely: it was unreadable.

"Fortunately, we are in a position to restore your funding, and on top of that give you the eighteen thousand you need for those critical carbon-14 dates. I myself have a personal interest in the subject. I'll never forget, as a boy, visiting those magnificent Chacoan ruins with Dr. Morris himself."

"Thank you, but—"

Again, the faint squeeze. "Please don't thank me. Mr. Brisbane was kind enough to bring this situation to my attention. The work you are doing here is important; it will bring credit to the Museum; and I personally would like to do anything I can to support it. If you need anything else, call me. Call *me*."

He released her hand ever so gently and turned to Brisbane. "I must be off to prepare my little speech. Thank you."

And he was gone.

She looked at Brisbane, but the face was still an opaque mask. "Now you know what will happen if you *do* get with the program," he said. "I'd rather not go into what will happen if you *don't*."

Brisbane turned back to the mirror, gave himself one last look.

"See you tonight, Dr. Kelly," he said mildly.

TWELVE

O'SHAUGHNESSY FOLLOWED PENDERGAST UP THE RED-carpeted steps toward the Museum's great bronze doors, convinced that every eye in the place was on him. He felt like a jerk in his policeman's uniform. He let his hand drop idly to the butt of his gun, and felt gratified as a nearby tuxedoed man gave him a decidedly nervous glance. He further consoled himself with the thought that he was getting time and a half for this dog-and-pony show—and time and a half from Captain Custer was nothing to sneeze at.

Cars were lining up along Museum Drive, disgorging beautiful and not-so-beautiful people. Velvet ropes held back a small, disconsolate-looking group of photographers and journalists. The flashes of the photographers' cameras were few and far between. A van with the logo of a local television station was already packing up and leaving.

"This opening for the new Primate Hall is rather smaller than others I've attended," said Pendergast as he glanced around. "Party fatigue, I expect. The Museum's been having so many these days."

"Primates? All these people are interested in monkeys?"

"I expect most of them are here to observe the primates *outside* the exhibition cases."

"Very funny."

They passed through the doors and across the Great Rotunda. Until two days ago, O'Shaughnessy hadn't been inside the Museum since he was a kid. But there were the dinosaurs, just like they'd always been. And beyond, the herd of elephants. The red carpet and velvet ropes led them onward, deeper into the building. Smiling young ladies were positioned along the way, pointing, nodding, indicating where to go. Very nice young ladies. O'Shaughnessy decided that another visit to the Museum, when he wasn't on duty, might be in order.

They wound through the African Hall, past a massive doorway framed in elephant tusks, and entered a large reception area. Countless little tables, set with votive candles, dotted the room. A vast buffet heaped with food ran along one wall, bookended by two well-stocked booze stations. A podium had been placed at the far end of the room. In a nearby corner, a string quartet sawed industriously at a Viennese waltz. O'Shaughnessy listened with incredulity. They were appalling. But at least it wasn't Puccini they were butchering.

The room was almost empty.

At the door stood a manic-looking man, a large name tag displayed below his white carnation. He spotted Pendergast, rushed over, and seized his hand with almost frantic gratitude. "Harry Medoker, head of public relations. Thank you for coming, sir, thank you. I think you'll love the new hall."

"Primate behavior is my specialty."

"Ah! Then you've come to the right place." The PR man caught a glimpse of O'Shaughnessy and froze in the act of pumping Pendergast's hand. "I'm sorry, Officer. Is there a problem?" His voice had lost all its conviviality.

"Yeah," said O'Shaughnessy in his most menacing tone.

The man leaned forward and spoke in most unwelcoming tones. "This is a private opening, Officer. I'm sorry, but you'll have to leave. We have no need of outside security—"

"Oh yeah? Just so you know, Harry, I'm here on the little matter of the *Museum cocaine ring.*"

"Museum cocaine ring?" Medoker looked like he was about to have a heart attack.

"Officer O'Shaughnessy," came Pendergast's mild warning.

O'Shaughnessy gave the man a little clap on the shoulder. "Don't breathe a word. Imagine how the press would run with it. Think of the *Museum,* Harry." He left the man white and shaking.

"I hate it when they don't respect the man in blue," said O'Shaughnessy.

For a moment, Pendergast eyed him gravely. Then he nodded toward the buffet. "Regulations may forbid drinking on the job, but they don't forbid eating *blini au caviar.*"

"Blini auwhat?"

"Tiny buckwheat pancakes topped with *crème fraîche* and caviar. Delectable."

O'Shaughnessy shuddered. "I don't like raw fish eggs."

"I suspect you've never had the real thing, Sergeant. Give one a try. You'll find them much more palatable than a *Die Walküre* aria, I assure you. However, there's also the smoked sturgeon, the foie gras, the prosciutto di Parma, and the Damariscotta River oysters. The Museum always serves an excellent table."

"Just give me the pigs in a blanket."

"Those can be obtained from the man with the cart on the corner of Seventy-seventh and Central Park West."

More people were trickling into the hall, but the crowd was still thin. O'Shaughnessy followed Pendergast over to the food table. He avoided the piles of sticky gray fish eggs. Instead, he took a few pieces of ham, cut a slice from a wheel of brie, and with some pieces of French bread made a couple of small ham-and-cheese sandwiches for himself. The ham was a little dry, and the cheese tasted a little like ammonia, but overall it was palatable.

"You had a meeting with Captain Custer, right?" Pendergast asked. "How did it go?"

O'Shaughnessy shook his head as he munched. "Not too good."

"I expect there was someone from the mayor's office."

"Mary Hill."

"Ah, Miss Hill. Of course."

"Captain Custer wanted to know why I hadn't told them about the journal, why I hadn't told them about the dress, why I hadn't told them about the note. But it was all in the report—which Custer hadn't read—so in the end I survived the meeting."

Pendergast nodded.

"Thanks for helping me finish that report. Otherwise, they'd have ripped me a new one."

"What a quaint expression." Pendergast looked over O'Shaughnessy's shoulder. "Sergeant, I'd like to introduce you to an old acquaintance of mine. William Smithback."

O'Shaughnessy turned to see a gangling, awkward-looking man at the buffet, a gravity-defying cowlick jutting from the top of his head. He was dressed in an ill-fitting tuxedo, and he seemed utterly absorbed in piling as much food onto his plate as possible, as quickly as possible. The man looked over, saw Pendergast, and started visibly. He glanced around uneasily, as if marking possible exits. But the FBI agent was smiling encouragingly, and the man named Smithback came toward them a little warily.

"Agent Pendergast," Smithback said in a nasal baritone. "What a surprise."

"Indeed. Mr. Smithback, I find you well." He grasped Smithback's hand and shook it. "How many years has it been?"

"Long time," said Smithback, looking like it had not been nearly long enough. "What are you doing in New York?"

"I keep an apartment here." Pendergast released the hand and looked the writer up and down. "I see you've graduated to Armani, Mr. Smithback," he said. "A rather better cut than those off-the-rack Fourteenth Street job-lot suits you used to sport. However, when you're ready to take a *real* sartorial step, might I recommend Brioni or Ermenegildo Zegna?"

Smithback opened his mouth to reply, but Pendergast continued smoothly. "I heard from Margo Green, by the way. She's up in Boston, working for the GeneDyne Corporation. She asked me to remember her to you."

Smithback opened his mouth again, shut it. "Thank you," he managed after a moment. "And—and Lieutenant D'Agosta? You keep in touch with him?"

"He also went north. He's now living in Canada, writing police procedurals, under the pen name of Campbell Dirk."

"I'll have to pick up one of his books."

"He hasn't made it big yet—not like you, Mr. Smithback—but I must say the books are readable."

By this point, Smithback had fully recovered. "And mine aren't?"

Pendergast inclined his head. "I can't honestly say I've

read any. Do you have one you could particularly recommend?"

"Very funny," said Smithback, frowning and looking about. "I wonder if Nora's going to be here."

"So you're the guy who wrote the article, right?" asked O'Shaughnessy.

Smithback nodded. "Made a splash, don't you think?"

"It certainly got everyone's attention," said Pendergast dryly.

"As well it should. Nineteenth-century serial killer, kidnapping and mutilating helpless kids from workhouses, all in the name of some experiment to extend his own wretched life. You know, they've awarded Pulitzers for less than that." People were arriving more quickly now, and the noise level was increasing.

"The Society for American Archaeology is demanding an investigation into how the site came to be destroyed. I understand the construction union is also asking questions. With this upcoming election, the mayor's on the defensive. As you can imagine, Moegen-Fairhaven wasn't terribly happy about it. Speak of the devil."

"What?" Smithback said, clearly surprised by this sudden remark.

"Anthony Fairhaven," Pendergast said, nodding toward the entrance.

O'Shaughnessy followed the glance. The man standing in the doorway to the hall was much more youthful than he'd expected; fit, with the kind of frame a bicyclist or rock climber might have—wiry, athletic. His tuxedo draped over his shoulders and chest with a lightness that made him look as if he'd been born in it. Even more surprising was the face. It was an open face, an honest-looking face; not the face of the rapacious money-grubbing real estate developer

Smithback had portrayed in the *Times* article. Then, most surprising of all: Fairhaven looked their way, noticed their glance, and smiled broadly at them before continuing into the hall.

A hissing came over the PA system; "Tales from the Vienna Woods" died away raggedly. A man was at the podium, doing a sound check. He retreated, and a hush fell on the crowd. After a moment, a second man, wearing a formal suit, mounted the podium and walked to the microphone. He looked grave, intelligent, patrician, dignified, at ease. In short, he was everything O'Shaughnessy hated.

"Who's that?" he asked.

"The distinguished Dr. Frederick Collopy," said Pendergast. "Director of the Museum."

"He's got a 29-year-old wife," Smithback whispered. "Can you believe it? It's a wonder he can even find the—Look, there she is now." He pointed to a young and extremely attractive woman standing to one side. Unlike the other women, who all seemed to be dressed in black, she was wearing an emerald-green gown with an elegant diamond tiara. The combination was breathtaking.

"Oh, God," Smithback breathed. "What a stunner."

"I hope the guy keeps a pair of cardiac paddles on his bedside table," O'Shaughnessy muttered.

"I think I'll go over and give him my number. Offer to spell him one of these nights, in case the old geezer gets winded."

Good evening, ladies and gentlemen, began Collopy. His voice was low, gravelly, without inflection. *When I was a young man, I undertook the reclassification of the Pongidae, the Great Apes . . .*

The level of conversation in the room dropped but did

not cease altogether. *People seemed far more interested in food and drink than in hearing this man talk about monkeys,* O'Shaughnessy thought.

. . . And I was faced with a problem: Where to put mankind? Are we in the Pongidae, or are we not? Are we a Great Ape, or are we something special? This was the question I faced . . .

"Here comes Dr. Kelly," said Pendergast.

Smithback turned, an eager, expectant, nervous look on his face. But the tall, copper-haired woman swept past him without so much as a glance, arrowing straight for the food table.

"Hey Nora! I've been trying to reach you all day!" O'Shaughnessy watched the writer hustle after her, then returned his attention to his ham-and-cheese sandwiches. He was glad he didn't have to do this sort of thing for a living. How could they bear it? Standing around, chatting aimlessly with people you'd never seen before and would never see again, trying to cough up a vestige of interest in their vapid opinions, all to a background obbligato of speechifying. It seemed inconceivable to him that there were people who actually liked going to parties like this.

. . . our closest living relatives . . .

Smithback was returning already. His tuxedo front was splattered with fish eggs and *crème fraîche.* He looked stricken.

"Have an accident?" asked Pendergast dryly.

"You might call it that."

O'Shaughnessy glanced over and saw Nora heading straight for the retreating Smithback. She did not look happy.

"Nora—" Smithback began again.

She rounded on him, her face furious. "How could you? I gave you that information in *confidence.*"

"But Nora, I did it for you. Don't you see? Now they can't touch—"

"You *moron.* My long-term career here is ruined. After what happened in Utah, and with the Lloyd Museum closing, this job was my last chance. And *you ruined it!*"

"Nora, if you could only look at it my way, you'd—"

"You *promised* me. And I trusted you! God, I can't believe it, I'm totally screwed." She looked away, then whirled back with redoubled ferocity. "Was this some kind of revenge because I wouldn't rent that apartment with you?"

"No, no, Nora, just the opposite, it was to *help* you. I swear, in the end you'll thank me—"

The poor man looked so helpless, O'Shaughnessy felt sorry for him. He was obviously in love with the woman— and he had just as obviously blown it completely.

Suddenly she turned on Pendergast. "And you!"

Pendergast raised his eyebrows, then carefully placed a blini back on his plate.

"Sneaking around the Museum, picking locks, fomenting suspicion. *You* started all this."

Pendergast bowed. "If I have caused you any distress, Dr. Kelly, I regret it deeply."

"Distress? They're going to crucify me. And there it all was, in today's paper. I could kill you! *All* of you!"

Her voice had risen, and now people were looking at her instead of at the man at the podium, still droning on about classifying his great apes.

Then Pendergast said, "Smile. Our friend Brisbane is watching."

Nora glanced over her shoulder. O'Shaughnessy followed the glance toward the podium and saw a well-groomed man—tall, glossy, with slicked-back dark hair—staring at them. He did not look happy.

Nora shook her head and lowered her voice. "Jesus, I'm not even supposed to be talking to you. I can't *believe* the position you've put me in."

"However, Dr. Kelly, you and I do need to talk," Pendergast said softly. "Meet me tomorrow evening at Ten Ren's Tea and Ginseng Company, 75 Mott Street, at seven o'clock. If you please."

Nora glared at him angrily, then stalked off.

Immediately, Brisbane glided over on long legs, planting himself in front of them. "What a pleasant surprise," he said in a chill undertone. "The FBI agent, the policeman, and the reporter. An unholy trinity if ever I saw one."

Pendergast inclined his head. "And how are you, Mr. Brisbane?"

"Oh, top form."

"I'm glad to hear it."

"I don't recall any of you being on the guest list. Especially you, Mr. Smithback. How did *you* slither past security?"

Pendergast smiled and spoke gently. "Sergeant O'Shaughnessy and I are here on law enforcement business. As for Mr. Smithback—well, I'm sure he would like nothing more than to be tossed out on his ear. What a marvelous follow-up that would make to his piece in today's edition of the *Times*."

Smithback nodded. "Thank you. It would."

Brisbane stood still, the smile frozen on his face. He looked first at Pendergast, then at Smithback. His eyes raked Smithback's soiled tux. "Didn't your mother teach you that caviar goes in the mouth, not on the shirt?" He walked off.

"Imbecile," Smithback murmured.

"Don't underestimate him," replied Pendergast. "He has

Moegen-Fairhaven, the Museum, and the mayor behind him. And he is no imbecile."

"Yeah. Except that I'm a reporter for the *New York Times.*"

"Don't make the mistake of thinking even that lofty position will protect you."

. . . and now, without more ado, let us unveil the Museum's latest creation, the Hall of Primates . . .

O'Shaughnessy watched as a ribbon beside the podium was cut with an oversized pair of scissors. There was a smattering of applause and a general drift toward the open doors of the new hall beyond. Pendergast glanced at him. "Shall we?"

"Why not?" Anything was better than standing around here.

"Count me out," said Smithback. "I've seen enough exhibitions in this joint to last me a lifetime."

Pendergast turned and grasped the reporter's hand. "I am sure we shall meet again. Soon."

It seemed to O'Shaughnessy that Smithback fairly flinched.

Soon they were through the doors. People drifted along the spacious hall, which was lined with dioramas of stuffed chimpanzees, gorillas, orangutans, and various monkeys and lemurs, displayed in their native habitats. With some surprise, O'Shaughnessy realized the dioramas were fascinating, beautiful in their own way. They were like magic casements opening onto distant worlds. How had these morons done it? But of course, they *hadn't* done it—it was the curators and artists who had. People like Brisbane were the deadwood at the top of the pile. He really needed to come here more often.

He saw a knot of people gathering around one case, which displayed a hooting chimpanzee swinging on a tree limb.

There was whispered conversation, muffled laughter. It didn't look any different from the other cases, and yet it seemed to have attracted half the people in the hall. O'Shaughnessy wondered what was so interesting about that chimpanzee. He looked about. Pendergast was in a far corner, examining some strange little monkey with intense interest. Funny man. A little scary, actually, when you got right down to it.

He strolled over to check out the case, standing at the fringe of the crowd. There were more murmurs, some stifled laughter, some disapproving clucks. A bejeweled lady was gesturing for a guard. When people noticed O'Shaughnessy was a cop, they automatically shuffled aside.

He saw that an elaborate label had been attached to the case. The label was made from a plaque of richly grained oak, on which gold letters were edged in black. It read:

ROGER C. BRISBANE III
FIRST VICE PRESIDENT

THIRTEEN

THE BOX WAS MADE OF FRUITWOOD. IT HAD LAIN, untouched and unneeded, for many decades, and was now covered in a heavy mantle of dust. But it had only taken one swipe of a soft velour cloth to remove the sediment of years, and a second swipe to bring out the rich, mellow sheen of the wood beneath.

Next, the cloth moved toward the brass corners, rubbing and burnishing. Then the brass hinges, shined and lightly oiled. Finally came the gold nameplate, fastened to the lid by four tiny screws. It was only when every inch, every element, of the box had been polished to brilliance that the fingers moved toward the latch, and—trembling slightly with the gravity of the moment—unsnapped the lock, lifted the lid.

Within, the tools gleamed from their beds of purple velvet. The fingers moved from one to the next, touching each lightly, almost reverently, as if they could impart some healing gift. As indeed they could—and had—and would again.

First came the large amputation knife. Its blade curved downward, as did all American amputation knives made between the Revolutionary and Civil Wars. In fact, this particular set dated from the 1840s, crafted by Wiegand & Snowden of Philadelphia. An exquisite set, a work of art.

The fingers moved on, a solitary ring of cat's-eye opal winking conspiratorially in the subdued light: metacarpal saw, Catlin knife, bone forceps, tissue forceps. At last, the fingers stopped on the capital saw. They caressed its length for a moment, then teased it from its molded slot. It was a beauty: long, built for business, its heavy blade breathtakingly sharp. As with the rest of the tools, its handle was made of ivory and gutta-percha; it was not until the 1880s, when Lister's work on germs was published, that surgical instruments began to be sterilized. All handles from that point on were made of metal: porous materials became mere collector's items. A pity, really; the old tools were so much more attractive.

It was a comfort to know that there would be no need for sterilization here.

The box contained two trays. With worshipful care, the fingers removed the upper tray—the amputation set—to expose the still greater beauty of the neurosurgical set below. Rows of skull trephines lay beside the more delicate saw blades. And encircling the rest was the greatest treasure of all: a medical chain saw, a long, thin band of metal covered in sharp serrated teeth, ivory hand grips at each end. It actually belonged among the amputation tools, but its great length consigned it to the lower tray. This was the thing to use when time, not delicacy, was of the essence. It was a horrifying-looking tool. It was consummately beautiful.

The fingers brushed each item in turn. Then, carefully, the upper tray was lowered back into position.

A heavy leather strop was brought from a nearby table and laid before the open box. The fingers rubbed a small amount of neat's-foot oil into the strop, slowly, without hurry.

It was important that there no longer be any hurry. Hurry had always meant mistakes, wasted effort.

At last, the fingers returned to the box, selected a knife, brought it to the light. Then—with lingering, loving care— laid it against the leather strop and began stroking back and forth, back and forth. The leather seemed almost to purr as the blade was stropped.

To sharpen all the blades in the surgical set to a razor edge would take many hours. But then, there would be time.

There would, in fact, be nothing but time.

the Appointed Time

ONE

PAUL KARP COULD HARDLY BELIEVE HE WAS ACTUALLY going to get some. *Finally.* Seventeen years old and now finally he was going to get some.

He pulled the girl deeper into the Ramble. It was the wildest, least visited part of Central Park. It wasn't perfect, but it would have to do.

"Why don't we just go back to your place?" the girl asked.

"My folks are home." Paul put his arms around her and kissed her. "Don't worry, this is great right here." Her face was flushed, and he could hear her breathing. He looked ahead for the darkest, the most private place he could find. Quickly, unwilling to lose the moment, he turned off the paved walk and plunged into a thicket of rhododendron bushes. She was following, gladly. The thought sent a little shiver of anticipation coursing through him. It only seemed deserted, he told himself. People came in here all the time.

He pushed his way into the densest part of the thicket. Even though the autumn sun still hovered low in the sky, the canopy of sycamores, laurels, and azaleas created a verdant half-light. He tried to tell himself it was cozy, almost romantic.

Finally they came to a hidden spot, a thick bed of myrtle surrounded by dark bushes. No one would see them here. They were utterly alone.

"Paul? What if a mugger—?"

"No mugger's going to see us in here," he quickly said, taking the girl in his arms and kissing her. She responded, first hesitantly, then more eagerly.

"Are you sure this place is okay?" she whispered.

"Sure. We're totally alone."

After a last look around, Paul lay down on the myrtle, pulling her beside him. They kissed again. Paul slid his hands up her blouse and she didn't stop him. He could feel her chest heaving, breasts rising and falling. The birds made a racket over their heads, and the myrtle rose around them like a thick, green carpet. It was very nice. Paul thought this was a great way for it to happen. He could tell the story later. But the important thing was it was *going* to happen. No longer would it be a joke among his friends: the last virgin of Horace Mann's senior class.

With renewed urgency, he pressed closer to her, undid some buttons.

"Don't push so hard," she whispered, squirming. "The ground is bumpy."

"Sorry." They wriggled on the thick myrtle, searching for a more comfortable spot.

"Now there's a branch digging into my back."

Suddenly she stopped.

"What?"

"I heard a rustle."

"It's just the wind." Paul shifted some more and they embraced again. His fingers felt thick and awkward as he unzipped her pants, unbuttoned the rest of her shirt. Her breasts swung free and at the sight he felt himself grow even harder. He put his hand on her bare midriff, sliding it downward. Her much more expert hand reached him first. As she took him in her cool gentle grasp, he gasped and thrust forward.

"Ouch. Wait. There's still a branch underneath me." She sat up, breathing hard, her blond hair falling over her shoulders. Paul sat up, too, frustration mingling with desire. He could see the flattened area where they had been lying. The myrtle was crushed and beneath he could see the outline of the light-colored branch. He stuck his hand through the myrtle and grabbed it, yanking at it angrily, struggling to wrest it free. *Goddamn branch.*

But something was very wrong: it felt strange, cold, rubbery, and as it came up out of the myrtle he saw it wasn't a branch at all, but an arm. Leaves slid away exposing the rest of the body, languorously, unwillingly. As his fingers went slack the arm fell away again, flopping back into the greenery.

The girl screamed first, scrambling backward, standing, tripping, standing up again and running, jeans unzipped and shirt flapping around her. Paul was on his feet but all he seemed able to hear was her crashing through the undergrowth. It had all happened so fast it seemed like some sort of dream. He could feel the lust dying away within him, horror flooding in to take its place. He turned to run. Then he paused and glanced wildly back, driven by some impulse to see if it were actually real. The fingers were partly curled, white skin smeared with mud. And in the dimness beyond, under the thick undergrowth, lay the rest of it.

TWO

DR. BILL DOWSON LOUNGED AGAINST THE SINK, EXAMINING his precisely trimmed fingernails without interest. *One more, then lunch. Thank God.* A cup of coffee and a BLT at the corner deli would hit the spot. He wasn't sure why he wanted a BLT, exactly: maybe it was the lividity of the last stiff that started him thinking about bacon. Anyway, that Dominican behind the deli counter had elevated the sandwich into an art form. Dowson could practically taste the crisp lettuce, the tang of tomato against the mayonnaise . . .

The nurse brought in the clipboard and he glanced up. She had short black hair and a trim body. He glanced at the clipboard without picking it up and smiled at her.

"What have we here?" he asked.

"Homicide."

He gave an exaggerated sigh, rolled his eyes. "What is that, the fourth today? It must be hunting season. Gunshot?"

"No. Some kind of multiple stabbing. They found it in Central Park, in the Ramble."

He nodded. "The dumping ground, eh? Figures." *Great. Another piece-of-shit killing.* He glanced at his watch. "Bring it in, please."

He watched the nurse walk out. Nice, very nice. She returned a moment later with a gurney, covered by a green sheet.

He made no move toward the body. "So, how about that dinner tonight?"

The nurse smiled. "I don't think it's a good idea, Doctor."

"Why not?"

"I've told you before. I don't date doctors. Especially ones I work with."

He nodded, pushed down his glasses, and grinned. "But I'm your soul mate, remember?"

She smiled. "Hardly."

But he could tell she was flattered by his interest. Better not push it, though, not these days. Sexual harassment and all that.

He sighed, eased himself off the sink. Then he pulled on a fresh pair of gloves. "Turn on the videocams," he said to the nurse as he prepped.

"Yes, Doctor."

He picked up the clipboard. "Says here we have a Caucasian woman, identified as Doreen Hollander, age 27, of Pine Creek, Oklahoma. Identified by her husband." He scanned the rest of the top sheet. Then he hung the clipboard on the gurney, drew on his surgical mask, and with the nurse's help lifted the sheeted corpse onto the stainless steel examining table.

He sensed a presence behind him and turned. In the doorway was a tall, slender man. His face and hands looked remarkably pale against the black of his suit. Behind the man stood a uniformed cop.

"Yes?" Dowson asked.

The man approached, opening his wallet. "I'm Special

Agent Pendergast, Dr. Dowson. And this is Sergeant O'Shaughnessy of the NYPD."

Dowson looked him over. This was very irregular. And there was something strange about the man: hair so very blond, eyes so very pale, accent so very, *very* southern. "And?"

"May I observe?"

"This an FBI case?"

"No."

"Where's your clearance?"

"I don't have one."

Dowson sighed with irritation. "You know the rules. You can't just watch for the hell of it."

The FBI agent took a step closer to him, closer than he liked, invading his personal space. He controlled an impulse to step backward.

"Look, Mr. Pendergast, get the necessary paperwork and come back. Okay?"

"That will be time-consuming," said the man named Pendergast. "It will hold you up considerably. I would appreciate your courtesy in letting us observe."

There was something in the man's tone that sounded a lot harder than the mellifluous accent and genteel words suggested. Dowson hesitated. "Look, with all due respect—"

"With all due respect, Dr. Dowson, I'm in no mood to bandy civilities with you. Proceed with the autopsy."

The voice was now cold as dry ice. Dowson remembered the videocam was on. He glanced covertly at the nurse. He had a strong sense that a humiliation at the hands of this man might be just around the corner. This would not look good and it might cause trouble later. The guy was FBI, after all. Anyway, his own ass was covered: he was on record stating the man needed clearance.

Dowson sighed. "All right, Pendergast. You and the sergeant, don scrubs."

He waited until they returned, then pulled back the sheet with a single motion. The cadaver lay on its back: blonde hair, young, fresh. The chill of the previous night had kept it from decomposing. Dowson leaned toward the mike and began a description. The FBI man was looking at the corpse with interest. But Dowson could see that the uniformed cop was beginning to look uneasy, shifting from one foot to another, lips pressed tight together. The last thing he needed was a puker.

"Is he going to be all right?" Dowson asked Pendergast in an undertone, nodding to the cop.

Pendergast turned. "You don't have to see this, Sergeant."

The cop swallowed, glancing from the corpse to Pendergast and back again. "I'll be in the lounge."

"Drop your scrubs in the bin on your way out," said Dowson with sarcastic satisfaction.

Pendergast watched the cop leave. Then he turned to Dowson. "I suggest you turn the body over before making your Y-incision."

"And why is that?"

Pendergast nodded toward the clipboard. "Page two."

Dowson picked it up, flipped over the top page. *Extensive lacerations . . . deep knife wounds* . . . Looked like the girl had been stabbed repeatedly in the lower back. Or worse. As usual, it was hard to make out from the police report what had actually taken place, from a medical standpoint. There had been no investigating ME. It had been given a low priority. This Doreen Hollander didn't count for much, it seemed.

Dowson returned the clipboard. "Sue, help me turn her over."

They turned the body, exposing the back. The nurse gasped and stepped away.

Dowson stared in surprise. "Looks like she died on the operating table, in the middle of an operation to remove a spinal tumor." Had they screwed up again downstairs? Just last week—twice—they had sent him the wrong paperwork with the wrong corpse. But immediately Dowson realized this was no hospital stiff. Not with dirt and leaves sticking to the raw wound that covered the entire lower back and sacrum area.

This was weird. Seriously weird.

He peered closer and began describing the wound for the benefit of the camera, trying to keep the surprise out of his voice.

"Superficially, this does not resemble the random knife slashing, stabbing, or cutting described in the report. It has the appearance of—of a dissection. The incision—if it is one—begins about ten inches below the scapula and seven inches above the belt line. It appears as if the entire cauda equina has been dissected out, starting at L1 and terminating at the sacrum."

At this, the FBI agent looked at him abruptly.

"The dissection includes the filum terminale." Dowson bent closer. "Nurse, sponge along here."

The nurse removed some of the debris around the wound. The room had fallen silent except for the whirr of the camera, and there was a clattering sound as twigs and leaves slid into the table's drainage channel.

"The spinal cord—more precisely, the cauda equina—is missing. It has been removed. The dissection extends peripherally to the neuroforamen and out to the transverse processes. Nurse, irrigate L1 to L5."

The nurse quickly irrigated the requested area.

"The, er, dissection has stripped off the skin, the subcutaneous tissue, and paraspinous musculature. It appears as if a self-retaining retractor was used. I can see the marks of it here, and here, and here." He carefully indicated the areas for the benefit of the video.

"The spinous processes and laminae have been removed, along with the ligamentum flavum. The dura is still present. There is a longitudinal incision in the dura from L1 to the sacrum, allowing full removal of the cord. It has the appearance of a . . . of a very professional incision. Nurse, the stereozoom."

The nurse rolled over a large microscope. Quickly, Dowson inspected the spinous processes. "It looks as if a rongeur has been used to remove the processes and laminae from the dura."

He straightened up, running a gowned arm across his forehead. This was not a standard dissection one would do in medical school. It was more like the kind of thing neurosurgeons practiced in advanced neuroanatomy classes. Then he remembered the FBI agent, Pendergast. He glanced at him, to see how he was taking it. He had seen a lot of shocked people at autopsies, but nothing like this: the man looked, not shocked exactly, so much as grim Death himself.

The man spoke. "Doctor, may I interrupt with a few questions?"

Dowson nodded.

"Was this dissection the cause of death?"

This was a new thought to Dowson. He shuddered. "If the subject were alive when this was done, yes, it would have caused death."

"At what point?"

"As soon as the incision was made in the dura, the cerebrospinal fluid would have drained. That alone would have been enough to cause death." He examined the wound again. It looked as if the operation had caused a great deal of bleeding from the epidural veins, and some of them had retracted—an indication of live trauma. Yet the dissector had not worked around the veins, as a surgeon on a live patient would have done, but had cut right through them. The operation, while done with great skill, had also apparently been done with haste. "A large number of veins have been cut, and only the largest—whose bleeding would have interfered with the work—have been ligated. The subject might have bled to death before the opening of the dura, depending on how fast the, er, person worked."

"But was the subject *alive* when the operation began?"

"It seems she was." Dowson swallowed weakly. "However, it seems no effort was made to *keep* the subject alive while the, ah, dissection was progressing."

"I would suggest some blood and tissue work to see if the subject had been tranquilized."

The doctor nodded. "It's standard."

"In your opinion, Doctor, how professional was this dissection?"

Dowson did not answer. He was trying to order his thoughts. This had the potential of being big and unpleasant. For the time being, no doubt they'd try to keep a low profile on this, try to fly it as long as possible beneath the radar of the New York press. But it would come out—it always did—and then there would be a lot of people second-guessing his actions. He'd better slow down, take it one step at a time. This was not the run-of-the-mill murder the police report indicated. Thank God he hadn't actually begun the autopsy. He had the FBI agent to thank for that.

He turned to the nurse. "Get Jones up here with the large-format camera and the camera for the stereozoom. And I want a second ME to assist. Who's on call?"

"Dr. Lofton."

"I need him within the half-hour. I also want to consult with our neurosurgeon, Dr. Feldman. Get him up here as soon as possible."

"Yes, Doctor."

He turned to Pendergast. "I'm not sure I can let you stay without some kind of official sanction."

To his surprise, the man seemed to accept this. "I understand, Doctor. I believe this autopsy is in good hands. I, personally, have seen enough."

So have I, thought Dowson. He now felt sure that a surgeon had done this. The thought made him feel sick.

O'Shaughnessy stood in the lounge. He debated whether to buy a cup of coffee from a vending machine, then decided against it. He felt distinctly embarrassed. Here he was, supposed to be a tough, sardonic New York City cop, and he'd wimped out. All but tossed his cookies right there on the examining room floor. The sight of that poor chubby naked girl on the table, blue and dirty, her young face all puffed up, eyes open, leaves and sticks in her hair . . . he shuddered afresh at the image.

He also felt a burning anger for the person who had done it. He wasn't a homicide cop, had never wanted to be one, even in the early days. He hated the sight of blood. But his own sister-in-law lived in Oklahoma. About this girl's age, too. Now, he felt he could stand whatever it took to catch that killer.

Pendergast glided through the stainless steel doors like a wraith. He barely glanced at O'Shaughnessy. The sergeant fell into step behind him, and they left the building and climbed into the waiting car in silence.

Something had definitely put Pendergast into a black mood. The guy was moody, but this was the darkest he had ever seen him. O'Shaughnessy still had no idea why Pendergast was suddenly so interested in this new murder, interrupting his work on the nineteenth-century killings. But somehow, this didn't seem to be the time to ask.

"We will drop the sergeant off at the precinct house," said Pendergast to his chauffeur. "And then you may take me home."

Pendergast settled back in the leather seat. O'Shaughnessy looked over at him.

"What happened?" he managed to ask. "What did you see?"

Pendergast looked out his window. "Evil." And he spoke no more.

THREE

WILLIAM SMITHBACK JR., IN HIS BEST SUIT (THE ARMANI, recently dry-cleaned), crispest white shirt, and most business-like tie, stood on the corner of Avenue of the Americas and Fifty-fifth Street. His eyes strayed upward along the vast glass-and-chrome monolith that was the Moegen-Fairhaven Building, rippling blue-green in the sunlight like some vast slab of water. Somewhere in that hundred-million-dollar pile was his prey.

He felt pretty sure he could talk his way into seeing Fairhaven. He was good at that kind of thing. This assignment was a lot more promising than that tourist murder in the Ramble his editor had wanted him to cover today. He conjured up the grizzled face of his editor, red eyes bug-big behind thick glasses, smoke-cured finger pointing, telling him that this dead lady from Oklahoma was going to be big. Big? Tourists were getting smoked all the time in New York City. It was too bad, but there it was. Homicide reporting was hackwork. He had a hunch about Fairhaven, the Museum, and these old killings Pendergast was so interested in. He always trusted his hunches. His editor wouldn't be disappointed. He was going to cast his fly onto the water, and by God Fairhaven might just bite.

Taking one more deep breath, he crossed the street—giving the finger to a cabbie that shot past inches away, horn blaring—and approached the granite and titanium entry. Another vast acreage of granite greeted him upon entering the interior. There was a large desk, manned by half a dozen security officers, and several banks of elevators beyond.

Smithback strode resolutely toward the security desk. He leaned on it aggressively.

"I'm here to see Mr. Fairhaven."

The closest guard was shuffling through a computer printout. "Name?" he asked, not bothering to look up.

"William Smithback Jr., of the *New York Times*."

"Moment," mumbled the guard, picking up a telephone. He dialed, then handed it to Smithback. A crisp voice sounded. "May I help you?"

"This is William Smithback Jr. of the *New York Times*. I'm here to see Mr. Fairhaven."

It was Saturday, but Smithback was gambling he'd be in his office. Guys like Fairhaven never took Saturdays off. And on Saturdays, they were usually less fortified with secretaries and guards.

"Do you have an appointment?" the female voice asked, reaching down to him from fifty stories.

"No. I'm the reporter doing the story on Enoch Leng and the bodies found at his jobsite on Catherine Street and I need to speak with him immediately. It's urgent."

"You need to call for an appointment." It was an utterly neutral voice.

"Good. Consider this the call. I'd like to make an appointment for"—Smithback checked his watch—"ten o'clock."

"Mr. Fairhaven is presently engaged," the voice instantly responded.

Smithback took a deep breath. So he *was* in. Time to press the attack. There were probably ten layers of secretaries beyond the one on the phone, but he'd gotten through that many before. "Look, if Mr. Fairhaven is too busy to talk to me, I'll just have to report in the article I'm writing for the Monday edition that he refused to comment."

"He is presently engaged," the robotic voice repeated.

"*No comment.* That'll do wonders for his public image. And come Monday, Mr. Fairhaven will be wanting to know who in his office turned away the reporter. Get my drift?"

There was a long silence. Smithback drew in some more air. This was often a long process. "You know when you're reading an article in the paper, and it's about some sleazy guy, and the guy says I have no comment? How does that make you feel about the guy? Especially a real estate developer. *No comment.* I could do a lot with *no comment.*"

There was more silence. Smithback wondered if she had hung up. But no, there was a sound on a line. It was a chuckle.

"That's good," said a low, pleasant, masculine voice. "I like that. Nicely done."

"Who's this?" Smithback demanded.

"Just some sleazy real estate developer."

"Who?" Smithback was not going to stand being made fun of by some lackey.

"Anthony Fairhaven."

"Oh." Smithback was momentarily struck speechless. He recovered quickly. "Mr. Fairhaven, is it *true* that—"

"Why don't you come on up, so we can talk face-to-face, like grown-up people? Forty-ninth floor."

"What?" Smithback was still surprised at the rapidity of his success.

"I said, come up. I was wondering when you'd call, being the ambitious, careerist reporter that you so evidently are."

Fairhaven's office was not quite what Smithback had envisioned. True, there were several layers of secretaries and assistants guarding the sanctum sanctorum. But when he finally gained Fairhaven's office, it wasn't the vast screw-you space of chrome-gold-ebony-old-master-paintings-African-primitives he'd expected. It was rather simple and small. True, there was art on the walls, but it consisted of some understated Thomas Hart Benton lithographs of yeoman farmers. Beside these was a glassed panel—locked and clearly alarmed—containing a variety of handguns, mounted on a black velvet backdrop. The sole desk was small and made of birch. There were a couple of easy chairs and a worn Persian rug on the floor. One wall was covered with bookshelves, filled with books that had clearly been read instead of purchased by the yard as furniture. Except for the gun case, it looked more like a professor's office than that of a real estate magnate. And yet, unlike any professor's office Smithback had ever been in, the space was meticulously clean. Every surface sparkled with an unblemished shine. Even the books appeared to have been polished. There was a faint smell of cleaning agents, a little chemical but not unpleasant.

"Please sit down," said Fairhaven, sweeping a hand toward the easy chairs. "Would you care for anything? Coffee? Water? Soda? Whisky?" He grinned.

"Nothing, thanks," said Smithback as he took a seat. He felt the familiar shudder of expectation that came before an intense interview. Fairhaven was clearly savvy, but he was rich and pampered; he no doubt lacked street-smarts. Smithback had interviewed—and skewered—dozens like him. It wouldn't even be a contest.

Fairhaven opened a refrigerator and took out a small bottle of mineral water. He poured himself a glass and then sat, not at his desk, but in an easy chair opposite Smithback. He crossed his legs, smiled. The bottle of water sparkled in the sunlight that slanted through the windows. Smithback glanced past him. The view, at least, was killer.

He turned his attention back to the man. Black wavy hair, strong brow, athletic frame, easy movements, sardonic look in the eye. Could be thirty, thirty-five. He jotted a few impressions.

"So," Fairhaven said with a small, self-deprecating smile, "the sleazy real estate developer is ready to take your questions."

"May I record this?"

"I would expect no less."

Smithback slipped a recorder out of his pocket. Of course he seemed charming. People like him were experts at charm and manipulation. But he'd never allow himself to be spun. All he had to do was remember who he was dealing with: a heartless, money-grubbing businessman who would sell his own mother for the back rent alone.

"Why did you destroy the site on Catherine Street?" he asked.

Fairhaven bowed his head slightly. "The project was behind schedule. We were fast-tracking the excavation. It would've cost me forty thousand dollars a day. I'm not in the archaeology business."

"Some archaeologists say you destroyed one of the most important sites to be discovered in Manhattan in a quarter-century."

Fairhaven cocked his head. "Really? Which archaeologists?"

"The Society for American Archaeology, for example."

A cynical smile broke out on Fairhaven's face. "Ah. I see. Well of course they'd be against it. If they had their way, no one in America would turn over a spadeful of soil without an archaeologist standing by with screen, trowel, and toothbrush."

"Getting back to the site—"

"Mr. Smithback, what I did was perfectly legal. When we discovered those remains, I *personally* stopped all work. I *personally* examined the site. We called in forensic experts, who photographed everything. We removed the remains with great care, had them examined, and then properly buried, all at my own expense. We did not restart work until we had direct authorization from the mayor. What more would you have me do?"

Smithback felt a small twinge. This was not proceeding quite as expected. He was letting Fairhaven control the agenda; that was the problem.

"You say you had the remains buried. Why? Was there anything perhaps you were trying to hide?"

At this Fairhaven actually laughed, leaning back in his chair, exposing beautiful teeth. "You make it sound suspicious. I'm a little embarrassed to admit that I'm a man with some small religious values. These poor people were killed in a hideous way. I wanted to give them a decent burial with an ecumenical service, quiet and dignified, free of the whole media circus. That's what I did—buried them together with their little effects in a real cemetery. I didn't want their bones ending up in a museum drawer. So I purchased a beautiful tract in the Gates of Heaven Cemetery in Valhalla, New York. I'm sure the cemetery director would be happy to show you the plot. The remains were my responsibility and, frankly, I had to do *something* with them. The city certainly didn't want them."

"Right, right," said Smithback, thinking. It would make a nice sidebar, this quiet burial under the leafy elms. But then he frowned. Christ, was he getting spun here?

Time for a new tack. "According to the records, you're a major donor to the mayor's re-election campaign. You get in a pinch at your construction site and he bails you out. Coincidence?"

Fairhaven leaned back in the chair. "Drop the wide-eyed, babe-in-the-woods look. You know perfectly well how things work in this town. When I give money to the mayor's campaign, I am exercising my constitutional rights. I don't expect any special treatment, and I don't ask for it."

"But if you get it, so much the better."

Fairhaven smiled broadly, cynically, but said nothing. Smithback felt another twinge of concern. This guy was being very careful about what he actually *said.* Trouble was, you couldn't record a cynical grin.

He stood and walked with what he hoped looked like casual confidence toward the paintings, hands behind his back, studying them, trying to frame a new strategy. Then he moved to the gun case. Inside, polished weapons gleamed. "Interesting choice of office decor," he said, gesturing at the case.

"I collect the rarest of handguns. I can afford to. That one you are pointing at, for example, is a Luger, chambered in .45. The only one ever made. I also have a collection of Mercedes-Benz roadsters. But they take up rather more display space, so I keep them at my place in Sag Harbor." Fairhaven looked at him, still smiling cynically. "We all collect things, Mr. Smithback. What's your passion?

Museum monographs and chapbooks, perhaps: removed for research, then not returned? By accident, of course."

Smithback looked at him sharply. Had the guy searched his apartment? But no: Fairhaven was merely fishing. He returned to the chair. "Mr. Fairhaven—"

Fairhaven interrupted him, his tone suddenly brisk, unfriendly. "Look, Smithback, I know you're exercising your constitutional right to skewer me. The big bad real estate developer is always an easy target. And you like easy targets. Because you fellows are all cut from the same cloth. You all think your work is *important*. But today's newspaper is lining tomorrow's bird cage. It's ephemera. What you do, in the larger scheme of things, is nugatory."

Nugatory? What the hell did that mean? It didn't matter: clearly it was an insult. He was getting under Fairhaven's skin. That was good—wasn't it?

"Mr. Fairhaven, I have reason to believe that you've been pressuring the Museum to stop this investigation."

"I'm sorry. What investigation?"

"The one into Enoch Leng and the nineteenth-century killings."

"That investigation? Why should I care one way or another about it? It didn't stop my construction project, and frankly that's all I care about. They can investigate it now until they're blue in the face, if they so choose. And I love this phrase all you journalists use: *I have reason to believe.* What you really mean is: *I want to believe but I haven't a shred of evidence.* All you fellows must've taken the same Journalism 101 class: Making an Ass of Yourself While Pretending to Get the Story." Fairhaven allowed himself a cynical laugh.

Smithback sat stiffly, listening to the laughter subside. Once again he tried to tell himself he was getting under

Fairhaven's skin. He spoke at last, keeping his voice as cool as possible.

"Tell me, Mr. Fairhaven, just why is it that you're so *interested* in the Museum?"

"I happen to love the Museum. It's my favorite museum in the world. I practically grew up in that place looking at the dinosaurs, the meteorites, the gems. I had a nanny who used to take me. She necked with her boyfriend behind the elephants while I wandered around by myself. But you're not interested in that, because it doesn't fit your image of the greedy real estate developer. Really, Smithback, I'm wise to your game."

"Mr. Fairhaven—"

Fairhaven grinned. "You want a confession?"

This temporarily stopped Smithback.

Fairhaven lowered his voice to confessional level. "I have committed two unforgivable crimes."

Smithback tried to maintain the hard-bitten reportorial look he cultivated in instances like these. He knew this was going to be some kind of trick, or joke.

"My two crimes are these—are you ready?"

Smithback checked to see if the recorder was still running.

"I am rich, and I am a developer. My two truly unforgivable sins. Mea culpa."

Against all his better journalistic instincts, Smithback found himself getting pissed off. He'd lost the interview. It was, in fact, a dead loss. The guy was a slimeball, but he was remarkably adroit at dealing with the press. So far Smithback had nothing, and he was going to get nothing. He made one last push anyway. "You still haven't explained—"

Fairhaven stood. "Smithback, if you only knew how utterly predictable you and your questions are—if you *only* knew how tiresome and mediocre *you* are as a reporter and, I'm sorry to say, as a human being—you'd be mortified."

"I'd like an explanation—"

But Fairhaven was pressing a buzzer. His voice smothered the rest of Smithback's question. "Miss Gallagher, would you kindly show Mr. Smithback out?"

"Yes, Mr. Fairhaven."

"This is rather abrupt—"

"Mr. Smithback, I am *tired.* I saw you because I didn't want to read about myself in the paper having refused comment. I was also curious to meet you, to see if you were perhaps a cut above the rest. Now that I've satisfied myself on that score, I don't see any reason to continue this conversation."

The secretary stood in the door, stout and unmovable. "Mr. Smithback? This way, please."

On his way out, Smithback paused in the outermost secretary's office. Despite his efforts at self-control, his frame was quivering with indignation. Fairhaven had been parrying a hostile press for more than a decade; naturally, he'd gotten damn good at it. Smithback had dealt with nasty interviewees before, but this one really got under his skin. Calling him tiresome, mediocre, ephemeral, nugatory (he'd have to look that up)—who did he think he was?

Fairhaven himself was too slippery to pin down. No big surprise there. There were other ways to find things out about people. People in power had enemies, and enemies loved to talk. Sometimes the enemies were working for them, right under their noses.

He glanced at the secretary. She was young, sweet, and looked more approachable than the battle-axes manning the inner offices.

"Here every Saturday?" He smiled nonchalantly.

"Most of them," she said, looking up from her computer. She was cute, with glossy red hair and a small splash of freckles. He winced inwardly, suddenly reminded of Nora.

"Works you hard, doesn't he?"

"Mr. Fairhaven? Sure does."

"Probably makes you work Sundays, too."

"Oh no," she said. "Mr. Fairhaven never works on Sunday. He goes to church."

Smithback feigned surprise. "Church? Is he Catholic?"

"Presbyterian."

"Probably a tough man to work for, I bet."

"No, he's one of the best supervisors I've had. He actually seems to care about us little folk."

"Never would have guessed it," Smithback said with a wink, drifting out the door. *Probably boning her and the other "little folk" on the side,* he thought.

Back on the street, Smithback allowed himself a most un-Presbyterian string of oaths. He was going to dig into this guy's past until he knew every detail, down to the name of his goddamn teddy bear. You couldn't become a big-time real estate developer in New York City and keep your hands clean. There would be dirt, and he would find it. Yes, there would be dirt. By *God,* there would be dirt.

FOUR

MANDY EKLUND CLIMBED THE FILTHY SUBWAY STAIRS TO First Street, turned north at Avenue A, and trudged toward Tompkins Square Park. Ahead, the park's anemic trees rose up against a sky faintly smeared with the purple stain of dawn. The morning star, low on the horizon, was fading into oblivion.

Mandy pulled her wrap more tightly around her shoulders in a futile attempt to keep out the early morning chill. She felt a little groggy, and her feet ached each time they hit the pavement. It had been a great night at Club Pissoir, though: music, free drinks, dancing. The whole Ford crowd had been there, along with a bunch of photographers, the *Mademoiselle* and *Cosmo* people, everyone who mattered in the fashion world. She really was making it. The thought still amazed her. Only six months before, she'd been working at Rodney's in Bismarck, giving free makeovers. Then, the right person happened to come through the shop. And now she was on the testing board at the Ford agency. Eileen Ford herself had taken her under her wing. It was all coming together faster than she'd ever dreamed possible.

Her father called almost every day from the farm. It was funny, kind of cute really, how worried he was about her living in New York City. He thought the place was a den of iniquity. He'd freak if he knew she stayed out till dawn. He still wanted her to go to college. And maybe she would— someday. But right now she was eighteen and having the time of her life. She smiled affectionately at the thought of her conservative old father, riding his John Deere, worrying himself about her. She'd make the call this time, give him a surprise.

She turned onto Seventh Street, passing the darkened park, keeping a wary eye out for muggers. New York was a lot safer now, but it was still wise to be careful. She felt into her purse, hand closing comfortingly around the small bottle of pepper spray attached to her key chain.

There were a couple of homeless sleeping on pieces of cardboard, and a man in a threadbare corduroy suit sat on a bench, drinking and nodding. An early breeze passed through the listless sycamore branches, rattling the leaves. They were just beginning to turn a jaundiced yellow.

Once again, she wished her walk-up apartment wasn't so far from a subway station. She couldn't afford cabs—not yet, anyway—and walking the nine blocks home at night was a hassle. At first it had seemed like a cool neighborhood, but the seediness was starting to get to her. Gentrification was creeping in, but not fast enough: the dingy squats and the old hollow buildings, sealed shut with cinderblock, were depressing. The Flatiron District would be better, or maybe even Yorkville. A lot of the Ford models, the ones who'd made it, lived up there.

She left the park behind and turned up Avenue C. Silent brownstones rose on either side, and the wind sent trash along the gutters with a dry, skittery sound. The faint ammoniac tang of urine floated out from dark doorways. Nobody picked up after their dogs, and she made her way with care through a disgusting minefield of dog shit. This part of the walk was always the worst.

She saw, ahead of her, a figure approaching down the sidewalk. She stiffened, considered crossing the street, then relaxed: it was an old man, walking painfully with a cane. As he approached she could see he was wearing a funny derby hat. His head was bowed, and she could make out its even brim, the crisp black lines of its crown. She didn't recall ever seeing anybody wearing a derby, except in old black-and-white movies. He looked very old-fashioned, shuffling along with cautious steps. She wondered what he was doing out so early. Probably insomnia. Old people had it a lot, she'd heard. Waking up at four in the morning, couldn't go back to sleep. She wondered if her father had insomnia.

They were almost even now. The old man suddenly seemed to grow aware of her presence; he raised his head and lifted his arm to grasp his hat. He was actually going to tip his hat to her.

The hat came up, the arm obscuring everything except the eyes. They were remarkably bright and cold, and they seemed to be regarding her intently. *Must be insomnia,* she thought—despite the hour, this old fellow wasn't sleepy at all.

"Good morning, miss," said an old, creaky voice.

"Good morning," she replied, trying to keep the surprise from her voice. Nobody ever said anything to you on the street. It was so un–New York. It charmed her.

As she passed him, she suddenly felt something whip around her neck with horrible speed.

She struggled and tried to cry out, but found her face

covered with a cloth, damp and reeking with a sickly-sweet chemical smell. Instinctively, she tried to hold her breath. Her hand scrabbled in her purse and pulled out the bottle of pepper spray, but a terrible blow knocked it to the sidewalk. She twisted and thrashed, moaning in pain and fear, her lungs on fire; she gasped once; and then all swirled into oblivion.

FIVE

IN HIS MESSY CUBICLE ON THE FIFTH FLOOR OF THE *TIMES* building, Smithback examined with dissatisfaction the list he had handwritten in his notebook. At the top of the list, the phrase "Fairhaven's employees" had been crossed out. He hadn't been able to get back into the Moegen-Fairhaven Building—Fairhaven had seen to that. Likewise, "neighbors" had also been crossed out: he'd been given the bum's rush at Fairhaven's apartment building, despite all his best stratagems and tricks. He'd looked into Fairhaven's past, to his early business associates, but they were either full of phony praise or simply refused comment.

Next, he'd checked out Fairhaven's charities. The New York Museum was a dead loss—no one who knew Fairhaven would talk about him, for obvious reasons—but he had more success with one of Fairhaven's other projects, the Little Arthur Clinic for Children. If success was the right word for it. The clinic was a small research hospital that cared for sick children with "orphaned" diseases: very rare illnesses that the big drug companies had no interest in finding cures for. Smithback had managed to get in posing as himself—a *New York Times* reporter interested in their work—without rousing suspicion. They had even given him an informal tour. But in the end that, too, had been a snow job: The doctors, nurses, parents, even the children sang hosannas for Fairhaven. It was enough to make you sick: turkeys at Thanksgiving, bonuses at Christmas, toys and books for the kids, trips to Yankee Stadium. Fairhaven had even attended a few funerals, which must have been tough. *And yet,* thought Smithback grumpily, *all it proved was that Fairhaven carefully cultivated his public image.*

The guy was a public relations pro from way back. Smithback had found nothing. Nothing.

That reminded him: he turned, grabbed a battered dictionary from a nearby shelf, flipped through the pages until he reached "n." Nugatory: of no importance, trifling.

Smithback put back the dictionary.

What was needed here was some deeper digging. Before the time when Fairhaven had gone pro with his life. Back when he was just another pimply high school kid. So Fairhaven thought Smithback was just another run-of-the-mill reporter, doing nugatory work? Well, he'd wouldn't be laughing so hard when he opened his Monday paper.

All it took was ten minutes on the Web to hit paydirt. Fairhaven's class at P.S. 1984, up on Amsterdam Avenue, had recently celebrated the fifteenth anniversary of their graduation. They had created a Web page reproducing their yearbook. Fairhaven hadn't shown up for the reunion, and he might not have even known of the Web page—but all the information about him from his old yearbook was posted, for all to see: photos, nicknames, clubs, interests, everything.

There he was: a clean-cut, all-around kid, smiling cockily out of a blurry graduation photograph. He was wearing a tennis sweater and a checked shirt—a typical well-heeled city boy. His father was in real estate, his mother a homemaker. Smithback quickly learned all kinds of things: that he was captain of the swim team; that he was born under the sign of Gemini; that he was head of the debating club; that his favorite rock group was the Eagles; that he played the guitar badly; that he wanted to be a doctor; that his favorite color was burgundy; and that he had been voted most likely to become a millionaire.

As Smithback scrolled through the Web site, the sinking feeling returned. It was all so unspeakably boring. But there was one detail that caught his eye. Every student had been given a nickname, and Fairhaven's was "The Slasher." He felt his disappointment abate just slightly. *The Slasher.* It would be nice if the nickname turned up a secret interest in torturing animals. It wasn't much, but it was something.

And he'd graduated only sixteen years ago. There would be people who remembered him. If there was anything unsavory, Smithback would find it. Let that bastard crack his paper next week and see how fast that smug smile got wiped off.

P.S. 1984. Luckily, the school was only a cab ride away. Turning his back on the computer, Smithback stood up and reached for his jacket.

The school stood on a leafy Upper West Side block between Amsterdam and Columbus, not far from the Museum, a long building of yellow brick, surrounded by a wrought iron fence. As far as New York City schools went, it was rather nice. Smithback strode to the front door, found it locked—security, of course—and buzzed. A policeman answered. Smithback flashed his press card and the cop let him in.

It was amazing how the place smelled: just like his own high school, far away and long ago. And there was the same taupe paint on the cinderblock walls, too. *All school principals must've read the same how-to manual,* Smithback thought as the cop escorted him through the metal detector and to the principal's office.

The principal referred him to Miss Kite. Smithback found her at her desk, working on student assignments between classes. She was a handsome, gray-haired woman, and when Smithback mentioned Fairhaven's name, he was gratified to see the smile of memory on her face.

"Oh yes," she said. Her voice was kind, but there was a no-nonsense edge to it that told Smithback this was no pushover granny. "I remember Tony Fairhaven well, because he was in my first twelfth-grade class, and he was one of our top students. He was a National Merit Scholar runner-up."

Smithback nodded deferentially and jotted a few notes. He wasn't going to tape-record this—that was a good way to shut people up.

"Tell me about him. Informally. What was he like?"

"He was a bright boy, quite popular. I believe he was the head of the swim team. A good, all-around, hardworking student."

"Did he ever get into trouble?"

"Sure. They all did."

Smithback tried to look casual. "Really?"

"He used to bring his guitar to school and play in the halls, which was against regulations. He played very badly and it was mostly to make the other students laugh." She thought for a moment. "One day he caused a hall jam."

"A hall jam." Smithback waited. "And then?"

"We confiscated the guitar and that ended it. We gave it back to him after graduation."

Smithback nodded, the polite smile freezing on his face. "Did you know his parents?"

"His father was in real estate, though of course it was Tony who really made such a success in the business. I don't remember the mother."

"Brothers? Sisters?"

"At that time he was an only child. Of course, there was the family tragedy."

Smithback involuntarily leaned forward. "Tragedy?"

"His older brother, Arthur, died. Some rare disease."

Smithback abruptly made the connection. "Did they call him Little Arthur, by any chance?"

"I believe they did. His father was Big Arthur. It hit Tony very hard."

"When did it happen?"

"When Tony was in tenth grade."

"So it was his older brother? Was he in the school, too?"

"No. He'd been hospitalized for years. Some very rare and disfiguring disease."

"What disease?"

"I really don't know."

"When you say it hit Fairhaven hard, how so?"

"He became withdrawn, antisocial. But he came out of it, eventually."

"Yes, yes. Let me see . . ." Smithback checked his notes. "Let's see. Any problems with alcohol, drugs, delinquency . . . ?" Smithback tried to make it sound casual.

"No, no, just the opposite," came the curt reply. The look on the teacher's face had hardened. "Tell me, Mr. Smithback, exactly *why* are you writing this article?"

Smithback put on his most innocent face. "I'm just doing a little biographical feature on Mr. Fairhaven. You understand, we want to get a well-rounded picture, the good and the bad. I'm not fishing for anything in particular." *Right.*

"I see. Well, Tony Fairhaven was a good boy, and he was

very anti-drug, anti-drinking, even anti-smoking. I remember he wouldn't even drink coffee." She hesitated. "I don't know, if anything, he might have been a little *too* good. And it was sometimes hard to tell what he was thinking. He was a rather closed boy."

Smithback jotted a few more pro forma notes.

"Any hobbies?"

"He talked about making money quite a bit. He worked hard after school, and he had a lot of spending money as a result. I don't suppose any of this is surprising, considering what he's done. I've read from time to time articles about him, how he pushed through this development or that over a neighborhood's protests. And of course I read your piece on the Catherine Street discoveries. Nothing surprising. The boy has grown into the man, that's all."

Smithback was startled: she'd given no indication she even knew who he was, let alone read his pieces.

"By the way, I thought your article was very interesting. And disturbing."

Smithback felt a flush of pleasure. "Thank you."

"I imagine that's why you're interested in Tony. Well, rushing in and digging up that site so he could finish his building was just like him. He was always very goal-oriented, impatient to get to the end, to finish, to succeed. I suppose that's why he's been so successful as a developer. And he could be rather sarcastic and impatient with people he considered his inferiors."

Right, thought Smithback.

"What about enemies. Did he have any?"

"Let me see . . . I just can't remember. He was the kind of boy that was never impulsive, always very deliberate in his actions. Although it seems to me there was something about a girl once. He got into a shoving match and was suspended for the afternoon. No blows were exchanged, though."

"And the boy?"

"That would have been Joel Amberson."

"What happened to Joel Amberson?"

"Why, nothing."

Smithback nodded, crossed his legs. This was getting nowhere. Time to move in for the kill. "Did he have any nicknames? You know how kids always seem to have a nickname in high school."

"I don't remember any other names."

"I took a look at the yearbook, posted on your Web site."

The teacher smiled. "We started doing that a few years ago. It's proven to be quite popular."

"No doubt. But in the yearbook, he had a nickname."

"Really? What was it?"

"The Slasher."

Her face furrowed, then suddenly cleared. "Ah, yes. *That.*"

Smithback leaned forward. "That?"

The teacher gave a little laugh. "They had to dissect frogs for biology class."

"And—?"

"Tony was a little squeamish—for two days he tried and tried but he couldn't do it. The kids teased him about it, and somebody started calling him that, The Slasher. It kind of stuck, as a joke, you know. He did eventually overcome his qualms—and got an A in biology, as I recall—but you know how it is once they start calling you a name."

Smithback didn't move a muscle. He couldn't believe it. It got worse and worse. The guy was a candidate for beatification.

"Mr. Smithback?"

Smithback made a show of checking his notes. "Anything else?"

The kindly gray-haired teacher laughed softly. "Look, Mr. Smithback, if it's dirt you're looking for on Tony—and I can see that it is, it's written all over your face—you're just not going to find it. He was a normal, all-around, high-achieving boy who seems to have grown into a normal, all-around, high-achieving man. And now, if you don't mind, I'd like to get back to my grading."

Smithback stepped out of P.S. 1984 and began walking, rather mournfully, in the direction of Columbus Avenue. This hadn't turned out the way he'd planned, at all. He'd wasted a colossal amount of time, energy, and effort, and without anything at all to show for it. Was it possible his instincts were wrong—that this was all a wild-goose chase, a dead end, inspired by a thirst for revenge? But no—that would be unthinkable. He was a seasoned reporter. When he had a hunch, it was usually right. So how was it he couldn't find the goods on Fairhaven?

As he reached the corner, his eye happened to stray toward a newsstand and the front page of a freshly printed *New York Post*. The headline froze him in his tracks.

EXCLUSIVE

SECOND MUTILATED BODY FOUND

The story that followed was bylined by Bryce Harriman.

Smithback fumbled in his pocket for change, dropped it

on the scarred wooden counter, and grabbed a paper. He read with trembling hands:

NEW YORK, Oct. 10—An as-yet-unidentified body of a young woman was discovered this morning in Tompkins Square Park, in the East Village. She is apparently the victim of the same brutal killer who murdered a tourist in Central Park two days ago.

In both cases, the killer dissected part of the spinal cord at the time of death, removing a section known as the cauda equina, a bundle of nerves at the base of the spinal cord that resembles a horse's tail, The Post has learned.

The actual cause of death appears to have been the dissection itself.

The mutilations in both cases appear to have been done with care and precision, possibly with surgical instruments. An anonymous source confirmed the police are investigating the possibility that the killer is a surgeon or other medical specialist.

The dissection mimics a description of a surgical procedure, discovered in an old document in the New York Museum. The document, found hidden in the archives, describes in detail a series of experiments conducted in the late nineteenth century by an Enoch Leng. These experiments were an attempt by Leng to prolong his own life span. On October 1, thirty-six alleged victims of Leng were uncovered during the excavation of a building foundation on Catherine Street. Nothing more is known about Leng, except that he was associated with the New York Museum of Natural History.

"What we have here is a copycat killer," said Police Commissioner Karl C. Rocker. "A very twisted individual read the article about Leng and is trying to duplicate his work." He declined to comment further on any details of the investigation, except to say that more than fifty detectives had been assigned to the case, and that it was being given "the highest priority."

Smithback let out a howl of anguish. The tourist in Central Park was the murder assignment that, like a complete fool, he'd turned down. Instead, he had promised his editor Fairhaven's head on a platter. Now, not only did he have nothing to show for his day of pounding the pavement, but he'd been scooped on the very story he himself had broken—and by none other than his old nemesis, Bryce Harriman.

It was his own head that would be on a platter.

SIX

NORA TURNED OFF CANAL STREET ONTO MOTT, MOVING slowly through the throngs of people. It was seven o'clock on a Friday evening, and Chinatown was packed. Sheets of densely printed Chinese newspapers lay strewn in the gutters. The stalls of the fish sellers were set up along the sidewalks, vast arrays of exotic-looking fish laid out on ice. In the windows, pressed duck and cooked squid hung on hooks. The buyers, primarily Chinese, pushed and shouted frantically, under the curious gaze of passing tourists.

Ten Ren's Tea and Ginseng Company was a few hundred feet down the block. She pushed through the door into a long, bright, orderly space. The air of the tea shop was perfumed with innumerable faint scents. At first she thought the shop was empty. But then, as she looked around once more, she noticed Pendergast at a rear table, nestled between display cases of ginseng and ginger. She could have sworn that the table had been empty just a moment before.

"Are you a tea drinker?" he asked as she approached, motioning her to a seat.

"Sometimes." Her subway had stalled between stations for twenty minutes, and she'd had plenty of time to rehearse what she would say. She would get it over with quickly and get out.

But Pendergast was clearly in no hurry. They sat in silence while he consulted a sheet filled with Chinese ideographs. Nora wondered if it was a list of tea offerings, but there seemed to be far too many items—surely there weren't that many kinds of tea in the world.

Pendergast turned to the shopkeeper—a small, vivacious woman—and began speaking rapidly.

"Nin hao, lao bin liang. Li mama hao ma?"

The woman shook her head. *"Bu, ta hai shi lao yang zi, shen ti bu hao."*

"Qing li Dai wo xiang ta wen an. Qing gei wo yi bei Wu Long cha hao ma?"

The woman walked away, returning with a ceramic pot from which she poured a minuscule cup of tea. She placed the cup in front of Nora.

"You speak Chinese?" Nora asked Pendergast.

"A little Mandarin. I confess to speaking Cantonese somewhat more fluently."

Nora fell silent. Somehow, she was not surprised.

"King's Tea of Osmanthus Oolong," said Pendergast, nodding toward her cup. "One of the finest in the world. From bushes grown on the sunny sides of the mountains, new shoots gathered only in the spring."

Nora picked up the cup. A delicate aroma rose to her nostrils. She took a sip, tasting a complex blend of green tea and other exquisitely delicate flavors.

"Very nice," she said, putting down the cup.

"Indeed." Pendergast glanced at her for a moment. Then he spoke again in Mandarin, and the woman filled up a bag, weighed it, and sealed it, scribbling a price on the plastic wrapping. She handed it to Nora.

"For me?" Nora asked.

Pendergast nodded.

"I don't want any gifts from you."

"Please take it. It's excellent for the digestion. As well as being a superb antioxidant."

Nora took it irritably, then saw the price. "Wait a minute, this is two hundred *dollars?*"

"It will last three or four months," said Pendergast. "A small price when one considers—"

"Look," said Nora, setting down the bag. "Mr. Pendergast, I came here to tell you that I can't work for you anymore. My career at the Museum is at stake. A bag of tea isn't going to change my mind, even if it is two hundred bucks."

Pendergast listened attentively, his head slightly bowed.

"They implied—and the implication was very clear— that I wasn't to work with you anymore. I *like* what I do. I keep this up, I'll lose my job. I already lost one job when the Lloyd Museum closed down. I can't afford to lose another. I *need* this job."

Pendergast nodded.

"Brisbane and Collopy gave me the money I need for my carbon dates. I've got a lot of work ahead of me now. I can't spare the time."

Pendergast waited, still listening.

"What do you need me for, anyway? I'm an archaeologist, and there's no longer any site to investigate. You've got a copy of the letter. You're FBI. You must have dozens of specialists at your beck and call."

Pendergast remained silent as Nora took a sip of tea. The cup rattled loudly in the saucer when she replaced it.

"So," she said. "Now that's settled."

Now Pendergast spoke. "Mary Greene lived a few blocks

from here, down on Water Street. Number 16. The house is still there. It's a five-minute walk."

Nora looked at him, eyebrows narrowing in surprise. It had never occurred to her how close they were to Mary Greene's neighborhood. She recalled the note, written in blood. Mary Greene had known she was going to die. Her want had been simple: not to die in complete anonymity.

Pendergast gently took her arm. "Come," he said.

She did not shrug him off. He spoke again to the shopkeeper, took the tea with a slight bow, and in a moment they were outside on the crowded street. They walked down Mott, crossing first Bayard, then Chatham Square, entering into a maze of dark narrow streets abutting the East River. The noise and bustle of Chinatown gave way to the silence of industrial buildings. The sun had set, leaving a glow in the sky that barely outlined the tops of the buildings. Reaching Catherine Street, they turned southeast. Nora glanced over curiously as they passed Henry and the site of Moegen-Fairhaven's new residential tower. The excavation was much bigger now; massive foundations and stem walls rose out of the gloom, rebar popping like reeds from the freshly poured concrete. Nothing was left of the old coal tunnel.

Another few minutes, and they were on Water Street. Old manufacturing buildings, warehouses, and decrepit tenements lined the street. Beyond, the East River moved sluggishly, dark purple in the moonlight. The Brooklyn Bridge loomed almost above them; and to its left, the Manhattan Bridge arced across the dark river, its span of brilliant lights reflected in the water below.

Near Market Slip, Pendergast stopped in front of an old tenement. It was still inhabited: a single window glowed with yellow light. A metal door was set into the first-floor facade. Beside it was a dented intercom and a series of buttons.

"Here it is," said Pendergast. "Number sixteen."

They stood in the gathering darkness.

Pendergast began to speak quietly in the gloom. "Mary Greene came from a working-class family. After her father's upstate farm failed, he brought his family down here. He worked as a stevedore on the docks. But both he and Mary's mother died in a minor cholera epidemic when the girl was fifteen. Bad water. She had a younger brother: Joseph, seven; and a younger sister: Constance, five."

Nora said nothing.

"Mary Greene tried to take in washing and sewing, but apparently it wasn't enough to pay the rent. There was no other work, no way to earn money. They were evicted. Mary finally did what she had to do to support her younger siblings, whom she evidently loved very much. She became a prostitute."

"How awful," Nora murmured.

"That's not the worst. She was arrested when she was sixteen. It was probably at that point her two younger siblings became street children. They called them guttersnipes in those days. There's no more record of them in any city files; they probably starved to death. In 1871 it was estimated there were twenty-eight thousand homeless children living on the streets of New York. In any case, later Mary was sent to a workhouse known as the Five Points Mission. It was basically a sweatshop. But it was better than prison. On the surface, that would have seemed to be Mary Greene's lucky break."

Pendergast fell silent. A barge on the river gave out a distant, mournful bellow.

"What happened to her then?"

"The paper trail ends at the lodging house door," Pendergast replied.

He turned to her, his pale face almost luminous in the gloaming. "Enoch Leng—*Doctor* Enoch Leng—placed himself and his medical expertise at the service of the Five Points Mission as well as the House of Industry, an orphanage that stood near where Chatham Square is today. He offered his time pro bono. As we know, Dr. Leng kept rooms on the top floor of Shottum's Cabinet throughout the 1870s. No doubt he had a house somewhere else in the city. He affiliated himself with the two workhouses about a year before Shottum's Cabinet burned down."

"We already know from Shottum's letter that Leng committed those murders."

"No question."

"Then why do you need my help?"

"There's almost nothing on record about Leng anywhere. I've tried the Historical Society, the New York Public Library, City Hall. It's as if he's been expunged from the historical record, and I have reason to think Leng himself might have eradicated his files. It seems that Leng was an early supporter of the Museum and an enthusiastic taxonomist. I believe there may be more papers in the Museum concerning Leng, at least indirectly. Their archives are so vast and disorganized that it would be virtually impossible to purge them."

"Why me? Why doesn't the FBI just subpoena the files or something?"

"Files have a way of disappearing as soon as they are officially requested. Even if one knew which files to request. Besides, I've seen how you operate. That kind of competence is rare."

Nora merely shook her head.

"Mr. Puck has been, and no doubt will continue to be, most helpful. And there's something else. Tinbury McFadden's daughter is still alive. She lives in an old house in Peekskill. She's ninety-five, but I understand very much *compos mentis.* She may have a lot to say about her father. She may have even known Leng. I have a sense she'd be more willing to speak to a young woman like yourself than to an agent of the Federal Bureau of Investigation."

"You've still never really explained why you've taken such an interest in this case."

"The reasons for my interest in the case are unimportant. What *is* important is that a human being should not be allowed to get away with a crime like this. Even if that person is long dead. We do not forgive or forget Hitler. It's important to *remember.* The past is part of the present. At the moment, in fact, it's all too much a part of the present."

"You're talking about these two new murders." The whole city was buzzing with the news. And the same words seemed to be on everyone's lips: *copycat killer.*

Pendergast nodded silently.

"But do you really think the murders are connected? That there's some madman out there who read Smithback's article, and is now trying to duplicate Leng's experiments?"

"I believe the murders are connected, yes."

It was now dark. Water Street and the piers beyond were deserted. Nora shuddered again. "Look, Mr. Pendergast, I'd like to help. But it's like I said. I just don't think there's anything more I can do for you. Personally, I think you'd do better to investigate the new murders, not the old."

"That is precisely what I am doing. The solution to the new murders lies in the old."

She looked at him curiously. "How so?"

"Now is not the time, Nora. I don't have sufficient

information to answer, not yet. In fact, I may have already said too much."

Nora sighed with irritation. "Then I'm sorry, but the bottom line is that I simply can't afford to put my job in jeopardy a second time. Especially without more information. You understand, don't you?"

There was a moment's silence. "Of course. I respect your decision." Pendergast bowed slightly. Somehow, he managed to give even this simple gesture a touch of elegance.

Pendergast asked the driver to let him out a block from his apartment building. As the Rolls-Royce glided silently away, Pendergast walked down the pavement, deep in thought. After a few minutes he stopped, staring up at his residence: the Dakota, the vast, gargoyle-haunted pile on a corner of Central Park West. But it was not this structure that remained in his mind: it was the small, crumbling tenement at Number 16 Water Street, where Mary Greene had once lived.

The house would contain no specific information; it had not been worth searching. And yet it possessed something less definable. It was not just the facts and figures of the past that he needed to know, but its shape and feel. Mary Greene had grown up there. Her father had been part of that great post–Civil War exodus from the farms to the cities. Her childhood had been hard, but it may well have been happy. Stevedores earned a living wage. Once upon a time, she had played on those cobbles. Her childish shouts had echoed off some of those very bricks. And then cholera carried away her parents and changed her life forever. There were at least thirty-five other stories like hers, all of which ended so cruelly in that basement charnel.

There was a faint movement at the end of the block, and Pendergast turned. An old man in black, wearing a derby hat and carrying a Gladstone bag, was painfully making his way up the sidewalk. He was bowed, moving with the help of a cane. It was almost as if Pendergast's musings had conjured a figure out of the past. The man slowly made his way toward him, his cane making a faint tapping noise.

Pendergast watched him curiously for a moment. Then he turned back toward the Dakota, lingering a moment to allow the brisk night air to clear his mind. But there was little clarity to be found; instead there was Mary Greene, the little girl laughing on the cobbles.

SEVEN

IT HAD BEEN DAYS SINCE NORA WAS LAST IN HER laboratory. She eased the old metal door open and flicked on the lights, pausing. Everything was as she had left it. A white table ran along the far wall: binocular microscope, flotation kit, computer. To the side stood black metal cabinets containing her specimens—charcoal, lithics, bone, other organics. The still air smelled of dust, with a faint overlay of smoke, piñon, juniper. It momentarily made her homesick for New Mexico. What was she doing in New York City, anyway? She was a Southwestern archaeologist. Her brother, Skip, was demanding she come home to Santa Fe on almost a weekly basis. She had told Pendergast she couldn't afford to lose her job here at the Museum. But what was the worst that could happen? She could get a position at the University of New Mexico, or Arizona State. They both had superb archaeology departments where she wouldn't have to defend the value of her work to cretins like Brisbane.

The thought of Brisbane roused her. Cretins or not, this was the *New York Museum*. She'd never get another opportunity like this again—not ever.

Briskly, she stepped into the office, closing and locking

the door behind her. Now that she had the money for the carbon-14 dates, she could get back to real work. At least that was one thing this whole fiasco had done for her: get her the money. Now she could prepare the charcoal and organics for shipping to the radiocarbon lab at the University of Michigan. Once she had the dates, her work on the Anasazi-Aztec connection could begin in earnest.

She opened the first cabinet and carefully removed a tray containing dozens of stoppered test tubes. Each was labeled, and each contained a single specimen: a bit of charcoal, a carbonized seed, a fragment of a corn cob, a bit of wood or bone. She removed three of the trays, placing them on the white table. Then she booted her workstation and called up the catalogue matrices. She began cross-checking, making sure every specimen had the proper label and site location. At $275 a shot for the dating, it was important to be accurate.

As she worked, her mind began to wander back to the events of the past few days. She wondered if the relationship with Brisbane could ever be repaired. He was a difficult boss, but a boss nonetheless. And he was shrewd; sooner or later he'd realize that it would be best for everyone if they could bury the hatchet and—

Nora shook her head abruptly, a little guilty about this selfish line of thought. Smithback's article hadn't just gotten *her* into hot water—it had apparently inspired a copycat killer the tabloids were already dubbing "The Surgeon." She couldn't understand how Smithback thought the article would help. She'd always known he was a careerist, but this was too much. A bumbling egomaniac. She remembered her first sight of him in Page, Arizona, surrounded by bimbos in bathing suits, giving out autographs. *Trying* to, anyway. What a joke. She should have trusted her first impression of him.

Her mind wandered from Smithback to Pendergast. A

strange man. She wasn't even sure he was authorized to be working on the case. Would the FBI just let one of their agents freelance like this? Why was he so evasive about his interest? Was he just secretive by nature? Whatever the situation, it was most peculiar. She was out of it now, and glad. Very glad.

And yet, as she went back to the tubes, she realized she wasn't feeling all that glad. Maybe it was just that this sorting and checking was tedious work, but she realized Mary Greene and her sad life were lingering in the back of her mind. The dim tenement, the pathetic dress, the pitiful note . . .

With an effort, she pushed it all away. Mary Greene and her family were long gone. It was tragic, it was horrifying—but it was no concern of hers.

Sorting completed, she began packing the tubes in their special Styrofoam shipping containers. Better to break it down into three batches, just in case one got lost. Sealing the containers, she turned to the bills of lading and FedEx shipping labels.

A knock sounded at the door. The knob turned, but the locked door merely rattled in its frame. She glanced over.

"Who is it?" she called.

The hoarse whisper was muffled by the door.

"Who?" She felt a sudden fear.

"Me. Bill." The furtive voice was louder.

Nora stood up with a mixture of relief and anger. "What are you doing here?"

"Open up."

"Are you kidding? Get out of here. Now."

"Nora, please. It's important."

"It's important that you stay the hell away from me. I'm warning you."

"I've *got* to talk to you."

"That's it. I'm calling security."

"No, Nora. *Wait*."

Nora picked up the phone, dialed. The officer she reached said he would be only too glad to remove the intruder. They would be there right away.

"Nora!" Smithback cried.

Nora sat down at her worktable, trying to compose her mind. She closed her eyes. Ignore him. Just ignore him. Security would be there in a moment.

Smithback continued to plead at the door. "Just let me in for a minute. There's something you have to know. Last night—"

She heard heavy footfalls and a firm voice. "Sir, you're in an off-limits area."

"Hey! Let go! I'm a reporter for—"

"You will come with us, please, sir."

There was the sound of a scuffle.

"Nora!"

A new note of desperation sounded strong in Smithback's voice. Despite herself, Nora went to the door, unlocked it, and stuck out her head. Smithback was being held between two burly security men. He glanced at her, cowlick bobbing reproachfully as he tried to extricate himself. "Nora, I can't *believe* you called security."

"Are you all right, miss?" one of the men asked.

"I'm fine. But that man shouldn't be here."

"This way, sir. We'll walk you to the door." The men started dragging Smithback off.

"Unhand me, oaf! I'll report you, Mister 3467."

"Yes, sir, you do that, sir."

"Stop calling me 'sir.' This is assault."

"Yes, sir."

The men, imperturbable, led him down the hall toward the elevator.

As Nora watched, she felt a turmoil of conflicting emotion. *Poor Smithback. What an undignified exit.* But then, he'd brought it on himself—hadn't he? He needed the lesson. He couldn't just show up like this, all mystery and high drama, and expect her to—

"Nora!" came the cry from down the hall. "You have to listen, *please!* Pendergast was attacked, I heard it on the police scanner. He's in St. Luke's–Roosevelt, down on Fifty-ninth. He—"

Then Smithback was gone, his shouts cut off by the elevator doors.

EIGHT

NOBODY WOULD TELL NORA ANYTHING. IT WAS MORE THAN an hour before the doctor could see her. At last he showed up in the lounge, very young: a tired, hunted look in his face and a two-day growth of beard.

"Dr. Kelly?" he asked the room while looking at his clipboard.

She rose and their eyes met. "How is he?"

A wintry smile broke on the doctor's face. "He's going to be fine." He looked at her curiously. "Dr. Kelly, are you a medical—?"

"Archaeologist."

"Oh. And your relationship to the patient?"

"A friend. Can I see him? What happened?"

"He was stabbed last night."

"My God."

"Missed his heart by less than an inch. He was very lucky."

"How is he?"

"He's in . . ." the doctor paused. The faint smile returned. "Excellent spirits. An odd fellow, Mr. Pendergast. He insisted on a local anesthetic for the operation—highly unusual, unheard of actually, but he refused to sign the consent forms otherwise. Then he demanded a mirror. We had to bring one up from obstetrics. I've never had quite such a, er, demanding patient. I thought for a moment I had a surgeon on my operating table. They make the worst patients, you know."

"What did he want a mirror for?"

"He insisted on watching. His vitals were dropping and he was losing blood, but he absolutely insisted on getting a view of the wound from various angles before he would allow us to operate. Very odd. What kind of profession is Mr. Pendergast in?"

"FBI."

The smile evaporated. "I see. Well, that explains quite a bit. We put him in a shared room at first—no private ones were available—but then we quickly had to make one available for him. Moved out a state senator to get it."

"Why? Did Pendergast complain?"

"No . . . *he* didn't." The doctor hesitated a moment. "He began watching the video of an autopsy. Very graphic. His roommate naturally objected. But it was really just as well. Because an hour ago, the things started to arrive." He shrugged. "He refused to eat hospital food, insisted on ordering in from Balducci's. Refused an IV drip. Refused painkillers—no OxyContin, not even Vicodin or Tylenol Number 3. He must be in dreadful pain, but doesn't show it. With these new patient-rights guidelines, my hands are tied."

"It sounds just like him."

"The bright side is that the most difficult patients usually make the fastest recovery. I just feel sorry for the nurses." The doctor glanced at his watch. "You might as well head over there now. Room 1501."

As Nora approached the room, she noticed a faint odor in the air: something out of place among the aromas of stale food and rubbing alcohol. Something exotic, fragrant. A shrill voice echoed out of the open door. She paused in the doorway and gave a little knock.

The floor of the room was stacked high with old books, and a riot of maps and papers lay across them. Tall sticks of sandalwood incense were propped inside silver cups, sending up slender coils of smoke. *That accounts for the smell,* Nora thought. A nurse was standing near the bed, clutching a plastic pill box in one hand and a syringe in the other. Pendergast lay on the bed in a black silk dressing gown. The overhead television showed a splayed body, grotesque and bloody, being worked on by no fewer than three doctors. One of the doctors was in the middle of lifting a wobbly brain out of the skull. She looked away. On the bedside table was a dish of drawn butter and the remains of coldwater lobster tails.

"Mr. Pendergast, I *insist* you take this injection," the nurse was saying. "You've just undergone a serious operation. You must have your sleep."

Pendergast withdrew his arms from behind his head, picked up a dusty volume lying atop the sheets, and began leafing through it nonchalantly. "Nurse, I have no intention of taking that. I shall sleep when I'm ready." Pendergast blew dust from the book's spine and turned the page.

"I'm going to call the doctor. This is completely unacceptable. And this filth is *highly* unsanitary." She waved her hand through the clouds of dust.

Pendergast nodded, leafed over another page.

The nurse stormed past Nora on her way out.

Pendergast glanced at her and smiled. "Ah, Dr. Kelly. Please come in and make yourself comfortable."

Nora took a seat in a chair at the foot of the bed. "Are you all right?"

He nodded.

"What happened?"

"I was careless."

"But who did it? Where? When?"

"Outside my residence," said Pendergast. He held up the remote and turned off the video, then laid the book aside. "A man in black, with a cane, wearing a derby hat. He tried to chloroform me. I held my breath and pretended to faint; then broke away. But he was extraordinarily strong and swift, and I underestimated him. He stabbed me, then escaped."

"You could have been killed!"

"That was the intention."

"The doctor said it missed your heart by an inch."

"Yes. When I realized he was going to stab me, I directed his hand to a nonvital place. A useful trick, by the way, if you ever find yourself in a similar position."

He leaned forward slightly. "Dr. Kelly, I'm convinced he's the same man who killed Doreen Hollander and Mandy Eklund."

Nora looked at him sharply. "What makes you say that?"

"I caught a glimpse of the weapon—a surgeon's scalpel with a myringotomy blade."

"But . . . but why you?"

Pendergast smiled, but the smile held more pain than mirth. "That shouldn't be hard to answer. Somewhere along the way, we brushed up a little too close to the truth. We flushed him out. This is a very positive development."

"A positive development? You could still be in danger!"

Pendergast raised his pale eyes and looked at her intently. "I am not the only one, Dr. Kelly. You and Mr. Smithback must take precautions." He winced slightly.

"You should have taken that painkiller."

"For what I plan to do, it's essential to keep my head clear.

People did without painkillers for countless centuries. As I was saying, you should take precautions. Don't venture out alone on the streets at night. I have a great deal of trust in Sergeant O'Shaughnessy." He slipped a card into her hand. "If you need anything, call him. I'll be up and about in a few days."

She nodded.

"Meanwhile, it might be a good idea for you to get out of town for a day. There's a talkative, lonely old lady up in Peekskill who would love to have visitors."

She sighed. "I told you why I couldn't help anymore. And you still haven't told me why you're spending your time with these old murders."

"Anything I told you now would be incomplete. I have more work of my own to do, more pieces of the puzzle to fit together. But let me assure you of one thing, Dr. Kelly: this is no frivolous field trip. It is *vital* that we learn more about Enoch Leng."

There was a silence.

"Do it for Mary Greene, if not for me."

Nora rose to leave.

"And Dr. Kelly?"

"Yes?"

"Smithback isn't such a bad fellow. I know from experience that he's a reliable man in a pinch. It would ease my mind if, while all this is going on, you two worked together—"

Nora shook her head. "No way."

Pendergast held up his hand with a certain impatience. "Do it for your own safety. And now, I need to get back to my work. I look forward to hearing back from you tomorrow."

His tone was peremptory. Nora left, feeling annoyed. Yet

again Pendergast had dragged her back into the case, and now he wanted to burden her with that ass Smithback. Well, forget Smithback. He'd just love to get his hands on part two of the story. Him and his Pulitzer. She'd go to Peekskill, all right. But she'd go by herself.

NINE

THE BASEMENT ROOM WAS SMALL AND SILENT. IN ITS
simplicity it resembled a monk's cell. Only a narrow-legged
wooden table and stiff, uncomfortable chair broke the
monotony of the uneven stone floor, the damp unfinished
walls. A black light in the ceiling threw a spectral blue pall
over the four items upon the table: a scarred and rotting
leather notebook; a lacquer fountain pen; a tan-colored length
of India-rubber; and a hypodermic syringe.

The figure in the chair glanced at each of the carefully
aligned items in turn. Then, very slowly, he reached for the
hypodermic. The needle glowed with strange enchantment
in the ultraviolet light, and the serum inside the glass tube
seemed almost to smoke.

He stared at the serum, turning it this way and that,
fascinated by its eddies, its countless miniature whorls. *This*
was what the ancients had been searching for: the
Philosopher's Stone, the Holy Grail, the one true name of
God. Much sacrifice had been made to get it—on his part,
on the part of the long stream of resources who had donated
their lives to its refinement. But any amount of sacrifice was
acceptable. Here before him was a universe of life, encased

in a prison of glass. *His* life. And to think it all started with a single material: the neuronal membrane of the cauda equina, the divergent sheaf of spinal ganglia with the longest nerve roots of all. To bathe all the cells of the body with the essence of neurons, the cells that did not die: such a simple concept, yet so damnably complicated in development.

The process of synthesis and refinement was tortuous. And yet he took great pleasure in it, just as he did in the ritual he was about to perform. Creating the final reduction, moving from step to step to step, had become a religious experience for him. It was like the countless Gnostic keys the believer must perform before true prayer can begin. Or the harpsichordist who works his way through the twenty-nine Goldberg Variations before arriving at the final, pure, unadorned truth Bach intended.

The pleasure of these reflections was troubled briefly by the thought of those who would stop him, if they could: who would seek him out, follow the carefully obscured trail to this room, put a halt to his noble work. The most troublesome one had already been punished for his presumption—though not as fully punished as intended. Still, there would be other methods, other opportunities.

Placing the hypodermic gently aside, he reached for the leather-bound journal, turned over the front cover. Abruptly, a new smell was introduced into the room: must, rot, decomposition. He was always struck by the irony of how a volume that, over the years, had itself grown so decayed managed to contain the secret that banished decay.

He turned the pages, slowly, lovingly, examining the early years of painstaking work and research. At last, he reached the end, where the notations were still new and fresh. He unscrewed the fountain pen and laid it by the last entry, ready to record his new observations.

He would have liked to linger further but did not dare: the serum required a specific temperature and was not stable beyond a brief interval. He scanned the tabletop with a sigh of something almost like regret. Though of course it was not regret, because in the wake of the injection would come nullification of corporeal poisons and oxidants and the arresting of the aging process—in short, that which had evaded the best minds for three dozen centuries.

More quickly now, he picked up the rubber strap, tied it off above the elbow of his right arm, tapped the rising vein with the side of a fingernail, placed the needle against the antecubital fossa, slid it home.

And closed his eyes.

TEN

NORA WALKED AWAY FROM THE RED GINGERBREAD peekskill station, squinting against the bright morning sun. It had been raining when she'd boarded the train at Grand Central. But here, only a few small clouds dotted the blue sky above the old riverfront downtown. Three-story brick buildings were set close together, faded facades looking toward the Hudson. Behind them, narrow streets climbed away from the river, toward the public library and City Hall. Farther still, perched on the rocky hillside, lay the houses of the old neighborhoods, their narrow lawns dotted with ancient trees. Between the aging structures lay a scattering of smaller and newer houses, a car repair shop, the occasional Spanish-American mini-market. Everything looked shabby and superannuated. It was a proud old town in uncomfortable transition, clutching to its dignity in the face of decay and neglect.

She checked the directions Clara McFadden had given her over the telephone, then began climbing Central Avenue. She turned right on Washington, her old leather portfolio swinging from one hand, working her way toward Simpson Place. It was a steep climb, and she found herself panting slightly. Across the river, the ramparts of Bear Mountain could be glimpsed through the trees: a patchwork of autumnal yellows and reds, interspersed with darker stands of spruce and pine.

Clara McFadden's house was a dilapidated Queen Anne, with a slate mansard roof, gables, and a pair of turrets decorated with oriel windows. The white paint was peeling. A wraparound porch surrounded the first floor, set off by a spindlework frieze. As she walked up the short drive, the wind blew through the trees, sending leaves swirling around her. She mounted the porch and rang the heavy bronze bell.

A minute passed, then two. She was about to ring again when she remembered the old lady had told her to walk in.

She grasped the large bronze knob and pushed; the door swung open with the creak of rarely used hinges. She stepped into an entryway, hanging her coat on a lone hook. There was a smell of dust, old fabric, and cats. A worn set of stairs swept upward, and to her right she could see a broad arched doorway, framed in carved oak, leading into what looked like a parlor.

A voice, riven with age but surprisingly strong, issued from within. "Do come in," it said.

Nora paused at the entrance to the parlor. After the bright day outside, it was shockingly dim, the tall windows covered with thick green drapes ending in gold tassels. As her eyes slowly adjusted, she saw an old woman, dressed in crepe and dark bombazine, ensconced on a Victorian wing chair. It was so dark that at first all Nora could see was a white face and white hands, hovering as if disconnected in the dimness. The woman's eyes were half closed.

"Do not be afraid," said the disembodied voice from the deep chair.

Nora took another step inside. The white hand moved,

indicating another wing chair, draped with a lace antimacassar. "Sit down."

Nora took a seat gingerly. Dust rose from the chair. There was a rustling sound as a black cat shot from behind a curtain and disappeared into the dim recesses of the room.

"Thank you for seeing me," Nora said.

The bombazine crackled as the lady raised her head. "What do you want, child?"

The question was unexpectedly direct, and the tone of the voice behind it sharp.

"Miss McFadden, I wanted to ask you about your father, Tinbury McFadden."

"My dear, you're going to have to tell me your name again. I am an old lady with a fading memory."

"Nora Kelly."

The old woman's claw reached out and pulled the chain of a lamp that stood beside her chair. It had a heavy tasseled lamp shade, and it threw out a dim yellow light. Now Nora could see Clara McFadden more clearly. Her face was ancient and sunken, pale veins showing through parchment-paper skin. The lady examined her for a few minutes with a pair of glittering eyes.

"Thank you, Miss Kelly," she said, turning off the lamp again. "What exactly do you want to know about my father?"

Nora took a folder out of the portfolio, squinting through the dimness at the questions she'd scribbled on the train north from Grand Central. She was glad she'd come prepared; the interview was becoming unexpectedly intimidating.

The old woman picked up something from a small table beside the wing chair: an old-fashioned pint bottle with a green label. She poured a bit of the liquid into a teaspoon, swallowed it, replaced the spoon. Another black cat, or perhaps the same one, leapt into the old lady's lap. She began stroking it and it rumbled with pleasure.

"Your father was a curator at the New York Museum of Natural History. He was a colleague of John Canaday Shottum, who owned a cabinet of curiosities in lower Manhattan."

There was no response from the old lady.

"And he was acquainted with a scientist by the name of Enoch Leng."

Miss McFadden seemed to grow very still. Then she spoke with acidic sharpness, her voice cutting through the heavy air. It was as if the name had woken her up. "Leng? What about Leng?"

"I was curious if you knew anything about Dr. Leng, or had any letters or papers relating to him."

"I certainly do know about Leng," came the shrill voice. "He's the man who murdered my father."

Nora sat in stunned silence. There was nothing about a murder in anything she had read about McFadden. "I'm sorry?" she said.

"Oh, I know they all said he merely disappeared. But they were wrong."

"How do you know this?"

There was another rustle. "How? Let me tell you how."

Miss McFadden turned on the light again, directing Nora's attention to a large, old framed photograph. It was a faded portrait of a young man in a severe, high-buttoned suit. He was smiling: two silver front teeth gleamed out of the frame. A roguish eyepatch covered one eye. The man had Clara McFadden's narrow forehead and prominent cheekbones.

She began to speak, her voice unnaturally loud and angry. "That was taken shortly after my father lost his right eye in

Borneo. He was a collector, you must understand. As a young man, he spent several years in British East Africa. He built up quite a collection of African mammals and artifacts collected from the natives. When he returned to New York he became a curator at the new museum just started by one of his fellow Lyceum members. The New York Museum of Natural History. It was very different back then, Miss Kelly. Most of the early Museum curators were gentlemen of leisure, like my father. They did not have systematic scientific training. They were amateurs in the best sense of the word. My father was always interested in oddities, queer things. You are familiar, Miss Kelly, with the cabinets of curiosities?"

"Yes," Nora said as she scribbled notes as quickly as she could. She wished she had brought a voice recorder.

"There were quite a few in New York at the time. But the New York Museum quickly started putting them out of business. It became my father's role at the Museum to acquire these bankrupt cabinet collections. He corresponded with many of the cabinet owners: the Delacourte family, Phineas Barnum, the Cadwalader brothers. One of these cabinet owners was John Canaday Shottum." The old lady poured herself another spoonful from the bottle. In the light, Nora could make out the label: *Lydia Pinkham's Vegetable Tonic.*

Nora nodded. "J. C. Shottum's Cabinet of Natural Productions and Curiosities."

"Precisely. There was only a small circle of scientific men in those days, and they all belonged to the Lyceum. Men of varying abilities, I might add. Shottum belonged to the Lyceum, but he was as much a showman as he was a scientist. He had opened a cabinet down on Catherine Street, where he charged a minimal admission. It was mostly patronized by the lower classes. Unlike most of his colleagues, Shottum had these notions of bettering the plight of the poor through education. That's why he situated his cabinet in such a disagreeable neighborhood. He was especially interested in using natural history to inform and educate the young. In any case, he needed help with identifying and classifying his collections, which he had acquired from the family of a young man who had been killed by natives in Madagascar."

"Alexander Marysas."

There was a rustle from the old lady. Once again, she extinguished the light, shrouding the room in darkness, throwing the portrait of her father into shadow. "You seem to know a great deal about this, Miss Kelly," Clara McFadden said suspiciously. "I hope I am not annoying you with my story."

"Not at all. Please go on."

"Shottum's was a rather wretched cabinet. My father helped him from time to time, but it was burdensome to him. It was not a good collection. Very haphazard, not systematic. To lure in the poor, especially the urchins, his exhibits tended toward the sensational. There was even something he called a 'gallery of unnatural monstrosities.' It was, I believe, inspired by Madame Tussaud's Chamber of Horrors. There were rumors that some people who went into that gallery never came out again. All rubbish, of course, most likely cooked up by Shottum to increase foot traffic."

Clara McFadden removed a lace handkerchief and coughed into it. "It was around that time a man named Leng joined the Lyceum. *Enoch* Leng." Her voice conveyed a depth of hatred.

Nora felt her heart quicken. "Did you know Leng?"

"My father talked about him a great deal. Especially

toward the end. My father, you see, had a bad eye and bad teeth. Leng helped him get some silver bridgework and a special pair of eyeglasses with an unusually thick lens. He seemed to be something of a polymath."

She tucked the handkerchief back into some fold of her clothing, took another spoonful of the elixir. "It was said he came from France, a small mountain town near the Belgian border. There was talk that he was a baron, born into a noble family. These scientists are all gossips, you know. New York City at the time was a very provincial place and Leng made quite an impression. No one doubted he was a very learned man. He called himself a doctor, by the way, and it was said he had been a surgeon and a chemist." She made a vinegary sound.

Motes drifted in the heavy air. The cat's purr rumbled on endlessly, like a turbine.

The strident voice cut the air again. "Shottum was looking for a curator for his cabinet. Leng took an interest in it, although it was certainly the poorest curatorial appointment among the cabinets of curiosities. Nevertheless, Leng took rooms on the top floor of the cabinet."

So far, all this matched the details provided in Shottum's letter. "And when was this?" Nora asked.

"In the spring of 1870."

"Did Leng live at the cabinet?"

"A man of Leng's breeding, *living* in the Five Points? Certainly not. But he kept to himself. He was a strange, elusive man, very formal in his diction and mannerisms. No one, not even my father, knew where he lived. Leng did not encourage intimacy.

"He spent most of his time at Shottum's or the Lyceum. As I recall, his work at Shottum's Cabinet was originally supposed to last only a year or two. At first, Shottum was very pleased with Leng's work. Leng catalogued the collection, wrote up label copy for everything. But then something happened—my father never knew what—and Shottum seemed to grow suspicious of Leng. Shottum wanted to ask him to leave, but was reluctant. Leng paid handsomely for the use of the third floor, and Shottum needed the money."

"What kind of experiments did Leng perform?"

"I expect the usual. All scientific men had laboratories. My father had one."

"You said your father never knew what made Shottum suspicious?" That would mean McFadden never read the letter hidden in the elephant's-foot box.

"That's correct. My father didn't press him on the subject. Shottum had always been a rather eccentric man, prone to opium and fits of melancholy, and my father suspected he might be mentally unstable. Then, one summer evening in 1881, Shottum's Cabinet burned. It was such a fierce fire that they found only a few crumbling remains of Shottum's bones. It was said the fire started on the first floor. A faulty gas lamp." Another bitter noise.

"But you think otherwise?"

"My father became convinced that Leng started that fire."

"Do you know why?"

The lady slowly shook her head. "He did not confide in me."

After a moment, she continued. "It was around the time of the fire that Leng stopped attending the meetings at the Lyceum. He stopped coming to the New York Museum. My father lost touch with him. He seemed to disappear from scientific circles. Thirty years must have passed before he resurfaced."

"When was this?"

"During the Great War. I was a little girl at the time. My father married late, you see. He received a letter from Leng. A very friendly letter, wishing to renew the acquaintance. My father refused. Leng persisted. He began coming to the Museum, attending my father's lectures, spending time in the Museum's archives. My father became disturbed, and after a while even frightened. He was so concerned I believe he even consulted certain fellow Lyceum members he was close to on the subject. James Henry Perceval and Dumont Burleigh are two names that come to mind. They came to the house more than once, shortly before the end."

"I see." Nora scribbled some more notes. "But you never met Leng?"

There was a pause. "I met him once. He came to our house late one night, with a specimen for my father, and was turned away at the door. He left the specimen behind. A graven artifact from the South Seas, of little value."

"And?"

"My father disappeared the next day."

"And you're convinced it was Leng's doing?"

"Yes."

"How?"

The old lady patted her hair. Her sharp eyes fixed on hers. "My dear child, how could I possibly know that?"

"But *why* would Leng murder him?"

"I believe my father found out something about Leng."

"Didn't the Museum investigate?"

"No one had seen Leng in the Museum. No one had seen him visit my father. There was no proof of anything. Neither Perceval nor Burleigh spoke up. The Museum found it easier to smear my father's name—to imply that he ran away for some unknown reason—than to investigate. I was just a girl at the time. When I grew older and demanded a reopening of the case, I had nothing to offer. I was rebuffed."

"And your mother? Was she suspicious?"

"She was dead by that time."

"What happened to Leng?"

"After his visit to my father, nobody ever saw or heard from him again."

Nora took a breath. "What did Leng look like?"

Clara McFadden did not answer immediately. "I'll never forget him," she said at last. "Have you read Poe's 'Fall of the House of Usher'? There's a description in the story that, when I came upon it, struck me terribly. It seemed to describe Leng precisely. It's stayed with me to this day, I can still quote the odd line of it from memory: 'a cadaverousness of complexion; an eye large, liquid, and very luminous . . . finely molded chin, speaking, in its want of prominence, of a want of moral energy.' Leng had blond hair, blue eyes, an aquiline nose. Old-fashioned black coat, formally dressed."

"That's a very vivid description."

"Leng was the kind of person who stayed with you long after he was gone. And yet, you know, it was his voice I remember most. It was low, resonant, strongly accented, with the peculiar quality of sounding like two people speaking in unison."

The gloom that filled the parlor seemed inexplicably to deepen. Nora swallowed. She had already asked all the questions she had planned to. "Thank you very much for your time, Ms. McFadden," she said as she rose.

"Why do you bring all this up now?" the old lady asked abruptly.

Nora realized that she must not have seen the newspaper article or heard anything about the recent copycat killings of the Surgeon. She wondered just what she should say. She looked about the room, dark, frozen in shadowy Victorian clutter. She did not want to be the one to upset this woman's world.

"I'm researching the early cabinets of curiosities."

The old lady transfixed her with a glittering eye. "An interesting subject, child. And perhaps a dangerous one."

ELEVEN

SPECIAL AGENT PENDERGAST LAY IN THE HOSPITAL BED, motionless save for his pale eyes. He watched Nora Kelly leave the room and close the door. He glanced over at the wall clock: nine P.M. precisely. A good time to begin.

He thought back over each word Nora had uttered during her visit, looking for any trivial fact or passing reference that he might have overlooked on first hearing. But there was nothing more.

Her visit to Peekskill had confirmed his darkest suspicions: Pendergast had long believed Leng killed Shottum and burned the cabinet. And he felt sure that McFadden's disappearance was also at the hands of Leng. No doubt Shottum had challenged Leng shortly after placing his letter in the elephant's-foot box. Leng had murdered him, and covered it up with the fire.

Yet the most pressing questions remained. *Why* had Leng chosen the cabinet as his base of operations? Why did he begin volunteering his services at the houses of industry a year before killing Shottum? And where did he relocate his laboratory after the cabinet burned?

In Pendergast's experience, serial killers were messy: they

were incautious, they left clues. But Leng was, of course, very different. He was not, strictly speaking, a serial killer. He had been remarkably clever. Leng had left a kind of negative imprint wherever he went; the man seemed defined by how little was known about him. There was more to be learned, but it was deeply hidden in the masses of information strewn about his hospital room. There was only one way to coax this information out. Research alone would not suffice.

And then there was the growing problem of his increasing lack of objectivity regarding this case, his growing emotional involvement. If he did not bring himself sharply under control, if he did not reassert his habitual discipline, he would fail. And he could not fail.

It was time to make his journey.

Pendergast's gaze shifted to the massings of books, maps, and old periodicals that filled half a dozen surgical carts in his room. His eyes moved from surface to tottering surface. The single most important piece of paper lay on his bedside table: the plans for Shottum's Cabinet. One last time, he picked it up and gazed at it, memorizing every detail. The seconds ticked on. He laid down the yellowing plat.

It was time. But first, something had to be done about the intolerable landscape of noise that surrounded him.

After his condition was upgraded from serious to stable, Pendergast had himself transferred from St. Luke's–Roosevelt to Lenox Hill Hospital. The old facility on Lexington Avenue had the thickest walls of any building in the city, save for his own Dakota. Even here, however, he was assaulted by sounds: the bleat of the blood-oxygen meter above his bed; the gossiping voices at the nurses' station; the hissings and beepings of the telemetry machines and ventilators; the adenoidal patient snoring in the adjacent room; the rumble of the forced-air ducts deep in the walls and ceiling. There was nothing he could do that would physically stop these sounds; yet they could be made to disappear through other means. It was a powerful mind game he had developed, an adaptation of *Chongg Ran,* an ancient Bhutanese Buddhist meditative practice.

Pendergast closed his eyes. He imagined a chessboard inside his head, on a wooden table, standing in a pool of yellow light. Then he created two players. The first player made his opening move; the second followed. A game of speed chess ensued; and then another, and another. The two players changed strategies, forming adaptive counterattacks: Inverted Hanham, Two Knights Defense, Vienna Gambit.

One by one, the more distant noises dropped away.

When the final game ended in a draw, Pendergast dissolved the chess set. Then, in the darkness of his mind's eye, he created four players, seated around a card table. Pendergast had always found bridge a nobler and subtler game than chess, but he rarely played it with others because, outside of his late family, he had found few worthy partners. Now the game began, each player ignorant of all but his own thirteen cards, each player with his own strategies and intellectual capabilities. The game began, with ruffs and slams and deep finesses. Pendergast toyed with the players, shifting Blackwood, Gerber, and Stayman conventions, positing a forgetful declarer, misunderstood signals between East and West.

By the time the first rubber was completed, all distractions were gone. The noises had ceased. In his mind, only a profound silence reigned. Pendergast turned further inward.

It was time for the memory crossing to begin.

Several minutes of intense mental concentration passed. Finally, he felt ready.

In his mind's eye, he rose from his bed. He felt light, airy, like a ghost. He saw himself walk through the empty hospital corridors, down the stairwell, across the arched foyer, and out onto the wide front steps of the hospital.

Only the building was no longer a hospital. A hundred and twenty years before, it had been known as the New York Rest Home for Consumptives.

Pendergast stood on the steps for a moment, glancing around in the gathering dusk. To the west, toward Central Park, the Upper East Side had become a patchwork of hog farms, wild lands, and rocky eminences. Small groups of hovels sprouted up here and there, huddled together as if for protection against the elements. Gas lamps stood along the avenue, infrequent this far north of the populous downtown, throwing small circles of light down onto the dusky macadam.

The prospect was vague, indistinct: detail at this location was unimportant. Pendergast did, however, allow himself to sample the air. It smelled strongly of coal smoke, damp earth, and horse manure.

He descended the steps, turning onto Seventy-sixth Street and walking east toward the river. Here it was more thickly settled, newer brownstones abutting old wood-and-frame structures. Carriages swayed down the straw-strewn street. People passed him silently, the men dressed in long suits with thin lapels, women in bustles and veiled hats.

At the next intersection he boarded a streetcar, paying five cents for the ride down to Forty-second Street. There, he transferred to the Bowery & Third Avenue elevated railway, paying another twenty cents. This extravagant price ensured him a palace car, with curtained windows and plush seats. The steam locomotive heading the train was named the *Chauncey M. Depew*. As it hurtled southward, Pendergast sat without moving in his velveteen chair. Slowly, he allowed sound to intrude once more into his world: first the clatter of the wheels on the tracks, and then the chatter of his passengers. They were engrossed with the concerns of 1881: the president's recovery and the imminent removal of the pistol ball; the Columbia Yacht Club sailing regatta on the Hudson earlier that afternoon; the miraculous curative properties of the Wilsonia Magnetic Garment.

There were still gaps, of course—hazy dark patches, like fog—about which Pendergast had little or no information. No memory crossing was ever complete. There were details of history that had been irrevocably lost.

When the train at last reached the lower stretches of the Bowery, Pendergast disembarked. He stood on the platform a moment, looking around a little more intently now. The elevated tracks were erected over the sidewalks, rather than along the middle of the street, and the awnings below were covered in a greasy film of oil drippings and ash. The *Chauncey M. Depew* gave a shriek, beginning its furious dash to the next stop. Smoke and hot cinders belched from its stack, scattering into the leaden air.

He descended skeletal wooden stairs to ground level, alighting outside a small shop. He glanced at its signboard: *George Washington Abacus, Physiognomic Operator and Professor of the Tonsorial Art.* The broad thoroughfare before him was a sea of bobbing plug hats. Trams and horsecars went careering down the center of the road. Peddlers of all kinds jostled the narrow sidewalk, crying out their trade to all who would listen. "Pots and pans!" called a tinker. "Mend your pots and pans!" A young woman trundling a steaming cauldron on wheels cried, "Oysters! Here's your brave, good oysters!" At Pendergast's left elbow, a man selling hot corn out of a baby's perambulator fished out an ear, smeared it with a butter-soaked rag, and held it out invitingly. Pendergast shook his head and eased his way into the milling crowd. He was jostled; there was a momentary fog, a loss of concentration; and then Pendergast recovered. The scene returned.

He moved south, gradually bringing all five senses fully alive to the surroundings. The noise was almost overwhelming: clattering horseshoes, countless snatches of music and song, yelling, screaming, whinnying, cursing. The air was supercharged with the odors of sweat, dung, cheap perfume, and roasting meats.

Down the street, at 43 Bowery, Buffalo Bill was playing in the *Scout of the Plains* stage show at the Windsor. Several other theaters followed, huge signs advertising current performances: *Fedora, Peck's Bad Boy, The Darkness to the North, Kit, the Arkansas Traveler.* A blind Civil War veteran lay between two entrances, cap held out imploringly.

Pendergast glided past with barely a glance.

At a corner, he paused to get his bearings, then turned onto East Broadway Street. After the frenzy of Bowery, he entered a more silent world. He moved past the myriad shops of the old city, shuttered and dark at this hour: saddleries, millinery shops, pawnbrokers, slaughterhouses. Some of these buildings were distinct. Others—places Pendergast had not succeeded in identifying—were vague and shadowy, shrouded in that same indistinct fog.

At Catherine Street he turned toward the river. Unlike on East Broadway, all the establishments here—grog shops, sailors' lodging houses, oyster-cellars—were open. Lamps cast lurid red stripes out into the street. A brick building loomed at the corner, low and long, streaked with soot. Its granite cornices and arched lintels spoke of a building done in a poor imitation of the Neo-Gothic style. A wooden sign, gold letters edged in black, hung over the door:

J. C. SHOTTUM'S CABINET
OF
NATURAL PRODUCTIONS
&
CURIOSITIES

A trio of bare electric bulbs in metal cages illuminated the doorway, casting a harsh glare onto the street. Shottum's was open for business. A hired hawker shouted at the door. Pendergast could not catch the words above the noise and bustle. A large signboard standing on the pavement in front advertised the featured attractions—*See the Double-Brained Child & Visit Our New Annex Showing Bewitching Female Bathers in Real Water.*

Pendergast stood on the corner, the rest of the city fading into fog as he focused his concentration on the building ahead, meticulously reconstructing every detail. Slowly, the walls came into sharper focus—the dingy windows, the interiors, the bizarre collections, the maze of exhibit halls—as his mind integrated and shaped the vast quantity of information he had amassed.

When he was ready, he stepped forward and queued up. He paid his two pennies to a man in a greasy stovepipe hat and stepped inside. A low foyer greeted his eye, dominated on the far side with a mammoth skull. Standing next to it was a moth-eaten Kodiak bear, an Indian birchbark canoe, a petrified log. His eyes traveled around the room. The large thighbone of an *Antediluvian Monster* stood against the far wall, and there were other eclectic specimens laid out, helter-skelter. The better exhibits, he knew, were deeper inside the cabinet.

Corridors ran off to the left and right, leading to halls packed with teeming humanity. In a world without movies, television, or radio—and where travel was an option only for the wealthiest—the popularity of this diversion was not surprising. Pendergast bore left.

The first part of the hall consisted of a systematic collection of stuffed birds, laid out on shelves. This exhibit, a feeble attempt to insinuate a little education, held no interest to the crowd, which streamed past on the way to less edifying exhibits ahead.

The corridor debouched into a large hall, the air hot and close. In the center stood what appeared to be a stuffed man, brown and wizened, with severely bowed legs, gripping a post. The label pinned below it read: *Pygmy Man of Darkest Africa, Who Lived to Be Three Hundred Fifty-Five Years of Age Before Death by Snakebite.* Closer inspection revealed it to be a shaved orangutan, doctored to look human, apparently preserved through smoking. It gave off a fearful smell. Nearby was an Egyptian mummy, standing against the wall in a wooden sarcophagus. There was a mounted skeleton missing its skull, labeled *Remains of the Beautiful Countess Adele de Brissac, Executed by Guillotine, Paris, 1789.* Next to it was a rusty piece of iron, dabbed with red paint, marked: *The Blade That Cut Her.*

Pendergast stood at the center of the hall and turned his attention to the noisy audience. He found himself mildly surprised. There were many more young people than he had assumed, as well as a greater cross section of humanity, from high to low. Young bloods and fancy men strolled by, puffing on cigars, laughing condescendingly at the exhibits. A group of tough-looking youths swaggered past, sporting the red flannel firemen's shirts, broadcloth pantaloons, and greased "soap-lock" hair that identified them as Bowery Boys. There were workhouse girls, whores, urchins, street peddlers, and barmen. It was, in short, the same kind of crowd that thronged the streets outside. Now that the workday was done for many, they came to Shottum's for an evening's entertainment. The two-penny admission was within reach of all.

Two doors at the far end of the hall led to more exhibits, one to the bewitching ladies, the other marked *Gallery of Unnatural Monstrosities.* This latter was narrow and dark, and it was the exhibit that Pendergast had come to see.

The sounds of the crowds were muffled here, and there were fewer visitors, mostly nervous, gaping youngsters. The carnival atmosphere had changed into something quieter, more eerie. The darkness, the closeness, the stillness, all conspired to create the effect of fear.

At the first turn of the gallery stood a table, on which was a large jar of thick glass, stoppered and sealed, containing a floating human baby. Two miniature, perfectly formed arms stuck out from its forehead. Pendergast peered closer and saw that, unlike many of the other exhibits, this one had not been doctored. He passed on. There was a small alcove containing a dog with a cat's head, this one clearly fake, the sewing marks visible through the thinning hair. It stood next to a giant clam, propped open, showing a skeletonized foot inside. The label copy told the gruesome story of the hapless pearl diver. Around another corner, there was a great miscellany of objects in jars of formaldehyde: a Portuguese man-of-war, a giant rat from Sumatra, a hideous brown thing the size of a flattened watermelon, marked *Liver, from a Woolly Mammoth Frozen in Siberian Ice.* Next to it was a Siamese-twinned giraffe fetus. The next turn revealed a shelf with a human skull with a hideous bony growth on the forehead, labeled *The Rhinoceros Man of Cincinnati.*

Pendergast paused, listening. Now the sounds of the crowd were very faint, and he was alone. Beyond, the darkened hall made one last sharp turn. An elaborately stylized arrow pointed toward an unseen exhibit around the corner. A sign read: *Visit Wilson One-Handed: For Those Who Dare.*

Pendergast glided around the corner. Here, it was almost silent. At the moment, there were no other visitors. The hall terminated in a small alcove. In the alcove was a single exhibit: a glass case containing a desiccated head. The shriveled tongue still protruded from the mouth, looking like a cheroot clamped between the twisted lips. Next to it lay what appeared to be a dried sausage, about a foot long, with a rusty hook attached to one end by leather straps. Next to that, the frayed end of a hangman's noose.

A label identified them:

THE HEAD

OF THE NOTORIOUS MURDERER

AND ROBBER

WILSON ONE-HANDED

HUNG BY THE NECK UNTIL DEAD

DAKOTA TERRITORY

JULY 4, 1868

THE NOOSE

FROM WHICH HE SWUNG

THE FOREARM STUMP AND HOOK OF

WILSON ONE-HANDED

WHICH BROUGHT IN A BOUNTY

OF ONE THOUSAND DOLLARS

Pendergast examined the cramped room. It was isolated and very dark. It was cut off from view of the other exhibits by a sharp turn of the corridor. It would comfortably admit only one person at a time.

A cry for help here would be unheard, out in the main galleries.

The little alcove ended in a cul-de-sac. As Pendergast stared at it, pondering, the wall wavered, then disappeared, as fog once again enshrouded his memory construct and the mental image fell away. But it did not matter: he had seen enough, threaded his way through sufficient passages, to understand.

And now—at last—he knew how Leng had procured his victims.

TWELVE

PATRICK O'SHAUGHNESSY STOOD ON THE CORNER OF Seventy-second and Central Park West, staring at the facade of the Dakota apartment building. There was a vast arched entrance to an inner courtyard, and beyond the entrance the building ran at least a third of the way down the block. It was there, in the darkness, that Pendergast had been attacked.

In fact, it probably looked just about like this when Pendergast was stabbed—except for the old man, of course; the one Pendergast had seen wearing a derby hat. Astonishing that the guy had almost managed to overpower the FBI agent, even factoring in the element of surprise.

O'Shaughnessy wondered again just what the hell he was doing here. He was off duty. He should be in J.W.'s hoisting a few with friends, or messing about his apartment, listening to that new recording of *The Bartered Bride*. They weren't paying him: so why should he care?

But he found, strangely enough, that he did care.

Custer, naturally, had dismissed it as a simple mugging: "Friggin' rube out-of-towner, no surprise he got his ass mugged." Well, O'Shaughnessy knew Pendergast was no rube. The man probably played up his New Orleans roots just to keep people like Custer off guard. And he didn't think Pendergast had gotten mugged, either. But now it was time to decide: just what was he going to do about it?

Slowly, he began to walk toward the site of the attack.

Earlier in the day, he'd visited Pendergast in the hospital. Pendergast had hinted to him that it would be useful—more than useful—to have the coroner's report on the bones found at the construction site. To get it, O'Shaughnessy realized, he would have to go around Custer. Pendergast also wanted more information on the developer, Fairhaven—who Custer had made it clear was off-limits. It was then O'Shaughnessy realized he had crossed some invisible line, from working for Custer to working for Pendergast. It was a new, almost heady feeling: for the first time in his life, he was working with someone he respected. Someone who wasn't going to pre-judge him on old history, or treat him as a disposable, fifth-generation Irish cop. *That* was the reason he was here, at the Dakota, on his night off. That's what a partner did when the other one got into trouble.

Pendergast, as usual, was silent on the attack. But to O'Shaughnessy, it had none of the earmarks of a mugging. He remembered, dimly, his days at the academy, all the statistics on various types of crimes and how they were committed. Back then, he had big ideas about where he was going in the force. That was before he took two hundred bucks from a prostitute because he felt sorry for her.

And—he had to admit to himself—because he needed the money.

O'Shaughnessy stopped, coughed, spat on the sidewalk.

Back at the academy, it had been Motive, Means, Opportunity. Take motive, for starters. Why kill Pendergast?

Put the facts in order. One: the guy is investigating a 130-year-old serial killer. No motive there: killer's dead.

Two: a copycat killer springs up. Pendergast is at the autopsy before there's even an autopsy. *Christ,* thought O'Shaughnessy, *he must have known what was going on even before the doctor did. Pendergast had already made the connection between the murder of the tourist and the nineteenth-century killings.*

How?

Three: Pendergast gets attacked.

Those were the facts, as O'Shaughnessy saw them. So what could he conclude?

That Pendergast *already* knew something important. And the copycat serial killer knew it, too. Whatever it was, it was important enough that this killer took a big risk in targeting him, on Seventy-second Street—not exactly deserted, even at nine o'clock in the evening—and had almost succeeded in killing him, which was the most astonishing thing of all.

O'Shaughnessy swore. The big mystery here was Pendergast himself. He wished Pendergast would level with him, share more information. The man was keeping him in the dark. Why? Now *that* was a question worth asking.

He swore again. Pendergast was asking a hell of a lot, but he wasn't giving anything in return. Why was he wasting a fine fall evening tramping around the Dakota, looking for clues that weren't there, for a guy who didn't want help?

Cool it, O'Shaughnessy told himself. Pendergast was the most logical, methodical guy he'd ever met. He'd have his reasons. All in good time. Meanwhile, this was a waste. Time for dinner and the latest issue of *Opera News.*

O'Shaughnessy turned to head home. And that's when he saw the tall, shadowy figure come into view at the corner.

Instinctively, O'Shaughnessy shrank into the nearest doorway. He waited. The figure stood on the corner, precisely where he himself had stood only a few minutes before, glancing around. Then it started down the street toward him, slowly and furtively.

O'Shaughnessy stiffened, receding deeper into the shadows. The figure crept down to the angle of the building, pausing right at the spot where Pendergast had been assaulted. The beam of a flashlight went on. He seemed to be inspecting the pavement, looking around. He was dressed in a long dark coat, which could easily be concealing a weapon. He was certainly no cop. And the attack had not been in the papers.

O'Shaughnessy made a quick decision. He grasped his service revolver in his right hand and pulled out his shield with his left. Then he stepped out of the shadows.

"Police officer," he said quietly but firmly. "Don't move. Keep your hands where I can see them."

The figure jumped sideways with a yelp, holding up a pair of gangly arms. "Wait! Don't shoot! I'm a reporter!"

O'Shaughnessy relaxed as he recognized the man. "So it's you," he said, holstering his gun, feeling disappointed.

"Yeah, and it's you," Smithback lowered his trembling arms. "The cop from the opening."

"Sergeant O'Shaughnessy."

"Right. What are you doing here?"

"Same as you, probably," said O'Shaughnessy. Then he stopped abruptly, remembering he was speaking to a reporter. It wouldn't be good for this to get back to Custer.

Smithback mopped his brow with a soiled handkerchief. "You scared the piss out of me."

"Sorry. You looked suspicious."

Smithback shook his head. "I imagine I did." He glanced around. "Find anything?"

"No."

There was a brief silence.

"Who do you think did it? Think it was just some mugger?"

Although Smithback was echoing the same question he'd asked himself moments before, O'Shaughnessy merely shrugged. The best thing to do was to keep his mouth shut.

"Surely the police have some kind of theory."

O'Shaughnessy shrugged again.

Smithback stepped closer, lowering his voice. "Look, I understand if it's confidential. I can quote you 'not for attribution.'"

O'Shaughnessy wasn't going to fall into that trap.

Smithback sighed, looking up at the buildings with an air of finality. "Well, there's nothing much else to be seen around here. And if you're going to clam up, I might as well go get a drink. Try to recover from that fright you gave me." He snugged the handkerchief back into his pocket. "Night, Officer."

He began to walk away. Then he stopped, as if struck by an idea.

"Want to come along?"

"No, thanks."

"Come on," the reporter said. "You don't look like you're on duty."

"I said no."

Smithback took a step closer. "You know, now that I think about it, maybe we could help each other out here. Know what I mean? I need to keep in touch with this investigation into the Surgeon."

"The Surgeon?"

"Haven't you heard? That's what the *Post* is calling this serial killer. Cheesy, huh? Anyway, I need information, and I'll bet you need information. Am I right?"

O'Shaughnessy said nothing. He did need information.

But he wondered if Smithback really had something, or was just bullshitting.

"I'll level with you, Sergeant. I got scooped on that tourist killing in Central Park. And now, I have to scramble to get new developments, or my editor will have my ass for brunch. A little advance notice here and there, nothing too specific, just a nod from a friend—you, for instance. That's all."

"What kind of information do you have?" O'Shaughnessy asked guardedly. He thought back a minute to what Pendergast had said. "Do you have anything on, say, Fairhaven?"

Smithback rolled his eyes. "Are you kidding? I've got a sackful on him. Not that it'll do you much good, but I'm willing to share. Let's talk about it over a drink."

O'Shaughnessy glanced up and down the street. Despite his better judgment, he found himself tempted. Smithback might be a hustler, but he seemed a decent sort of hustler. And he'd even worked with Pendergast in the past, though the reporter didn't seem too eager to reminisce about it. And finally, Pendergast had asked him to put together a file on Fairhaven.

"Where?"

Smithback smiled. "Are you kidding? The best bars in New York City are just one block west, on Columbus. I know a great place, where all the Museum types go. It's called the Bones. Come on, the first round's on me."

THIRTEEN

THE FOG GREW THICKER FOR A MOMENT. PENDERGAST waited, maintaining his concentration. Then through the fog came flickerings of orange and yellow. Pendergast felt heat upon his face. The fog began to clear.

He was standing outside J. C. Shottum's Cabinet of Natural Productions and Curiosities. It was night. The cabinet was burning. Angry flames leapt from the first- and second-story windows, punching through billowing clouds of black, acrid smoke. Several firemen and a bevy of police were frantically roping off the street around the building and pushing curious onlookers back from the conflagration. Inside the rope, several knots of firefighters arced hopeless streams of water into the blaze, while others scurried to douse the gaslights along the sidewalk.

The heat was a physical force, a wall. Standing on the street corner, Pendergast's gaze lingered appreciatively on the fire engine: a big black boiler on carriage wheels, belching steam, *Amoskeag Manufacturing Company* in gold letters on its sweating sides. Then he turned toward the onlookers. Would Leng be among them, admiring his handiwork? No, he would have been long gone. Leng was no pyromaniac. He would be safely ensconced in his uptown house, location unknown.

The location of the house was a great question. But another, perhaps more pressing, question remained: where had Leng moved his *laboratory?*

There was a tremendous, searing crack; roof timbers collapsed inward with a roiling shower of sparks; an appreciative murmur rose from the crowd. With a final look at the doomed structure, Pendergast began threading his way through the crowd.

A little girl rushed up, no older than six, threadbare and frighteningly gaunt. She had a battered straw broom in her hand, and she swept the street corner ahead of him industriously, clearing away the dung and pestilential garbage, hoping pathetically for a coin. "Thank you," Pendergast said, tossing her several broad copper pennies. She looked at the coins, eyes wide at her good fortune, then curtsied awkwardly.

"What's your name, child?" Pendergast asked gently.

The girl looked up at him, as if surprised to hear an adult speak to her in a solicitous tone. "Constance Greene, sir," she said.

"Greene?" Pendergast frowned. "Of Water Street?"

"No, sir. Not—not anymore." Something seemed to have frightened the girl, and, with another curtsy, she turned and melted away down a crowded side street.

Pendergast stared down the foul street and its seething crowds for some time. Then, with a troubled expression on his face, he turned and slowly retraced his steps. A barker stood in the doorway of Brown's Restaurant, delivering the bill of fare in a loud, breathless, ceaseless litany:

Biledlamancapersors.
Rosebeefrosegoorosemuttonantaters—
Biledamancabbage, vegetaybles—
Walkinsirtakaseatsir.

Pendergast moved on thoughtfully, listening to the City Hall bell toll the urgent fire alarm. Making his way to Park Street, he passed a chemist's shop, closed and shuttered, an array of bottles in diverse sizes and colors decorating the window: *Paine's Celery Compound; Swamp Root; D. & A. Younce's Indian Cure Oil (Good for Man and Beast).*

Two blocks down Park, he stopped abruptly. He was fully attentive now, eyes open to every detail. He had painstakingly researched this region of old New York, and the fog of his memory construct retreated well into the distance. Here, Baxter and Worth Streets angled in sharply, creating a crazy-quilt of intersections known as the Five Points. In the bleak landscape of urban decay that stretched before him, there was none of the carefree revelry Pendergast had found earlier, along Bowery.

Thirty years before, in the 1850s, the "Points" had been the worst slum in all New York, in all America, worse even than London's Seven Dials. It remained a miserable, squalid, dangerous place: home to fifty thousand criminals, drug addicts, prostitutes, orphans, confidence men, villains of all shape and description. The uneven streets were broken and scored into dangerous ruts, brimming with garbage and offal. Hogs wandered about, rooting and wallowing in the fouled gutters. The houses seemed prematurely aged, their windows broken, tarpaper roofs hanging free, timbers sagging. A single gas lamp threw light into the intersection. On all sides, narrow streets marched off into endless darkness. The doors of the first-floor taverns were flung wide against the summer heat. The smells of liquor and cigar smoke issued forth. Women, bare-breasted, lolled in the doorways, exchanging obscene jeers with whores in the neighboring saloons or soliciting passersby in lurid tones. Across the way, nickel-a-night flophouses, riddled with vermin and pestilence, sat between the shabby cow-sheds of fencers of stolen goods.

Pendergast gazed carefully around at the scene, scrutinizing the topography, the architecture, for any clue, any hidden link that a mere study of historical records could not provide. At last he turned eastward, where a vast, five-story structure sat, decayed and listing, dark even in the light of the gas lamp. This was the former Old Brewery, at one time the worst of all the Five Points tenements. Children who had the misfortune to be born within were known to pass months or even years without tasting the outside air. Now, thanks to the efforts of a charitable group, it had been rebuilt as the Five Points Mission. An early urban renewal project for which, in 1880, the good Dr. Enoch Leng had volunteered his medical services, pro bono. He had continued to work there into the early '90s, when the historical record on Leng vanished abruptly.

Pendergast walked slowly toward the building. An ancient sign for the Old Brewery remained painted along its upper story, dominating the far newer and cleaner Five Points Mission sign beneath. He considered entering the building, then decided against it. There was another visit he had to make first.

Behind the Five Points Mission, a tiny alley ran north into a dark cul-de-sac. Moist, fetid air seeped out from the darkness. Many years before, when the Points region had been a marshy pond known as the Collect, Aaron Burr had installed a large subterranean pump for the natural springs at this spot, founding the New Amsterdam Water Company. The pond grew increasingly foul, however, and eventually had been filled in to make way for tenements.

Pendergast paused thoughtfully. Later, this alleyway had been known as Cow Bay, the most dangerous street in the Five Points. It had been crowded with tall wooden tenements with names like "Brickbat Mansion" and "The Gates of Hell," tenanted by violent alcoholics who would stab a man for the clothes on his back. Like many structures in the Five Points, these were warrens of vile-smelling chambers, honeycombed with secret panels and doors that connected to other houses on adjoining streets by networks of underground passageways, allowing criminals easy escape from pursuing law enforcement. In the mid-nineteenth century, the street had averaged a murder a night. Now it was home to an ice delivery company, a slaughterhouse, and an abandoned substation of the city's waterworks, shut down in 1879 when the uptown reservoir rendered it obsolete.

Pendergast moved on another block, then turned left onto Little Water Street. At the far corner was the Five Points House of Industry, the other orphanage graced with the medical attention of Enoch Leng. It was a tall Beaux Arts building, punctuated along its north end by a tower. A small rectangular widow's walk, buttressed by iron fencing, sat atop its mansard roof. The building looked woefully out of place among the shabby wooden houses and ramshackle squatteries.

He stared up at the heavy-browed windows. Why had Leng chosen to lend his services to these two missions, one after the other, in 1880—the year *before* Shottum's Cabinet burned? If he was looking for an endless source of impoverished victims whose absence would cause no alarm, the cabinet was a better choice than a workhouse. After all, one could have only so many mysterious disappearances before someone grew suspicious. And why had Leng chosen *these* missions in particular? There were countless others in lower Manhattan. Why had Leng decided to work—and, presumably, draw his pool of victims—from this spot?

Pendergast stepped back onto the cobbles, glancing up and down the lane, thinking. Of all the streets he had traveled, Little Water Street was the only one no longer extant in the twentieth century. It had been paved over, built upon, forgotten. He had seen old maps that showed it, naturally; but no map ever drawn had superimposed its course onto *present-day* Manhattan . . .

An incredibly shabby man with a horse and cart came down the street, ringing a bell, collecting garbage for tips, a brace of tame hogs following behind. Pendergast did not heed him. Instead, he glided back down the narrow road, pausing at the entrance to Cow Bay. Although with the disappearance of Little Water Street it was difficult to tell on modern maps, Pendergast now saw that the two missions would *both* have backed onto these terrible old tenements. Those dwellings were gone, but the warren of tunnels that once served their criminal residents would have remained.

He glanced down both sides of the alley. Slaughterhouse, ice factory, abandoned waterworks . . . It suddenly made perfect sense.

More slowly now, Pendergast walked away, headed for Baxter Street and points north. He could, of course, have ended his journey at this point—have opened his eyes to the present-day books and tubes and monitor screens—but he preferred to continue the discipline of this mental exercise, to take the long way back to Lenox Hill Hospital. He was curious to see if the fire at Shottum's Cabinet had been brought under control. Perhaps he would hire a carriage uptown. Or better yet, walk up past the Madison Square Garden circus, past Delmonico's, past the palaces of Fifth Avenue. There was much to think about, much more than he had previously imagined—and 1881 was as good a place as any to do it in.

FOURTEEN

NORA STOPPED AT THE NURSES' STATION TO ASK DIRECTIONS to Pendergast's new room. A sea of hostile faces greeted the question. *Clearly,* Nora thought, *Pendergast was as popular at Lenox as he had been at St. Luke's–Roosevelt.*

She found him lying up in bed, the blinds shut tight against the sun. He looked very tired, his face gray. His blond-white hair hung limply over his high forehead, and his eyes were closed. As she entered, they slowly opened.

"I'm sorry," Nora said. "This is a bad time."

"Not at all. I did ask you to see me. Please clear off that chair and sit down."

Nora moved the stack of books and papers from the chair to the floor, wondering again what this was about. She'd already given him her report about her visit with the old lady and told him it would be her last assignment for him. He had to understand that it was time for her to get back to her own career. As intriguing as it was, she was not about to commit professional *hara kiri* over this business.

Pendergast's eyes had drooped until they were almost closed, but she could still see the pale irises behind the slitted lids.

"How are you?" Courtesy required she ask that question, but there wouldn't be any others. She'd listen to what he had to say, then leave.

"Leng acquired his victims from the cabinet itself," Pendergast said.

"How do you know?"

"He captured them at the back of one of the halls, most likely a small cul-de-sac housing a particularly gruesome exhibit. He would lie in wait until a visitor was alone, then he'd snatch his victim, take the unfortunate through a door at the rear of the exhibit, which led down the back stairs to the coal cellar. It was a perfect setup. Street people vanished all the time in that neighborhood. Undoubtably, Leng selected victims that would not be missed: street urchins, workhouse boys and girls."

He spoke in a monotone, as if reviewing his findings within his own mind instead of explaining them to her.

"From 1872 to 1881 he used the cabinet for this purpose. Nine years. Thirty-six victims that we know of, perhaps many more Leng disposed of in some other way. As you know, there had in fact been rumors of people vanishing in the cabinet. These no doubt served to increase its popularity."

Nora shuddered.

"Then in 1881 he killed Shottum and burned the cabinet. We of course know why: Shottum found out what he was up to. He said as much in his letter to McFadden. But that letter has, in its own way, been misleading me all this time. Leng would have killed Shottum anyway." Pendergast paused to take a few breaths. "The confrontation with Shottum merely gave him the excuse he needed to burn the cabinet. You see, phase one of his work was complete."

"Phase one?"

"He had achieved what he set out to do. He perfected his formula."

"You don't seriously mean Leng was able to prolong his own life?"

"He clearly *believed* he could. In his mind, the experimentation phase could cease. Production could begin. Victims would still be required, but many fewer than before. The cabinet, with its high volume of foot traffic, was no longer necessary. In fact, it had become a liability. It was imperative for Leng to cover his tracks and start afresh."

There was a silence. Then Pendergast resumed.

"A year before the cabinet burned, Leng offered his services to two workhouses in the vicinity—the Five Points House of Industry and the Five Points Mission. The two were connected by the warren of old underground tunnels that riddled the entire Five Points area in the nineteenth century. In Leng's day, a foul alley known as Cow Bay lay between the workhouses. Along with the sordid tenements you'd expect, Cow Bay was home to an ancient subterranean pumping station dating back to the days of the Collect Pond. The waterworks were shut down and sealed for good about a month before Leng allied himself with the workhouses. That is no mere coincidence of dates."

"What are you saying?"

"The abandoned waterworks was the site of Leng's *production* laboratory. The place he went after burning Shottum's Cabinet. It was secure, and better still it provided easy underground access to both workhouses. An ideal place to begin production of the substance he believed would prolong his life. I have the old plans for the waterworks, here." Pendergast waved his hand, weakly.

Nora glanced over at the complex set of diagrams. She wondered what had so exhausted the agent. He had seemed much better the day before. She hoped he hadn't taken a turn for the worse.

"Today, of course, the workhouses, the tenements, even many of the streets are gone. A three-story brownstone was built directly above the site of Leng's production laboratory. Number 99 Doyers Street, erected in the 1920s off Chatham Square. Broken into one-bedroom flats, with a separate two-bedroom apartment in the basement. Any traces of Leng's laboratory would lie under that building."

Nora thought for a moment. Excavating Leng's production laboratory would no doubt be a fascinating archaeological project. There would be evidence there, and as an archaeologist she could find it. She wondered, once again, why Pendergast was so interested in these nineteenth-century murders. It would be of some historical solace to know that Mary Greene's killer had been brought to light— She abruptly terminated the line of thought. She had her own work to do, her own career to salvage. She had to remind herself once again that this was history.

Pendergast sighed, turned slightly in the bed. "Thank you, Dr. Kelly. Now, you'd better go. I'm badly in need of sleep."

Nora glanced at him in surprise. She had been expecting another plea for her help. "Why did you ask to see me, exactly?"

"You've been a great help to me in this investigation. More than once, you've asked for more information than I could give you. I assumed you wished to know what I've discovered. You've earned that, at the very least. There's a detestable term one hears bandied about these days: 'closure.' Detestable, but in this case appropriate. I hope this knowledge will bring you some degree of closure, and allow you to continue your work at the Museum without a sense of unfinished business. I offer my sincerest thanks for your help. It has been invaluable."

Nora felt a twinge of offense at this abrupt dismissal. She reminded herself that this was what she had wanted . . . Wasn't it? After a moment she spoke. "Thanks for saying so. But if you ask me, this business sounds totally unfinished. If you're right about this, 99 Doyers Street seems like the next logical stop."

"That is correct. The basement apartment is currently unoccupied, and an excavation below the living room floor would be most instructive. I plan to rent the apartment myself and undertake that excavation. And that is why I must recover as quickly as possible. Take care, Dr. Kelly." He shifted with an air of finality.

"Who's going to do the excavation?" she asked.

"I will find another archaeologist."

Nora looked at him sharply. "Where?"

"Through the New Orleans field office. They are most flexible when it comes to my, ah, projects."

"Right," said Nora briskly. "But this isn't a job for just any archaeologist. This requires someone with special skills in—"

"Are you offering?"

Nora was silent.

"Of course you're not. That's why I didn't ask. You've more than once expressed your desire to return to a more normal course of work. I've imposed upon you too much as it is. Besides, this investigation has taken a dangerous turn, far more so than I initially assumed. An assumption I have paid for, as you can see. I would not wish you exposed to any more danger than you have been already."

Nora stood up.

"Well," she said, "I guess that's settled. I've enjoyed

working with you, Mr. Pendergast—if 'enjoy' is the right word. It's certainly been interesting." She felt vaguely dissatisfied with this outcome, even though it was what she had come down here to achieve.

"Indeed," said Pendergast. "Most interesting."

She began to walk toward the door, then stopped, remembering something. "But I may be in touch with you again. I got a note from Reinhart Puck in the Archives. Says he's found some new information, asked me to stop by later this afternoon. If it seems useful, I'll pass it on."

Pendergast's pale eyes were still regarding her attentively. "Do that. And again, Dr. Kelly, you have my thanks. Be very careful."

She nodded, then turned to leave, smiling at the baleful stares that greeted her as she passed the nurses' station.

FIFTEEN

THE DOOR TO THE ARCHIVES GAVE OUT A SHARP CREAK AS Nora eased it open. There had been no response to her knocking, and the door was unlocked, in clear violation of regulations. Very strange.

The smell of old books, papers, and the odor of corruption that seemed to suffuse the entire Museum hung in her nostrils. Puck's desk lay in the center of a pool of light, a wall of darkness beyond. Puck himself was nowhere to be seen.

Nora checked her watch. Four P.M. She was right on time.

She released the door and it sighed back into place. She turned the lock, then approached the desk, heels clicking on the marble floor. She signed in automatically, scrawling her name at the top of a fresh page in the logbook. Puck's desk was neater than usual, and a single typewritten note sat in the middle of the green felt pad. She glanced at it. *I'm on the triceratops in the back.*

The triceratops, Nora thought, looking into the gloom. Leave it to Puck to be off dusting old relics. But where the hell was the triceratops? She didn't recall having seen one. And there were no lights on in the back that she could see.

The damn triceratops could be anywhere. She looked around: no diagram of the Archives, either. Typical.

Feeling an undercurrent of irritation, she moved to the banks of ivory light switches. She snapped a few on at random. Lights sprang up here and there, deep within the Archives, casting long shadows down the rows of metal shelving. *Might as well turn them all on,* she thought, flipping whole rows of switches with the edge of her hand. But even with all the lights, the Archives remained curiously shadowy and dim, large pools of darkness and long dim aisles predominating.

She waited, half expecting Puck to call out to her. There was no sound except the distant ticking of steam pipes and the hiss of the forced-air ducts.

"Mr. Puck?" she called tentatively.

Her voice reverberated and died. No answer.

She called again, louder this time. The Archives were so vast she wondered if her voice could penetrate to the rear.

For a minute, she considered coming back another time. But Puck's message had been most insistent.

Vaguely, she recalled seeing some mounted fossil skeletons on her last visit. Maybe she would find the triceratops among them.

With a sigh, she began walking down one of the aisles, listening to the clatter of her shoes against the marble. Although the entrance to the aisle had been brightly lit, it soon grew shadowy and dim. It was amazing how poorly illuminated the place was; in the middle sections of the aisles, far from the lights, one almost needed a flashlight to make out the objects stacked on the shelves.

At the next pool of light, Nora found herself at a junction from which several aisles wandered away at a variety of angles. She paused, considering which to take. *It's like*

Hansel and Gretel in here, she thought. *And I'm fresh out of bread crumbs.*

The aisle closest to her left went in a direction that, she remembered, led to a grouping of stuffed animals. But its few lights were burned out and it vanished into darkness. Nora shrugged and took the next aisle over.

It felt so different, walking these passages alone. The last time, she'd been with Pendergast and Puck. She had been thinking about Shottum and hadn't paid much attention to her surroundings. With Puck guiding their steps, she hadn't even bothered to notice the strange jogs these aisles took, the odd angles at which they met. It was the most eccentric layout imaginable, made even more eccentric by its vast size.

Her thoughts were interrupted as the aisle took a sharp turn to the left. Around the corner, she unexpectedly came upon a number of freestanding African mammals—giraffes, a hippo, a pair of lions, wildebeests, kudu, water buffalo. Each was wrapped in plastic, bestowing a muffled, ghostly appearance.

Nora stopped. No sign of a triceratops. And once again, the aisles led away in half a dozen directions. She chose one at random, followed it through one jog, then another, coming abruptly to another intersection.

This was getting ridiculous. "Mr. Puck!" she called out loudly.

The echoes of her voice gradually faded away. The hiss of forced air filled the ensuing silence.

She didn't have time for this. She would come back later, and she'd call first to make sure Puck was waiting at his desk. Better still, she'd just tell him to take whatever it was he wanted to show her directly to Pendergast. She was off the case, anyway.

She turned to walk out of the Archives, taking what she

thought would be the shortest path. After a few minutes, she came to a stop beside a rhino and several zebras. They looked like lumpy sentinels beneath the omnipresent plastic, giving off a strong smell of paradichlorobenzene.

These aisles didn't look familiar. And she didn't seem to be any closer to the exit.

For a moment, she felt a small current of anxiety. Then she shook it away with a forced laugh. She'd just make her way back to the giraffes, then retrace her steps from there.

As she turned, her foot landed in a small puddle of water. She looked up just as a drop of water splattered on her forehead. Condensation from the pipes far overhead. She shook it away and moved on.

But she couldn't seem to find her way back to the giraffes.

This was crazy. She'd navigated through trackless deserts and dense rainforests. How could she be lost in a museum in the middle of New York City?

She looked around, realizing it was her sense of direction she had lost. With all these angled aisles, these dimly lit intersections, it had become impossible to tell where the front desk was. She'd have to—

She abruptly froze, listening intently. A soft pattering sound. It was hard to tell where it had come from, but it was close.

"Mr. Puck? Is that you?"

Nothing.

She listened, and the pattering sound came again. *Just more water dripping somewhere,* she thought. Even so, she was more eager than ever to find the door.

She chose an aisle at random and moved down it at a brisk walk, heels clicking rapidly against the marble. On both sides of the aisle, the shelves were covered with bones stacked like cordwood, each with a yellowing tag tied to its end. The tags flapped and fluttered in the dead air stirred by her passage. The place was like a crypt. Amid the silence, the darkness, and the ghoulish specimens, it was hard not to think about the set of grisly murders that had occurred just a few years before, within this very subbasement. It was still the subject of rumor and speculation in the staff lounge.

The aisle ended in another jog.

Damn it, thought Nora, looking up and down the long rows of shelving that vanished into the gloom. Another welling of anxiety, harder to fight down this time. And then, once again, she heard—or thought she heard—a noise from behind. This time it wasn't a pattering, so much as the scrape of a foot on stone.

"Who's there?" she demanded, spinning around. "Mr. Puck?"

Nothing save the hiss of steam and the drip of water.

She began walking again, a little faster now, telling herself not to be afraid; that the noises were merely the incessant shiftings and settlings of an old, decrepit building. The very corridors seemed watchful. The click of her heels was unbearably loud.

She turned a corner and stepped in another puddle of water. She pulled back in disgust. Why didn't they do something about these old pipes?

She looked at the puddle again. The water was black, greasy—not, in fact, water at all. Oil had leaked on the floor, or maybe some chemical preservative. It had a strange, sour smell. But it didn't look like it had leaked from anywhere: she was surrounded by shelves covered with mounted birds, beaks open, eyes wide, wings upraised.

What a mess, she thought, turning her expensive Bally shoe sideways to find that the oily liquid had soiled the sole and part of the stitching. This place was a disgrace. She pulled an oversized handkerchief from her pocket—a necessary accoutrement to working in a dusty museum—and wiped it along the edge of the shoe. And then, abruptly, she froze. Against the white background of the handkerchief, the liquid was not black. It was a deep, glistening red.

She dropped the handkerchief and took an involuntary step back, heart hammering. She looked at the pool, stared at it with sudden horror. It was blood—a whole lot of blood. She looked around wildly: where had it come from? Had it leaked out of a specimen? But it seemed to be just sitting there, all alone—a large pool of blood in the middle of the aisle. She glanced up, but there was nothing: just the dim ceiling thirty feet above, crisscrossed with pipes.

Then she heard what sounded like another footfall, and, through a shelf of specimens, she glimpsed movement. Then, silence returned.

But she had definitely heard something. *Move, move,* all her instincts cried out.

Nora turned and walked quickly down the long aisle. Another sound came—fast footsteps? The rustle of fabric?—and she paused again to listen. Nothing but the faint drips from the pipes. She tried to stare through the isolated gaps in the shelves. There was a wall of specimen jars, snakes coiled in formaldehyde, and she strained to see through. There seemed to be a shape on the other side, large and black, rippled and distorted by the stacks of glass jars. She moved . . . and it moved in turn. She was sure of it.

She backtracked quickly, breath coming faster, and the dark shape moved as well. It seemed to be pacing her in the next aisle—perhaps waiting for her to reach either one end or the other.

She slowed and, struggling to master her fear, tried walking as calmly as she could toward the end of the aisle.

She could see, hear, the shape—so near now—moving as well, keeping pace.

"Mr. Puck?" she ventured, voice quavering.

There was no answer.

Suddenly, Nora found herself running. She arrowed down the aisle, sprinting as fast as she could. Swift footfalls sounded in the adjoining aisle.

Ahead was a gap, where her aisle joined the next. She had to get past, outrun the person in the adjoining aisle.

She dashed through the gap, glimpsing for a split second a huge black figure, metal flashing in its gloved hand. She sprinted down the next aisle, through another gap, and on down the aisle again. At the next gap, she veered sharply right, heading down a new corridor. Selecting another aisle at random, she turned into it and ran on through the dimness ahead.

Halfway to the next intersection, she stopped again, heart pounding. There was silence, and for a moment relief surged through her: she had managed to lose her pursuer.

And then she caught the sound of faint breathing from the adjoining aisle.

Relief disappeared as quickly as it had come. She had not outrun him. No matter what she did, no matter where she ran, he had continued to pace her, one aisle over.

"Who are you?" she asked.

There was a faint rustle, then an almost silent laugh.

Nora looked to the left and right, fighting back panic, desperately trying to determine the best way out. These shelves were covered with stacks of folded skins, parchment-dry, smelling fearfully of decay. Nothing looked familiar.

Twenty feet farther down the aisle, she spied a gap in the shelving, on the side away from the unknown presence. She sprinted ahead and turned into the gap, then doubled back into yet another adjoining aisle. She stopped, crouched, waited.

Footfalls sounded several aisles over, coming closer, then receding again. He had lost her.

Nora turned and began moving, as stealthily as possible, through the aisles, trying to put as much distance as possible between herself and the pursuer. But no matter which way she turned, or how fast she ran, whenever she stopped she could hear the footfalls, rapid and purposeful, seeming to keep pace.

She *had* to figure out where she was. If she kept running around aimlessly, eventually he—it—would catch her.

She looked around. This aisle ended in a wall. She was at the edge of the Archives. Now, at least, she could follow the wall, make her way to the front.

Crouching, she moved along as quickly as she could, listening intently for the sound of footsteps, her eye scanning the dimness ahead. Suddenly, something yawned out from the gloom: it was a triceratops skull, mounted on the wall, its outlines shadowy and vague in the poor light.

Relief flooded through her. Puck must be around here somewhere; the intruder wouldn't dare approach them simultaneously.

She opened her mouth to call out softly. But then she paused, looking more closely at the dim outline of the dinosaur. Something was odd—the silhouette was all wrong. She began to move cautiously toward it. And then, abruptly, she stopped once again.

There, impaled on the horns of the triceratops, hung a body, naked from the waist up, arms and legs hanging loose. Three bloody horns stuck right through the man's back. It looked as if the triceratops had gored the person, hoisting him into the air.

Nora took a step back. Her mind took in the details, as if from a long distance away: the balding head with a fringe of gray hair; the flabby skin; the withered arms. Where the horns had speared through the lower back, the flesh was one long, open wound. Blood had collected around the base of the horns, running in dark rivulets around the torso and dripping onto the marble.

I'm on the triceratops in the back.

In the back.

She heard a scream, realized that it had come from her own throat.

Blindly, she wheeled away and ran, veering once, and again, and then again, racing down the aisles as quickly as she could move her legs. And then, abruptly, she found herself in a cul-de-sac. She spun to retrace her steps—and there, blocking the end of the row, stood an antique, black-hatted figure.

Something gleamed in his gloved hands.

There was nowhere to go but up. Without an instant's thought, she turned, grabbed the edge of a shelf, and began climbing.

The figure came flying down the aisle, black cloak billowing behind.

Nora was an experienced rock climber. Her years as an archaeologist in Utah, climbing to caves and Anasazi cliff dwellings, were not forgotten. In a minute she had reached the top shelf, which swayed and groaned under the unexpected weight. She turned frantically, grabbed the first thing that came to hand—a stuffed falcon—and looked down once again.

The black-hatted man was already below, climbing, face obscured in deep shadow. Nora aimed, then threw.

The falcon bounced harmlessly off one shoulder.

She looked around desperately for something else. A box of papers; another stuffed animal; more boxes. She threw one, then another. But they were too light, useless.

Still the man climbed.

With a sob of terror, she swung over the top shelf and started descending the other side. Abruptly, a gloved hand darted *between* the shelving, caught hold of her shirt. Nora screamed, ripping herself free. A dim flash of steel and a tiny blade swept past her, missing her eye by inches. She swung away as the blade made another glittering arc toward her. Pain abruptly blossomed in her right shoulder.

She cried out, lost her grip. Landing on her feet, she broke her fall by rolling to one side.

On the far side of the shelving, the man had quickly climbed back down to the ground. Now he began climbing directly through the shelf, kicking and knocking specimen jars and boxes aside.

Again she ran, running wildly, blindly, from aisle to aisle.

Suddenly, a vast shape rose out of the dimness before her. It was a woolly mammoth. Nora recognized it immediately: she'd been here, once before, with Puck.

But which direction was out? As she looked around, Nora realized she would never make it—the pursuer would be upon her in a matter of seconds.

Suddenly, she knew there was only one thing to do.

Reaching for the light switches at the end of the aisle, she brushed them off with a single movement, plunging the surrounding corridors once again into darkness. Quickly, she felt beneath the mammoth's scratchy belly. There it was: a wooden lever. She tugged, and the trap door fell open.

Trying to make as little noise as possible, she climbed into the hot, stuffy belly, pulling the trapdoor up behind her.

Then she waited, inside the mammoth. The air stank of rot, dust, jerked meat, mushrooms.

She heard a rapid series of clicks. The lights came back on. A stray beam worked through a small hole in the animal's chest: an eyehole, for the circus worker.

Nora looked out, trying to control her rapid breathing, to push away the panic that threatened to overwhelm her. The man in the derby hat stood not five feet away, back turned. Slowly, he rotated himself through 360 degrees, looking, listening intently. He was holding a strange instrument in his hands: two polished ivory handles joined by a thin, flexible steel saw with tiny serrations. It looked like some kind of dreadful antique surgical instrument. He flexed it, causing the steel wire to bend and shimmy.

His gaze came to rest on the mammoth. He took a step toward it, his face in shadow. It was as if he knew this was where she was hiding. Nora tensed, readying herself to fight to the end.

And then, just as suddenly as he'd approached, he was gone.

"Mr. Puck?" a voice was calling. "Mr. Puck, I'm here! Mr. Puck?"

It was Oscar Gibbs.

Nora waited, too terrified to move. The voice came closer and, finally, Oscar Gibbs appeared around the corner of the aisle.

"Mr. Puck? Where are you?"

With a trembling hand, Nora reached down, unlatched the trapdoor, and lowered herself out of the belly of the mammoth. Gibbs turned, jumped back, and stood there, staring at her open-mouthed.

"Did you see him?" Nora gasped. "Did you see him?"

"Who? What were you doing in there? Hey, you're bleeding!"

Nora looked at her shoulder. There was a spreading stain of blood where the scalpel had nicked her.

Gibbs came closer. "Look, I don't know what you're doing here, or what's going on, but let's get you to the nurse's office. Okay?"

Nora shook her head. "No. Oscar, you have to call the police, right away. Mr. Puck"—her voice broke for a moment—"Mr. Puck's been murdered. And the murderer is right here. In the Museum."

Many Worm

ONE

BILL SMITHBACK HAD MANAGED, WITH A LITTLE NAME-dropping here and a little intimidation there, to get the best seat in the house. "The house" was the press room of One Police Plaza, a cavernous space painted the institutional color known universally as Vomit Green. It was now filled to overflowing with scurrying television news crews and frantic journalists. Smithback loved the electric atmosphere of a big press conference, called hastily after some dreadful event, packed with city officials and police brass laboring under the misapprehension that they could spin the unruly fourth estate of New York.

He remained in his seat, calm, legs folded, tape recorder loaded, and shotgun mike poised, while pandemonium raged around him. To his professional nose, it smelled different today. There was an undertone of fear. More than fear, actually: closer to ill-suppressed hysteria. He'd seen it as he'd ridden the subway downtown that morning, walked the streets around City Hall. These three copycat killings, one on top of another, were just too strange. People were talking of nothing else. The whole city was on the verge of panic.

Off to one side he caught sight of Bryce Harriman,

expostulating with a policeman who refused to let him move closer to the front. All that fine vocational training at Columbia journalism school, wasted on the *New York Post.* He should have taken a nice quiet professorship at his old alma mater, teaching callow youth how to write a flawless inverted pyramid. True, the bastard had scooped him on the second murder, on the copycat angle, but surely that was just luck. Wasn't it?

There was a stir in the crowd. The wing doors of the press room belched out a group of blue suits, followed by the mayor of New York City, Edward Montefiori. The man was tall and solid, very much aware that all eyes were upon him. He paused, nodding to acquaintances here and there, his face reflecting the gravity of the moment. The New York City mayoral race was in full swing, being conducted as usual at the level of two-year-olds. It was imperative that he catch this killer, bring the copycat murders to an end; the last thing the mayor wanted was to give his rival yet more fodder for his nasty television advertisements, which had been decrying the city's recent upsurge in crime.

More people were coming onto the stage. The mayor's spokesperson, Mary Hill, a tall, extremely poised African-American woman; the fat police captain Sherwood Custer, in whose precinct this whole mess had started; the police commissioner, Rocker—a tall, weary-looking man—and, finally, Dr. Frederick Collopy, director of the Museum, followed by Roger Brisbane. Smithback felt a surge of anger when he saw Brisbane, looking urbane in a neatly tailored gray suit. Brisbane was the one who had screwed up everything between him and Nora. Even after Nora's horrible discovery of Puck's murdered corpse, after being chased and nearly caught herself by the Surgeon, she had refused to see him, to let him comfort her. It was almost as if she blamed him for what happened to Puck and Pendergast.

The noise level in the room was becoming deafening. The mayor mounted the podium and raised his hand. At the gesture, the room quickly fell silent.

The mayor read from a prepared statement, his Brooklyn accent filling the room.

"Ladies and gentlemen of the press," he began. "From time to time our great city, because of its size and diversity, has been stalked by serial killers. Thankfully, it has been many years since the last such plague. Now, however, it appears we are faced with a new serial killer, a true psychopath. Three people have been murdered in the space of a week, and in a particularly violent way. While the city is now enjoying the lowest murder rate of any major metropolitan area in the country—thanks to our vigorous enforcement efforts and zero tolerance for lawbreaking—this is clearly three murders too many. I called this press conference to share with the public the strong and effective steps we are taking to find this killer, and to answer as best we can questions you might have about this case and its somewhat sensational aspects. As you know, openness has always been a top priority of my administration. I therefore have brought with me Karl Rocker, the police commissioner; Sherwood Custer, precinct captain; Director Frederick Collopy and Vice President Roger Brisbane of the New York Museum of Natural History, where the latest homicide was discovered. My spokesperson, Mary Hill, will field the questions. But first, I will ask Commissioner Rocker to give you a briefing on the case."

He stepped back and Rocker took the microphone.

"Thank you, Mr. Mayor." His low, intelligent voice, dry as parchment, filled the room. "Last Thursday, the body of a young woman, Doreen Hollander, was discovered in Central Park. She had been murdered, and a peculiar kind of dissection or surgical operation performed on her lower back. While the official autopsy was in progress and the results were being evaluated, a second killing took place. Another young woman, Mandy Eklund, was found in Tompkins Square Park. Forensic analysis indicated that her manner of death, and the violence done to her person, matched the killing of Doreen Hollander. And yesterday, the body of a fifty-four-year-old man, Reinhart Puck, was discovered in the Archives of the New York Museum. He was the Museum's head archivist. The body showed mutilations identical to Ms. Eklund's and Ms. Hollander's."

There was a flurry of raised hands, shouts, gestures. The commissioner quelled them by holding up both hands. "As you know, a letter was discovered in these same Archives, referring to a nineteenth-century serial killer. This letter described similar mutilations, conducted as a scientific experiment by a doctor named Leng, in lower Manhattan, one hundred and twenty years ago. The remains of thirty-six individuals were discovered at a building site on Catherine Street, presumably the spot where Dr. Leng did his depraved work."

There was another flurry of shouts.

Now, the mayor broke in again. "An article about the letter appeared in last week's *New York Times*. It described, in detail, the kind of mutilations Leng had performed on his victims more than a century ago, as well as the reason why he had carried them out."

The mayor's eyes roved the crowd and paused momentarily on Smithback. The journalist felt a shiver of pride at the implied recognition. *His* article.

"That article appears to have had an unfortunate effect: it

appears to have stimulated a copycat killer. A modern psychopath."

What was this? Smithback's smugness vanished before a quickly rising sense of outrage.

"I am told by police psychiatrists this killer believes, in some twisted way, that by killing these people he will accomplish what Leng tried to accomplish a century ago— that is, extend his life span. The, er, sensationalistic approach of the *Times* article we believe inflamed the killer and stimulated him to act."

This was outrageous. The mayor was blaming *him*.

Smithback looked around and saw that many eyes in the room were on him. He stifled his first impulse to stand up and protest. He had been doing his job as a reporter. It was just a story. How *dare* the mayor make him the scapegoat?

"I am not blaming anyone in particular," Montefiori droned on, "but I would ask *you*, ladies and gentlemen of the press, to please show restraint in your coverage. We already have three brutal killings on our hands. We are determined not to allow any more. All leads are being followed up vigorously. Let us not inflame the situation further. Thank you."

Mary Hill stepped forward to take questions. There was a roar, an instant outcry, as everyone stood up, gesturing madly. Smithback remained seated, flushing deeply. He felt violated. He tried to collect his thoughts, but his shock and outrage made him unable to think.

Mary Hill was taking the first question.

"You said the murderer performed an operation on his victims," somebody asked. "Can you elaborate?"

"Basically, the lower portion of the spinal cord had been removed in all three victims," the commissioner himself answered.

"It's being said that the latest operation was actually *performed* in the Museum," shouted another reporter. "Is that so?"

"It is true that a large pool of blood was discovered in the Archives, not far from the victim. It appears the blood was, in fact, from the victim, but more forensic tests are underway. Whether the, er, *operation* was actually performed there must await further lab work."

"I understand that the FBI have been on the scene," a young woman shouted. "Could you tell us the nature of their involvement?"

"That is not entirely correct," Rocker answered. "An FBI agent has taken an unofficial interest in the nineteenth-century serial killings. But he has no connection to this case."

"Is it true that the third body was impaled on the horns of a dinosaur?"

The commissioner winced slightly. "Yes, the body was found affixed to a triceratops skull. Clearly, we are dealing with a seriously deranged individual."

"About the mutilation of the bodies. Is it true that only a surgeon could have done it?"

"It is one lead we are following up."

"I just want to clarify one point," another reporter said. "Are you saying that the Smithback piece in the *Times* caused these murders?"

Smithback turned. It was Bryce Harriman, the shit.

Commissioner Rocker frowned. "What Mayor Montefiori said was—"

Once again, the mayor intervened. "I was merely calling for restraint. To be sure, we *wish* that article had never appeared. Three people might be alive today. And the methods the reporter used to acquire his information bear some ethical scrutiny, to my mind. But no, I've not said the article *caused* the killings."

Another reporter: "Isn't it a bit of a diversion, Your Honor, to blame a reporter who was only doing his job?"

Smithback craned his neck. Who said that? He was going to buy that man a drink.

"That is not what I said. I merely said—"

"But you clearly *implied* that the article triggered the killings."

He was going to buy that man drinks *and* dinner. As Smithback looked around, he could see many of the returning glances were sympathetic. The mayor, in attacking him, had indirectly attacked the entire press corps. Harriman had shot himself in the foot by bringing up the subject. He felt emboldened: now they would have to call on him. They would *have* to.

"May I have the next question, please?" Mary Hill asked.

"Do you have any suspects?"

"We've been given a very clear description of the suspect's attire," Commissioner Rocker said. "A tall slender Caucasian male, between six foot and six foot two, wearing an old-fashioned black coat and a derby hat, was seen in the Archives around the time Mr. Puck's body was found. A similarly dressed man, with a rolled umbrella or cane, was also seen in the vicinity of the second crime scene. I'm not at liberty to give any details beyond that."

Smithback stood up, waved. Mary Hill ignored him.

"Ms. Perez of *New York* magazine. Your question, please."

"I have a question for Dr. Collopy of the Museum. Sir, do you think the killer known as the Surgeon is a Museum employee? Given that the most recent victim seems to have been killed and dissected in the Museum, I mean."

Collopy cleared his throat and stepped forward. "I believe the police are looking into that," he said in a well-modulated voice. "It seems highly unlikely. All our employees now go through criminal background checks, are psychologically profiled, and are thoroughly drug-tested. And it hasn't been proven that the killing actually took place in the Museum, I might add."

There was another roar as Hill looked for more questions. Smithback shouted and waved his hands along with the rest. Christ, they weren't really going to ignore him?

"Mr. Diller of *Newsday,* your question please."

She *was* avoiding him, the witch.

"I'd like to address my question to the mayor. Mr. Mayor, how is it that the site on Catherine Street was 'inadvertently' destroyed? Wasn't this a site of major historical importance?"

The mayor stepped forward. "No. It was not of historical significance—"

"No historical significance? The largest serial killing in the nation's history?"

"Mr. Diller, this press conference is about the present-day homicides. Please, let's not conflate the two. We had no legal reason to stop construction of a hundred-million-dollar building. The bones and effects were photographed, studied by the medical examiner, and removed for further analysis. Nothing more could be done."

"Is it perhaps because Moegen-Fairhaven is a major donor to your campaign—"

"Next question," rapped out Hill.

Smithback stood up and shouted, "Mr. Mayor, since aspersions have been cast—"

"Ms. Epstein of WNBC," cried Mary Hill, her powerful voice drowning him out. A slender newswoman stood up, holding a mike, a camera turned on her.

"Excuse ME!" Smithback quickly took advantage of the temporary lull. "Ms. Epstein, since I have been personally attacked, may I respond?"

The famous anchorwoman didn't pause for a second. "Of course," she said graciously, and turned to her cameraman to make sure he got it on tape.

"I'd like to address my question to Mr. Brisbane," Smithback continued, not pausing for a second. "Mr. Brisbane, why has the letter that started all this been put off limits, along with all the items from the Shottum collection? The Museum isn't trying to *hide* something, is it?"

Brisbane rose with an easy smile. "Not at all. Those materials have merely been temporarily removed for conservation. It's standard Museum procedure. In any case, the letter has already inflamed one copycat murderer into action—to release it now would be irresponsible. The materials are still available to qualified researchers."

"Is it not true that you tried to prevent employees from working on the case?"

"Not at all. We've cooperated all along. The record speaks for itself."

Shit. Smithback thought fast. "Mr. Brisbane—"

"Mr. Smithback, care to give someone else a turn?" Mary Hill's voice once again sliced through the air.

"No!" Smithback cried, to scattered laughter. "Mr. Brisbane, isn't it true that Moegen-Fairhaven, which gave the Museum two million dollars last year—not to mention the fact that Fairhaven himself sits on your board—has put pressure on the Museum to stop this investigation?"

Brisbane colored and Smithback knew his question had hit home. "That is an irresponsible allegation. As I said, we've cooperated all along—"

"So you *deny* threatening your employee, Dr. Nora Kelly,

forbidding her to work on the case? Keep in mind, Mr. Brisbane, that we have yet to hear from Nora Kelly herself. The one who found the third victim's body, I might add—and who was chased by the Surgeon and almost killed in turn."

The clear implication was that Nora Kelly might have something to say that would not agree with Brisbane's account. Brisbane's face darkened as he realized he'd been backed into a corner. "I will not answer these hectoring questions." Beside him, Collopy looked grim.

Smithback felt a swell of triumph.

"*Mister* Smithback," said Mary Hill acidly, "are you quite done monopolizing this press conference? Clearly the nineteenth-century homicides have nothing to do with the current serial killings, except as inspiration."

"And how do you know *that?*" Smithback cried out, his triumph now secure.

The mayor now turned to him. "Are you suggesting, sir," he said facetiously, "that Dr. Leng is still alive and continuing his business?"

There was a solid round of laughter in the hall.

"Not at all—"

"Then I suggest you sit down, my friend."

Smithback sat down, amid more laughter, his feelings of triumph squashed. He had scored a hit, but they knew how to hit back.

As the questions droned on, it slowly dawned on him just what he had done, dragging Nora's name into the press conference. It didn't take him nearly as long to figure out how she would feel about it.

TWO

DOYERS STREET WAS A SHORT, NARROW DOGLEG OF A lane at the southeastern edge of Chinatown. A cluster of tea shops and grocery stores stood at the far end, festooned with bright neon signs in Chinese. Dark clouds scudded across the sky, whipping scraps of paper and leaves off the sidewalk. There was a distant roll of thunder. A storm was coming.

O'Shaughnessy paused at the entrance of the deserted lane, and Nora stopped beside him. She shivered, with both fear and cold. She could see him peering up and down the sidewalk, eyes alert for any sign of danger, any possibility that they had been followed.

"Number ninety-nine is in the middle of the block," he said in a low voice. "That brownstone, there."

Nora followed the indicated direction with her eyes. It was a narrow building like all the others: a three-story structure of dirty green brick.

"Sure you don't want me to go in with you?" O'Shaughnessy asked.

Nora swallowed. "I think it'd be better if you stayed here and watched the street."

O'Shaughnessy nodded, then slipped into the shadow of a doorway.

Taking a deep breath, Nora started forward. The sealed envelope containing Pendergast's banknotes felt like a lead weight within her purse. She shivered again, glancing up and down the dark street, fighting her feeling of agitation.

The attack on her, and Puck's brutal murder, had changed everything. It had proven these were no mere psychotic copycat killings. It had been carefully planned. The murderer had access to the Museum's private spaces. He had used Puck's old Royal typewriter to type that note, luring her to the Archives. He had pursued her with terrifying coolness. She'd felt the man's presence, mere inches away from her, there in the Archives. She'd even felt the sting of his scalpel. This was no lunatic: this was someone who knew exactly what he was doing, and why. Whatever the connection between the old killings and the new, this had to be stopped. If there was anything—*anything*—she could do to get the killer, she was willing to do it.

There were answers beneath the floor of Number 99 Doyers Street. She was going to find those answers.

Her mind returned to the terrifying chase, in particular to the flash of the Surgeon's scalpel as it flicked toward her, faster than a striking snake. It was an image that she found herself unable to shake. Then the endless police questioning; and afterward her trip to Pendergast's bedside, to tell him she had changed her mind about Doyers Street. Pendergast had been alarmed to hear of the attack, reluctant at first, but Nora refused to be swayed. With or without him, she was going down to Doyers. Ultimately, Pendergast had relented: on the condition that Nora keep O'Shaughnessy by her side at all times. And he had arranged for her to receive the fat packet of cash.

She mounted the steps to the front door, steeling herself for the task at hand. She noticed that the apartment names beside the buzzers were written in Chinese. She pressed the buzzer for Apartment 1.

A voice rasped out in Chinese.

"I'm the one interested in renting the basement apartment," she called out.

The lock snapped free with a buzz, she pushed on the door, and found herself in a hallway lit by fluorescent lights. A narrow staircase ascended to her right. At the end of the hallway she could hear a door being endlessly unbolted. It opened at last and a stooped, depressed-looking man appeared, in shirtsleeves and baggy slacks, peering down the hall at her.

Nora walked up. "Mr. Ling Lee?"

He nodded and held the door open for her. Beyond was a living room with a green sofa, a Formica table, several easy chairs, and an elaborate red- and gold-carved bas-relief on the wall, showing a pagoda and trees. A chandelier, grossly oversized for the space, dominated the room. The wallpaper was lilac, the rug red and black.

"Sit down," the man said. His voice was faint, tired.

She sat down, sinking alarmingly into the sofa.

"How you hear about this apartment?" Lee asked. Nora could see from his expression he was not pleased to see her.

Nora launched into her story. "A lady who works in the Citibank down the block from here told me about it."

"What lady?" Lee asked, more sharply. In Chinatown, Pendergast had explained, most landlords preferred to rent to their own.

"I don't know her name. My uncle told me to talk to her, said that she knew where to find an apartment in this area. She told me to call you."

"Your uncle?"

"Yes. Uncle Huang. He's with the DHCR."

This bit of information was greeted with a dismayed silence. Pendergast figured that having a Chinese relative would make it easier for her to get the apartment. That he worked for the Department of Housing and Community Renewal—the city division that enforced the rent laws— made it all the better.

"Your name?"

"Betsy Winchell."

Nora noticed a large, dark presence move from the kitchen into the doorway of the living room. It was apparently Lee's wife, arms folded, three times his size, looking very stern.

"Over the phone, you said the apartment was available. I'm prepared to take it right away. Please show it to me."

Lee rose from the table and glanced at his wife. Her arms tightened.

"Follow me," he said.

They went back into the hall, out the front door, and down the steps. Nora glanced around quickly, but O'Shaughnessy was nowhere to be seen. Lee removed a key, opened the basement apartment door, and snapped on the lights. She followed him in. He closed the door and made a show of relocking no fewer than four locks.

It was a dismal apartment, long and dark. The only window was a small, barred square beside the front door. The walls were of painted brick, once white but now gray, and the floor was covered with old brick pavers, cracked and chipped. Nora looked at them with professional interest. They were laid but not cemented. What was beneath? Dirt? Sand? Concrete? The floor looked just uneven and damp enough to have been laid on dirt.

"Kitchen and bedroom in back," said Lee, not bothering to point.

Nora walked to the rear of the apartment. Here was a cramped kitchen, leading into two dark bedrooms and a bath. There were no closets. A window in the rear wall, below grade, allowed feeble brown light from an air shaft to enter between thick steel bars.

Nora emerged. Lee was examining the lock on the front door. "Have to fix lock," he said in a portentous tone. "Many robber try to get in."

"You have a lot of break-ins?"

Lee nodded enthusiastically. "Oh yes. Many robber. Very dangerous."

"Really?"

"Many robber. Many mugger." He shook his head sadly.

"The apartment looks safe, at least." Nora listened. The ceiling seemed fairly soundproof—at least, she could hear nothing from above.

"Neighborhood not safe for girl. Every day, murder, mugging, robber. Rape."

Nora knew that, despite its shabby appearance, Chinatown was one of the safest neighborhoods in the city. "I'm not worried," she said.

"Many rule for apartment," said Lee, trying another tack.

"Is that right?"

"No music. No noise. No man at night." Lee seemed to be searching his mind for other strictures a young woman would find objectionable. "No smoke. No drink. Keep clean every day."

Nora listened, nodding her agreement. "Good. That sounds perfect. I like a neat, quiet place. And I have no boyfriend." With a renewed flash of anger she thought of Smithback and how he had dragged her into this mess by publishing that article. To a certain extent Smithback *had* been responsible for these copycat killings. Just yesterday, he'd had the nerve to bring up her name at the mayor's news conference, for the whole city to hear. She felt certain that, after what happened in the Archives, her long-term prospects at the Museum were even more questionable than before.

"Utility not include."

"Of course."

"No air-condition."

Nora nodded.

Lee seemed at a loss, then his face brightened with a fresh idea. "After suicide, no allow gun in apartment."

"Suicide?"

"Young woman hang herself. Same age as you."

"A hanging? I thought you mentioned a gun."

The man looked confused for a moment. Then his face brightened again. "She hang, but it no work. Then shoot herself."

"I see. She favored the comprehensive approach."

"Like you, she no have boyfriend. Very sad."

"How terrible."

"It happen right in there," said Lee, pointing into the kitchen. "Not find body for three day. Bad smell." He rolled his eyes and added, in a dramatic undertone: *"Many worm."*

"How dreadful," Nora said. Then she smiled. "But the apartment is just perfect. I'll take it."

Lee's look of depression deepened, but he said nothing.

She followed him back up to his apartment. Nora sat back down at the sofa, uninvited. The wife was still there, a formidable presence in the kitchen doorway. Her face was screwed into an expression of suspicion and displeasure. Her crossed arms looked like balsa-colored hams.

The man sat down unhappily.

"So," said Nora, "let's get this over with. I want to rent the apartment. I need it immediately. Today. Right now."

"Have to check reference," Lee replied feebly.

"There's no time and I'm prepared to pay cash. I need the apartment tonight, or I won't have a place to sleep." As she spoke, she removed Pendergast's envelope. She reached in and took out a brick of hundred-dollar bills.

The appearance of the money brought a loud expostulation from the wife. Lee did not respond. His eyes were on the cash.

"I have here first month's rent, last month's rent, and a month's deposit." Nora thumped the roll on the tabletop. "Six thousand six hundred dollars. Cash. Bring out the lease."

The apartment was dismal and the rent bordered on outrageous, which was probably why it wasn't gone already. She hoped that hard cash was something Lee could not afford to ignore.

There was another sharp comment from the wife. Lee ignored her. He went into the back, and returned a few minutes later, laying two leases in front of her. They were in Chinese. There was a silence.

"Need reference," said the wife stolidly, switching to English for Nora's benefit. "Need credit check."

Nora ignored her. "Where do I sign?"

"There," the man pointed.

Nora signed *Betsy Winchell* with a flourish on both leases, and then handwrote on each lease a crude receipt: *$6,600 received by Mr. Ling Lee.* "My Uncle Huang will translate it for me. I hope for your sake there's nothing illegal in it. Now you sign. Initial the receipt."

There was a sharp noise from the wife.

Lee signed his name in Chinese; emboldened, it seemed, by the opposition of his wife.

"Now give me the keys and we're done."

"Have to make copy of keys."

"You give me those keys. It's my apartment now. I'll make the copies for you at my own expense. I need to start moving in right away."

Lee reluctantly handed her the keys. Nora took them, folded one of the leases into her pocket, and stood up. "Thank you very much," she said cheerfully, holding out her hand.

Lee shook it limply. As the door closed, Nora heard another sharp irruption of displeasure from the wife. This one sounded as if it might go on for a long time.

THREE

NORA IMMEDIATELY RETURNED TO THE APARTMENT BELOW. O'Shaughnessy appeared by her side as she unlocked the door. Together, they slipped into the living room, and Nora secured the door with deadbolts and chains. Then she moved to the barred window. Two nails stuck out from either side of the lintel, on which someone had once hung a makeshift curtain. She removed her coat and hung it across the nails, blocking the view from outside.

"Cozy place," O'Shaughnessy said, sniffing. "Smells like a crime scene."

Nora didn't answer. She was staring at the floor, already working out the dig in her mind.

While O'Shaughnessy cased the apartment, Nora made a circuit of the living room, examining the floor, gridding it off, plotting her lines of attack. Then she knelt and, taking a penknife from her pocket—a knife her brother, Skip, had given her for her sixteenth birthday and which she never traveled without—eased it between the edges of two bricks. Slowly, deliberately, she cut her way through the crust of grime and old floor wax. She rocked the knife back and forth between the bricks, gently loosening the stonework. Then, bit by bit, she began to work the closest brick from its socket. In a moment it was free. She pulled it out.

Earth. The damp smell rose toward her nostrils. She poked her finger into it: cool, moist, a little slimy. She probed with the penknife, found it compact but yielding, with little gravel or rocks. *Perfect.*

She straightened up, looked around. O'Shaughnessy was standing behind her, looking down curiously.

"What are you doing?" he asked.

"Checking the subflooring."

"And?"

"It's old fill, not cement."

"Is that good?"

"It's outstanding."

"If you say so."

She tapped the brick back into place, then stood. She checked her watch. Three o'clock, Friday afternoon. The Museum would close in two hours.

She turned to O'Shaughnessy. "Look, Patrick, I need you to get up to my office at the Museum, plunder my field locker for some tools and equipment I'll need."

O'Shaughnessy shook his head. "Nothing doing. Pendergast said I was to stay with you."

"I remember. But I'm here now, safe. There must be five locks on that door, I won't be going anywhere. I'll be a lot safer here than walking the streets. Besides, the killer knows where I work. Would you rather *I* went uptown and *you* waited here?"

"Why go anywhere? What's the hurry? Can't we wait until Pendergast is out of the hospital?"

She stared at him. "The clock's ticking, Patrick. There's a killer out there."

O'Shaughnessy looked at her. Hesitated.

"We can't afford to just sit around. I hope you're not going to give me a hard time. I need those tools, and I need them now."

Still, hesitation.

Nora felt her anger rise. "Just do it. Okay?"

O'Shaughnessy sighed. "Double-lock the door behind me, and don't open it for anybody. Not the landlord, not the fire department, not Santa Claus. Only me. Promise?"

Nora nodded. "I promise."

"Good, I'll be back ASAP."

She drew up a quick list of items, gave O'Shaughnessy directions, and locked the door carefully behind him, shutting out the sound of the growing storm. Slowly, she stepped away from the door, her eyes swiveling around the room, coming to rest at last on the brickwork beneath her feet. One hundred years before, Leng, for all his genius, could not have anticipated the reach of modern archaeology. She would excavate this site with the greatest care, sifting through his old laboratory layer by layer, bringing all her skills to bear in order to capture even the smallest piece of evidence. And there *would* be evidence, she knew that. There was no such thing as a barren archaeological site. People—wherever they went, whatever they did—always left a record.

Taking out her penknife, she knelt and, once again, began easing the blade between the old bricks. There was a sudden peal of thunder, louder than any that had come before; she paused, heart beating wildly with terror. She forced her feelings back under control, shaking her head ruefully. No killer was going to stop her from finding out what was beneath this floor. She wondered briefly what Brisbane would say to this work. *The hell with him,* she thought.

She turned the penknife over in her hands, closed it with a sigh. All her professional life, she had unearthed and catalogued human bones without emotion—with no connection to the ancient skeletons beyond a shared humanity. But Mary Greene had proven utterly different. There, outside the girl's house, Pendergast had thrown Mary Greene's short life and awful death into sharp relief. For the first time, Nora realized she had excavated, *handled,* the bones of someone that she could understand, grieve for. More and more, Pendergast's tale of Mary Greene was sinking in, despite her attempts to keep a professional distance. And now, she had almost become another Mary Greene.

That made it personal. Very personal.

Her thoughts were interrupted by the rattle of wind at the door, and another, fainter, rumble of thunder. Nora rose to her knees, opened the penknife again, and began scraping vigorously at the brickwork beneath her feet. It was going to be a long night.

FOUR

THE WIND SHOOK THE BARRED DOOR, AND OCCASIONAL flickers of lightning and grumblings of thunder penetrated the room. Now that O'Shaughnessy had returned, the two worked together, the policeman moving the dirt, Nora focusing on uncovering the details. They labored by the light of a single yellow bulb. The room smelled strongly of decaying earth. The air was close, humid, and stifling.

She had opened a four-square-meter dig in the living room floor. It had been carefully gridded off, and she had stepped down the excavation, each meter grid to a different level, allowing her to climb in and out of the deepening hole. The floor bricks were neatly piled against the far wall. The door leading to the kitchen was open, and through it a large pile of brown dirt was visible, piled in the center of the room atop a sheet of heavy plastic. Beside it was a smaller sheet of plastic, containing bagged items recovered from the digsite.

At last Nora paused, putting her trowel aside to take stock. She removed her safety helmet, drew the back of her hand across her brow, replaced the helmet on her head. It was well past midnight, and she felt exhausted. The excavation at its deepest point had gone down more than four feet below grade: a lot of work. It was difficult, also, to work this rapidly while maintaining a professional excavation.

She turned to O'Shaughnessy. "Take five. I'd like to examine this soil profile."

"About time." He straightened up, resting on his shovel. His brow was streaming with sweat.

Nora shone her flashlight along the carefully exposed wall of dirt, reading it as one might read a book. Occasionally she would shave off a little with a trowel to get a clearer view.

There was a layer of clean fill on the top going down six inches—laid, no doubt, as a base for the more recent brick floor. Below was about three feet of coarser fill, laced with bits of post-1910 crockery and china. But she could see nothing from Leng's laboratory—at least, nothing obvious. Still, she had flagged and bagged everything, by the book.

Beneath the coarse fill, they had struck a layer containing bits of trash, rotting weeds, pieces of mold-blown bottles, soup bones, and the skeleton of a dog: ground debris from the days when the site had been a vacant lot. Under that was a layer of bricks.

O'Shaughnessy stretched, rubbed his back. "Why do we have to dig so far down?"

"In most old cities, the ground level rises at a fixed rate over time: in New York it's about three quarters of a meter every hundred years." She pointed toward the bottom of the hole. "Back then, that *was* ground level."

"So these old bricks below are the original basement flooring?"

"I think so. The floor of the laboratory." *Leng's laboratory.*

And yet it had yielded few clues. There was a remarkable lack of debris, as if the floor had been swept clean. She had found some broken glassware wedged into the cracks of the brick; an old fire grate with some coal; a button; a rotten trolley ticket, a few other odds and ends. It seemed that Leng had wanted to leave nothing behind.

Outside, a fresh flash of lightning penetrated the coat Nora had hung over the window. A second later, thunder rumbled. The single bulb flickered, browned, then brightened once again.

She continued staring thoughtfully at the floor. At last, she spoke. "First, we need to widen the excavation. And then, I think we'll have to go deeper."

"Deeper?" said O'Shaughnessy, a note of incredulity in his voice.

Nora nodded. "Leng left nothing *on* the floor. But that doesn't mean he left nothing *beneath* it."

There was a short, chilly silence.

Outside, Doyers Street lay prostrate under a heavy rain. Water ran down the gutters and disappeared into the storm drains, carrying with it trash, dog turds, drowned rats, rotting vegetables, the guts of fish from the market down the street. The occasional flash of lightning illuminated the darkened facades, shooting darts of light into the curling fogs that licked and eddied about the pavement.

A stooped figure in a derby hat, almost obscured beneath a black umbrella, made its way down the narrow street. The figure moved slowly, painfully, leaning on a cane as it approached. It paused, ever so briefly, before Number 99 Doyers Street; then it drifted on into the miasma of fog, a shadow merging with shadows until one could hardly say that it had been there at all.

FIVE

CUSTER LEANED BACK IN HIS OVERSIZED MEDITERRANEAN office chair with a sigh. It was a quarter to twelve on Saturday morning, and by rights he should have been out with the bowling club, drinking beer with his buddies. He was a precinct commander, for chrissakes, not a homicide detective. Why did they want him in on a frigging Saturday? Goddamn pointless public relations bullshit. He'd done nothing but sit on his ass all morning, listening to the asbestos rattle in the heating ducts. A waste of a perfectly good weekend.

At least Pendergast was out of action for the time being. But what, exactly, had he been up to? When he'd asked O'Shaughnessy about it, the man was damned evasive. You'd think a cop with a record like his would do himself a favor, learn what to kiss and when. Well, Custer had had enough. Come Monday, he was going to tighten the leash on that puppy, but good.

The buzzer on his desk rang, and Custer poked at it angrily. "What the hell is it now? I was not to be disturbed."

"Commissioner Rocker is on line one, Captain," came Noyes's voice, carefully neutral.

Omigod holy shit sonofabitch, thought Custer. His shaking hand hovered over the blinking light on his telephone. What the hell did the commissioner want with him? Hadn't he done everything they'd asked him to do, the mayor, the chief, everybody? Whatever it was, it wasn't his fault . . .

A fat, trembling finger depressed the button.

"Custer?" The commissioner's desiccated voice filled his ear.

"What is it, sir?" Custer squeaked, making a belated effort to lower the pitch of his voice.

"Your man. O'Shaughnessy."

"Yes sir? What about O'Shaughnessy?"

"I'm a little curious here. Why, *exactly,* did he request a copy of the forensic report from the ME's office on the remains found down on Catherine Street? Did you authorize this?" The voice was slow, weary.

What the hell was O'Shaughnessy up to? Custer's mind raced. He could tell the truth, say that O'Shaughnessy must have been disobeying his orders. But that would make him look like a fool, a man who couldn't control his own. On the other hand, he could lie.

He chose the latter, more habitual course.

"Commissioner?" he managed to bring his voice down to a relatively masculine pitch. "I authorized it. You see, we didn't have a copy down here for our files. It's just a formality, you know, dotting every t and crossing every i. We do things by the book, sir."

There was a silence. "Custer, since you are so nimble with aphorisms, you surely know the expression 'Let sleeping dogs lie'?"

"Yes, sir."

"I thought the *mayor* made it clear we were going to let

that *particular* sleeping dog lie." Rocker didn't sound like he had the greatest faith in the mayor's judgment.

"Yes, sir."

"O'Shaughnessy isn't freelancing, is he, Custer? He's not, by any chance, helping that FBI agent while he's laid up—is he?"

"He's a solid officer, loyal and obedient. I asked him to get the report."

"In that case, I'm surprised at you, Custer. Surely you know that once the report is down at the precinct, every cop there will have access to it. Which is one step from laying it on the doorstep of the *New York Times*."

"I'm sorry, sir. I didn't think of that."

"I want that report—*every* copy of that report—sent back up to me. Personally. By courier. You understand? No copy is to remain at precinct."

"Yes, sir." Christ, how was he going to do that? He would have to get it from O'Shaughnessy, the son of a bitch.

"I get the funny feeling, Custer, that you don't quite appreciate the full situation here. This Catherine Street business has nothing to do with any criminal investigation. It is a historical matter. That forensic report *belongs* to Moegen-Fairhaven. It's private property. They paid for it and the remains were found on their land. Those remains have been given a respectful but anonymous burial in a private cemetery, with the appropriate religious ceremonies, all arranged by Moegen-Fairhaven. The matter is closed. Follow me so far?"

"Yes, sir."

"Now, Moegen-Fairhaven is a good friend of the mayor— as the mayor has taken pains to point out to me—and Mr. Fairhaven himself is working very hard to see that he is re-elected. But if this situation gets any more botched up,

Fairhaven might not be so enthusiastic in his support. He might decide to sit this one out. He might even decide to throw his weight behind the other fellow who's running."

"I understand, sir."

"Good. Now we've got a psychopath out there, this so-called Surgeon, carving people up. If you'd focus your talents on that, Custer, I'd appreciate it. Good day."

There was a click as the line went abruptly dead.

Custer sat up in his chair, gripping the phone, his porcine frame trembling. He swallowed, brought his shaking voice under control, and pressed the buzzer on his desk. "Get O'Shaughnessy on the line. Try whatever you need, radio, emergency frequency, cell, home number, whatever."

"He's off duty, Captain," Noyes said.

"I don't give a rat's ass what he is. Get him."

"Yes, sir." And the speaker crackled back into silence.

SIX

NORA TOOK HER TROWEL, KNELT, AND BEGAN PRYING UP one of the old bricks that made up the ancient floor. It was rotten and waterlogged, and it crumbled under the trowel. She quickly plucked out the pieces, then began prying up its neighbors, one after the other. O'Shaughnessy stood above her, watching. They had worked through the night, and past noon of the following day, widening the excavation to eight square meters. She felt weary beyond description. But this was still one task she wanted to do herself.

Once he'd gotten wind of their progress, Pendergast had forced himself out of his hospital bed—despite the fearful protests of the doctors and nurses—and made the journey down to Doyers Street himself. Now he lay near the digsite on an orthopedic mattress, newly delivered from Duxiana. He remained there, arms across his chest, eyes closed, moving infrequently. With his black suit and pallid face, he looked alarmingly like a corpse. At Pendergast's request Proctor, his chauffeur, had delivered a variety of items from the Dakota apartment: a small table, a Tiffany lamp, and an array of medicines, unguents, and French chocolates, along with a stack of obscure books and maps.

The soil beneath the floor of Leng's old laboratory was waterlogged and foul-smelling. Nora cleared a one-meter square of the floor bricks, then began digging a diagonal test trench with her trowel. Anything under the floor would not be deep. There wasn't much farther to go. She was almost in the water table.

She struck something. A deft bit of brushwork revealed a rusted, rotten nineteenth-century umbrella, only its whalebone skeleton intact. She carefully cleared around it, photographed it in situ, then removed it and laid its rotting pieces on a sheet of acid-free specimen paper.

"You've found something?" Pendergast asked, eyes still closed. A long white hand removed a chocolate from a box and placed it in his mouth.

"The remains of an umbrella." She worked more quickly. The dirt was looser, muddier.

Fourteen inches down, in the left-hand corner of the grid, her trowel struck heavily against something. She began clearing away the sodden dirt around it. Then her brush hand jerked aside reflexively. It was a circlet of hair about a smooth dome of brown bone.

A distant rumble of thunder pierced the silence. The storm was still upon them.

She heard a faint intake of breath from O'Shaughnessy.

"Yes?" Pendergast's voice came instantly.

"We've got a skull here."

"Keep digging, if you please." Pendergast didn't sound surprised.

Working carefully with the brush, heart pounding uncomfortably in her chest, Nora cleared away more dirt. The frontal bone came slowly into view, then two eye sockets, slimy, sticky matter still clinging inside. A foul smell rose and she gagged involuntarily. This was no clean Anasazi skeleton that had been buried a thousand years in dry sand.

Plucking her T-shirt up over her nose and mouth, she continued. A bit of nasal bone became exposed, the opening cradling a twisted piece of cartilage. Then, as the maxilla was exposed, came a flash of metal.

"Please describe." Again Pendergast's weak voice broke the silence of the room.

"Give me another minute."

Nora brushed, working down the craniofacial bones. When the face was exposed, she sat back on her heels.

"All right. We have a skull of an older adult male, with some hair and soft matter remaining, probably due to the anaerobic environment of the site. Just below the maxilla there are two silver teeth, partly fallen from the upper jaw, attached to some old bridgework. Below that, just inside the jaws, I see a pair of gold spectacles, one lens of which has black opaque glass."

"Ah. You have found Tinbury McFadden." There was a pause and Pendergast added, "We must keep going. Still to be found are James Henry Perceval and Dumont Burleigh, members of the Lyceum and colleagues of our Dr. Leng. Two people unlucky enough to have also received J. C. Shottum's confidences. The little circle is complete."

"That reminds me," Nora said. "I remembered something, while I was digging last night. The first time I asked Puck to show me the Shottum material, he said in passing that Shottum was quite popular these days. I didn't pay much attention to it then. But after what happened, I began to wonder who had—" She stopped.

"Who had made that particular journey ahead of us," Pendergast finished the thought for her.

Suddenly there was the rattle of the doorknob.

All eyes turned.

The knob rattled, turned, turned again.

There was a series of concussive raps on the door, which reverberated through the small apartment. A pause followed; then a second volley of frantic pounding.

O'Shaughnessy looked up, hand dropping to his automatic. "Who's that?"

A shrill female voice sounded outside the door. "What go on here? What that smell? What you do in there? Open up!"

"It's Mrs. Lee," Nora said as she rose to her feet. "The landlady."

Pendergast lay still. His pale cat's eyes flitted open for a moment, then closed again. He looked as if he was settling in for a nap.

"Open up! What go on in there?"

Nora climbed out of the trench, moved to the door. "What's the problem?" she said, keeping her voice steady. O'Shaughnessy joined her.

"Problem with smell! Open up!"

"There's no smell in here," said Nora. "It must be coming from somewhere else."

"It come from here, up through floor! I smell all night, it much worse now when I come out of apartment. Open up!"

"I'm just cooking, that's all. I've been taking a cooking class, but I guess I'm not very good yet, and—"

"That no cooking smell! Smell like shit! This nice apartment building! I call police!" Another furious volley of pounding.

Nora looked at Pendergast, who lay still, wraith-like, eyes closed. She turned to O'Shaughnessy.

"She wants the police," he said with a shrug.

"But you're not in uniform."

"I've got my shield."

"What are you going to say?"

The pounding continued.

"The truth, of course." O'Shaughnessy slid toward the door, undid the locks, and let the door fall open.

The squat, heavyset landlady stood in the door. Her eyes darted past O'Shaughnessy, saw the gigantic hole in the living room floor, the piles of dirt and bricks beyond, the exposed upper half of a skeleton. A look of profound horror blossomed across her face.

O'Shaughnessy opened his wallet to display his shield, but the woman seemed not to notice. She was transfixed by the hole in the floor, the skeleton grinning up at her from the bottom.

"Mrs.—Lee, was it? I'm Sergeant O'Shaughessy of the New York Police Department."

Still the lady stared, slack-jawed.

"There's been a murder in this apartment," O'Shaughnessy said matter-of-factly. "The body was buried under the floor. We're investigating. I know it's a shock. I'm sorry, Mrs. Lee."

Finally, the woman seemed to take notice of him. She turned slowly, looking first at his face, then at his badge, then at his gun. "Wha—?"

"A murder, Mrs. Lee. In your apartment."

She looked back at the huge hole. Within it, the skeleton lay peacefully, wrapped in its mantle of earth. Above, in the bed, Pendergast lay still, arms crossed over his chest, in a similar attitude of repose.

"Now, Mrs. Lee, I'm going to ask you to go back quietly to your apartment. Tell no one about this. *Call* no one. Lock and bolt your door. Do not let anyone in unless they show you one of these." O'Shaughnessy shoved the badge closer to her face.

"Do you understand, Mrs. Lee?"

She nodded dumbly, eyes wide.

"Now go on upstairs. We need twenty-four hours of absolute quiet. Then of course there will be a large group of police arriving. Medical examiners, forensic experts—it will be a mess. *Then* you can talk. But for now—" He lifted a finger to his lips and pantomimed an exaggerated *shhhhhh*.

Mrs. Lee turned and shuffled up the stairs. Her movements were slow, like a sleepwalker's. Nora heard the upstairs door open, then close. And then all was quiet once again.

In the silence, Pendergast opened one eye. It swiveled around to O'Shaughnessy, then to Nora.

"Well done, you two," he said in a weak voice. And the faintest of smiles played about his lips.

SEVEN

As the squad car carrying Captain Sherwood Custer turned the corner onto Doyers Street, the captain stared through the windshield, tensing at the noisy group of reporters. It was a smallish group, but he could see they were the worst of the lot.

Noyes angled the car into the curb and Custer opened his door, heaving his frame out onto the street. As he approached the brownstone, the reporters began calling to him. And there was the worst of all, that man—Smithbutt, or whatever—arguing with the uniformed officer standing on the front steps. "It isn't fair!" he was crying in an outraged tone, oversized cowlick jiggling atop his head. "You let *him* in, so you've got to let *me* in!"

The officer ignored this, stepping aside to let Custer pass the yellow crime scene tape.

"Captain Custer!" the reporter cried, turning to him: "Commissioner Rocker has refused to speak with the press. Will you comment on the case, please?"

Custer did not respond. *The commissioner,* he thought. The commissioner himself was here. He was going to be chewed out but good. *Let this particular sleeping dog lie,* the man had said. Custer had not only wakened the dog, but it had bitten him in the ass. Thanks to O'Shaughnessy.

They signed him in at the door and Custer stepped through, Noyes following at his heels. They made their way quickly down to the basement apartment. Outside, the reporter could still be heard, voice raised in protest.

The first thing Custer noticed when he stepped into the apartment was a big hole, lots of dirt. There were the usual photographers, lights, forensics, an ME, the SOC people. And there was the commissioner.

The commissioner glanced up and spotted him. A spasm of displeasure went across his face. "Custer!" he called, nodding him over.

"Yes, sir." Custer swallowed, gritted his teeth. *This was it.*

"Congratulations."

Custer froze. Rocker's sarcasm was a bad sign. And right in front of everybody, too.

He stiffened. "I'm sorry, sir, this was completely unauthorized from beginning to end, and I'm personally going to—"

He felt the commissioner's arm snake around his shoulder, pull him closer. Custer could smell stale coffee on his breath. "Custer?"

"Yes sir?"

"Please, just listen," the commissioner muttered. "Don't speak. I'm not here to attend to excuses. I'm here to put you in charge of this investigation."

This was a *really* bad sign. He'd been victimized by the commissioner's sarcasm before, but not like this. Never like this.

Custer blinked. "I'm truly sorry, sir—"

"You're not listening to me, Captain." Arm still around his shoulder, the commissioner steered Custer away from the press of officials, back into the rear of the narrow apartment. "I understand your man O'Shaughnessy had something to do with uncovering this site."

"Yes, and I am going to severely reprimand—"

"Captain, will you let me finish?"

"Yes, sir."

"The mayor has called me twice this morning. He's delighted."

"Delighted?" Custer wasn't sure if this was more sarcasm, or something even worse.

"Delighted. The more attention that gets deflected from the new copycat murders, the happier he is. New murders are very bad for approval ratings. Thanks to this discovery, you're the cop of the hour. For the mayor, at least."

Silence. It was clear to Custer that Rocker didn't fully share the mayor's good opinion.

"So are we crystal-clear, Captain? This is now officially your case."

"What case?" Custer was momentarily confused. Were they opening an official investigation into these old killings, too?

"The *Surgeon* case." Rocker waved his hand dismissively at the huge hole with their skeletons. "This is nothing. This is archaeology. This is not a case."

"Right. Thank you, sir," Custer said.

"Don't thank me. Thank the mayor. It was his, ah, *suggestion* that you handle it."

Rocker let his arm slip from Custer's shoulder. Then he stood back and looked at the captain: a long, appraising glance. "Feel you can do this, Captain?"

Custer nodded. The numbness was beginning to fade.

"The first order of business is damage control. These old murders will give you a day, maybe two, before the public's attention returns to the Surgeon. The mayor may like seeing these old murders getting the attention, but frankly I don't. It'll give the copycat killer ideas, egg him on." He jerked a thumb over his shoulder. "I brought in Bryce Harriman. You know him?"

"No."

"He's the one who first put a finger on the copycat angle. We need to keep him where we can see him. We'll give him an exclusive, but we'll control the information he gets. Understand?"

"Yes, sir."

"Good. He's a nice sort, eager to please. He's waiting out front. Remember to keep the conversation on the *old* bones and on *this* site. Not on the Surgeon or the new killings. The public may be confounding the two, but we're sure as hell not."

Custer turned back toward the living room. But Rocker put out a hand to stop him.

"And, Captain? Once you're done with Harriman, I'd suggest you get to work on this new case of yours. Get *right* to work. Catch that killer. You don't want another, fresher stiff turning up on your watch—do you? Like I said, you've got a little breathing space here. Make use of it."

"Yes, sir."

Rocker continued to peer at him from beneath lowered brows. Then he grunted, nodded, and gestured Custer on ahead of him.

The living room was, if possible, even more crowded than it had been moments before. At the commissioner's signal, a tall, slender man stepped out of the shadows: horn-rimmed glasses, slicked-back hair, tweed jacket, blue oxford shirt, tasseled loafers.

"Mr. Harriman?" Rocker said. "This is Captain Custer."

Harriman gave Custer's hand a manly shake. "Nice to meet you in person, sir."

Custer returned the handshake. Despite his instinctive distrust of the press, he found himself approving of the man's deferential attitude. *Sir.* When was the last time a reporter had called him *sir*?

The commissioner glanced gravely from one man to the other. "Now, if you'll excuse me, Captain? I have to get back to One Police Plaza."

Custer nodded. "Of course, sir."

He watched the man's broad back as it disappeared through the door.

Noyes was suddenly there, in front of Custer, hand extended. "Allow me to be the first to congratulate you, sir."

Custer shook the limp hand. Then he turned back to Harriman, who was smiling beneath the horn-rims, impeccably knotted repp tie snugged against a buttoned-down collar. A dweeb, without doubt. But a very useful dweeb. It occurred to Custer that giving Harriman an exclusive would take that other pesky reporter—the one whose voice was still clamoring out in the street—down a few notches. Slow him down, get him off their asses for a while. It was bracing how quickly he was adjusting to his new responsibility.

"Captain Custer?" the man said, notebook poised.

"Yeah?"

"May I ask you a few questions?"

Custer gestured magnanimously. "Shoot."

EIGHT

O'SHAUGHNESSY STEPPED INTO THE CAPTAIN'S OUTER office, automatically looking around for Noyes. He had a pretty good idea why Custer wanted to see him. He wondered if the subject of the prostitute's two hundred bucks would come up, as it sometimes did when he got a little too independent for some ass-kisser's taste. Normally he wouldn't care; he'd had years to practice letting it all roll off his back. *Ironic,* he thought, *that the shit was about to come down now—now, just when he'd gotten on an investigation he found himself caring about.*

Noyes came around the corner, chewing gum, his arms full of papers, his perpetually wet lower lip hanging loose from a row of brown teeth. "Oh," he said. "It's you." He dropped the pile on his desk, took his sweet time sitting down, then leaned toward a speaker.

"He's here," he called into it.

O'Shaughnessy sat down, watching Noyes. The man always chewed that nasty, old-fashioned, violet-scented gum favored by dowagers and alcoholics. The outer office reeked of it.

Ten minutes later the captain appeared in the door, hiking

up his pants and tucking in his shirt. He jerked his chin at O'Shaughnessy to indicate he was ready for him.

O'Shaughnessy followed him back into the office. The captain sank heavily into his chair. He rolled his eyes toward O'Shaughnessy with a stare that was meant to be tough but only looked baleful.

"Jesus Christ, O'Shaughnessy." He wagged his head from side to side, jowls flapping like a beagle. "Jesus *H.* Christ."

There was a silence.

"Gimme the report."

O'Shaughnessy took a long breath. "No."

"Whaddya mean, *no?*"

"I don't have it anymore. I gave it to Special Agent Pendergast."

The captain stared at O'Shaughnessy for at least a minute. "You *gave* it to that prick?"

"Yes, sir."

"May I ask why?"

O'Shaughnessy did not answer immediately. Fact was, he didn't want to get put off this case. He liked working with Pendergast. He liked it a lot. For the first time in years, he found himself lying awake at night, thinking about the case, trying to fit the pieces together, dreaming up new lines of investigation. Still, he wasn't going to kiss ass. Let the showdown come.

"He requested it. For his investigation. You asked me to assist him, and that's what I did."

The jowls began to quiver. "O'Shaughnessy, I thought I made it clear that you were to *seem* to be helpful, not to *be* helpful."

O'Shaughnessy tried to look puzzled. "I don't think I quite understand you, sir."

The captain rose from his chair with a roar. "You know damn well what I'm talking about."

O'Shaughnessy stood his ground, feigning surprise now as well as puzzlement. "No, sir, I don't."

The jowls began to shake with rage. "O'Shaughnessy, you impudent little—" Custer broke off, swallowed, tried to get himself under control. Sweat had broken out above his thick, rubbery upper lip. He took a deep breath. "I'm putting you down for administrative leave."

God damn it. "On what grounds?"

"Don't give me that. You know why. Disobeying my direct orders, freelancing for that FBI agent, undermining the department—not to mention getting involved in that *excavation* down on Doyers Street."

O'Shaughnessy knew well that the discovery had been a boon to Custer. It had temporarily taken the heat off the mayor, and the mayor had thanked Custer by putting him in charge of the investigation.

"I followed procedure, sir, in my liaison work with Special Agent Pendergast."

"The hell you did. You've kept me in the dark every step of the way, despite these endless goddamn reports you keep filing which you know damn well I don't have time to read. You went way around me to get that report. Christ, O'Shaughnessy, I've given you every opportunity here, and all you do is piss on me."

"I'll file a grievance with the union, sir. And I'd like to state for the record that, as a Catholic, I am deeply offended by your profanity involving the name of Our Savior."

There was an astonished silence, and O'Shaughnessy saw that Custer was about to lose it completely. The captain spluttered, swallowed, clenched and unclenched his fists.

"As for the police union," said Custer, in a strained, high

voice, "bring 'em on. As for the other, don't think you can out-Jesus me, you sanctimonious prick. I'm a churchgoing man myself. Now lay your shield and piece down *here*"— he thumped his desk— "and get your Irish ass out. Go home and boil some potatoes and cabbage. You're on admini-strative leave pending the result of an Internal Affairs investigation. *Another* Internal Affairs investigation, I might add. And at the union hearing, I'm going to ask for your dismissal from the force. With your record, that won't be too hard to justify."

O'Shaughnessy knew this wasn't an empty threat. He removed his gun and badge and dropped them one at a time on the table.

"Is that all, sir?" he asked, as coolly as possible.

With satisfaction, he saw Custer's face blacken with rage yet again. "Is that all? Isn't that enough? You better start pulling your résumé together, O'Shaughnessy. I know a McDonald's up in the South Bronx that needs a rent-a-cop for the graveyard shift."

As O'Shaughnessy left, he noticed that Noyes's eyes— brimming with wet sycophantic satisfaction—followed him out the door.

He paused on the steps of the station house, momentarily blinded by the sunlight. He thought of the many times he'd trudged up and down these stairs, on yet another aimless patrol or pointless piece of bureaucratic busywork. It seemed a little odd that—despite his carefully groomed attitude of nonchalance—he felt more than a twinge of regret. Pendergast and the case would have to make do without him. Then he sighed, shrugged, and descended the steps. His career was over, and that was that.

To his surprise, a familiar car—a Rolls-Royce Silver Wraith—was idling silently at the curb. The door was opened by the invisible figure in the rear. O'Shaughnessy approached, leaned his head inside.

"I've been put on administrative leave," he said to the occupant of the rear seat.

Pendergast, leaning back against the leather, nodded. "Over the report?"

"Yup. And that mistake I made five years ago didn't help any."

"How unfortunate. I apologize for my role in your misfortune. But get in, if you please. We don't have much time."

"Didn't you hear what I said?"

"I did. You're working for me now."

O'Shaughnessy paused.

"It's all arranged. The paperwork is going through as we speak. From time to time, I have need of, ah, consulting specialists." Pendergast patted a sheaf of papers lying on the seat beside him. "It's all spelled out in here. You can sign them in the car. We'll stop by the FBI office downtown and get you a photo ID. It's not a shield, unfortunately, but it should serve almost as well."

"I'm sorry, Mr. Pendergast, but you should know, they're opening an—"

"I know all about it. Get in, please."

O'Shaughnessy climbed in and closed the door behind him, feeling slightly dazed.

Pendergast gestured toward the papers. "Read them, you won't find any nasty surprises. Fifty dollars an hour, guaranteed minimum thirty hours a week, benefits, and the rest."

"Why are you doing this?"

Pendergast gazed at him mildly. "Because I've seen you rise to the challenge. I need a man with the courage of his convictions. I've seen how you work. You know the streets, you can talk to the people in a way I can't. You're one of them. I'm not. Besides, I can't push this case alone. I need someone who knows his way around the byzantine workings of the NYPD. And you have a certain compassion. Remember, I saw that tape. I'm going to need compassion."

O'Shaughnessy reached for the papers, still dazed. Then he stopped.

"On one condition," he said. "You know a lot more about this than you've let on. And I don't like working in the dark."

Pendergast nodded. "You're quite right. It's time we had a talk. And once we've processed your papers, that's the next order of business. Fair enough?"

"Fair enough." And O'Shaughnessy took the papers, scanned them quickly.

Pendergast turned to the driver. "Federal Plaza, please, Proctor. And quickly."

NINE

NORA PAUSED BEFORE THE DEEP ARCHWAY, CARVED OF sand-colored stone streaked with gray. Although it had been recently cleaned, the massive Gothic entrance looked old and forbidding. It reminded Nora of Traitor's Gate at the Tower of London. She half expected to see the iron teeth of a portcullis winking from the ceiling, defenestrating knights peering out of arrow slits above, cauldrons of boiling pitch at the ready.

At the base of an adjoining wall, before a low iron railing, Nora could see the remains of half-burnt candles, flower petals, and old pictures in broken frames. It looked almost like a shrine. And then she realized this arch must be the doorway in which John Lennon was shot, and these trinkets the remains of offerings still left by the faithful. And Pendergast himself had been stabbed nearby, not halfway down the block. She glanced upward. The Dakota rose above her, its Gothic facade overhung with gables and stone decorations. Dark clouds scudded above the grim, shadow-haunted towers. *What a place to live,* she thought. She looked carefully around, studying the landscape with a caution that had become habitual since the chase in the Archives. But there was no obvious sign of danger. She moved toward the building.

Beside the archway, a doorman stood in a large sentry box of bronze and glass, staring implacably out at Seventy-second Street, silent and erect as a Buckingham Palace guard. He seemed oblivious of her presence. But when she stepped beneath the archway, he was before her in a flash, pleasant but unsmiling.

"May I help you?" he asked.

"I have an appointment to see Mr. Pendergast."

"Your name?"

"Nora Kelly."

The guard nodded, as if expecting her. "Southeast lobby," he said, stepping aside and pointing the way. As Nora walked through the tunnel toward the building's interior courtyard, she saw the guard return to his sentry box and pick up a telephone.

The elevator smelled of old leather and polished wood. It rose several floors, came to an unhurried stop. Then the doors slid open to reveal an entryway, a single oak door at its far end, standing open. Within the doorway stood Agent Pendergast, his slender figure haloed in the subdued light.

"So glad you could come, Dr. Kelly, " he said in his mellifluous voice, stepping aside to usher her in. His words were, as always, exceedingly gracious, but there was something tired, almost grim, in his tone. *Still recovering,* Nora thought. He looked thin, almost cadaverous, and his face was even whiter than usual, if such a thing were possible.

Nora stepped forward into a high-ceilinged, windowless room. She looked around curiously. Three of the walls were painted a dusky rose, framed above and below by black molding. The fourth was made up entirely of black marble, over which a continuous sheet of water ran from ceiling to floor. At the base, where the water gurgled quietly into a pool, a cluster of lotus blossoms floated. The room was filled with the soft, pleasant sound of water and the faint perfume of flowers. Two tables of dark lacquer stood nearby. One held a mossy tray in which grew a setting of bonsai trees—dwarf maples, by the look of them. On the other, inside an acrylic display cube, the skull of a cat was displayed on a spider mount. Coming closer, Nora realized that the skull was, in fact, carved from a single piece of Chinese jade. It was a work of remarkable, consummate artistry, the stone so thin it was diaphanous against the black cloth of the base.

Sitting nearby on one of several small leather sofas was Sergeant O'Shaughnessy, in mufti. He was crossing and uncrossing his legs and looking uncomfortable.

Pendergast closed the door and glided toward Nora, hands behind his back.

"May I get you anything? Mineral water? Lillet? Sherry?"

"Nothing, thanks."

"Then if you will excuse me for a moment." And Pendergast disappeared through a doorway that had been set, almost invisibly, into one of the rose-colored walls.

"Nice place," she said to O'Shaughnessy.

"You don't know the half of it. Where'd he get all the dough?"

"Bill Smi— That is, a former acquaintance of mine said he'd heard it was old family money. Pharmaceuticals, something like that."

"Mmm."

They lapsed into silence, listening to the whispering of the water. Within a few minutes, the door opened again and Pendergast's head reappeared.

"If the two of you would be so kind as to come with me?" he asked.

They followed him through the door and down a long, dim hallway. Most of the doors they passed were closed, but Nora caught glimpses of a library—full of leather- and buckram-bound volumes and what looked like a rosewood harpsichord—and a narrow room whose walls were covered with oil paintings, four or five high, in heavy gilt frames. Another, windowless, room had rice paper walls and tatami mats covering its floor. It was spare, almost stark, and—like the rest of the rooms—very dimly lit. Then Pendergast ushered them into a vast, high-ceilinged chamber of dark, exquisitely wrought mahogany. An ornate marble fireplace dominated the far end. Three large windows looked out over Central Park. To the right, a detailed map of nineteenth-century Manhattan covered an entire wall. A large table sat in the room's center. Upon it, several objects resting atop a plastic sheet: two dozen fragments of broken glass pieces, a lump of coal, a rotten umbrella, and a punched tram car ticket.

There was no place to sit. Nora stood back from the table while Pendergast circled it several times in silence, staring intently, like a shark circling its prey. Then he paused, glancing first at her, then at O'Shaughnessy. There was an intensity, even an obsession, in his eyes that she found disturbing.

Pendergast turned to the large map, hands behind his back once again. For a moment, he simply stared at it. Then he began to speak, softly, almost to himself.

"We know where Dr. Leng did his work. But now we are confronted with an even more difficult question. Where did he live? Where did the good doctor hide himself on this teeming island?

"Thanks to Dr. Kelly, we now have some clues to narrow our search. The tram ticket you unearthed was punched for the West Side Elevated Tramway. So it's safe to assume Dr. Leng was a West Sider." He turned to the map, and, using a red marker, drew a line down Fifth Avenue, dividing Manhattan into two longitudinal segments.

"Coal carries a unique chemical signature of impurities, depending on where it is mined. This coal came from a long-defunct mine near Haddonfield, New Jersey. There was only one distributor for this coal in Manhattan, Clark & Sons. They had a delivery territory that extended from 110th Street to 139th Street."

Pendergast drew two parallel lines across Manhattan, one at 110th Street and one at 139th Street.

"Now we have the umbrella. The umbrella is made of silk. Silk is a fiber that is smooth to the touch, but under a microscope shows a rough, almost toothy texture. When it rains, the silk traps particles—in particular, pollen. Microscopic examination of the umbrella showed it to be heavily impregnated with pollen from a weed named *Trismegistus gonfalonii,* commonly known as marsh dropseed. It used to grow in bogs all over Manhattan, but by 1900 its range had been restricted to the marshy areas along the banks of the Hudson River."

He drew a red line down Broadway, then pointed to the small square it bordered. "Thus, it seems reasonable to assume that our Dr. Leng lived west of this line, no more than one block from the Hudson."

He capped the marker, then glanced back at Nora and O'Shaughnessy. "Any comments so far?"

"Yes," said Nora. "You said Clark & Sons delivered coal to this area uptown. But why was this coal found downtown in his laboratory?"

"Leng ran his laboratory in secret. He couldn't have coal delivered there. So he would have brought small amounts of coal down from his house."

"I see."

Pendergast continued to scrutinize her. "Anything else?"

The room was silent.

"Then we can assume our Dr. Leng lived on Riverside Drive between 110th Street and 139th Street, or on one of the side streets between Broadway and Riverside Drive. That is where we must concentrate our search."

"You're still talking hundreds, maybe thousands, of apartment buildings," said O'Shaughnessy.

"Thirteen hundred and five, to be exact. Which brings me to the glassware."

Pendergast silently took another turn around the table, then reached out and picked up a fragment of glass with a pair of rubber-tipped tweezers, holding it into the light.

"I analyzed the residue on this glass. It had been carefully washed, but with modern methods one can detect substances down to parts per trillion. There was a very curious mix of chemicals on this glassware. I found similar chemicals on the glass bits I recovered from the floor of the charnel. Quite a frightening mixture, when you begin to break it down. And there was one rare organic chemical, 1,2 alumino phospho-cyanate, the ingredients for which could only be purchased in five chemists' shops in Manhattan at the time, between 1890 and 1918, when Leng appears to have used his downtown laboratory. Sergeant O'Shaughnessy was most helpful in tracking down their locations."

He made five dots on the map with his marker.

"Let us first assume Dr. Leng purchased his chemicals at the most convenient place. As you can see, there is no shop near his lab downtown, so let us postulate he purchased his chemicals near his house uptown. We can thus eliminate these two East Side shops. That leaves three on the West Side. But this one is too far downtown, so we can eliminate it as well." He made crosses through three of the five dots. "That leaves these two others. The question is, which one?"

Once again, his question was greeted by silence. Pendergast laid down the piece of glass and circled the table yet again, then stopped in front of the map. "He shopped at neither one."

He paused. "Because 1,2 alumino phosphocyanate is a dangerous poison. A person buying it might attract attention. So let us assume, instead, that he shopped at the chemist *farthest* from his haunts: his house, the Museum, the downtown lab. A place where he would not be recognized. Clearly, that has to be *this* one, here, on East Twelfth Street. New Amsterdam Chemists." He drew a line around the dot. "*This* is where Leng shopped for his chemicals."

Pendergast spun around, pacing back and forth before the map. "In a stroke of good fortune, it turns out New Amsterdam Chemists is still in business. There may be records, even be some residual memory." He turned to O'Shaughnessy. "I will ask you to investigate. Visit the establishment, and check their old records. Then search for old people who grew up in the neighborhood, if necessary. Treat it as you would a police investigation."

"Yes, sir."

There was a brief silence. Then Pendergast spoke again.

"I'm convinced Dr. Leng didn't live on any of the side streets between Broadway and Riverside Drive. He lived on Riverside Drive itself. That would narrow things down from over a thousand buildings to less than a hundred."

O'Shaughnessy stared at him. "How do you know Leng lived on the Drive?"

"The grand houses were all along Riverside Drive. You can still see them, mostly broken up into tiny apartments or abandoned now, but they're still there—some of them, anyway. Do you really think Leng would have lived on a side street, in middle-class housing? This man had a great deal of money. I've been thinking about it for some time. He wouldn't want a place that could be walled in by future construction. He'd want light, a healthy flow of fresh air, and a pleasant view of the river. A view that could never be obstructed. I *know* he would."

"But *how* do you know?" O'Shaughnessy asked.

Suddenly, Nora understood. "Because he expected to be there *for a very, very long time.*"

There was a long silence in the cool, spacious room. A slow, and very uncharacteristic, smile gathered on Pendergast's face. "Bravo," he said.

He went to the map, and drew a red line down Riverside Drive, from 139th Street to 110th. "*Here* is where we must look for Dr. Leng."

There was an abrupt, uncomfortable silence.

"You mean, Dr. Leng's house," said O'Shaughnessy.

"No," said Pendergast, speaking very deliberately. "I mean *Dr. Leng.*"

Horse's Tail

ONE

WITH A HUGE SIGH, WILLIAM SMITHBACK JR. SETTLED INTO the worn wooden booth in the rear of the Blarney Stone Tavern. Situated directly across the street from the New York Museum's southern entrance, the tavern was a perennial haunt of Museum staffers. They had nicknamed the place the Bones because of the owner's penchant for hammering bones of all sizes, shapes, and species into every available surface. Museum wags liked to speculate that, were the police to remove the bones for examination, half of the city's missing persons cases still on the books would be solved immediately.

Smithback had spent many long evenings here in years past, notebooks and beer-spattered laptop in attendance, working on various books: his book about the Museum murders; his follow-up book about the Subway Massacre. It had always seemed like a home away from home to him, a refuge against the troubles of the world. And yet tonight, even the Bones held no consolation for him. He recalled a line he'd read somewhere—Brendan Behan, perhaps—about having a thirst so mighty it cast a shadow. That's how he felt.

It had been the worst week of his life—from this terrible

business with Nora to his useless interview with Fairhaven. And to top it all, he'd just been scooped by the frigging *Post*—by his old nemesis Bryce Harriman, no less—twice. First on the tourist murder in Central Park, and then on the bones discovered down on Doyers Street. By rights, that was *his* story. How had that weenie Harriman gotten an exclusive? He couldn't get an exclusive from his own girlfriend, for chrissakes. Who did he know? To think he, Smithback, had been kept outside with the milling hacks while Harriman got the royal treatment, *the inside story* . . . Christ, he needed a drink.

The droopy-eared waiter came over, hangdog features almost as familiar to Smithback as his own.

"The usual, Mr. Smithback?"

"No. You got any of the fifty-year-old Glen Grant?"

"At thirty-six dollars," the waiter said dolefully.

"Bring it. I want to drink something as old as I feel."

The waiter faded back into the dark, smoky atmosphere. Smithback checked his watch and looked around irritably. He was ten minutes late, but it looked like O'Shaughnessy was even later. He hated people who were even later than he was, almost as much as he hated people who were on time.

The waiter rematerialized, carrying a brandy snifter with an inch of amber-colored liquid in the bottom. He placed it reverently before Smithback.

Smithback raised it to his nose, swirled the liquid about, inhaled the heady aroma of Highland malt, smoke, and fresh water that, as the Scots said, had flowed through peat and over granite. He felt better already. As he lowered the glass, he could see Boylan, the proprietor, in the front, handing a black-and-tan over the bar with an arm that looked like it had been carved from a twist of chewing tobacco. And past

Boylan was O'Shaughnessy, just come in and looking about. Smithback waved, averting his eyes from the cheap polyester suit that practically sparkled, despite the dim light and cigar fumes. How could a self-respecting man wear a suit like that?

"'Tis himself," said Smithback in a disgraceful travesty of an Irish accent as O'Shaughnessy approached.

"Ach, aye," O'Shaughnessy replied, easing into the far side of the booth.

The waiter appeared again as if by magic, ducking deferentially.

"The same for him," said Smithback, and then added, "you know, the twelve-year-old."

"Of course," said the waiter.

"What is it?" O'Shaughnessy asked.

"Glen Grant. Single malt scotch. The best in the world. On me."

O'Shaughnessy grinned. "What, you forcing a bluidy Presbyterian drink down me throat? That's like listening to Verdi in translation. I'd prefer Powers."

Smithback shuddered. "That stuff? Trust me, Irish whisky is better suited to degreasing engines than to drinking. The Irish produce better writers, the Scots better whisky."

The waiter went off, returning with a second snifter. Smithback waited as O'Shaughnessy sniffed, winced, took a swig.

"Drinkable," he said after a moment.

As they sipped in silence, Smithback shot a covert glance at the policeman across the table. So far he'd gotten precious little out of their arrangement, although he'd given him a pile on Fairhaven. And yet he found he had come to like the guy: O'Shaughnessy had a laconic, cynical, even fatalistic outlook on life that Smithback understood completely.

Smithback sighed and sat back. "So what's new?"

O'Shaughnessy's face instantly clouded. "They fired me."

Smithback sat up again abruptly. "What? When?"

"Yesterday. Not fired, exactly. Not yet. Put on administrative leave. They're opening an investigation." He glanced up suddenly. "This is just between you and me."

Smithback sat back. "Of course."

"I've got a hearing next week before the union board, but it looks like I'm done for."

"Why? Because you did a little moonlighting?"

"Custer's pissed. He'll bring up some old history. A bribe I took, five years ago. That, along with insubordination and disobeying orders, will be enough to drag me down."

"That fat-assed bastard."

There was another silence. *There's one potential source shot to hell,* Smithback thought. *Too bad. He's a decent guy.*

"I'm working for Pendergast now," O'Shaughnessy added in a very low voice, cradling his drink.

This was even more of a shock. "Pendergast? How so?" Perhaps all was not lost.

"He needed a Man Friday. Someone to pound the pavement for him, help track things down. At least, that's what he said. Tomorrow, I'm supposed to head down to the East Village, snoop around a shop where Pendergast thinks Leng might have bought his chemicals."

"Jesus." Now, this was an interesting development indeed: O'Shaughnessy working for Pendergast, no longer shackled by the NYPD rules about talking to journalists. Maybe this was even better than before.

"If you find something, you'll let me know?" Smithback asked.

"That depends."

"On what?"

"On what you can do for us with that something."

"I'm not sure I understand."

"You're a reporter, right? You do research?"

"It's my middle name. Why, you guys need my help with something?" Smithback suddenly glanced away. "I don't think Nora would like that."

"She doesn't know. Neither does Pendergast."

Smithback looked back, surprised. But O'Shaughnessy didn't look like he planned to say anything else about it. *No use trying to force anything out of this guy,* Smithback thought. *I'll wait till he's good and ready.*

He took a different tack. "So, how'd you like my file on Fairhaven?"

"Fat. Very fat. Thanks."

"Just a lot of bullshit, I'm afraid."

"Pendergast seemed pleased. He told me to congratulate you."

"Pendergast's a good man," Smithback said cautiously.

O'Shaughnessy nodded, sipped. "But you always get the sense he knows more than he lets on. All this talk about how we have to be careful, how our lives are in danger. But he refuses to spell it all out. And then, out of nowhere, he drops a bomb on you." His eyes narrowed. "And that's where you may come in."

Here we go. "Me?"

"I want you to do a little digging. Find something out for me." There was a slight hesitation. "See, I worry the injury may have hit Pendergast harder than we realized. He's got this crazy theory. So crazy, when I heard it, I almost walked out right then."

"Yeah?" Smithback took a casual sip, carefully concealing his interest. He knew very well what a "crazy theory" of Pendergast's could turn out to mean.

"Yeah. I mean, I like this case. I'd hate to turn away from it. But I can't work on something that's nuts."

"I hear that. So what's Pendergast's crazy theory?"

O'Shaughnessy hesitated, longer this time. He was clearly struggling with himself over this.

Smithback gritted his teeth. *Get the man another drink.*

He waved the waiter over. "We'll have another round," he said.

"Make mine Powers."

"Have it your way. Still on me."

They waited for the next round to arrive.

"How's the newspaper business?" O'Shaughnessy asked.

"Lousy. Got scooped by the *Post*. Twice."

"I noticed that."

"I could've used some help there, Patrick. The phone call about Doyers Street was nice, but it didn't get me inside."

"Hey, I gave you the tip, it's up to you to get your ass inside."

"How'd Harriman get the exclusive?"

"I don't know. All I know is, they hate you. They blame you for triggering the copycat killings."

Smithback shook his head. "Probably going to can me now."

"Not for a scoop."

"Two scoops. And Patrick, don't be so naive. This is a bloodsucking business, and you either suck or get sucked." The metaphor didn't have quite the ring Smithback intended, but it conveyed the message.

O'Shaughnessy laughed mirthlessly. "That about sums it up in my business, too." His face grew graver. "But I know what it's like to be canned."

Smithback leaned forward conspiratorially. Time to push a little. "So what's Pendergast's theory?"

O'Shaughnessy took a sip of his drink. He seemed to arrive at some private decision. "If I tell you, you'll use your resources, see if there's any chance it's true?"

"Of course. I'll do whatever I can."

"And you'll keep it to yourself? No story—at least, not yet?"

That hurt, but Smithback managed to nod in agreement.

"Okay." O'Shaughnessy shook his head. "Not that you could print it, anyway. It's totally unpublishable."

Smithback nodded. "I understand." This was sounding better and better.

O'Shaughnessy glanced at him. "Pendergast thinks this guy Leng is still alive. He thinks Leng succeeded in prolonging his life."

This stopped Smithback cold. He felt a shock of disappointment. "Shit, Patrick, that *is* crazy. That's *absurd.*"

"I told you so."

Smithback felt a wave of desperation. This was worse than nothing. Pendergast had gone off the deep end. Everybody knew a copycat killer was at work here. Leng, still alive after a century and a half? The story he was looking for seemed to recede further into the distance. He put his head in his hands. "How?"

"Pendergast believes that the examination of the bones on Doyers Street, the Catherine Street autopsy report, and the Doreen Hollander autopsy results, all show the same exact pattern of marks."

Smithback continued to shake his head. "So Leng's been killing all this time—for, what, the last hundred and thirty years?"

"That's what he thinks. He thinks the guy is still living up on Riverside Drive somewhere."

For a moment, Smithback was silent, toying with the matches. Pendergast needed a long vacation.

"He's got Nora examining old deeds, identifying which houses dating prior to 1900 weren't broken into apartments. Looking for property deeds that haven't gone into probate for a very, very long time. That sort of thing. Trying to track Leng down."

A total waste, Smithback thought. *What's going on with Pendergast?* He finished his now tasteless drink.

"Don't forget your promise. You'll look into it? Check the obituaries, comb old issues of the *Times* for any crumbs you can find? See if there's even a chance Pendergast might be right?"

"Sure, sure." *Jesus, what a joke.* Smithback was now sorry he'd agreed to the arrangement. All it meant was more wasted time.

O'Shaughnessy looked relieved. "Thanks."

Smithback dropped the matches into his pocket, drained his glass. He flagged down the waiter. "What do we owe you?"

"Ninety-two dollars," the man intoned sadly. As usual, there was no tab: Smithback was sure a goodly portion went into the waiter's own pockets.

"Ninety-two dollars!" O'Shaughnessy cried. "How many drinks did you have before I arrived?"

"The good things in life, Patrick, are not free," Smithback said mournfully. "That is especially true of single malt Scotch."

"Think of the poor starving children."

"Think of the poor thirsty journalists. Next time, you pay. Especially if you come armed with a story that crazy."

"I told you so. And I hope you won't mind drinking Powers. No Irishman would be caught dead paying a tab like that. Only a Scotsman would dare charge that much for a drink."

Smithback turned onto Columbus Avenue, thinking. Suddenly, he stopped. While Pendergast's theory was ridiculous, it had given him an idea. With all the excitement about the copycat killings and the Doyers Street find, no one had really followed up on Leng himself. Who was he? Where did he come from? Where did he get his medical degree? What was his connection to the Museum? Where had he lived?

Now this was good.

A story on Dr. Enoch Leng, mass murderer. Yes, yes, this was it. This might just be the thing to save his ass at the *Times.*

Come to think of it, this was better than good. This guy antedated Jack the Ripper. *Enoch Leng: A Portrait of America's First Serial Killer.* This could be a cover story for the *Times Sunday Magazine.* He'd kill two birds with one stone: do the research he'd promised O'Shaughnessy, while getting background on Leng. And he wouldn't be betraying any confidences, of course—because once he'd determined when the man died, that would be the end of Pendergast's crazy theory.

He felt a sudden shiver of fear. What if Harriman was already pursuing the story of Leng? He'd better get to work right away. At least he had one big advantage over Harriman: he was a hell of a researcher. He'd start with the newspaper morgue—look for little notes, mentions of Leng or Shottum or McFadden. And he'd look for more killings with the Leng modus operandi: the signature dissection of the spinal cord. Surely Leng had killed more people than had been found at

Catherine and Doyers Streets. Perhaps some of those other killings had come to light and made the papers.

And then there were the Museum's archives. From his earlier book projects, he'd come to know them backward and forward. Leng had been associated with the Museum. There would be a gold mine of information in there, if only one knew where to find it.

And there would be a side benefit: he might just be able to pass along to Nora the information she wanted about where Leng lived. A little gesture like that might get their relationship back on track. And who knows? It might get Pendergast's investigation back on track, as well.

His meeting with O'Shaughnessy hadn't been a total loss, after all.

TWO

EAST TWELFTH STREET WAS A TYPICAL EAST VILLAGE STREET, O'Shaughnessy thought as he turned the corner from Third Avenue: a mixture of punks, would-be poets, '60s relics, and old-timers who just didn't have the energy or money to move. The street had improved a bit in recent years, but there was still a superfluity of beaten-down tenements among the head shops, wheat-grass bars, and used-record vendors. He slowed his pace, watching the people passing by: slumming tourists trying to look cool; aging punk rockers with very dated spiked purple hair; artists in paint-splattered jeans lugging canvases; drugged-out skinheads in leather with dangling chrome doohickeys. They seemed to give him a wide berth: nothing stood out on a New York City street quite like a plainclothes police officer, even one on administrative leave and under investigation.

Up ahead now, he could make out the shop. It was a little hole-in-the-wall of black-painted brick, shoehorned between brownstones that seemed to sag under the weight of innumerable layers of graffiti. The windows of the shop were thick with dust, and stacked high with ancient boxes and displays, so faded with age and sun that their labels were indecipherable. Small greasy letters above the windows spelled out *New Amsterdam Chemists.*

O'Shaughnessy paused, examining the shopfront. It seemed hard to believe that an old relic like this could survive, what with a Duane Reade on the very next corner. Nobody seemed to be going in or out. The place looked dead.

He stepped forward again, approaching the door. There was a buzzer, and a small sign that read *Cash Only.* He pressed the buzzer, hearing it rasp far, far within. For what seemed a long time, there was no other noise. Then he heard the approach of shuffling footsteps. A lock turned, the door opened, and a man stood before him. At least, O'Shaughnessy thought it was a man: the head was as bald as a billiard ball, and the clothes were masculine, but the face had a kind of strange neutrality that made sex hard to determine.

Without a word, the person turned and shuffled away again. O'Shaughnessy followed, glancing around curiously. He'd expected to find an old pharmacy, with perhaps an ancient soda fountain and wooden shelves stocked with aspirin and liniment. Instead, the shop was an incredible rat's nest of stacked boxes, spiderwebs, and dust. Stifling a cough, O'Shaughnessy traced a complex path toward the back of the store. Here he found a marble counter, scarcely less dusty than the rest of the shop. The person who'd let him in had taken up a position behind it. Small wooden boxes were stacked shoulder high on the wall behind the shopkeeper. O'Shaughnessy squinted at the paper labels slid into copper placards on each box: amaranth, nux vomica, nettle, vervain, hellebore, nightshade, narcissus, shepherd's purse, pearl trefoil. On an adjoining wall were hundreds of glass beakers, and beneath were several rows of boxes, chemical symbols scrawled on their faces in red marker. A book titled *Wortcunning* lay on the counter.

The man—it seemed easiest to think of him as a man—stared back at O'Shaughnessy, pasty face expectant.

"O'Shaughnessy, FBI consultant," O'Shaughnessy said, displaying the identity card Pendergast had secured for him. "I'd like to ask you a few questions, if I might."

The man scrutinized the card, and for a minute O'Shaughnessy thought he was going to challenge it. But the shopkeeper merely shrugged.

"What kind of people visit your shop?"

"It's mostly those wiccans." The man screwed up his face.

"Wiccans?"

"Yeah. Wiccans. That's what they call themselves these days."

Abruptly, O'Shaughnessy understood. "You mean witches."

The man nodded.

"Anybody else? Any, say, doctors?"

"No, nobody like that. We get chemists here, too. Sometimes hobbyists. Health supplement types."

"Anybody who dresses in an old-fashioned, or unusual fashion?"

The man gestured in the vague direction of East Twelfth Street. "They *all* dress in an unusual fashion."

O'Shaughnessy thought for a moment. "We're investigating some old crimes that took place near the turn of the century. I was wondering if you've got any old records I could examine, lists of clientele and the like."

"Maybe," the man said. The voice was high, very breathy.

This answer took O'Shaughnessy by surprise. "What do you mean?"

"The shop burned to the ground in 1924. After it was

rebuilt, my grandfather—he was running the place back then—started keeping his records in a fireproof safe. After my father took over, he didn't use the safe much. In fact, he only used it for storing some possessions of my grandfather's. He passed away three months ago."

"I'm sorry to hear that," O'Shaughnessy said. "How did he die?"

"Stroke, they said. So anyway, a few weeks later, an antiques dealer came by. Looked around the shop, bought a few old pieces of furniture. When he saw the safe, he offered me a lot of money if there was anything of historical value inside. So I had it drilled." The man sniffed. "But there was nothing much. Tell the truth, I'd been hoping for some gold coins, maybe old securities or bonds. The fellow went away disappointed."

"So what was inside?"

"Papers. Ledgers. Stuff like that. That's why I told you, maybe."

"Can I have a look at this safe?"

The man shrugged. "Why not?"

The safe stood in a dimly lit back room, amid stacks of musty boxes and decaying wooden crates. It was shoulder high, made of thick green metal. There was a shiny cylindrical hole where the lock mechanism had been drilled out.

The man pulled the door open, then stepped back as O'Shaughnessy came forward. He knelt and peered inside. Dust motes hung like a pall in the air. The contents of the safe lay in deep shadow.

"Can you turn on some more lights?" O'Shaughnessy asked.

"Can't. Aren't any more."

"Got a flashlight handy?"

The man shook his head. "But hold on a second." He shuffled away, then returned a minute later, carrying a lighted taper in a brass holder.

Jesus, this is unbelievable, O'Shaughnessy thought. But he accepted the candle with murmured thanks and held it inside the safe.

Considering its large size, the safe was rather empty. O'Shaughnessy moved the candle around, making a mental inventory of its contents. Stacks of old newspapers in one corner; various yellowed papers, tied into small bundles; several rows of ancient-looking ledger books; two more modern-looking volumes, bound in garish red plastic; half a dozen shoe boxes with dates scrawled on their faces.

Setting the candle on the floor of the safe, O'Shaughnessy grabbed eagerly at the old ledgers. The first one he opened was simply a shop inventory, for the year 1925: page after page of items, written in a spidery hand. The other volumes were similar: semiannual inventories, ending in 1942.

"When did your father take over the shop?" O'Shaughnessy asked.

The man thought for a moment. "During the war. '41 maybe, or '42."

Makes sense, O'Shaughnessy thought. Replacing the ledgers, he flipped through the stack of newspapers. He found nothing but a fresh cloud of dust.

Moving the candle to one side, and fighting back a rising sense of disappointment, he reached for the bundles of papers. These were all bills and invoices from wholesalers, covering the same period: 1925 to 1942. No doubt they would match the inventory ledgers.

The red plastic volumes were clearly far too recent to be of any interest. That left just the shoe boxes. *One more chance.* O'Shaughnessy plucked a shoe box from the top of the pile, blew the dust from its lid, opened it.

Inside were old tax returns.

Damn it, O'Shaughnessy thought as he replaced the box. He chose another at random, opened the lid. More returns.

O'Shaughnessy sat back on his haunches, candle in one hand and shoe box in the other. *No wonder the antiques dealer left empty-handed,* he thought. *Oh, well. It was worth a try.*

With a sigh, he leaned forward to replace the box. As he did so, he glanced once again at the red plastic folders. It was strange: the man said his father only used the safe for storing things of the grandfather. But plastic was a recent invention, right? Surely later than 1942. Curious, he plucked up one of the volumes and flipped it open.

Within, he saw a dark-ruled page, full of old, handwritten entries. The page was sooty, partially burned, its edges crumbling away into ash.

He glanced around. The proprietor of the shop had moved away, and was rummaging inside a cardboard box.

Eagerly O'Shaughnessy snatched both the plastic volume and its mate from the safe. Then he blew out the candle and stood up.

"Nothing much of interest, I'm afraid." He held up the volumes with feigned nonchalance. "But as a formality, I'd like to take these down to our office, just for a day or two. With your permission, of course. It'll save you and me lots of paperwork, court orders, all that kind of thing."

"Court orders?" the man said, a worried expression coming over his face. "Sure, sure. Keep them as long as you want."

Outside on the street, O'Shaughnessy paused to brush dust from his shoulders. Rain was threatening, and lights were coming on in the shotgun flats and coffeehouses that lined the street. A peal of distant thunder sounded over the hum of traffic. O'Shaughnessy turned up the collar of his jacket and tucked the volumes carefully under one arm as he hurried off toward Third Avenue.

From the opposite sidewalk, in the shadow of a brownstone staircase, a man watched O'Shaughnessy depart. Now he came forward, derby hat low over a long black coat, cane tapping lightly on the sidewalk, and—after looking carefully left and right—slowly crossed the street, in the direction of New Amsterdam Chemists.

THREE

BILL SMITHBACK LOVED THE NEW YORK TIMES NEWSPAPER morgue: a tall, cool room with rows of metal shelves groaning under the weight of leather-bound volumes. On this particular morning, the room was completely empty. It was rarely used anymore by other reporters, who preferred to use the digitized, online editions, which went back only twenty-five years. Or, if necessary, the microfilm machines, which were a pain but relatively fast. Still, Smithback found there was nothing more interesting, or so curiously useful, as paging through the old numbers themselves. You often found little strings of information in successive issues—or on adjoining pages—that you would have missed by cranking through reels of microfilm at top speed.

When he proposed to his editor the idea of a story on Leng, the man had grunted noncommittally—a sure sign he liked it. As he was leaving, he heard the bug-eyed monster mutter: "Just make damn sure it's better than that Fairhaven piece, okay? Something with *marrow*."

Well, it would be better than Fairhaven. It *had* to be.

It was afternoon by the time he settled into the morgue. The librarian brought him the first of the volumes he'd requested, and he opened it with reverence, inhaling the smell of decaying wood pulp, old ink, mold, and dust. The volume was dated January 1881, and he quickly found the article he was looking for: the burning of Shottum's cabinet. It was a front-page story, with a handsome engraving of the flames. The article mentioned that the eminent Professor John C. Shottum was missing and feared dead. Also missing, the article stated, was a man named Enoch Leng, who was vaguely billed as a boarder at the cabinet and Shottum's "assistant." Clearly, the writer knew nothing about Leng.

Smithback paged forward until he found a follow-up story on the fire, reporting that remains believed to be Shottum had been found. No mention was made of Leng.

Now working backward, Smithback paged through the city sections, looking for articles on the Museum, the Lyceum, or any mention of Leng, Shottum, or McFadden. It was slow going, and Smithback often found himself sidetracked by various fascinating, but unrelated, articles.

After a few hours, he began to get a little nervous. There were plenty of articles on the Museum, a few on the Lyceum, and even occasional mentions of Shottum and his colleague, Tinbury McFadden. But he could find nothing at all on Leng, except in the reports of the meetings of the Lyceum, where a "Prof. Enoch Leng" was occasionally listed among the attendees. Leng clearly kept a low profile.

This is going nowhere, fast, he thought.

He launched into a second line of attack, which promised to be much more difficult.

Starting in 1917, the date that Enoch Leng abandoned his Doyers Street laboratory, Smithback began paging forward, looking for any murders that fit the profile. There were 365 editions of the *Times* every year. In those days, murders were a rare enough occurrence to usually land on the front page,

so Smithback confined himself to perusing the front pages—
and the obituaries, looking for the announcement of Leng's
death which would interest O'Shaughnessy as well as
himself.

There were many murders to read about, and a number of
highly interesting obituaries, and Smithback found himself
fascinated—too fascinated. It was slow going.

But then, in the September 10, 1918, edition, he came
across a headline, just below the fold: *Mutilated Body in
Peck Slip Tenement.* The article, in an old-fashioned attempt
to preserve readers' delicate sensibilities, did not go into
detail about what the mutilations were, but it appeared to
involve the lower back.

He read on, all his reporter's instincts aroused once again.
So Leng was still active, still killing, even after he abandoned
his Doyers Street lab.

By the end of the day he had netted a half-dozen
additional murders, about one every two years, that could
be the work of Leng. There might have been others,
undiscovered; or it might be that Leng had stopped hiding the
bodies and was simply leaving them in tenements in widely
scattered sections of the city. The victims were always
homeless paupers. In only one case was the body even
identified. They had all been sent to Potter's Field for burial.
As a result, nobody had remarked on the similarities. The
police had never made the connection among them.

The last murder with Leng's modus operandi seemed to
occur in 1930. After that, there were plenty of murders, but
none involving the "peculiar mutilations" that were Leng's
signature.

Smithback did a quick calculation: Leng appeared in New
York in the 1870s—probably as a young man of, say, thirty.

In 1930, he would have been over eighty. So why did the murders cease?

The answer was perfectly obvious: Leng had died. He hadn't found an obituary; but then, Leng had kept such a low profile that an obituary would have been highly unlikely.

So much for Pendergast's theory, thought Smithback.

And the more he thought about it, the more he felt sure that Pendergast couldn't really believe such an absurd thing. No; Pendergast was throwing this out as a red herring for some devious purpose of his own. That was Pendergast through and through—artful, winding, oblique. You never knew what he was really thinking, or what his plan was. He would explain all this to O'Shaughnessy the next time he saw him; no doubt the cop would be relieved to hear Pendergast hadn't gone off the deep end.

Smithback scanned another year's worth of obituaries, but nothing on Leng appeared. Figures: the guy just cast no shadow at all on the historical record. It was almost creepy.

He checked his watch: quitting time. He'd been at it for ten straight hours.

But he was off to a good start. In one stroke, he'd uncovered another half-dozen unsolved murders which could likely be attributed to Leng. He had maybe two more days before his editor started demanding results. More, if he could show his work was turning up some nuggets of gold.

He eased himself out of the comfortable chair, rubbed his hands together. Now that he'd combed the public record, he was ready to take the next step: Leng's private record.

One thing the day's research had revealed was that Leng had been a guest researcher at the Museum. Smithback knew that, back then, all visiting scientists had to undergo an academic review in order to gain unfettered access to the collections. The review gave such details as the person's age, education, degrees, fields of specialty, publications, marital status, and address. This might lead to other treasure troves of documents—deeds, leases, legal actions, so forth. Perhaps Leng could hide from the public eye—but the Museum's records would be a different story.

By the time Smithback was done, he would know Leng like a brother.

The thought gave him a delicious shudder of anticipation.

FOUR

O'SHAUGHNESSY STOOD ON THE STEPS OUTSIDE THE
Jacob Javits Federal Building. The rain had stopped, and
puddles lay here and there in the narrow streets of lower
Manhattan. Pendergast had not been at the Dakota, and he
was not here, at the Bureau. O'Shaughnessy felt an odd blend
of emotions: impatience, curiosity, eagerness. He'd been
almost disappointed that he couldn't show his find to
Pendergast right away. Pendergast would surely see the value
of the discovery. Maybe it would be the clue they needed to
break the case.

He ducked behind one of the building's granite pillars to
inspect the journals once again. His eye ran down the
columned pages, the countless entries of faded blue ink. It
had everything: names of purchasers, lists of chemicals,
amounts, prices, delivery addresses, dates. Poisons were
listed in red. Pendergast was going to *love* this. Of course,
Leng would have made his purchases under a pseudonym,
probably using a false address—but he would have had to
use the *same* pseudonym for each purchase. Since
Pendergast had already compiled a list of at least some of
the rare chemicals Leng had used, it would be a simple matter

to match that with the purchases in this book, and, through that, discover Leng's pseudonym. If it was a name Leng used in other transactions, this little book was going to take them very far indeed.

O'Shaughnessy glanced at the volumes another minute, then tucked them back beneath his arm and began walking thoughtfully down Broadway, toward City Hall and the subway. The volumes covered the years 1917 through 1923, antedating the fire that burned the chemist's shop. Clearly, they'd been the only things to survive the fire. They had been in the possession of the grandfather, and the father had had them rebound. That was why the antiques dealer hadn't bothered to examine them: they looked modern. It had been sheer luck that he himself had—

Antiques dealer. Now that he thought about it, it seemed suspicious that some dealer just happened to walk into the store a few weeks after the old man's death, interested in the safe. Perhaps that death hadn't been an accident, after all. Perhaps the copycat killer had been there *before* him, looking for more information on Leng's chemical purchases. But no—that was impossible. The copycat killings had begun as a result of the article. This had happened before. O'Shaughnessy chastised himself for not getting a description of the dealer. Well, he could always go back. Pendergast might want to come along himself.

Suddenly, he stopped. Of their own accord, his feet had taken him past the subway station to Ann Street. He began to turn back, then hesitated. He wasn't far, he realized, from 16 Water Street, the house where Mary Greene had lived. Pendergast had already been down there with Nora, but O'Shaughnessy hadn't seen it. Not that there was anything to see, of course. But now that he was committed to this case, he wanted to see everything, miss nothing. He thought back to the Metropolitan Museum of Art: to the pathetic bit of dress, the desperate note.

It was worth a ten-minute detour. Dinner could wait.

He continued down Ann Street, then turned onto Gold, whistling *Casta Diva* from Bellini's *Norma.* It was Maria Callas's signature piece, and one of his favorite arias. He was in high spirits. Detective work, he was rediscovering, could actually be fun. And he was rediscovering something else: he had a knack for it.

The setting sun broke through the clouds, casting his own shadow before him, long and lonely down the street. To his left lay the South Street Viaduct and, beyond, the East River piers. As he walked, office and financial buildings began giving way to tenements—some sporting re-pointed brick facades, others vacant and hollow-looking.

It was growing chilly, but the last rays of the sun felt good on his face. He cut left onto John Street, heading toward the river. Ahead lay the rows of old piers. A few had been asphalted and still in use; others tilted into the water at alarming angles; and some were so decayed they were nothing more than double rows of posts, sticking out of the water. As the sun dipped out of sight, a dome of afterglow lay across the sky, deep purple grading to yellow against a rising fog. Across the East River, lights were coming on in the low brownstones of Brooklyn. He quickened his pace, seeing his breath in the air.

It was as he passed Pearl Street that O'Shaughnessy began to feel that he was being followed. He wasn't sure why, exactly; if, subliminally, he had heard something, or if it was simply the sixth sense of a beat cop. But he kept walking, not checking his stride, not turning around. Administrative leave or no, he had his own .38 Special strapped under his arm, and he knew how to use it. Woe to the mugger who thought he looked like an easy target.

He stopped, glancing along the tiny, crooked maze of streets that led down to the waterfront. As he did so, the feeling grew stronger. O'Shaughnessy had long ago learned to trust such feelings. Like most beat cops, he had developed a highly sensitive street radar that sensed when something was wrong. As a cop, you either developed this radar fast, or you got your ass shot off and returned to you, gift-wrapped by St. Peter in a box with a nice pretty red ribbon. He'd almost forgotten he had the instinct. It had seen years of disuse, but such things died hard.

He continued walking until he reached the corner of Burling Slip. He turned the corner, stepping into the shadows, and quickly pressed himself against the wall, removing his Smith & Wesson at the same time. He waited, breathing shallowly. He could hear the faint sound of water lapping the piers, the distant sound of traffic, a barking dog. But there was nothing else.

He cast an eye around the corner. There was still enough light to see clearly. The tenements and dockside warehouses looked deserted.

He stepped out into the half-light, gun ready, waiting. If somebody was following, they'd see his gun. And they would go away.

He slowly reholstered the weapon, looked around again, then turned down Water Street. Why did he still feel he was being followed? Had his instincts rung a false alarm, after all?

As he approached the middle of the block, and Number 16, he thought he saw a dark shape disappear around the corner, thought he heard the scrape of a shoe on pavement.

He sprang forward, thoughts of Mary Greene forgotten, and whipped around the corner, gun drawn once again.

Fletcher Street stretched ahead of him, dark and empty. But at the far corner a street lamp shone, and in its glow he could see a shadow quickly disappearing. It had been unmistakable.

He sprinted down the block, turned another corner. Then he stopped.

A black cat strolled across the empty street, tail held high, tip twitching with each step. He was a few blocks downwind of the Fulton Fish Market, and the stench of seafood wafted into his nostrils. A tugboat's horn floated mournfully up from the harbor.

O'Shaughnessy laughed ruefully to himself. He was not normally predisposed to paranoia, but there was no other word for it. He had been chasing a cat. This case must be getting to him.

Hefting the journals, he continued south, toward Wall Street and the subway.

But this time, there was no doubt: footsteps, and close. A faint cough.

He turned, pulled his gun again. Now it was dark enough that the edges of the street, the old docks, the stone doorways, lay in deep shadow. Whoever was following him was both persistent and good. This was not some mugger. And the cough was bullshit. The man *wanted* him to know he was being followed. The man was trying to spook him, make him nervous, goad him into making a mistake.

O'Shaughnessy turned and ran. Not because of fear, really, but because he wanted to provoke the man into following. He ran to the end of the block, turned the corner, continuing halfway down the next block. Then he stopped, silently retraced his steps, and melted into the shadow of a doorway. He thought he heard footsteps running down the block. He braced himself against the door behind him, and waited, gun drawn, ready to spring.

Silence. It stretched on for a minute, then two, then five. A cab drove slowly by, twin headlights lancing through the fog and gloom. Cautiously, O'Shaughnessy eased his way out of the doorway, looked around. All was deserted once again. He began making his way back down the sidewalk in the direction from which he'd come, moving slowly, keeping close to the buildings. Maybe the man had taken a different turn. Or given up. Or maybe, after all, it was only his imagination.

And that was when the dark figure lanced out of an adjacent doorway—when something came down over his head and tightened around his neck—when the sickly sweet chemical odor abruptly invaded his nostrils. One of O'Shaughnessy's hands reached for the hood, while the other convulsively squeezed off a shot. And then he was falling, falling without end . . .

The sound of the shot reverberated down the empty street, echoing and reechoing off the old buildings, until it died away. And silence once more settled over the docks and the now empty streets.

FIVE

PATRICK O'SHAUGHNESSY AWOKE VERY SLOWLY. HIS HEAD felt as if it had been split open with an axe, his knuckles throbbed, and his tongue was swollen and metallic in his mouth. He opened his eyes, but all was darkness. Fearing he'd gone blind, he instinctively drew his arms toward his face. He realized, with a kind of leaden numbness, that they were restrained. He tugged, and something rattled.

Chains. He was shackled with chains.

He moved his legs and found they were chained as well.

Almost instantly, the numbness fled, and cold reality flooded over him. The memory of the footsteps, the cat-and-mouse in the deserted streets, the smothering hood, returned with stark, pitiless clarity. For a moment, he struggled fiercely, a terrible panic bubbling up in his chest. Then he lay back, trying to master himself. *Panic's not going to solve anything. You have to think.*

Where was he?

In a cell of some sort. He'd been taken prisoner. But by whom?

Almost as soon as he asked this question, the answer came: by the copycat killer. By the Surgeon.

The fresh wave of panic that greeted this realization was cut short by a sudden shaft of light—bright, even painful after the enveloping darkness.

He looked around quickly. He was in a small, bare room of rough-hewn stone, chained to a floor of cold, damp concrete. One wall held a door of rusted metal, and the light was streaming in through a small slot in its face. The light suddenly diminished, and a voice sounded in the slot. O'Shaughnessy could see wet red lips moving.

"Please do not discompose yourself," the voice said soothingly. "All this will be over soon. Struggle is unnecessary."

The slot rattled shut, and O'Shaughnessy was once again plunged into darkness.

He listened as the retreating steps rang against the stone floor. It was all too clear what was coming next. He'd seen the results at the medical examiner's office. The Surgeon would come back; he'd come back, and . . .

Don't think about that. Think about how to escape.

O'Shaughnessy tried to relax, to concentrate on taking long, slow breaths. Now his police training helped. He felt calmness settle over him. No situation was ever hopeless, and even the most cautious criminals made mistakes.

He'd been stupid, his habitual caution lost in his excitement over finding the ledgers. He'd forgotten Pendergast's warning of constant danger.

Well, he wouldn't be stupid any longer.

All this will be over soon, the voice had said. That meant it wouldn't be long before he'd be coming back. O'Shaughnessy would be ready.

Before the Surgeon could do anything, he'd have to remove the shackles. And that's when O'Shaughnessy would jump him.

But the Surgeon was clearly no fool. The way he'd

shadowed him, ambushed him: that had taken cunning, strong nerves. If O'Shaughnessy merely pretended to be asleep, it wouldn't be enough.

This was it: do or die. He'd have to make it good.

He took a deep breath, then another. And then, closing his eyes, he smashed the shackles of his arm against his forehead, raking them laterally from left to right.

The blood began to flow almost at once. There was pain, too, but that was good: it kept him sharp, gave him something to think about. Wounds to the forehead tended to bleed a lot; that was good, too.

Now he carefully lay to one side, positioning himself to look as if he'd passed out, scraping his head against the rough wall as he slumped to the floor. The stone felt cold against his cheek; the blood warm as it trickled through his eyelashes, down his nose. It would work. It would work. He didn't want to go out like Doreen Hollander, torn and stiff on a morgue gurney.

Once again, O'Shaughnessy quelled a rising panic. It would be over soon. The Surgeon would return, he'd hear the footsteps on the stones. The door would open. When the shackles were removed, he'd surprise the man, overwhelm him. He'd escape with his life, collar the copycat killer in the process.

Stay calm. Stay calm. Eyes shut, blood trickling onto the cold damp stone, O'Shaughnessy deliberately turned his thoughts to opera. His breathing grew calmer. And soon, in his mind, the bleak walls of the little cell began to ring with the exquisitely beautiful strains of *O Isis Und Osiris,* rising effortlessly toward street level and the inviolate sky far above.

SIX

PENDERGAST STOOD ON THE BROAD PAVEMENT, SMALL brown package beneath one arm, looking thoughtfully up at the brace of lions that guarded the entrance to the New York Public Library. A brief, drenching rain had passed over the city, and the headlights of the buses and taxis shimmered in countless puddles of water. Pendergast raised his eyes from the lions to the facade behind them, long and imposing, heavy Corinthian columns rising toward a vast architrave. It was past nine P.M., and the library had long since closed: the tides of students, researchers, tourists, unpublished poets and scholars that swirled about its portals by day had receded hours before.

He glanced around once more, eyes sweeping the stone plaza and the sidewalk beyond. Then he adjusted the package beneath his arm, and made his way slowly up the broad stairs.

To one side of the massive entrance, a smaller door had been set into the granite face of the library. Pendergast approached it, rapped his knuckles lightly on the bronze. Almost immediately it swung inward, revealing a library guard. He was very tall, with closely cropped blond hair, heavily muscled. A copy of *Orlando Furioso* was in one meaty hand.

"Good evening, Agent Pendergast," the guard said. "How are you this evening?"

"Quite well, Francis, thank you," Pendergast replied. He nodded toward the book. "How are you enjoying Ariosto?"

"Very much. Thanks for the suggestion."

"I believe I recommended the Bacon translation."

"Nesmith in the microfiche department has one. The others are on loan."

"Remind me to send you down a copy."

"I'll do that, sir. Thanks."

Pendergast nodded again and passed on, through the entrance hall and up the marble stairs, hearing nothing but the sound of his own footsteps. At the entrance to Room 315—the Main Reading Room—he paused again. Inside, ranks of long wooden tables lay beneath yellow pools of light. Pendergast entered, gliding toward a vast construction of dark wood that divided the Reading Room into halves. By day, this was the station from which library workers accepted book requests from patrons and sent them down to the subterranean stacks by pneumatic tube. But now, with the fall of night, the receiving station was silent and empty.

Pendergast opened a door at one end of the receiving station, stepped inside, and made his way to a small door, set into a frame beside a long series of dumbwaiters. He opened it and descended the staircase beyond.

Beneath the Main Reading Room were seven levels of stacks. The first six levels were vast cities of shelving, laid out in precise grids that went on, row after row, stack after stack. The ceilings of the stacks were low, and the tall shelves of books claustrophobic. And yet, as he walked in the faint light of the first level—taking in the smell of dust, and mildew, and decomposing paper—Pendergast felt a rare sense of peace. The pain of his stab wound, the heavy burden of the case at hand, seemed to ease. At every turn, every intersection, his mind filled with the memory of some prior perambulation: journeys of discovery, literary expeditions that had frequently ended in investigative epiphanies, abruptly solved cases.

But there was no time now for reminiscing, and Pendergast moved on. Reaching a narrow, even steeper staircase, he descended deeper into the stacks.

At last, Pendergast emerged from the closet-like stairwell onto the seventh level. Unlike the flawlessly catalogued levels above it, this was an endless rat's nest of mysterious pathways and cul-de-sacs, rarely visited despite some astonishing collections known to be buried here. The air was close and stuffy, as if it had—like the volumes it surrounded—not circulated for decades. Several corridors ran away from the stairwell, framed by bookcases, crossing and recrossing at strange angles.

Pendergast paused momentarily. In the silence, his hyperacute sense of hearing picked up a very faint scratching: colonies of silverfish, gorging their way through an endless supply of pulp.

And there was another sound, too: louder and sharper. *Snip.*

Pendergast turned toward the sound, tracking it through the stacks of books, angling first one way, then another. The sound grew nearer.

Snip. Snip.

Up ahead, Pendergast made out a halo of light. Turning a final corner, he saw a large wooden table, brilliantly lit by a dentist's O-ring lamp. Several objects were arrayed along one edge of the table: needle, a spool of heavy filament, a pair of white cotton gloves, a bookbinder's knife, a glue pen. Next to them was a stack of reference works: Blades's *The Enemies of Books*; Ebeling's *Urban Entomology*; Clapp's *Curatorial Care of Works of Art on Paper.* On a book truck beside the table sat a tall pile of old volumes in various states of decomposition, covers frayed, hinges broken, spines torn.

A figure sat at the table, back to Pendergast. A confusion of long hair, white and very thick, streamed down from the skull onto the hunched shoulders. *Snip.*

Pendergast leaned against the nearest stack and—keeping a polite distance—rapped his knuckles lightly against the metal.

"I hear a knocking," the figure quoted, in a high yet clearly masculine tone. He did not turn his head. *Snip.*

Pendergast knocked again.

"Anon, anon!" the man responded.

Snip.

Pendergast knocked a third time, more sharply.

The man straightened his shoulders with an irritable sigh. "Wake Duncan with thy knocking!" he cried. "I would thou couldst."

Then he laid aside a pair of library scissors and the old book he had been rebinding, and turned around.

He had thin white eyebrows to match the mane of hair, and the irises of his eyes were yellow, giving him a gaze that seemed leonine, almost feral. He saw Pendergast, and his old withered face broke into a smile. Then he caught sight of the package beneath Pendergast's arm, and the smile broadened.

"If it isn't Special Agent Pendergast!" he cried. "The extra-special, *Special* Agent Pendergast."

Pendergast inclined his head. "How are you, Wren?"

"I humbly thank thee, well, well." The man gestured a

bony hand toward the book truck, the pile of books waiting to be repaired. "But there is so little time, and so many damaged children."

The New York Public Library harbored many strange souls, but none was stranger than the specter known as Wren. Nobody seemed to know anything about him: whether Wren was his first name, or his last, or even his real name at all. Nobody seemed to know where he'd come from, or whether he was officially employed by the library. Nobody knew where or what he ate—some speculated that he dined on library paste. The only things known about the man was that he had never been seen to leave the library, and that he had a pathfinder's instinct for the lost treasures of the seventh level.

Wren looked at his guest, venal yellow eyes sharp and bright as a hawk's. "You don't look like yourself today," he said.

"No doubt." Pendergast said no more, and Wren seemed not to expect it.

"Let's see. Did you find—what was it again? Oh, yes— that old Broadway Water Company survey and the Five Points chapbooks useful?"

"Very much so."

Wren gestured toward the package. "And what are you lending me today, *hypocrite lecteur?*"

Pendergast leaned away from the bookcase, brought the package out from beneath his arm. "It's a manuscript of *Iphigenia at Aulis,* translated from the ancient Greek into Vulgate."

Wren listened, his face betraying nothing.

"The manuscript was illuminated at the old monastery of Sainte-Chapelle in the late fourteenth century. One of the last works they produced before the terrible conflagration of 1397."

A spark of interest flared in the old man's yellow eyes.

"The book caught the attention of Pope Pius III, who pronounced it sacrilegious and ordered every copy burnt. It's also notable for the scribbles and drawings made by the scribes in the margins of the manuscript. They are said to depict the lost text of Chaucer's fragmentary 'Cook's Tale.'"

The spark of interest abruptly burned hot. Wren held out his hands.

Pendergast kept the package just out of reach. "There is one favor I'd request in return."

Wren retracted his hands. "Naturally."

"Have you heard of the Wheelwright Bequest?"

Wren frowned, shook his head. White locks flew from side to side.

"He was the president of the city's Land Office from 1866 to 1894. He was a notorious packrat, and ultimately donated a large number of handbills, circulars, broadsides, and other period publications to the Library."

"That explains why I haven't heard of it," Wren replied. "It sounds of little value."

"In his bequest, Wheelwright also made a sizable cash donation."

"Which explains why the bequest would still be extant."

Pendergast nodded.

"But it would have been consigned to the seventh level."

Pendergast nodded again.

"What's your interest, *hypocrite lecteur*?"

"According to the obituaries, Wheelwright was at work on a scholarly history of wealthy New York landowners when he died. As part of his research, he'd kept copies of all the Manhattan house deeds that passed through his office for properties over $1,000. I need to examine those house deeds."

Wren's expression narrowed. "Surely that information could be more easily obtained at the New-York Historical Society."

"Yes. So it should have been. But some of the deeds are inexplicably missing from their records: a swath of properties along Riverside Drive, to be precise. I had a man at the Society look for them, without success. He was most put out by their absence."

"So you've come to me."

In response, Pendergast held out the package.

Wren took it eagerly, turned it over reverently in his hands, then slit the wrapping paper with his knife. He placed the package on the table and began carefully peeling away the bubble wrap. He seemed to have abruptly forgotten Pendergast's presence.

"I'll be back to examine the bequest—and retrieve my illuminated manuscript—in forty-eight hours," Pendergast said.

"It may take longer," Wren replied, his back to Pendergast. "For all I know, the bequest no longer exists."

"I have great faith in your abilities."

Wren murmured something inaudible. He donned the gloves, gently unbuckled the cloisonné enamel fastenings, stared hungrily at the hand-lettered pages.

"And Wren?"

Something in Pendergast's tone made the old man look over his shoulder.

"May I suggest you find the bequest *first,* and contemplate the manuscript *later*? Remember what happened two years ago."

Wren's face took on a look of shock. "Agent Pendergast, you know I *always* put your interests first."

Pendergast looked into the crafty old face, now full of hurt and indignation. "Of course you do."

And then he abruptly vanished into the shadowy stacks.

Wren blinked his yellow eyes, then turned his attention back to the illuminated manuscript. He knew exactly where the bequest was—it would be a work of fifteen minutes to locate. That left forty-seven and three-quarter hours to examine the manuscript. Silence quickly returned. It was almost as if Pendergast's presence had been merely a dream.

SEVEN

THE MAN WALKED UP RIVERSIDE DRIVE, HIS STEPS SHORT and precise, the metal ferrule of his cane making a rhythmic click on the asphalt. The sun was rising over the Hudson River, turning the water an oily pink, and the trees in Riverside Park stood silently, motionless, in the chill autumn air. He inhaled deeply, his olfactory sense working through the trackless forest of city smells: the tar and diesel coming off the water, dampness from the park, the sour reek of the streets.

He turned the corner, then paused. In the rising light, the short street was deserted. One block over, he could hear the sounds of traffic on Broadway, see the faint light from the shops. But here it was very quiet. Most of the buildings on the street were abandoned. His own building, in fact, stood beside a site where, many years before, a small riding ring for Manhattan's wealthiest young ladies had been. The ring was long gone, of course, but in its place stood a small, unnamed service drive off the main trunk of Riverside, which served to insulate his building from traffic. The island formed by the service drive sported grass and trees, and a statue of Joan of Arc. It was one of the quieter, more forgotten places on the island of Manhattan—forgotten by all, perhaps, save him. It had the additional advantage of being roamed by nocturnal gangs and having a reputation for being dangerous. It was all very convenient.

He slipped down a carriageway, through a side door and into a close, musty space. By feel—it was dark, with the windows securely boarded over—he made his way down a dim corridor, then another, to a closet door. He opened it. The closet was empty. He stepped inside, turned a knob in the rear wall. It opened noiselessly, revealing stone steps leading down.

At the bottom of the steps, the man stopped, feeling along the wall until his fingers found the ancient light switch. He twisted it, and a series of bare bulbs came on, illuminating an old stone passageway, dank and dripping with moisture. He hung his black coat on a brass hook, placed his bowler hat on an adjoining hat rack, and dropped his cane into an umbrella stand. Then he moved down the passageway, feet ringing against the stonework, until he reached a heavy iron door, a rectangular slot set high into its face.

The slot was closed.

The man paused a moment outside the room. Then he reached into his pocket for a key, unlocked the iron door, and pushed it open.

Light flooded into the cell, revealing a bloodstained floor and wall, chains and cuffs lying in disorganized bands of metal.

The room was empty. Of course. He swept it with his eyes, smiled. Everything was ready for the next occupant.

He closed the door and locked it again, then proceeded down the hall to a large subterranean room. Switching on the bright electric lights, he approached a stainless steel gurney. Atop the gurney lay an old-fashioned Gladstone bag and two journals, bound in cheap red plastic. The man picked up the top journal, turning its pages with great interest. It was all so wonderfully ironic. By rights, these journals should have perished in flames long ago. In the wrong hands, they could have done a great deal of damage. *Would* have done a great deal of damage, had he not come along at the right time. But now, they were back where they belonged.

He replaced the journal and, more slowly, opened the medical valise.

Inside, a cylindrical container of hard gray hospital plastic lay on a smoking bed of dry ice chips. The man pulled on a pair of latex gloves. Then he removed the container from the briefcase, placed it on the gurney, and unlatched it. He reached in, and, with infinite caution, withdrew a long, gray, ropy mass. Had it not been for the blood and matter that still adhered to the tissue, it would have resembled the kind of heavy cable that supports a bridge, the red-streaked outer lining filled with thousands of tiny, fibrous strings. A small smile curled the man's lips, and his pale eyes glittered as he stared. He held the mass up to the light, which shone through it with a glow. Then he brought it to a nearby sink, where he carefully irrigated it with a bottle of distilled water, washing off the bone chips and other offal. Next, he placed the cleaned organ in a large machine, closed its top, and turned it on. A high whine filled the stone room as the tissue was blended into a paste.

At timed intervals, the man consulted the pages of a notebook, then added some chemicals through a rubber bladder in the machine's lid with deft, precise movements. The paste lightened; clarified. And then, his movements ever so careful, the man detached the ultrablender and poured the paste into a long stainless tube, placed it in a nearby centrifuge, closed the cover, and turned a switch. There was a humming noise that grew rapidly in pitch, then stabilized.

Centrifuging out the serum would take 20.5 minutes. It was only the first stage in a long process. One had to be absolutely precise. The slightest error at any step only magnified itself until the final product was useless. But now that he'd decided to do all further harvesting here in the laboratory, rather than in the field, no doubt things would proceed with even greater consistency.

He turned to the sink, in which sat a large, carefully rolled towel. Taking it by one edge, he raised it, letting it unroll. Half a dozen bloodstained scalpels slid into the basin. He began to clean them, slowly, lovingly. They were the old-fashioned kind: heavy, nicely balanced. Of course, they weren't as handy as the modern Japanese models with the snap-in blades, but they felt good in the hand. And they kept an edge. Even in this age of ultrablenders and DNA sequencing machines, old tools still had their place.

Placing the scalpels in an autoclave to dry and sterilize, the man removed the gloves, washed his hands very carefully, then dried them on a linen towel. He glanced over, checking the progress of the centrifuge. And then he moved to a small cabinet, opened it, and withdrew a piece of paper. He placed it on the gurney, beside the briefcase. On the paper, in an elegant copperplate script, were five names:

Pendergast
Kelly
Smithback
O'Shaughnessy
Puck

The last name had already been crossed out. Now, the man plucked a fountain pen of inlaid lacquer from his pocket. And then—neatly, formally, with long slender fingers—he drew a beautifully precise line through the fourth name, ending with a little curlicue flourish.

EIGHT

AT HIS FAVORITE NEIGHBORHOOD COFFEE SHOP, SMITHBACK lingered over his breakfast, knowing the Museum did not open its doors until ten. Once more, he glanced over the photocopies of articles he'd culled from back issues of the *Times*. The more he read them, the more he was sure the old murders were the work of Leng. Even the geography seemed consistent: most of the murders had taken place on the Lower East Side and along the waterfront, about as far away from Riverside Drive as you could get.

At nine-thirty he called for the bill and set off down Broadway for a bracing fall walk to the Museum. He began to whistle. While he still had the relationship with Nora to repair, he was an eternal optimist. If he could bring her the information she wanted on a silver platter, that would be a start. She couldn't stay mad at him forever. They had so much in common, shared both good and bad times together. If only she didn't have such a temper!

He had other reasons to be happy. Although every now and then his instincts failed him—the thing with Fairhaven was a good example—most of the time his journalist's nose was infallible. And his article on Leng had gotten off to a good start. Now all he needed was to dig up a few personal nuggets to bring the madman to life—maybe even a photograph. And he had an idea of where to get all of it.

He blinked in the bright fall light, inhaled the crisp air.

Years before—during the time he'd spent writing what had started out as a history of the Museum's superstition exhibition—Smithback had grown to know the Museum very well. He knew its eccentric ways, the ins and outs, the shortcuts, the curiosa, the hidden corners and miscellaneous archives. If there was any information about Leng hidden within those walls, Smithback would find it.

When the great bronze doors opened, Smithback made sure he buried himself within the throngs, staying as anonymous as possible. He paid the suggested admission and pinned on his button, strolling through the Great Rotunda, gaping like all the others at the soaring skeletons.

Soon he broke away from the tourists and worked his way down to the first floor. One of the least known, but most useful, archives in the Museum was here. Colloquially known as Old Records, it housed cabinet upon filing cabinet of personnel records, running from the Museum's founding to about 1986, when the system was computerized and moved to a gleaming new space on the fourth floor and given the shiny new name of Human Resources. How well he remembered Old Records: the smell of mothballs and foxed paper, the endless files on long-dead Museum employees, associates, and researchers. Old Records still contained some sensitive material, and Smithback remembered that it was kept locked and guarded. The last time he was in here, it was on official business and he had a signed permission. This time, he was going to have to use a different approach. The guards might recognize him; then again, after several years, they might not.

He walked through the vast Hall of Birds, echoing and empty, considering how best to proceed. Soon he found himself before the twin riveted copper doors labeled *Personnel Records, Old.* Peering through the crack between them, he could see two guards, sitting at a table, drinking coffee.

Two guards. Twice the chance of being recognized, half the chance of pulling a fast one on them. He had to get rid of one.

He took a turn around the hall, still thinking, as a plan began to take shape. Abruptly, he turned on his heel and walked out into the corridor, up the stairs, and into the huge Selous Memorial Hall. There, the usual cadre of cheerful old ladies had taken their places at the information desk. Smithback plucked the visitor's button from his lapel and tossed it in a trash bin. Then he strode up to the nearest lady.

"I'm Professor Smithback," he said, with a smile.

"Yes, Professor. What can I do for you?" The lady had curly white hair and violet eyes.

Smithback gave her his most charming smile. "May I use your phone?"

"Of course." The woman handed him the phone from under the desk. Smithback looked through the nearby museum phone book, found the number, and dialed.

"Old Records," a gruff voice answered.

"Is Rook on duty there?" Smithback barked.

"Rook? There's no Rook here. You got the wrong number, pal."

Smithback expelled an irritated stream of air into the phone. "Who's on in Records, then?"

"It's me and O'Neal. Who's this?" The voice was truculent, stupid.

" 'Me'? Who's *'me'*?"

"What's your problem, friend?" came the reply.

Smithback put on his coldest, most officious voice. "Allow me to repeat myself. May I be so presumptuous to ask who *you* are, sir, and whether you want to be written up for insubordination?"

"I'm Bulger, sir." The guard's gruff manner wilted instantly.

"Bulger. I see. You're the man I need to talk to. This is Mr. Hrumrehmen in Human Resources." He spoke rapidly and angrily, deliberately garbling the name.

"Yes, I'm sorry, I didn't realize. How can I help you, Mr.—?"

"You certainly can help me, Bulger. There's a problem here with certain, ah, *asseverations* in your personnel file, Bulger."

"What kind of problem?" The man sounded suitably alarmed.

"It's confidential. We'll discuss it when you get here."

"When?"

"*Now,* of course."

"Yes, sir, but I didn't catch your name—"

"And tell O'Neal I'm sending someone down to review your procedures in the meantime. We've had some disturbing reports about laxity."

"Yes, sir, of course, but—?"

Smithback replaced the phone. He looked up to find the elderly volunteer eyeing him curiously, even suspiciously.

"What was that all about, Professor?"

Smithback grinned and drew a hand over his cowlick. "Just a little trick on a coworker. We've got this running joke, see . . . Gotta do something to lighten up this old pile."

She smiled. *The dear innocent,* Smithback thought a little guiltily as he made a beeline back down the stairs to Old

Records. On the way, he passed one of the guards he'd seen through the crack: huffing down the hall, belly jiggling as he walked, panic writ large on his face. The Human Resources office at the Museum was a notoriously feared place, overstaffed like the rest of the administration. It would take the guard ten minutes to get there, ten minutes to wander around looking for the nonexistent Mr. Hrumrehmen, and ten minutes to get back. That would give Smithback thirty minutes to talk his way inside and find what he was looking for. It wasn't a lot of time, but Smithback knew the Museum's archival systems inside and out. He had infinite confidence in his ability to find what he needed in short order.

Once again, he strode down the hall to the copper doors of Old Records. He straightened his shoulders, took a deep breath. Raising one hand, he knocked imperiously.

The door was opened by the remaining security officer. He looked young, barely old enough to be out of high school. He was already spooked. "Yes, how can I help you?"

Smithback grasped the man's surprised, limp hand while stepping inside at the same time.

"O'Neal? I'm Maurice Fannin from Human Resources. They sent me down here to straighten things out."

"Straighten things out?"

Smithback slid his way inside, looking at the rows of old metal filing cabinets, the scarred table covered with foam coffee cups and cigarette butts, the piss-yellow walls.

"This is a disgrace," he said.

There was an uncomfortable silence.

Smithback drilled his eyes into O'Neal. "We've been doing a little looking into your area here, and let me tell you, O'Neal, we are *not* pleased. Not pleased at all."

O'Neal was immediately and utterly cowed. "I'm sorry, sir. Maybe you should talk to my supervisor, Mr. Bulger—"

"Oh, we are. We're having a *long* discussion with him." Smithback looked around again. "When was the last time you had a file check, for example?"

"A what?"

"A *file check*. When was the last time, O'Neal?"

"Er, I don't know what that is. My supervisor didn't tell me anything about a file check—"

"Strange, he thought you knew all about the procedure. Now, that's what I mean here, O'Neal: sloppy. Very sloppy. Well, from now on, we will be *requiring* a monthly file check." Smithback narrowed his eyes, strode over to a filing cabinet, pulled on a drawer. It was, as he expected, locked.

"It's locked," said the guard.

"I can *see* that. Any idiot can see that." He rattled the handle. "Where's the key?"

"Over there." The poor guard nodded toward a wall box. It, too, was locked.

It occurred to Smithback that the climate of fear and intimidation the new Museum administration had fostered was proving most helpful. The man was so terrified, the last thing he would think of doing was challenging Smithback or asking for his ID.

"And the key to that?"

"On my chain."

Smithback looked around again, his quick eyes taking in every detail under the pretense of looking for further violations. The filing cabinets had labels on them, each with a date. The dates seemed to run back to 1865, the founding year of the Museum.

Smithback knew that any outside researchers who were issued a pass to the collections would have to have been approved by a committee of curators. Their deliberations, and the files the applicant had to furnish, should still be in here. Leng almost certainly had such a collections pass. If his file were still here, it would contain a wealth of personal information: full name, address, education, degrees, research specialization, list of publications—perhaps even copies of some of those publications. It might even contain a photograph.

He rapped with a knuckle on the cabinet marked *1880.* "Like this file. When was the last time you file-checked this drawer?"

"Ah, as far as I know, never."

"Never?" Smithback sounded incredulous. "Well, what are you waiting for?"

The guard hustled over, unlocked the wall cabinet, fumbled for the right key, and unlocked the drawer.

"Now let me show you how to do a file check." Smithback opened the drawer and plunged his hands into the files, rifling them, stirring up a cloud of dust, thinking fast. A yellowed index card was poking from the first file, and he whipped it out. It listed every file in the drawer by name, alphabetized, dated, cross-referenced. This was beautiful. Thank God for the early Museum bureaucrats.

"See, you start with this index card." He waved it in the guard's face.

The guard nodded.

"It lists every file in the cabinet. Then you check to see if all the files are there. Simple. That's a file check."

"Yes, sir."

Smithback quickly scanned the list of names on the card. No Leng. He shoved the card back and slammed the drawer.

"Now we'll check 1879. Open the drawer, please."

"Yes, sir."

Smithback drew out the 1879 index card. Again, no Leng was listed. "You'll need to institute much more careful procedures down here, O'Neal. These are extremely valuable historical files. Open the next one. '78."

"Yes, sir."

Damn. Still no Leng.

"Let's take a quick look at some of the others." Smithback had him open up more cabinets and check the yellow index cards on each, all the while giving O'Neal a steady stream of advice about the importance of file-checking. The years crept inexorably backward, and Smithback began to despair.

And then, in 1870, he found the name. *Leng.*

His heart quickened. Forgetting all about the guard, Smithback flipped quickly through the files themselves, pausing at the Ls. Here he slowed, carefully looked at each one, then looked again. He went through the Ls three times. But the corresponding Leng file was missing.

Smithback felt crushed. It had been such a good idea.

He straightened up, looked at the guard's frightened, eager face. The whole idea was a failure. What a waste of energy and brilliance, frightening this poor guy for nothing. It meant starting over again, from scratch. But first, he'd better get his ass out of there before Bulger returned, disgruntled, spoiling for an argument.

"Sir?" the guard prompted.

Smithback wearily closed the drawer. He glanced at his watch. "I have to be getting back. Carry on. You're doing a good job here, O'Neal. Keep it up." He turned to go.

"Mr. Fannin?"

For a moment Smithback wondered who the man was talking to. Then he remembered. "Yes?"

"Do the carbons need a file check also?"

"Carbons?" Smithback paused.

"The ones in the vault."

"Vault?"

"The vault. Back there."

"Er, yes. Of course. Thank you, O'Neal. My oversight. Show me the vault."

The young guard led the way through a rear door to a large, old safe with a nickel wheel and a heavy steel door. "In here."

Smithback's heart sank. It looked like Fort Knox. "Can you open this?"

"It's not locked anymore. Not since the high-security area was opened."

"I see. What are these carbons?"

"Duplicates of the files back there."

"Let's take a look. Open it up."

O'Neal wrestled the door open. It revealed a small room, crammed with cabinets.

"Let's take a look at, say, 1870."

The guard glanced around. "There it is."

Smithback made a beeline for the drawer, yanking it open. The files were on some early form of photocopy paper, like glossy sepia-toned photographs, faded and blurred. He quickly pawed through to the Ls.

There it was. A security clearance for Enoch Leng, dated 1870: a few sheets, tissue-thin, faded to light brown, covered in long spidery script. With one swift stroke Smithback slipped them out of the file and into his jacket pocket, covering the motion with a loud cough.

He turned around. "Very good. All this will need to be file-checked, too, of course."

He stepped out of the vault. "Listen, O'Neal, other than the file check, you're doing a fine job down here. I'll put in a good word for you."

"Thank you, Mr. Fannin. I try, I really do—"

"Wish I could say the same for Bulger. Now there's someone with an *attitude*."

"You're right, sir."

"Good day, O'Neal." And Smithback beat a hasty retreat.

He was just in time. In the hall, he again passed Bulger, striding back, his face red and splotchy, thumbs hooked in his belt loops, lips and belly thrust forward aggressively, keys swaying and jingling. He looked *pissed*.

As Smithback made for the nearest exit, it almost felt as if the pilfered papers were burning a hole in the lining of his jacket.

The
Old, Dark House

ONE

SAFELY ON THE STREET, SMITHBACK DUCKED THROUGH THE Seventy-seventh Street gate into Central Park and settled on a bench by the lake. The brilliant fall morning was already warming into a lovely Indian summer day. He breathed in the air and thought once again of what a dazzling reporter he was. Bryce Harriman couldn't have gotten his hands on these papers if he had a year to do it and all the makeup people of Industrial Light and Magic behind him. With a sense of delicious anticipation, he removed the three sheets from his pocket. The faint scent of dust reached his nose as sunlight hit the top page.

It was an old brown carbon, faint and difficult to read. At the top of the first sheet was printed: *Application for Access to the Collections: The New York Museum of Natural History*

Applicant: *Prof. Enoch Leng, M.D., Ph.D. (Oxon.), O.B.E., F.R.S. &tc.*

Recommender: *Professor Tinbury McFadden, Department of Mammalogy*

Seconder: *Professor Augustus Spragg, Department of Ornithology*

The applicant will please describe to the committee, in brief, the purposes of his application:

The applicant, Dr. Enoch Leng, wishes access to the collections of anthropology and mammalogy to conduct research on taxonomy and classification, and to prepare comparative essays in physical anthropology, human osteology, and phrenology.

The applicant will please state his academic qualifications, giving degrees and honors, with appropriate dates:

The applicant, Prof. Enoch Leng, graduated Artium Baccalaurei, with First Honors, from Oriel College, Oxford; Doctor of Natural Philosophy, New College, Oxford, with First Honors; Elected Fellow of the Royal Society 1865; Elected to White's, 1868; Awarded Order of the Garter, 1869.

The applicant will please state his permanent domicile and his current lodgings in New York, if different:

Prof. Enoch Leng
891 Riverside Drive, New York
New York

Research laboratory at
Shottum's Cabinet of Natural Productions and Curiosities

Catherine Street, New York
New York

The applicant will please attach a list of publications, and will supply offprints of at least two for the review of the Committee.

Smithback looked through the papers, but realized he had missed this crucial piece.

The disposition of the Committee is presented below:

Professor is hereby given permission to the free and open use of the Collections and Library of the New York Museum of Natural History, this 27th Day of March, 1870.

Authorized Signatory: *Tinbury McFadden*

Signed: *E. Leng.*

Smithback swore under his breath. He felt abruptly deflated. This was thin—thin indeed. It was too bad that Leng hadn't gotten his degree in America—that would have been much easier to follow up. But maybe he could pry the information out of Oxford over the telephone—although it was possible the academic honors were false. The list of publications would have been much easier to check, and far most interesting, but there was no way he could go back and get it now. It had been such a good idea, and he'd pulled it off so well. *Damn.*

Smithback searched through the papers again. No photograph, no curriculum vitae, no biography giving place and date of birth. The only thing here at all was an address.

Damn. Damn.

But then, a new thought came to him. He recalled the address was what Nora had been trying to find. Here, at least, was a peace offering.

Smithback did a quick calculation: 891 Riverside lay uptown, in Harlem somewhere. There were a lot of old mansions still standing along that stretch of Riverside Drive: those that remained were mostly abandoned or broken up into apartments. Chances were, of course, that Leng's house had been torn down a long time ago. But there was a chance it might still stand. That might make a good picture, even if it was an old wreck. *Especially* if it was an old wreck. Come to think of it, there might even be bodies buried about the premises, or walled up in the basement. Perhaps Leng's own body might be there, moldering in a corner. That would please O'Shaughnessy, help Nora. And what a great capstone for his own article—the investigative journalist finding the corpse of America's first serial killer. Of course, it was very unlikely, but even so . . .

Smithback checked his watch. Almost one o'clock.

Oh, God. Such a brilliant bit of detective work and all he'd really got was the damn address. Well, it was a matter of an hour or two to simply go check and see if the house was still standing.

Smithback stuffed the papers back into his pocket and strolled to Central Park West. There wasn't much point in flagging down a cab—they'd refuse to take him that far uptown, and once there he'd never find a cab to take him home again. Even though it was broad daylight, he had no intention of doing any wandering around in that dangerous neighborhood.

The best thing to do might be to rent a car. The *Times* had a special arrangement with Hertz, and there was a branch not far away on Columbus. Now that he thought about it, if the house did still exist, he'd probably want to check inside, talk to current tenants, find out if anything unusual had come to light during renovations, that sort of thing.

It might be dark before he was through.

That did it: he was renting a car.

Forty-five minutes later, he was heading up Central Park West in a silver Taurus. His spirits had risen once again. This still could be a big story. After he'd checked on the house, he could do a search of the New York Public Library, see if he could turn up any published articles of Leng. Maybe he could even search the police files to see if anything unusual had happened in the vicinity of Leng's house during the time he was alive.

There were still a lot of strong leads to follow up here. Leng could be as big as Jack the Ripper. The similarities were there. All it took was a journalist to make it come alive.

With enough information, *this* could be his next book.

He, Smithback, would be a shoo-in for that Pulitzer which always seemed to elude him. And even more important— well, just as important, at least—he'd have a chance to square himself with Nora. This would save her and Pendergast a lot of time wading through city deeds. And it would please Pendergast, who he sensed was a silent ally. Yes: all in all, this was going to work out well.

Reaching the end of the park, he headed west on

Cathedral Parkway, then turned north onto Riverside Drive. As he passed 125th Street he slowed, scanning the addresses of the broken buildings. Six Hundred Seventy. Seven Hundred One. Another ten blocks went by. As he continued north, he slowed still further, holding his breath in anticipation.

And then his eye alighted on 891 Riverside Drive.

The house was still standing. He couldn't believe his luck: Leng's own house.

He gave it a long, searching look as he passed by, then turned right at the next street, 138th, and circled the block, heart beating fast.

Eight Ninety-one was an old Beaux Arts mansion that took up the entire block, sporting a pillared entryway, festooned with Baroque Revival decorations. There was even a damn coat of arms carved above the door. It was set back from the street by a small service road, forming a triangle-shaped island that adjoined Riverside Drive. There were no rows of buzzers beside the door, and the first-floor windows had been securely boarded up and covered with tin. The place, it seemed, had never been broken into apartments. Like so many old mansions along the Drive, it had simply been abandoned years before—too expensive to maintain, too expensive to tear down, too expensive to revamp. Almost all such buildings had reverted to the city for unpaid taxes. The city simply boarded them up and warehoused them.

He leaned over the passenger seat, squinting for a better look. The upper-story windows were not boarded up, and none of the panes appeared to be broken. It was perfect. It looked just like the house of a mass murderer. *Front page photo, here we come.* Smithback could just see his story generating a police search of the place, the discovery of more bodies. This was getting better and better.

So how best to proceed? A little peek through a window might be in order—provided he could find a place to park.

Pulling away from the curb, he circled the block again, then drove down Riverside, looking for a parking spot. Considering how poor the neighborhood was, there were a remarkable number of cars: junkers, aging Eldorado pimpmobiles, fancy SUVs with huge speakers tilting up from their rear beds. It was six or seven blocks before he finally found a semilegal parking spot on a side street off Riverside. He should have hired a livery driver, damn it, and had him wait while he inspected the house. Now, he had to walk nine blocks through Harlem. Just what he had tried to avoid.

Nudging the rental car into the space, he glanced carefully around. Then he got out of the car, locked it, and—quickly, but not so quickly as to attract attention—walked back up to 137th Street.

When he reached the corner, he slowed, sauntering down the block until he came to the porte-cochère entrance. Here, he paused to look at the house more carefully, trying to look as casual as possible.

It had once been very grand: a four-story structure of marble and brick, with a slate mansard roof, oval windows, towers, and a widow's walk. The facade was encrusted with carved limestone details set into brick. The streetfront was surrounded by a tall spiked iron fence, broken and rusty. The yard was filled with weeds and trash, along with a riot of sumac and ailanthus bushes and a pair of dead oaks. Its dark-browed upper-story windows looked out over the Hudson and the North River Water Pollution Control Plant.

Smithback shivered, glanced around one more time, then crossed the service road and started down the carriageway. Gang graffiti was sprayed all over the once elegant marble and brick. Windblown trash had accumulated several feet deep in the recesses. But in the rear of the carriage drive, he could see a stout door made of oak. It, too, had been sprayed with graffiti, but still looked operable. It had neither window nor peephole.

Smithback slipped farther down the carriageway, keeping close to the outside wall. The place stank of urine and feces. Someone had dropped a load of used diapers beside the door, and a pile of garbage bags lay in a corner, torn apart by dogs and rats. As if on cue, an enormously fat rat waddled out of the trash, dragging its belly, looked insolently at him, then disappeared back into the garbage.

He noticed two small, oval windows, set on each side of the door. Both were covered with tin, but there might be a way to pry one loose. Advancing, Smithback carefully pressed his hand against the closest, testing it. It was solid as a rock: no cracks, no way to see in. The other was just as carefully covered. He inspected the seams, looking for holes, but there were none. He laid a hand on the oaken door: again, it felt totally solid. This house was locked up tight, nigh impregnable. Perhaps it had been locked up since the time of Leng's death. There might well be personal items inside. Once again, Smithback wondered if the remains of victims might also be there.

Once the police got their hands on the place, he'd lose his chance to learn anything more.

It would be very interesting to see inside.

He looked up, his eye following the lines of the house. He'd had some rock climbing experience, gained from a trip to the canyon country of Utah. The trip where he'd met Nora. He stepped away, studying the facade. There were lots of cornices and carvings that would make good handholds. Here, away from the street, he wasn't as likely to be noticed.

With a little luck, he might be able to climb to one of the second-story windows. Just for a look.

He glanced back down the carriageway. The street was deserted, the house deathly silent.

Smithback rubbed his hands together, smoothed his cowlick. And then he set his left wing tip into a gap in the lower course of masonry and began to climb.

TWO

CAPTAIN CUSTER CHECKED THE CLOCK ON THE WALL OF HIS office. It was nearly noon. He felt a growl in his capacious stomach and wished, for at least the twentieth time, that noon would hurry up and come so he could head out to Dilly's Deli, purchase a double corned beef and swiss on rye with extra mayo, and place the monstrous sandwich in his mouth. He always got hungry when he was nervous, and today he was very, very nervous. It had been barely forty-eight hours since he'd been put in charge of the Surgeon case, but already he was getting impatient calls. The mayor had called, the commissioner had called. The three murders had the entire city close to panicking. And yet he had nothing to report. The breathing space he'd bought himself with that article on the old bones was just about used up. The fifty detectives working the case were desperately following up leads, for all the good it did them. But to where? Nowhere. He snorted, shook his head. Incompetent ass-wipes.

His stomach growled again, louder this time. Pressure and agitation encircled him like a damp bathhouse towel. If this was what it felt like to be in charge of a big case, he wasn't sure he liked it.

He glanced at the clock again. Five more minutes. Not going to lunch before noon was a matter of discipline with him. As a police officer, he knew discipline was key. That was what it was all about. He couldn't let the pressure get to him.

He remembered how the commissioner had stared sidelong at him, back in that little hovel on Doyers Street when he'd assigned him the investigation. Rocker hadn't seemed exactly confident in his abilities. Custer remembered, all too clearly, his words of advice: *I'd suggest you get to work on this new case of yours. Get* right *to work. Catch that killer. You don't want another, fresher stiff turning up on your watch—do you?*

The minute hand moved another notch.

Maybe more manpower is the answer, he thought. He should put another dozen detectives on that murder in the Museum Archives. That was the most recent murder, that's where the freshest clues would be. That curator who'd found the corpse—the frosty bitch, what's her name—had been pretty closemouthed. If he could—

And then, just as the second hand swept toward noon, he had the revelation.

The Museum Archives. The Museum curator . . .

It was so overwhelming, so blinding, that it temporarily drove all thoughts of corned beef from his head.

The Museum. The Museum was the center around which everything revolved.

The third murder, the brutal operation? *It took place in the Museum.*

That archaeologist, Nora Kelly? *Worked for the Museum.*

The incriminating letter that reporter, Smithbank or whatever, had leaked? The letter that started the whole thing? *Found in the Museum's Archives.*

That creepy old guy, Collopy, who'd authorized the removal of the letter? *Director of the Museum.*

Fairhaven? *On the Museum's board.*

The nineteenth-century killer? *Connected to the Museum.*

And the archivist himself, Puck, had been murdered. Why? *Because he had discovered something. Something in the Archives.*

Custer's mind, unusually clear, began racing over the possibilities, the myriad combinations and permutations. What was needed was strong, decisive action. *Whatever it was Puck had found, he would find, too. And that would be key to the murderer.*

There was no time to lose, not one minute.

He stood up and punched the intercom. "Noyes? Get in here. Right away."

The man was in the doorway even before Custer's finger was off the button.

"I want the top ten detectives assigned to the Surgeon case over here for a confidential briefing in my office. Half an hour."

"Yes, Captain." Noyes raised a quizzical, but appropriately obsequious, eyebrow.

"I've got it. Noyes, I've figured it out."

Noyes ceased his gum chewing. "Sir?"

"The key to the Surgeon killings is in the Museum. It's there, in the Archives. God knows, maybe even the murderer himself is in there, on the Museum's staff." Custer grabbed his jacket. "We're going in there hard and fast, Noyes. They won't even know what hit them."

THREE

USING CORNICES AND ESCUTCHEONS AS HAND- AND
footholds, Smithback slowly pulled his way up the wall
toward the stone embrasure of a second-story window. It had
been harder than he expected, and he'd managed to scrape
a cheek and mash a finger in the process. And, of course, he
was ruining a two-hundred-and-fifty-dollar pair of handmade
Italian shoes. Maybe the *Times* would pay. Spreadeagled
against the side of the house, he felt ridiculously exposed.
There must be an easier way to win a Pulitzer, he thought.
He grabbed for the window ledge, pulled himself upward
with a grunt of effort. Gaining the wide ledge, he remained
there a moment, catching his breath, looking around. The
street was still quiet. Nobody seemed to have noticed
anything. He turned his attention back to the rippled glass
of the window.

The room beyond seemed utterly empty and dark. Dust
motes hung in the anemic shafts of light that slanted inward.
He thought he could make out a closed door in the far wall.
But there was nothing to give him any indication of what
lay beyond, in the rest of the house.

If he wanted to learn anything more, he'd have to get inside.

What could the harm be? The house had clearly been deserted for decades. It was probably city property now, public property. He'd come this far, done this much. If he left now, he'd have to start all over again. The image of his editor's face, shaking a fistful of copy, eyes popping with anger, filled his mind. If he was going to charge them for the shoes, he better have something to show for it.

He tried the window, and, as expected, found it locked—or, perhaps, frozen shut with age. He experienced a moment of indecision, looked around again. The thought of clambering back down the wall was even less pleasant than climbing up had been. What he could see from the window told him nothing. He *had* to find a way in—just for the briefest look. He sure as hell couldn't stay on the ledge forever. If anyone happened by and saw him . . .

And then he spotted the cop car a few blocks south on Riverside Drive, cruising slowly north. It would not be good at all if they caught sight of him up here—and he had no way to get down in time.

Quickly, he pulled off his jacket, stuffed it into a ball, and placed it against one of the lowest of the large panes. Using his shoulder, he pressed until it gave with a sharp crack. He pried out the pieces of glass, laid them on the ledge, and crawled through.

Inside the room, he stood up and peered through the window. All was calm; his entry hadn't been noticed. Then he turned around, listening intently. Silence. He sniffed the air. It smelled, not unpleasantly, of old wallpaper and dust—it was not the stale air he'd been expecting. He took a few deep breaths.

Think of the story. Think of the Pulitzer. Think of Nora. He would do a quick reconnaissance and then get out.

He waited, allowing his eyes to adjust to the dimness. There was a shelf in the back, and a single book lay on it. Smithback walked over and picked it up. It was an old nineteenth-century treatise titled *Mollusca,* with a gold engraving of a conch on the cover. Smithback felt a slight quickening of his heart: a natural history book. He opened it, hoping to find a bookplate reading *Ex Libris Enoch Leng.* But there was nothing. He flipped the pages, looking for notes, then put the book back.

Nothing else for it: time to explore the house.

He carefully removed his shoes, placed them by the window, and proceeded in stockinged feet. With careful steps he made his way to the closed door. The floor creaked, and he stopped. But the profound silence remained. It was unlikely that anyone would be in the house—it looked like even the junkies and bums had been successfully kept out—but caution would be wise nonetheless.

He placed his hand on the doorknob, turned it ever so slowly, eased the door open an inch. He peered through the crack. Blackness. He pushed it wider, allowing the dim afternoon light from the window behind him to spill into the hallway. He saw that it was very long, quite grand, with flocked wallpaper in a heavy green design. On the walls, in gilded alcoves, were paintings draped with white sheets. The sheets clung to the heavy frames. At the far end of the hall, a broad set of marble stairs swept downward, disappearing into a pool of deeper darkness. At the top of the stairs stood something—a statue, perhaps?—draped in yet another white sheet.

Smithback held his breath. It really did look as if the house had been shut up and deserted since Leng's death. It was fantastic. Could all this stuff be Leng's?

He ventured a few steps down the hall. As he did so, the smell of mold and dust became suffused with something less pleasant: something organic, sweet, decayed. It was as if the rotten old heart of the house had finally died.

Perhaps his suspicions were right, and Leng had entombed the bodies of his victims behind the heavy Victorian wallpaper.

He paused, an arm's length from one of the paintings. Curious, he reached out, took the corner of the white sheet, and lifted. The rotting sheet fell away in a cloud of dust and tatters, and he stepped back, momentarily startled. A dark painting stood revealed. Smithback peered closer. It depicted a pack of wolves ripping apart a deer in a deep wood. It was ghoulish in its anatomical detail, but beautifully executed nevertheless, and no doubt worth a fortune. Curiosity aroused, Smithback stepped to the next alcove and plucked at the sheet, which also turned to powder at his touch. This painting showed a whale hunt—a great sperm whale, draped with harpoon lines, thrashing about in its death throes, a huge jet of bright arterial blood rising from its spouter, while its flukes dashed a boatful of harpooners into the sea.

Smithback could hardly believe his luck. He had struck paydirt. But then, it wasn't luck: it was the result of hard work and careful research. Even Pendergast hadn't yet figured out where Leng lived. This would redeem his job at the *Times,* maybe even redeem his relationship with Nora. Because he was sure that—whatever information about Leng Nora and Pendergast were looking for—it was *here.*

Smithback waited, listening intently, but there were no sounds from below. He moved down the carpeted hallway in slow, small, noiseless steps. Reaching the covered statue at the top of the banister, he reached up and grasped at the sheet. As rotten as the others, it fell apart, dropping to the ground in a dissolving heap. A cloud of dust, dry rot, and mold billowed up into the air.

At first Smithback felt a frisson of fear and incomprehension at the sight, until his mind began to understand just what he was looking at. It was, in fact, nothing more than a stuffed chimpanzee, hanging from a tree branch. Moths and rats had chewed away most of the face, leaving pits and holes that went down to brown bone. The lips were gone as well, giving the chimpanzee the agonized grin of a mummy. One ear hung by a thread of dried flesh, and even as Smithback watched it fell to the ground with a soft thud. One of the chimp's hands was holding a wax fruit; the other was clutching its stomach, as if in pain. Only the beady glass eyes looked fresh, and they stared at Smithback with maniacal intensity.

Smithback felt his heart quicken. Leng had, after all, been a taxonomist, collector, and member of the Lyceum. Did he, like McFadden and the rest, also have a collection, a so-called cabinet of curiosities? Was this decayed chimp part of his collection?

He again experienced a moment of indecision. *Should he leave now?*

Taking a step back from the chimpanzee, he peered down the staircase. There was no light except what little filtered in from behind nailed boards and wooden shutters. Gradually, he began to make out the dim outlines of what seemed to be a reception hall, complete with parqueted oak floor. Lying across it were exotic skins—zebra, lion, tiger, oryx, cougar. Ranged about were a number of dark objects, also draped in white sheets. The paneled walls were lined with old cabinets, covered with rippled glass doors. On them sat a number of shadowy objects in display cases, each with a brass plate affixed below it.

Yes, it *was* a collection—Enoch Leng's collection.

Smithback stood, clutching the upper knob of the banister. Despite the fact that nothing seemed to have been touched in the house for a hundred years, he could feel, deep in his gut, that the house hadn't been empty all this time. It looked, somehow, *tended.* It bespoke the presence of a caretaker. He should turn around now and get out.

But the silence was profound, and he hesitated. The collections below were worth a brief look. The interior of this house and its collections would play a big role in his article. He would go down for a moment—just a moment—to see what lay beneath some of the sheets. He took a careful step, and then another . . . and then he heard a soft click behind him. He spun around, heart pounding.

At first, nothing looked different. And then he realized that the door from which he'd entered the hallway must have closed. He breathed a sigh of relief: a gust of wind had come through the broken window and pushed the door shut.

He continued down the sweeping marble staircase, hand clutching the banister. At the bottom he paused, screwing up his eyes, peering into the even more pronounced darkness. The smell of rot and decay seemed stronger here.

His eyes focused on an object in the center of the hall. One of the sheets had become so decayed that it had already fallen from the object it covered. In the darkness it looked strange, misshapen. Smithback took a step forward, peering intently—and suddenly he realized what it was: the mounted specimen of a small carnivorous dinosaur. But this dinosaur was extraordinarily well preserved, with fossilized flesh still clinging to the bones, some fossilized internal organs, even huge swaths of fossilized skin. And covering the skin were the unmistakable outlines of *feathers*.

Smithback stood, dumbstruck. It was an astounding specimen, of incalculable value to science. Recent scientists had theorized that some dinosaurs, even T. Rex, might have had a covering of feathers. Here was the proof. He glanced down: a brass label read *Unknown coeloraptor from Red Deer River, Alberta, Canada*.

Smithback turned his attention to the cabinets, his eye falling on a series of human skulls. He moved closer. The little brass label below them read: *Hominidae series from Swartkopje Cave, South Africa*. Smithback could hardly believe his eyes. He knew enough about hominid fossils to know they were exceedingly rare. These dozen skulls were some of the most complete he had ever seen. They would revolutionize hominid studies.

His eye caught a gleam from the next cabinet. He stepped up to it. It was crowded with gemstones, and his eye landed on a large, green cut stone the size of a robin's egg. The label below read *Diamond, flawless specimen from Novotney Terra, Siberia, 216 carats, believed to be the only green diamond in existence*. Next to it, in an especially large case, were immense star rubies, sapphires, and more exotic stones with names he could hardly pronounce, winking in the dim recesses—gemstones equal to the finest ones at the New York Museum. They seemed to have been given star billing among the other exhibits. On a nearby shelf lay a series of gold crystals, perfectly beautiful, lacy as frost, one as large as a grapefruit. Below lay rows of tektites, mostly black misshapen things, but some with a beautiful deep green or violet coloring.

Smithback took a step back, his mind wrestling with the richness and variety of the display. *To think all this has stood here, in this ruined house, for a hundred years* . . . He turned away and, on impulse, reached out and twitched off the sheet from a small specimen behind him. The sheet dissolved, and a strange stuffed animal greeted his eye: a large, tapirlike mammal with a huge muzzle, powerful forelegs, bulbous head, and curving tusks. It was like nothing he had ever seen before; a freak. He bent down to make out the dim label: *Only known specimen of the Tusked Megalopedus, described by Pliny, thought to be fantastical until this specimen was shot in the Belgian Congo by the English explorer Col. Sir Henry F. Moreton, in 1869.*

Good lord, thought Smithback: could it be true? A large mammal, completely unknown to science? Or was it a fake? Suddenly the thought occurred to him: could all these be fakes? But as he looked around, he realized they were not. Leng would not have collected fakes, and even in the dim light he could see that these were real. *These were real.* And if the rest of the collections in the house were like this, they constituted possibly the greatest natural history collection in the world. This was no mere cabinet of curiosities. It was too dark to take notes, but Smithback knew he wouldn't need notes: what he had seen had been imprinted upon his mind forever.

Only once in a lifetime was a reporter given such a story.

He jerked away another sheet, and was greeted by the massive, rearing fossil skeleton of a short-faced cave bear, caught in a silent roar, its black teeth like daggers. The engraved brass label on the oak mounting stand indicated it had been pulled from the Kutz Canyon Tar Pits, in New Mexico.

He whispered through the reception hall on his stockinged feet, pulling off additional sheets, exposing a whole row of Pleistocene mammals—each one a magnificent specimen as fine or finer than any in a museum—ending with a series of Neanderthal skeletons, perfectly preserved, some with weapons, tools, and one sporting some sort of necklace made out of teeth.

Glancing to one side, he noticed a marble archway leading into a room beyond. In its center of the room was a huge, pitted meteorite, at least eight feet in diameter, surrounded by rows upon rows of additional cabinets.

It was *ruby* in color.

This was almost beyond belief.

He looked away, turning his attention to the objects ranged about mahogany shelves on a nearby wall. There were bizarre masks, flint spearpoints, a skull inlaid with turquoise, bejeweled knives, toads in jars, thousands of butterflies under glass: everything arranged with the utmost attention to systematics and classification.

He noticed that the light fixtures weren't electric. They were *gas,* each with a little pipe leading up into a mantle, covered by a cut-glass shade. It was incredible. It *had* to be Leng's house, just as he had left it. It was as if he had walked out of the house, boarded it up, and left . . .

Smithback paused, his excitement suddenly abating. Obviously, the house hadn't remained like this, untouched, since Leng's death. There must be a caretaker who came regularly. Somebody had put tin over the windows and draped the collections. The feeling that the house was not empty, that someone was still there, swept over him again.

The silence; the watchful exhibits and grotesque specimens; the overpowering darkness that lay in the corners of the room—and, most of all, the rising stench of rot—brought a growing unease that would not be denied. He shuddered involuntarily. What was he doing? There was already enough here for a Pulitzer. He had the story: now, be smart and get the hell out.

He turned and swiftly climbed the stairs, passing the chimpanzee and the paintings—and then he paused. All the doors along the hall were closed, and it seemed even darker than it had a few minutes before. He realized he had forgotten which door he had come through. It was near the end of the hall, that much he remembered. He approached the most likely, tried the handle, and to his surprise found it locked. *Must have guessed wrong,* he thought, moving to the next.

That, too, was locked.

With a rising sense of alarm he tried the door on the other side. It was locked, as well. So was the next, and the next. With a chill prickling his spine, he tried the rest—all, every one, securely locked.

Smithback stood in the dark hallway, trying to control the sudden panic that threatened to paralyze his limbs.

He was locked in.

FOUR

CUSTER'S UNMARKED CRUISER PULLED UP WITH A
satisfying squeal of rubber before the Museum's security
entrance, five squad cars skidding up around him, sirens
wailing, light bars throwing red and white stripes across the
Romanesque Revival facade. He rolled out of the squad car
and strode decisively up the stone steps, a sea of blue in his
wake.

At the impromptu meeting with his top detectives, and
then in the ride uptown to the Museum, the theory that had
hit him like a thunderclap became a firm, unshakable
conviction. *Surprise and speed is the way to go in this case,*
he thought as he looked up at the huge pile of granite. Hit 'em
hard and fast, leave them reeling—that was what his
instructor at the Police Academy had always said. It was
good advice. The commissioner wanted action. And it
was action, in the form of Captain Sherwood Custer, that he
was going to get.

A Museum security guard stood at the doorway, the police
lights reflecting off his glasses. He looked bewildered. Several
other guards were coming up behind him, staring down the
steps, looking equally perplexed. A few tourists were

approaching up Museum Drive, cameras dangling, guidebooks in hand. They stopped when they saw the cluster of police cars. After a brief parley, the group turned around and headed back toward a nearby subway entrance.

Custer didn't bother to show the grunt his badge. "Captain Custer, Seventh Precinct," he rapped out. "Brevetted to Homicide."

The guard swallowed painfully. "Yes, Captain?"

"Is the Museum's security chief in?"

"Yes, sir."

"Get him down here. Right away."

The guards scurried around, and within five minutes a tall man in a tan suit, black hair combed back with a little too much grease, arrived. *He's an unsavory-looking fellow,* Custer thought; but then, so many people in private security were. Not good enough to join the real force.

The man held out his hand and Custer took it reluctantly. "Jack Manetti, director of security. What can I do for you, officers?"

Without a word, Custer displayed the embossed, signed, and notarized bench warrant he'd managed to get issued in close to record time. The security director took it, read it over, handed it back to Custer.

"This is highly unusual. May I ask what's happened?"

"We'll get to the specifics shortly," Custer replied. "For now, this warrant should be all you need to know. My men will need unlimited access to the Museum. I'm going to require an interrogation room set up for the questioning of selected staff. We'll work as quickly as we can, and everything will go smoothly—provided we get cooperation from the Museum." He paused, thrust his hands behind his back, looked around imperiously. "You realize, of course, that we have the authority to impound any items that, in our judgment, are germane to the case." He wasn't sure what the word *germane* meant, but the judge had used it in the warrant, and it sounded good.

"But that's impossible, it's almost closing time. Can't this wait until tomorrow?"

"Justice doesn't wait, Mr. Manetti. I want a complete list of Museum staff. We'll single out the individuals we want to question. If certain staff members have gone home early, they'll need to be called back in. I'm sorry, but the Museum will just have to be inconvenienced."

"But this is unheard of. I'm going to have to check with the Museum's director—"

"You do that. In fact, let's go see him in person. I want to make sure we're clear, clear as *crystal,* on all points of order, so that once our investigations are underway we will not be inconvenienced or delayed. Understood?"

Manetti nodded, displeasure contracting his face. *Good,* thought Custer: the more upset and flustered everyone became, the quicker he'd be able to flush out the killer. Keep them guessing, don't give them time to think. He felt exhilarated.

He turned. "Lieutenant Detective Cannell, take three officers and have these gentlemen show you to the staff entrance. I want everyone leaving the premises to be ID'd and checked against personnel records. Get phone numbers, cell numbers, and addresses. I want everyone available to be called back at a moment's notice, if necessary."

"Yes, sir."

"Lieutenant Detective Piles, you come with me."

"Yes, sir."

Custer turned a stern eye back on Manetti. "Show us the way to Dr. Collopy's office. We have business to discuss."

"Follow me," said the security director, even more unhappily.

Custer motioned to the rest of his men, and they followed him through great echoing halls, up several floors in a giant elevator, and along yet more halls filled with displays— Christ, this place had more than its share of weird shit—until at last they reached a grand paneled door leading to an even grander paneled office. The door was half open, and beyond sat a small woman at a desk. She rose at their approach.

"We're here to see Dr. Collopy," said Custer, looking around, wondering why a secretary had such a fancy office.

"I'm sorry, sir," the woman said. "Dr. Collopy's not here."

"He's not?" Custer and Manetti said in chorus.

The secretary shook her head, looking flustered. "He hasn't been back since lunch. Said he had some important business to take care of."

"But lunch was hours ago," Custer said. "Isn't there some way he can be reached?"

"There's his private cell phone," the secretary said.

"Dial it." Custer turned to Manetti. "And you, call around to some of the other top brass. See if they know where this Collopy is."

Manetti moved off to another desk, picked up a phone. The large office fell silent, save for the beep of numbers being dialed. Custer looked around. The space was paneled in very dark wood, and it was chock-full of bleak oil paintings and forbidding-looking displays parked behind glass-fronted cabinets. Christ, it was like a house of horrors.

"The cell phone's turned off, sir," the secretary said.

Custer shook his head. "Isn't there any other number you can call? His house, for example?"

The secretary and Manetti exchanged looks. "We aren't

supposed to call there," she said, looking even more flustered.

"I don't care what you're *supposed* to do. This is urgent police business. Call his house."

The secretary unlocked a desk drawer, rummaged through a file of index cards, plucked one out. She looked at it a moment, shielding it from Custer's and Manetti's view. Then she replaced the card, locked the drawer, and dialed a number.

"Nobody's picking up," she said after a moment.

"Keep ringing."

Half a minute went by. Finally, the secretary replaced the phone in its cradle. "There's no answer."

Custer rolled his eyes. "All right, listen. We can't waste any more time. We have good reason to believe that the key to the serial killer known as the Surgeon—perhaps even the killer himself—will be found here in the Museum. Time is of the essence. I'm going to personally supervise a thorough search of the Archives. Lieutenant Detective Piles will be in charge of questioning certain staff members."

Manetti was silent.

"With the Museum's cooperation, I think we can get through this by midnight, if not sooner. We'll need a room for interrogation. We will require power for our recording machinery, a sound engineer, and an electrician. I will require identification from everyone, and access to personnel files on an ongoing basis."

"Just which staff members are you going to question?" Manetti asked.

"We will determine that from the files."

"We have two thousand five hundred employees."

This temporarily floored Custer. *Twenty-five hundred people to run a museum? What a welfare program.* He took a breath, carefully recomposing his features. "We will deal with that. As a start, we'll need to interview, let's see . . . night watchmen who might have noticed any unusual comings or goings. And that archaeologist who excavated those skeletons, found the others down on Doyers Street, and—"

"Nora Kelly."

"Right."

"The police have already spoken with her, I believe."

"So we'll be speaking with her again. And we'll want to talk to the head of security—that's you—about your security arrangements, in the Archives and elsewhere. I want to question everyone connected with the Archives and the discovery of, ah, Mr. Puck's body. How's that for a start?" He gave a quick, artificial smile.

There was a silence.

"Now, direct me to the Archives, please."

For a moment, Manetti just stared at him, as if the situation was beyond his powers of comprehension.

"Direct me to the Archives, Mr. Manetti, and make it now, if you please."

Manetti blinked. "Very well, Captain. If you'll follow me."

As they walked down the storied halls, cops and administrators in tow, Custer felt a huge swelling of excitement at his newly found self-confidence. He'd finally discovered his true calling. Homicide was where he should have been all along. It was obvious he was a natural; he had a knack for the work. His being put in charge of this case had not been a fluke. It had been destiny.

FIVE

SMITHBACK STOOD IN THE DARK HALL, STRUGGLING TO control his fright. It was fright that was his problem here, not locked doors. Clearly, at least one of them must be unlocked: he had just come through it.

As deliberately as he could, he went down the hall once again, trying all the doors, shaking harder this time, even at the cost of making some noise, pushing at the jambs, making sure they weren't simply stuck. But no, it wasn't his imagination. They were all securely locked.

Had somebody locked the door behind him? But that was impossible: the room had been empty. A gust of wind had closed it. He shook his head, searching unsuccessfully for amusement in his own paranoia.

The doors, he decided, must lock automatically when shut. Maybe that was a feature of old houses like this. No problem: he would find another way out of the house. Downstairs, through the reception hall and out a first floor window or door. Perhaps out the porte-cochère door, which had every appearance of being functional—in fact it was probably the very door used by the custodian. Relief coursed through him at this thought. It would be easier; it would save him the trouble of having to climb back down that outside wall.

All he had to do was find his way to it through the dark house.

He stood in the hall, waiting for his heartbeat to slow. The place was so quiet, so unusually quiet, that he found his ears alert for the faintest sound. The silence, he told himself, was a good sign. No custodian was around. He probably came only once a week, at most; or maybe only once a year, given all the dust in the place. Smithback had all the time in the world.

Feeling a little sheepish, he made his way back to the head of the stairs and peered down. The carriage door, it seemed to him, should be to the left, somewhere off the reception hall. He descended the stairs and paused warily at the bottom, peering again at the strange, endless displays. Still, no sound. The place was clearly deserted.

He remembered Pendergast's theory. *What if Leng really had succeeded . . . ?*

Smithback forced himself to laugh out loud. What the hell was he thinking about? Nobody could live 150 years. The darkness, the silence, the mysterious collections were getting to him.

He paused, taking stock. A passage ran off from the hall to the left, in what he thought was the right direction. It lay in complete darkness, yet it seemed the most promising. He should have thought to bring a damn flashlight. No matter: he would try that first.

Stepping carefully, avoiding the display cases and sheeted objects, he walked across the hall and into the side passage. His pupils refused to dilate further and the corridor remained pitch black, the darkness an almost palpable presence around him. He fumbled in his pocket, found the box of matches he'd picked up at the Blarney Stone. He lit one, the scraping and flaring of the match unpleasantly loud in the still air.

The flickering light revealed a passage leading into another large room, also crammed with wooden cabinets. He took a few steps forward until the matchlight died away. Then he went on as far as he dared into the blackness, felt around with his hand, found the doorframe of the room, drew himself forward again. Once he was inside, he lit another match.

Here was a different kind of collection: rows and rows of specimens in jars of formaldehyde. He caught a quick glimpse of rows of gigantic, staring eyeballs in jars—whale eyeballs? Trying not to waste the light, he hurried forward, stumbling over a large glass jeroboam on a marble pedestal, filled with what looked like a huge floating bag. As he got back on his feet and lit another match, he caught a glimpse of the label: *Mammoth stomach, containing its last meal, from the icefields of Siberia* . . .

He went quickly on, passing as fast as he could between the rows of cabinets, until he arrived at a single wooden door, battered and scarred. There was a sudden sharp pain as the match burned his fingers. Cursing, he dropped it, then lit another. In the renewed flare of light, he opened the door. It led into a huge kitchen, tiled in white and black. There was a deep stone fireplace set into one wall. The rest of the room was dominated by a huge iron stove, a row of ovens, and several long tables set with soapstone sinks. Dozens of pots of greenish copper were suspended from ceiling hooks. Everything looked decayed, covered with a thick layer of dust, cobwebs, and mouse droppings. It was a dead end.

The house was huge. The matches wouldn't last forever. What would he do when they ran out?

Get a grip, Smithback, he told himself. Clearly, no one

had cooked in this kitchen in a hundred years. Nobody lived in the house. What was he worrying about?

Relying on memory, without lighting any more matches, he backtracked into the large room, feeling his way along the glass-fronted cases. At one point he felt his shoulder brush against something. A second later, there was a tremendous crash at his feet, and the sudden biting stench of formaldehyde. He waited, nerves taut, for the echoes to abate. He prepared to light a match, thought better of it— was formaldehyde flammable? Better not experiment now. He took a step, and his stockinged foot grazed something large, wet, and yielding. *The specimen in the jar.* He gingerly stepped around it.

There had been other doors set into the passageway beyond. He would try them one at a time. But first, he paused to remove his socks, which were sodden with formaldehyde. Then, stepping into the passageway, he ventured another match. He could see four doors, two on the left wall, two on the right.

He opened the closest, found an ancient, zinc-lined bathroom. Sitting in the middle of the tiled floor was the grinning skull of an allosaurus. The second door fronted a large closet full of stuffed birds; the third, yet another closet, this one full of stuffed lizards. The fourth opened into a scullery, its walls pocked and scarred, ravaged by traceries of mildew.

The match went out and Smithback stood in the enfolding darkness. He could hear the sound of his own stertorous breathing. He felt in the matchbook, counted with his fingers: six left. He fought back—less successfully this time—the scrabbling panic that threatened to overwhelm him. He'd been in tough situations before, tougher than this. *It's an empty house. Just find your way out.*

He made his way back to the reception hall and its shrouded collections. Being able to see again, no matter how faintly, calmed him a little—there was something utterly terrifying about absolute darkness. He looked around again at the astounding collections, but all he could feel now was a rising dread. The foul smell was stronger here: the sickly-sweet odor of decay, of something that by all rights belonged under several feet of earth . . .

Smithback took a series of deep, calming breaths. The thick layers of undisturbed dust on the floor proved the place was deserted; that even the caretaker, if there was one, hardly ever came.

He glanced around again, eyes wide against the faint light. On the far side of the hall, a shadowy archway led into what looked like a large room. He walked across the hall, bare feet padding on the parquet floor, and passed beneath the archway. The walls of the room beyond were paneled in dark wood, rising to a coffered ceiling. This room, too, was filled with displays: some shrouded, others raised on plinths or armatures. But the displays themselves were utterly different from what he had seen before. He stepped forward, looking around, bafflement mixing with the sharp sense of trepidation. There were large steamer trunks, some with glass sides, bound in heavy leather straps; galvanized containers like antique milk cans, their lids studded with heavy bolts; an oddly shaped, oversized wooden box, with copper-lined circles cut out of its top and sides; a coffin-shaped crate, pierced by half a dozen swords. On the walls hung ropes, strings of moldering kerchiefs tied end-to-end; straitjackets, manacles, chains, cuffs of various sizes. It was an inexplicable, eerie display, made the more unsettling by its lack of relation to what he had seen before.

Smithback crept on into the center of the room, keeping

away from the dark corners. The front of the house, he figured, would be straight ahead. The other side of the house had proven a dead end; surely he would have better luck this way. If need be, he would batter down the front door.

At the far end of the room, another passageway led off into darkness. He stepped gingerly into it, feeling his way along one wall, sliding his feet forward with small, tentative steps. In the faintest of light he could see the hall ended in another room, much smaller and more intimate than the ones he had passed through before. The specimens were fewer here—just a few cabinets filled with seashells and some mounted dolphin skeletons. It seemed to have once been a drawing room or parlor of some kind. Or perhaps—and at the thought, fresh hope surged within him—an entryway?

The only illumination came from a single pinprick of light in the far wall, which sent a pencil-thin beam of light through the dusty air. A tiny hole in one of the boarded windows. With a huge sense of relief he quickly crossed the room and began feeling along the wall with his fingers. There was a heavy oak door here. The hope that was rising within him grew stronger. His fingers fell on a marble doorknob, oversized and terribly cold in his hands. He grasped it eagerly, turned.

The knob refused to budge.

With desperate strength, he tried again. No luck.

He stepped back and, with a groan of despair, felt along the edge of the door with his hands, searching for a deadbolt, lock, *anything*. An overwhelming sense of fear returned.

Heedless of the noise now, he threw himself against the door, once, twice, rushing at it with all his weight, trying desperately to break it down. The hollow thumps echoed through the room and down the hall. When the door still refused to budge, he stopped and leaned against it with a gasp of panic.

As the last echoes died away, something stirred from within the well of blackness in a far corner of the room. A voice, low and dry as mummy dust, spoke.

"My dear fellow, leaving so soon? You've only just got here."

SIX

CUSTER BURST THROUGH THE DOOR TO THE ARCHIVES AND planted himself in the middle of the entryway, hands on his hips. He could hear the patter of heavy-shod feet as his officers fanned out behind him. *Fast and furious,* he reminded himself. *Don't give 'em time to think.* He observed—with more than a little satisfaction—the consternation of the two staff members who had leapt up at the sight of a dozen uniformed officers bearing down on them.

"This area is to be searched," Custer barked out. Noyes, stepping forward out of Custer's shadow, held up the warrant in a superfluous gesture. Custer noted, with approval, that Noyes was glaring almost as balefully at the archivists as he was himself.

"But, Captain," he heard Manetti protest, "the place has already *been* searched. Right after the body of Puck was found, the NYPD had forensics teams, dogs, fingerprint sweepers, photographers, and—"

"I've seen the report, Manetti. But that was then. This is now. We have new evidence, important evidence." Custer looked around impatiently. "Let's get some light in here, for chrissakes!"

One of the staff jumped and, passing his hand over a vast cluster of ancient-looking switches, turned on a bank of lights within.

"Is that the best you can do? It's as dark as a tomb in here."

"Yes, sir."

"All right." Custer turned to his detectives. "You know what to do. Work row by row, shelf by shelf. Leave no stone unturned."

There was a pause.

"Well? Get to it, gentlemen!"

The men exchanged brief, uncertain glances. But without a questioning word they dutifully fanned out into the stacks. In a moment they were gone, like water absorbed into a sponge, leaving Manetti and Custer and the two frightened staffers alone by the reference desk. The sound of thumping, banging, and rattling began to echo back down the stacks as Custer's men started to pull things off the shelves. It was a satisfying sound, the sound of progress.

"Have a seat, Manetti," said Custer, unable now to keep condescension completely out of his voice. "Let's talk."

Manetti looked around, saw no available chairs, and remained standing.

"Okay." Custer removed a leather-covered notebook and gold pen—purchased in Macy's just after the commissioner gave him the new assignment—and prepared to take notes. "So, what we got here in these Archives? A bunch of papers? Newspapers? Old takeout menus? What?"

Manetti sighed. "The Archives contain documents, as well as specimens not considered important enough for the main collections. These materials are available to historians and others with a professional interest. It's a low-security area."

"Low security is right," Custer replied. "Low enough to get this man Puck's ass hoisted on a goddamned petrified antler. So where's the valuable stuff kept?"

"What's not in the general collection is kept in the Secure Area, a location with a separate security system."

"What about signing in to these Archives, and all that?"

"There's a logbook."

"Where's the book?"

Manetti nodded at a massive volume on the desk. "It was photocopied for the police after Puck's death."

"And what does it record?"

"Everybody who enters or leaves the Archives area. But the police already noticed that some of the most recent pages were razored out—"

"Everybody? Staff as well as visiting researchers?"

"Everybody. But—"

Custer turned to Noyes, then pointed at the book. "Bag it."

Manetti looked at him quickly. "That's Museum property."

"It was. Now it's evidence."

"But you've already taken all the important evidence, like the typewriter those notes were written on, and the—"

"When we're done here, you'll get a receipt for everything." *If you ask nicely,* Custer thought to himself. "So, what we got here?" he repeated.

"Dead files, mostly, from other Museum departments. Papers of historical value, memos, letters, reports. Everything but the personnel files and some departmental files. The Museum saves everything, naturally, as a public institution."

"What about that letter found here? The one reported in the papers, describing those killings. How was that found?"

"You'll have to ask Special Agent Pendergast, who found it along with Nora Kelly. He found it hidden in some kind of box. Made out of an elephant's foot, I believe."

That Nora Kelly again. Custer made a mental note to question her himself once he was done here. She'd be his prime suspect, if he thought her capable of hoisting a heavyset man onto a dinosaur horn. Maybe she had accomplices.

Custer jotted some notes. "Has anything been moved in or out of here in the past month?"

"There may have been some routine additions to the collection. I believe that once a month or so they send dead files down here." Manetti paused. "And, after the discovery of the letter, it and all related documents were sent upstairs for curating. Along with other material."

Custer nodded. "And Collopy ordered that, did he not?"

"Actually, I believe it was done at the order of the Museum's vice president and general counsel, Roger Brisbane."

Brisbane: he'd heard that name before, too. Custer made another note. "And what, exactly, did the related documents consist of?"

"I don't know. You'll have to ask Mr. Brisbane."

Custer turned to the two museum employees behind the desk. "This guy, Brisbane. You see him down here a lot?"

"Quite a bit, recently," said one.

"What's he been doing?"

The man shrugged. "Just asking a lot of questions, that's all."

"What kind of questions?"

"Questions about Nora Kelly, that FBI guy . . . He wanted to know what they'd been looking at, where they went, that kind of thing. And some journalist. He wanted to know if a journalist had been in here. I can't remember the name."

"Smithbrick?"

"No, but something like that."

Custer picked up his notebook, flipped through it. There it was. "William Smithback, Junior."

"That's it."

Custer nodded. "How about this Agent Pendergast? Any of you see him?"

The two exchanged glances. "Just once," the first man said.

"Nora Kelly?"

"Yup," said the same man: a young fellow with hair so short he looked almost bald.

Custer turned toward him. "Did you know Puck?"

The man nodded.

"Your name?"

"Oscar. Oscar Gibbs. I was his assistant."

"Gibbs, did Puck have any enemies?"

Custer noticed the two men exchanging another glance, more significant this time.

"Well . . ." Gibbs hesitated, then began again. "Once, Brisbane came down here and really lit into Mr. Puck. Screaming and yelling, threatening to bury him, to have him fired."

"Is that right? Why?"

"Something about Mr. Puck leaking damaging information, failing to respect the Museum's intellectual property rights. Things like that. I think he was mad because Human Resources hadn't backed up his recommendation to fire Mr. Puck. Said he wasn't through with him, not by a long shot. That's really all I remember."

"When was this, exactly?"

Gibbs thought a moment. "Let's see. That would have been the thirteenth. No, the twelfth. October twelfth."

Custer picked up his notebook again and made another notation, longer this time. He heard a shattering crash from the bowels of the Archives; a shout; then a protracted ripping noise. He felt a warm feeling of satisfaction. There would be no more letters hidden in elephants' feet when he was done. He turned his attention back to Gibbs.

"Any other enemies?"

"No. To tell you the truth, Mr. Puck was one of the nicest people in the whole Museum. It was a big shock to see Brisbane come down on him like that."

This Brisbane's not a popular guy, thought Custer. He turned to Noyes. "Get this man Brisbane for me, will you? I want to talk to him."

Noyes moved toward the front desk just as the Archives door burst open. Custer turned to see a man dressed in a tuxedo, his black tie askew, brilliantined hair hanging across his outraged face.

"What the hell is going on here?" the man shouted in Custer's direction. "You just can't come bursting in here like this, turning the place upside down. Let me see your warrant!"

Noyes began fumbling for the warrant, but Custer stayed him with a single hand. It was remarkable, really, how steady his hand felt, how calm and collected he was during all this, the turning point of his entire career. "And who might you be?" he asked in his coolest voice.

"Roger C. Brisbane III. First vice president and general counsel of the Museum."

Custer nodded. "Ah, Mr. Brisbane. You're just the man I wanted to see."

SEVEN

SMITHBACK FROZE, STARING INTO THE POOL OF DARKNESS
that lay at the far corner of the room. "Who is that?" he
finally managed to croak.

There was no response.

"Are you the caretaker?" He gave a strained laugh. "Can
you believe it? I've locked myself in."

Again, silence.

Perhaps the voice had been his imagination. God knows,
he'd seen enough in this house to cure him of ever wanting
to watch another horror movie.

He tried again. "Well, all I can say is, I'm glad you
happened by. If you could help me find my way to the
door—"

The sentence was choked off by an involuntary spasm of
fright.

A figure had stepped out into the dim light. It was muffled
in a long dark coat, features in deep shadow under a derby
hat. In one upraised hand was a heavy, old-fashioned scalpel.
The razor edge gleamed faintly as the man turned it slowly,
almost lovingly, between slender fingers. In the other hand,
a hypodermic syringe winked and glimmered.

"An unexpected pleasure to see you here," the figure said in a low, dry voice as he caressed the scalpel. "But convenient. In fact, you've arrived just in time."

Some primitive instinct of self-preservation, stronger even than the horror that had seized him, spurred Smithback into action. He spun and ran. But it was so dark, and the figure moved so blindingly fast . . .

Later—he didn't know how much later—Smithback woke up. There was a torpor, and a strange, languorous kind of confusion. He'd had a dream, a terrible dream, he remembered; but it was over now and everything was fine, he would wake to a beautiful fall morning, the hideous fragmented memories of the nightmare melting away into his subconscious. He'd rise, dress, have his usual breakfast of red flannel hash at his favorite Greek coffeeshop, and slowly take on once again, as he did every morning, his mundane, workaday life.

But as his mind gradually grew more alert, he realized that the broken memories, the horrible hinted fragments, were not evaporating. He had somehow been caught. In the dark. In Leng's house.

Leng's house . . .

He shook his head. It throbbed violently at the movement. The man in the derby hat was the Surgeon. In Leng's house.

Suddenly, Smithback was struck dumb by shock and fear. Of all the terrible thoughts that darted through his mind at that terrible moment, one stood out from the rest: *Pendergast was right. Pendergast was right all along.*

Enoch Leng was still alive.

It was Leng himself who was the Surgeon.

And Smithback had walked *right into his house.*

That noise he was hearing, that hideous gasping, was his own hyperventilation, the suck of air through tape covering his mouth. He forced himself to slow down, to take stock. There was a strong smell of mold around him, and it was pitch black. The air was cold, damp. The pain in his head increased. Smithback moved his arm toward his forehead, felt it stop abruptly—felt the tug of an iron cuff around his wrist, heard the clank of a chain. What the hell was this?

His heart began to race, faster and faster, as one by one the holes in his memory filled: the endless echoing rooms, the voice from the darkness, the man stepping out of the shadows . . . the glittering scalpel. *Oh, God, was it really Leng? After 130 years? Leng?*

He tried to stand in automatic groggy panic but fell back again immediately, to a chorus of clinks and clatterings. He was stark naked, chained to the ground by his arms and legs, his mouth sealed with heavy tape.

This couldn't be happening. Oh, Jesus, this was insane.

He hadn't told anyone he was coming up here. Nobody knew where he was. Nobody even knew he was missing. If only he'd told someone, the pool secretary, O'Shaughnessy, his great-grandfather, his half-sister, *anyone* . . .

He lay back, head pounding, hyperventilating again, heart battering in his rib cage.

He had been drugged and chained by the man in black— the man in the derby hat. That much was clear. The same man who tried to kill Pendergast, no doubt; the same man, probably, who had killed Puck and the others. The Surgeon. He was in the dungeon of the Surgeon.

The Surgeon. Professor Enoch Leng.

The sound of a footfall brought him to full alertness. There was a scraping noise, then a painfully bright rectangle of light appeared in the wall of darkness ahead. In the reflected light, Smithback could see he was in a small basement room with a cement floor, stone walls and an iron door. He felt a surge of hope, even gratitude.

A pair of moist lips appeared at the iron opening. They moved.

"Please do not discompose yourself," came the voice. "All this will be over soon. Struggle is unnecessary."

There was something almost familiar in that voice, and yet inexpressibly strange and terrible, like the whispered tones of nightmare.

The slot slid shut, leaving Smithback in darkness once more.

All those Dreadful Little Cuts

ONE

THE BIG ROLLS-ROYCE GLIDED ITS WAY ALONG THE ONE-lane road that crossed Little Governors Island. Fog lay thick in the marshes and hollows, obscuring the surrounding East River and the ramparts of Manhattan that lay beyond. The headlights slid past a row of ancient, long-dead chestnut trees, then striped their way across heavy wrought iron gates. As the car stopped, the lights came to rest on a bronze plaque: *Mount Mercy Hospital for the Criminally Insane.*

A security guard stepped out of a booth into the glare and approached the car. He was heavyset, tall, friendly looking. Pendergast lowered the rear window and the man leaned inside.

"Visiting hours are over," he said.

Pendergast reached into his jacket, removed his shield wallet, opened it for the guard.

The man gave it a long look, and then nodded, as if it was all in a day's work.

"And how may we help you, Special Agent Pendergast?"

"I'm here to see a patient."

"And the name of the patient?"

"Pendergast. Miss Cornelia Delamere Pendergast."

There was a short, uncomfortable silence.

"Is this official law enforcement business?" The security guard didn't sound quite so friendly anymore.

"It is."

"All right. I'll call up to the big house. Dr. Ostrom is on duty tonight. You can park your car in the official slot to the left of the main door. They'll be waiting for you in reception."

Within a few minutes Pendergast was following the well-groomed, fastidious-looking Dr. Ostrom down a long, echoing corridor. Two guards walked in front, and two behind. Fancy wainscoting and decorative molding could still be glimpsed along the corridor, hidden beneath innumerable layers of institutional paint. A century before, in the days when consumption ravaged all classes of New York society, Mount Mercy Hospital had been a grand sanatorium, catering to the tubercular offspring of the rich. Now, thanks in part to its insular location, it had become a high-security facility for people who had committed heinous crimes but were found not guilty by reason of insanity.

"How is she?" Pendergast asked.

There was a slight hesitation in the doctor's answer. "About the same," he said.

They stopped at last in front of a thick steel door, a single barred window sunk into its face. One of the forward guards unlocked the door, then stood outside with his partner while the other two guards followed Pendergast within.

They were standing in a small "quiet room" almost devoid of decoration. No pictures hung on the lightly padded walls. There was a plastic sofa, a pair of plastic chairs, a single table. Everything was bolted to the floor. There was no clock, and the sole fluorescent ceiling light was hidden behind heavy wire mesh. There was nothing that could be used as a weapon, or to assist a suicide. In the far wall stood another steel door, even thicker, without a window. *Warning: Risk of Elopement* was posted above it in large letters.

Pendergast took a seat in one of the plastic chairs, and crossed his legs.

The two forward attendants disappeared through the inner door. For a few minutes the small room fell into silence, punctuated only by the faint sounds of screams and an even fainter, rhythmic pounding. And then, louder and much nearer, came the shrill protesting voice of an old woman. The door opened, and one of the guards pushed a wheelchair into the room. The chair's five-point leather restraint was almost invisible beneath the heavy layer of rubber that covered every metal surface.

In the chair, securely bound by the restraints, sat a prim, elderly dowager. She was wearing a long, old-fashioned black taffeta dress, Victorian button-up shoes, and a black mourning veil. When she saw Pendergast her complaints abruptly ceased.

"Raise my veil," she commanded. One of the guards lifted it from her face, and, standing well away, laid it down her back.

The woman stared at Pendergast, her palsied, liver-spotted face trembling slightly.

Pendergast turned to Dr. Ostrom. "Will you kindly leave us alone?"

"Someone must remain," said Ostrom. "And please give the patient some distance, Mr. Pendergast."

"The last time I visited, I was allowed a private moment with my great-aunt."

"If you will recall, Mr. Pendergast, the last time you visited—" Ostrom began rather sharply.

Pendergast held up his hand. "So be it."

"This is a rather late hour to be visiting. How much time do you need?"

"Fifteen minutes."

"Very well." The doctor nodded to the attendants, who took up places on either side of the exit. Ostrom himself stood before the outer door, as far from the woman as possible, crossed his arms, and waited.

Pendergast tried to pull the chair closer, remembered it was bolted to the floor, and leaned forward instead, gazing intently at the old woman.

"How are you, Aunt Cornelia?" he asked.

The woman bent toward him. She whispered hoarsely, "My dear, how lovely to see you. May I offer you a spot of tea with cream and sugar?"

One of the guards snickered, but shut up abruptly when Ostrom cast a sharp glance in his direction.

"No, thank you, Aunt Cornelia."

"It's just as well. The service here has declined dreadfully these past few years. It's so hard to find good help these days. Why haven't you visited me sooner, my dear? You know that at my age I cannot travel."

Pendergast leaned nearer.

"Mr. Pendergast, not quite so close, if you please," Dr. Ostrom murmured.

Pendergast eased back. "I've been working, Aunt Cornelia."

"Work is for the middle classes, my dear. Pendergasts do not work."

Pendergast lowered his voice. "There's not much time, I'm afraid, Aunt Cornelia. I wanted to ask you some questions. About your great-uncle Antoine."

The old lady pursed her lips in a disapproving line. "Great-uncle Antoine? They say he went north, to New York

City. Became a Yankee. But that was many years ago. Long before I was born."

"Tell me what you know about him, Aunt Cornelia."

"Surely you've heard the stories, my boy. It is an unpleasant subject for all of us, you know."

"I'd like to hear them from you, just the same."

"Well! He inherited the family tendency to madness. There but for the grace of God . . ." The old woman sighed pityingly.

"What kind of madness?" Pendergast knew the answer, of course; but he needed to hear it again. There were always details, nuances, that were new.

"Even as a boy he developed certain dreadful obsessions. He was quite a brilliant youth, you know: sarcastic, witty, strange. At seven you couldn't beat him in a game of chess or backgammon. He excelled at whist, and even suggested some refinements that, I understand, helped develop auction bridge. He was terribly interested in natural history, and started keeping quite a collection of horrid things in his dressing room—insects, snakes, bones, fossils, that sort of thing. He also had inherited his father's interest in elixirs, restoratives, chemicals. And poisons."

A strange gleam came into the old lady's black eyes at the mention of poisons, and both attendants shifted uneasily.

Ostrom cleared his throat. "Mr. Pendergast, how much longer? We don't want to unduly disturb the patient."

"Ten minutes."

"No more."

The old lady went on. "After the tragedy with his mother, he grew moody and reclusive. He spent a great deal of time alone, mixing up chemicals. But then, no doubt you know the cause of *that* fascination."

Pendergast nodded.

"He developed his own variant of the family crest, like an old apothecary's sign it was, three gilded balls. He hung it over his door. They say he poisoned the six family dogs in an experiment. And then he began spending a lot of time down . . . down *there*. Do you know where I mean?"

"Yes."

"They say he always felt more comfortable with the dead than with the living, you know. And when he wasn't there, he was over at St. Charles Cemetery, with that appalling old woman Marie LeClaire. You know, Cajun voodoo and all that."

Pendergast nodded again.

"He helped her with her potions and charms and frightful little stick dolls and making marks on graves. Then there was that unpleasantness with her tomb, after she died . . ."

"Unpleasantness?"

The old woman sighed, lowered her head. "The interference with her grave, the violated body and all those dreadful little cuts. Of course you *must* know that story."

"I've forgotten." Pendergast's voice was soft, gentle, probing.

"He believed he was going to bring her back to life. There was the question of whether she had put him up to it before she died, charged him with some kind of dreadful after-death assignment. The missing pieces of flesh were never found, not a one. No, that's not quite right. I believe they found an ear in the belly of an alligator caught a week later out of the swamp. The earring gave it away, of course." Her voice trailed off. She turned to one of the attendants, and spoke in a tone of cold command. "My hair needs attention."

One of the attendants—the one wearing surgical gloves—came over and gingerly patted the woman's hair back into place, keeping a wary distance.

She turned back to Pendergast.

"She had a kind of sexual hold over him, as dreadful as that sounds, considering the sixty-year difference in their ages." The old lady shuddered, half in disgust, half in pleasure. "Clearly, she encouraged his interest in reincarnation, miracle cures, silly things like that."

"What did you hear about his disappearance?"

"It happened at the age of twenty-one, when he came into his fortune. But 'disappearance' really isn't quite the word, you know: he was asked to leave the house. At least, so I've been told. He'd begun to talk about saving, healing the world—making up for what his father had done, I suppose—but that cut no mustard with the rest of the family. Years later, when his cousins tried to track down the money he'd inherited and taken with him, he seemed to have vanished into thin air. They were terribly disappointed. It was so *very* much money, you see."

Pendergast nodded. There was a long silence.

"I have one final question for you, Aunt Cornelia."

"What is it?"

"It is a moral question."

"A moral question. How curious. Is this connected by any chance with Great-Uncle Antoine?"

Pendergast did not answer directly. "For the past month, I have been searching for a man. This man is in possession of a secret. I am very close to discovering his whereabouts, and it is only a matter of time until I confront him."

The old woman said nothing.

"If I win the confrontation—which is by no means certain—I may be faced with the question of what to do with his secret. I may be called upon to make a decision that will have, possibly, a profound effect on the future of the human race."

"And what is this secret?"

Pendergast lowered his voice to the merest ghost of a whisper.

"I believe it is a medical formula that will allow anyone, by following a certain regimen, to extend his life by at least a century, perhaps more. It will not vanquish death, but it will significantly postpone it."

There was a silence. The old lady's eyes gleamed anew. "Tell me, how much will this treatment cost? Will it be cheap, or dear?"

"I don't know."

"And how many others will have access to this formula besides yourself?"

"I'll be the only one. I'll have very little time, maybe only seconds after it comes into my hands, to decide what to do with it."

The silence stretched on into minutes. "And how was this formula developed?"

"Suffice to say, it cost the lives of many innocent people. In a singularly cruel fashion."

"That adds a further dimension to the problem. However, the answer is quite clear. When this formula comes into your possession, you must destroy it immediately."

Pendergast looked at her curiously. "Are you quite sure? It's what medical science has most desired since the beginning."

"There is an old French curse: may your fondest wish come true. If this treatment is cheap and available to everyone, it will destroy the earth through overpopulation. If it is dear and available only to the very rich, it will cause riots, wars, a breakdown of the social contract. Either way, it will lead directly to human misery. What is the value of a long life, when it is lived in squalor and unhappiness?"

"What about the immeasurable increase in wisdom that this discovery will bring, when you consider the one, maybe two hundred years, of additional learning and study it will afford the brilliant mind? Think, Aunt Cornelia, of what someone like Goethe or Copernicus or Einstein could have done for humanity with a two-hundred-year life span."

The old woman scoffed. "The wise and good are outnumbered a thousand to one by the brutal and stupid. When you give an Einstein two centuries to perfect his science, you give a thousand others two centuries to perfect their brutality."

This time, the silence seemed to stretch into minutes. By the door, Dr. Ostrom stirred restlessly.

"Are you all right, my dear?" the old lady asked, looking intently at Pendergast.

"Yes."

He gazed into her dark, strange eyes, so full of wisdom, insight, and the most profound insanity. "Thank you, Aunt Cornelia," he said.

Then he straightened up. "Dr. Ostrom?"

The doctor glanced toward him.

"We're finished here."

TWO

CUSTER STOOD IN A POOL OF LIGHT BEFORE THE ARCHIVES desk. Clouds of dust—by-products of the ongoing investigation—billowed out from aisles in the dimness beyond. The pompous ass, Brisbane, was still protesting in the background, but Custer paid little attention.

The investigation, which had started so strongly, was bogging down. So far his men had found an amazing assortment of junk—old maps, charts, snakeskins, boxes of teeth, disgusting unidentifiable organs pickled in centuries-old alcohol—but not one thing that resembled an actual clue. Custer had been certain that, once in the Archives, the puzzle would immediately fall into place; that his newfound investigative skill would make the critical connection everyone else had overlooked. But so far there had been no brainstorm, no connection. An image of Commissioner Rocker's face—staring at him through lowered, skeptical brows—hung before his eyes. A feeling of unease, imperfectly suppressed, began to filter through his limbs. And the place was huge: it would take weeks to search at this rate.

The Museum lawyer was talking more loudly now, and Custer forced himself to listen.

"This is nothing but a fishing expedition," Brisbane was saying. "You can't just come in here and turn the place upside down." He gestured furiously at the NYPD evidence lockers lying on the floor, a riot of objects scattered within and around them. "And all that is Museum property!"

Absently, Custer gestured toward the warrant that Noyes was holding. "You've seen the warrant."

"Yes, I have. And it's not worth the paper it's written on. I've never seen such general language. I protest this warrant, and I am stating for the record that I will not permit the Museum to be further searched."

"Let's have your boss, Dr. Collopy, decide that. Has anybody heard from him yet?"

"As the Museum's legal counsel, I'm authorized to speak for Dr. Collopy."

Custer refolded his arms gloomily. There came another crash from the recesses of the Archives, some shouting, and a ripping sound. An officer soon appeared, carrying a stuffed crocodile, cotton pouring from a fresh slit in its belly. He laid it in one of the evidence lockers.

"What the hell are they doing back there?" Brisbane shouted. "Hey, you! Yes, you! You've damaged that specimen!"

The officer looked at him with a dull expression, then shambled back into the files.

Custer said nothing. His feeling of anxiety increased. So far, the questioning of Museum staff hadn't come up with anything either—just the same old stuff the earlier investigation had produced. This had been his call, his operation. His and his alone. If he was wrong—it almost didn't bear thinking, of course, but *if*—he'd be hung out to dry like last week's laundry.

"I'm going to call Museum security and have your men escorted out," Brisbane fumed. "This is intolerable. Where's Manetti?"

"Manetti was the man who let us in here," Custer said distractedly. What if he'd made a mistake—a huge mistake?

"He shouldn't have done that. Where is he?" Brisbane turned, found Oscar Gibbs, the Archives assistant. "Where's Manetti?"

"He left," Gibbs said.

Custer watched absently, noticing how the young man's insolent tone, his dark look, conveyed what he thought of Brisbane. *Brisbane's not popular,* Custer thought again. *Got a lot of enemies. Puck sure must have hated the guy, the way Brisbane came down on him. Can't say I blame him one bit for—*

And that was when the revelation hit him. Like his initial revelation, only bigger: much bigger. So obvious in retrospect, and yet so difficult to first perceive. This was the kind of brilliant leap of intuition one received departmental citations for. It was a leap of deduction worthy of Sherlock Holmes.

He turned now, watching Brisbane subtly, but intently. The man's well-groomed face was glistening, his hair askew, eyes glittering with anger.

"Left where?" Brisbane was demanding.

Gibbs shrugged insolently.

Brisbane strode over to the desk and picked up the phone. Custer continued to watch him. He dialed a few numbers, and left low, excited messages.

"Captain Custer," he said, turning back. "Once again, I am ordering you to remove your men from the premises."

Custer returned the glance from between lowered lids. He'd have to do this very carefully.

"Mr. Brisbane," he asked, taking what hoped sounded like a reasonable tone. "Shall we discuss this in your office?"

For a moment, Brisbane seemed taken aback. "My office?"

"It'll be more private. Perhaps we needn't search the Museum much longer. Perhaps we can settle this in your office, now."

Brisbane seemed to consider this. "Very well. Follow me."

Custer nodded to his man, Lieutenant Detective Piles. "You take over here."

"Yes, sir."

Then Custer turned toward Noyes. The merest crook of his fat finger brought the little man to his side.

"Noyes, I want you with me," he murmured. "Got your service piece on you?"

Noyes nodded, rheumy eyes glistening in the dusky light.

"Good. Then let's go."

THREE

THE SLOT OPENED AGAIN. IN THE ENDLESS PERIOD OF darkness and terror, Smithback had lost his perception of time. How long had it been? Ten minutes? An hour? A day?

The voice spoke, lips once again gleaming in the rectangle of light. "How kind of you to visit me in my very old and interesting house. I hope you enjoyed seeing my collections. I am particularly fond of the corydon. Did you, by chance, see the corydon?"

Smithback tried to respond, belatedly remembering that his mouth was taped.

"Ah! How thoughtless of me. Do not trouble yourself to answer. I will speak. You will listen."

Smithback's mind raced through the possibilities for escape. There were none.

"Yes, the corydon is most interesting. As is the mosasaur from the chalk beds of Kansas. And of course the durdag from Tibet is quite unusual, one of only two in the world. I understand it was fashioned from the skull of the fifteenth reincarnation of the Buddha."

Smithback heard a dry laugh, like the scattering of withered leaves.

"Altogether a most interesting cabinet of curiosities, my dear Mr. Smithback. I'm sorry that so few people have had a chance to see it, and that those so honored find themselves unable to make a return visit."

There was a silence. And then the voice continued, softly and gently: "I will do you well, Mr. Smithback. No effort will be spared."

A spasm of fear, unlike anything he had ever known, racked Smithback's limbs. *I will do you well . . .* Do *you well . . .* Smithback realized that he was about to die. In his extremity of terror, he did not immediately notice that Leng had called him by name.

"It will be a memorable experience—more memorable than those who have come before you. I have made great strides, remarkable strides. I have devised a most exacting surgical procedure. You will be awake to the very end. Consciousness, you see, is the key: I now realize that. *Painstaking* care will be taken, I assure you."

There was a silence as Smithback struggled to keep his reason about him.

The lips pursed. "I shouldn't want to keep you waiting. Shall we proceed to the laboratory?"

A lock rattled and the iron door creaked open. The dark figure in the derby hat who approached was now holding a long hypodermic needle. A clear drop trembled at its end. A pair of round, old-fashioned smoked glasses were pushed into his face.

"This is merely an injection to relax your muscles. Succinyl choline. Very similar to curare. It's a paralyzing agent; you'll find it tends to render the sort of weakness one feels in dreams. You know what I mean: the danger is coming, you try to escape, but you find yourself unable to move. Have no fear, Mr. Smithback: though you'll be unable to move, you *will* remain conscious throughout much of the operation, until the final excision and removal is performed. It will be much more interesting for you that way."

Smithback struggled as the needle approached.

"You see, it's a delicate operation. It requires a steady and highly expert hand. We can't have the patient thrashing about during the procedure. The merest slip of the scalpel and all would be ruined. You might as well dispose of the resource and start afresh."

Still the needle approached.

"I suggest you take a deep breath now, Mr. Smithback."

I will do *you well* . . .

With the strength born of consummate terror, Smithback threw himself from side to side, trying to tear free his chains. He opened his mouth against the heavy tape, trying desperately to scream, feeling the flesh of his lips tearing away from his skin under the effort. He jerked violently, fighting against the manacles, but the figure with the needle kept approaching inexorably—and then he felt the sting of the needle as it slid into his flesh, a sensation of heat spreading through his veins, and then a terrible weakness: the precise weakness Leng had described, that feeling of paralysis that happens in the very worst of dreams, at the very worst possible moment.

But this, Smithback knew, was no dream.

FOUR

POLICE SERGEANT PAUL J. FINESTER REALLY HATED THE
whole business. It was a terrible, criminal, waste of time. He
glanced around at the rows of wooden tables set up in parallel
lines across the library carpet; at the frumpy, tweed-wearing,
bug-eyed, moth-eaten characters who sat across the tables
from the cops. Some looked scared, others outraged. Clearly,
none of these museum wimps knew anything: they were just
a bunch of scientists with bad teeth and even worse breath.
Where did they find these characters? It made him mad to
think of his hard-earned tax dollars supporting this stone
shitpile. Not just that, but it was already ten P.M., and when
he got home his wife was going to kill him. Never mind that
it was his job, that he was being paid time and a half, that
they had a mortgage on the fancy Cobble Hill apartment she
forced him to buy and a baby who cost a fortune in diapers.
She was still going to kill him. He would come home, dinner
would be a blackened crisp in the oven—where it had been
since six o'clock, at 250 degrees—the ball and chain would
already be in bed with the light out, but still wide awake,
lying there like a ramrod, mad as hell, the baby crying and
unattended. The wife wouldn't say anything when he got

into the bed, just turn her back to him, with a huge self-pitying sigh, and—

"Finester?"

Finester turned to see his partner, O'Grady, staring at him. "You okay, Finester? You look like somebody died."

Finester sighed. "I wish it was me."

"Cheese it. We've got another."

There was something in O'Grady's tone that caused Finester to look across their set of desks. Instead of yet another geek, here was a woman—an unusually pretty woman, in fact—with long copper hair and hazel eyes, trim athletic body. He found himself straightening up, sucking in the gut, flexing the biceps. The woman sat down across from them, and he caught a whiff of her perfume: expensive, nice, very subtle. God, a real looker. He glanced at O'Grady and saw the same transformation. Finester grabbed his clipboard, ran his eye down the interrogation lineup. So this was Nora Kelly. The famous, infamous Nora Kelly. The one who found the third body, who'd been chased in the Archives. He hadn't expected someone so young. Or so attractive.

O'Grady beat him to the opening. "Dr. Kelly, please make yourself comfortable." His voice had taken on a silken, honeyed tone. "I am Sergeant O'Grady, and this is Sergeant Finester. Do we have permission to tape-record you?"

"If it's necessary," the woman said. Her voice wasn't quite as sexy as her looks. It was clipped, short, irritated.

"You have the right to a lawyer," continued O'Grady, his voice still low and soothing, "and you have the right to decline our questioning. We want you to understand this is voluntary."

"And if I refuse?"

O'Grady chuckled in a friendly way. "It's not my

decision, you understand, but they might subpoena you, make you come down to the station. Lawyers are expensive. It would be inconvenient. We just have a few questions here, no big deal. You're not a suspect. We're just asking for a little help."

"All right," the woman said. "Go ahead. I've been questioned several times before. I suppose once more won't hurt."

O'Grady began to speak again, but this time Finester was ready, and he cut O'Grady off. He wasn't going to sit there like an idiot while O'Grady did all the talking. The guy was as bad as his wife.

"Dr. Kelly," he said, hastily, perhaps a little too loud, quickly covering it with a smile of his own, "we're delighted you're willing to help us. For the record, please state your full name, address, the date, and time. There's a clock on the wall over there, but no, I see you're wearing a watch. It's just a formality, you know, so we can keep our tapes straight, not get them mixed up. We wouldn't want to arrest the wrong person." He chuckled at his joke and was a little disappointed when she didn't chuckle along with him.

O'Grady gave him a pitying, condescending look. Finester felt the irritation toward his partner rise. When you got down to it, he really couldn't stand the guy. So much for the unbreakable blue bond. He found himself wishing O'Grady would stop a bullet someday soon. Like tomorrow.

The woman stated her name. Then Finester jumped in again and recorded his own, O'Grady following a little grudgingly. After a few more formalities, Finester put the background sheet aside and reached for the latest list of prepared questions. The list seemed longer than before, and he was surprised to see some handwritten entries at the bottom. They must have just been added, obviously in haste.

Who the hell had been messing with their interrogation sheets? This whole thing was balls up. Totally balls up.

O'Grady seized on Finester's silence as an opportunity. "Dr. Kelly," he jumped in, "could you please describe in your own words your involvement in this case? Please take all the time you need to recall the details. If you don't remember something, or are unsure about it, feel free to let us know. I've found that it's better to say you can't remember than to give us details that may not be accurate." He gave her a broad smile, his blue eyes twinkling with an almost conspiratorial gleam.

Screw him, thought Finester.

The woman gave a testy sigh, crossed her long legs, and began to speak.

FIVE

SMITHBACK FELT THE PARALYSIS, THE DREADFUL helplessness, take complete possession of him. His limbs were dead, motionless, foreign. He could not blink his eyes. Worst of all—by far, the worst of all—he could not even fill his lungs with air. His body was immobilized. He panicked as he tried to work his lungs, struggled to draw in breath. It was like drowning, only worse.

Leng hovered over him now, a dark figure backlit by the rectangle of the door, spent needle in his hand. His face was a shadow beneath the brow of his derby hat.

A hand reached forward, grasped the edge of the duct tape that still partially sealed Smithback's mouth. "No need for this anymore," Leng said. With a sharp tug, it was ripped away. "Now, let's get you intubated. After all, it wouldn't do to have you asphyxiate before the procedure begins."

Smithback tried to draw breath for a scream. Nothing came but the barest whisper. His tongue felt thick and impossibly large in his mouth. His jaw sagged, a rivulet of saliva drooling down his chin. It was a consummate struggle just to draw in a spoonful of air.

The figure took a step back, disappearing beyond the door. There was a rattle in the hallway and Leng returned, wheeling a stainless steel gurney and a large, boxlike machine on rubber wheels. He positioned the gurney next to Smithback, then bent over and, with an old iron key, quickly unlocked the cuffs around the reporter's wrists and legs. Through his terror and despair Smithback could smell the musty, mothball odor of antique clothes, along with the tang of sweat and a faint whiff of eucalyptus, as if Leng had been sucking on a lozenge.

"I'm going to place you on the gurney now," Leng said.

Smithback felt himself being lifted. And then, cold unyielding metal pressed against his naked limbs. His nose was running but he could not raise his arm to brush it away. His need for oxygen was becoming acute. He was totally paralyzed—but, most terrible of all, he retained an utter clarity of consciousness and sensation.

Leng reappeared in his field of vision, a slender plastic tube in one hand. Placing his fingers on Smithback's jaw, Leng pulled the mouth wide. Smithback felt the tube knock roughly against the back of his throat, slide down his trachea. How awful to feel the intense, undeniable desire to retch— and yet be unable to make even the slightest movement. There was a hiss as the ventilating machine filled his lungs with air.

For a moment, the relief was so great Smithback momentarily forgot his predicament.

Now the gurney was moving. A low, brickwork ceiling was passing by overhead, punctuated occasionally by naked bulbs. A moment later, and the ceiling changed, rising into what seemed a cavernous space. The gurney swung around again, then came to rest. Leng bent down, out of sight. Smithback heard four measured clicks, one after the other, as the wheels were locked in place. There were banks of heavy lights, a whiff of alcohol and Betadine that covered a subtler, far worse, smell.

Leng slid his arms beneath Smithback, raised him up once again, and moved him from the gurney to another steel table, wider and even colder. The motion was gentle, almost loving.

And then—with a completely different motion, economical and amazingly strong—he turned Smithback over onto his stomach.

Smithback could not close his mouth, and his tongue pressed against the metal gurney, unwillingly sampling the sour chlorinated taste of disinfectants. It made him think about who else might have been on this table, and what might have happened to them. A wave of fear and nausea washed over him. The ventilator tube gurgled inside his mouth.

Then Leng approached and, passing his hand across Smithback's face, shut his eyelids.

The table was cold, so cold. He could hear Leng moving around. There was a pressure on his elbow, a brief sting as an intravenous needle was inserted near his wrist, the ripping sound of medical tape being pulled from its canister. He could smell the eucalyptus breath, hear the low voice. It spoke in a whisper.

"There will be some pain, I'm afraid," the voice said as straps were fixed to Smithback's limbs. "Rather a lot of pain, in fact. But good science is never really free from pain. So do not discompose yourself. And if I may offer a word of advice?"

Smithback tried to struggle, but his body was far away. The whisper continued, soft and soothing: *"Be like the gazelle in the jaws of the lion: limp, accepting, resigned. Trust me. That is the best way."*

There was the sound of water rushing in a sink, the clink of steel on steel, instruments sliding in a metal basin. The light in the room grew abruptly brighter. Smithback's pulse began to race wildly, faster and faster, until the table beneath him seemed almost to rock in time with the frantic beating of his heart.

SIX

NORA SHIFTED IN THE UNCOMFORTABLE WOODEN CHAIR, glanced at her watch for what had to be the fifth time. Ten-thirty. This was like the questioning she'd endured after finding Puck's body, only worse—much worse. Though she'd deliberately kept her story brief, reduced her answers to mere one-liners, the questions kept coming in an endless, moronic stream. Questions about her work at the Museum. Questions about being chased by the Surgeon in the Archives. Questions about the typewritten note Puck—or rather the murderer, pretending to be Puck—had sent her, which she'd given to the police long before. All questions she had already answered two or three times, to more intelligent and thoughtful police officers than these. Worse, the two cops sitting opposite her—one a beefed-up little troll, the other decent-looking but full of himself—showed no signs of reaching the end of their list. They kept interrupting each other, darting angry looks back and forth, competing for heaven only knew what reason. If there was bad blood between these two, they shouldn't be working together. God, what a performance.

"Dr. Kelly," said the short one, Finester—looking for the thousandth time at his notes—"we're almost through here."

"Praise be to God."

This comment was met with a short silence. Then O'Grady waded in once again, looking at a freshly scribbled sheet that had just been handed to him.

"You are familiar with a Mr. William Smithback?"

Nora felt her annoyance giving way to a sudden wariness. "Yes."

"What is your relationship to Mr. Smithback?"

"Ex-boyfriend."

O'Grady turned the paper over in his hands. "We have a report here that earlier today, Mr. Smithback impersonated a security officer and gained unauthorized clearance to some high-security files in the Museum. Would you know why?"

"No."

"When was the last time you spoke to Mr. Smithback?"

Nora sighed. "I don't remember."

Finester sat back in his seat, folded his beefy arms. "Take your time, please." He had a shiny, paste-colored dome of a head, topped by a tuft of hair so thick and coarse it looked like a hairy island in the middle of his bald head.

This was intolerable. "Maybe a week."

"Under what circumstances?"

"He was harassing me in my office."

"Why?"

"He wanted to tell me that Agent Pendergast had been stabbed. Museum security dragged him away. They'll have a record of it." What the hell was Smithback doing back in the Museum? The guy was incorrigible.

"You have no idea what Mr. Smithback was looking for?"

"I believe I just *said* that."

There was a short silence while O'Grady checked his notes. "It says here that Mr. Smithback—"

Nora interrupted impatiently. "Look, why aren't you pursuing some real leads here? Like those typewritten notes of the killer's, the one sent to me and the one left on Puck's desk? Obviously, the killer is somebody with access to the Museum. Why all these questions about Smithback? I haven't spoken to him in a week. I don't know anything about what he's up to and, frankly, I couldn't care less."

"We have to ask you these questions, Dr. Kelly," O'Grady replied.

"Why?"

"They're on my list. It's my job."

"Jesus." She passed a hand over her forehead. This whole episode was Kafkaesque. "Go ahead."

"After a warrant was put out on Mr. Smithback, we found his rented car parked on upper Riverside Drive. Would you know why he rented the car?"

"How many times do I have to tell you? I haven't spoken to him in a week."

O'Grady turned over the sheet. "How long have you known Mr. Smithback?"

"Almost two years."

"Where did you meet him?"

"In Utah."

"Under what circumstances?"

"On an archaeological expedition." Nora was suddenly having trouble paying attention to the questions. Riverside Drive? What the hell was Smithback doing up there?

"What kind of an archaeological expedition?"

Nora didn't answer.

"Dr. Kelly?"

Nora looked at him. "Where on Riverside Drive?"

O'Grady looked confused. "I'm sorry?"

"*Where* was Smithback's car found on Riverside Drive?"

O'Grady fumbled with the paper. "It says here upper Riverside. One hundred thirty-first and Riverside."

"One hundred thirty-first Street? What was he doing up there?"

"That's just what we were hoping you could tell us. Now, about that archaeological expedition—"

"And you say he came in this morning, gained access to some files? What files?"

"Old security files."

"Which ones?"

O'Grady flipped through some other sheets. "It says here it was an old personnel file."

"On who?"

"It doesn't say."

"How did he do it?"

"Well, it doesn't say, and—"

"For God's sake, can't you *find out?*"

Pink anger blossomed across O'Grady's face. "May we get back to the questions, please?"

"I know something about this," Finester suddenly broke in. "I was on duty earlier today. When you were out getting donuts and coffee, O'Grady. Remember?"

O'Grady turned. "In case you've forgotten, Finester, *we're* supposed to be the ones asking the questions."

Nora gave O'Grady her coldest stare. "How can I answer if you don't give me the information I need?"

O'Grady's rose-colored face grew redder. "I don't see why—"

"She's right, O'Grady. She has a right to know," Finester turned to Nora, pug face lit up by an ingratiating smile. "Mr. Smithback lured one of the security guards away with a phony telephone call, allegedly from the Human Resources office. Then he pretended to be from Human Resources himself and persuaded the remaining guard to unlock certain filing cabinets. Said he was conducting some kind of file inspection."

"He did?" Despite her concern, Nora couldn't help smiling to herself. It was vintage Smithback. "And what were those files, exactly?"

"Security clearances, dating back over a hundred years."

"And that's why he's in trouble?"

"That's the least of it. The guard thought he saw him take some papers out of one drawer. So you can add theft to—"

"*Which* file drawer?"

"It was the 1870 personnel file drawer, I believe," Finester recollected with obvious pride. "And after the guard's suspicions were aroused, they cross-checked the files and found that one of them was missing its cover sheets. It had been virtually emptied."

"Which one?"

"It was that one on the nineteenth-century serial killer, what's-his-name. The one written about in the *Times*. Clearly that's what he was after, more information on—"

"*Enoch Leng?*"

"Yeah. That's the guy."

Nora sat, stunned.

"Now, can we *please* get back to the questions, Dr. Kelly?" O'Grady interrupted.

"And his car was found up Riverside Drive? At 131st Street? How long had it been there?"

Finester shrugged. "He rented it right after he stole the file. It's staked out. As soon as he picks it up, we'll know."

O'Grady broke in again. "Finester, now that you've managed to reveal all the confidential details, maybe you can keep quiet for a minute. Now, Dr. Kelly, this archaeological expedition—"

Nora reached into her purse for her cell phone, found it, pulled it out.

"No cell phones, Dr. Kelly, until we're finished." It was O'Grady again, his voice rising in anger.

She dropped the phone back into her purse. "Sorry. I've got to go."

"You can go as soon as we *finish* the *questions.*" O'Grady was livid. "Now, *Doctor* Kelly, about that archaeological expedition . . ."

Nora didn't hear the rest. Her mind was racing.

"Dr. Kelly?"

"But can't we, ah, finish this later?" She tried to smile, tried to put on her most pleading look. "Something really important has just come up."

O'Grady didn't return the smile. "This is a *criminal* investigation, Dr. Kelly. *We'll* be *done* when *we* get to the end of the questions—not before."

Nora thought for a moment. Then she looked O'Grady in the eye. "I've got to go. Go, go to the bathroom, I mean."

"Now?"

She nodded.

"I'm sorry, but we'll have to accompany you, then. Those are the rules."

"Into the *bathroom*?"

He blushed. "Of course not, but to the facilities. We'll wait outside."

"Then you'd better hurry. I've really got to go. Bad kidneys."

O'Grady and Finester exchanged glances.

"Bacterial infection. From a dig in Guatemala."

The policemen rose with alacrity. They crossed the

Rockefeller Great Room, past the dozens of tables and the endless overlapping recitations of other staff members, out into the main library. Nora waited, biding her time, as they made their way toward the entrance. No point in sounding more of an alarm than was necessary.

The library itself was silent, researchers and scientists long since gone. The Great Room lay behind them now, the back-and-forth of questions and answers inaudible. Ahead were the double doors leading out into the hall and the rest rooms beyond. Nora approached the doors, the two cops trailing in her wake.

Then, with a sudden burst of speed, she darted through, swinging the doors behind her, back into the faces of the officers. She heard the thud of an impact, something clattering to the ground, a yelp of startled surprise. And then came a loud barking sound, like a seal giving the alarm, followed by shouts and running feet. She glanced back. Finester and O'Grady were through the doors and in hot pursuit.

Nora was very fit, but Finester and O'Grady surprised her. They were fast, too. At the far end of the hall, she glanced back and noticed that the taller sergeant, O'Grady, was actually gaining ground.

She flung open a stairwell door and began flying down the stairs, two at a time. Moments later, the door opened again: she heard loud voices, the pounding of feet.

She plunged downward even more quickly. Reaching the basement, she pushed the panic bar on the door and burst into the paleontological storage area. A long corridor ran ahead, arrow-straight, gray and institutional, illuminated by bare bulbs in wire cages. Doors lined both sides: *Probiscidia, Eohippii, Bovidae, Pongidae.*

The thudding of approaching feet filled the stairwell

behind her. Was it possible they were still gaining? Why couldn't she have gotten the two porkers at the table to her left?

She sprinted down the hallway, veered abruptly around a corner, and ran on, thinking fast. The vast dinosaur bone storage room was nearby. If she was going to lose these two, her best chance lay in there. She dug into her purse as she ran: thank God she'd remembered to bring her lab and storage keys along that morning.

She almost flew past the heavy door, fumbling with the keys. She turned, jammed her key into the lock, and pushed the door open just as the cops came into view around the corner.

Shit. They've seen me. Nora closed the door, locked it behind her, turned toward the long rows of tall metal stacks, preparing to run.

Then she had an idea.

She unlocked the door again, then took off down the closest aisle, turning left at the first crossing, then right, angling away from the door. At last she dropped into a crouch, pressing herself into the shadows, trying to catch her breath. She heard the tramp of feet in the corridor beyond. The door rattled abruptly.

"Open up!" came O'Grady's muffled roar.

Nora glanced around quickly, searching for a better place to hide. The room was lit only by the dim glow of emergency lighting, high up in the ceiling. Additional lights required a key—standard procedure in Museum storage rooms, where light could harm the specimens—and the long aisles were cloaked in darkness. She heard a grunt, the shiver of the door in its frame. She hoped they wouldn't be stupid enough to break down an unlocked door—that would ruin everything.

The door shivered under the weight of another heavy

blow. Then they figured it out: it was almost with relief that she heard the jiggling of the handle, the creak of the opening door. Warily, silently, she retreated farther into the vast forest of bones.

The Museum's dinosaur bone collection was the largest in the world. The dinosaurs were stored unmounted, stacked disarticulated on massive steel shelves. The shelves themselves were constructed of steel I-beams and angle iron, riveted together to make a web of shelving strong enough to support thousands of tons: vast piles of tree-trunk-thick legbones, skulls the size of cars, massive slabs of stone matrix with bones still imbedded, awaiting the preparator's chisel. The room smelled like the interior of an ancient stone cathedral.

"We know you're in here!" came the breathless voice of Finester.

Nora receded deeper into the shadows. A rat scurried in front of her, scrambling for safety within a gaping allosaurus eye socket. Bones rose on both sides like great heaps of cordwood, shelves climbing into the gloom. Like most of the Museum storage rooms, it was an illogical jumble of shelves and mismatched rows, growing by accretion over the last century and a half. A good place to get lost in.

"Running away from the police never did anyone any good, Dr. Kelly! Give yourself up now and we'll go easy on you!"

She shrank behind a giant turtle almost the size of a studio apartment, trying to reconstruct the layout of the vault in her head. She couldn't remember seeing a rear door in previous visits. Most storage vaults, for security purposes, had only one. There was only one way out, and they were blocking it. She had to get them to move.

"Dr. Kelly, I'm sure we can work something out! Please!"

Nora smiled to herself. What a pair of blunderers. Smithback would have had fun with them.

Her smile faded at the thought of Smithback. She was certain now of what he'd done. Smithback had gone to Leng's house. Perhaps he had heard Pendergast's theory—that Leng was alive and still living in his old house. Perhaps he'd wheedled it out of O'Shaughnessy. The guy could have made Helen Keller talk.

On top of that, he was a good researcher. He knew the Museum's files. While she and Pendergast were going through deeds, he'd gone straight to the Museum and hit paydirt. And knowing Smithback, he'd have run right up to Leng's house. That's why he'd rented a car, driven it up Riverside Drive. Just to check out the house. But Smithback could never merely check something out. *The fool, the damned fool . . .*

Cautiously, Nora tried dialing Smithback on her cell phone, muffling the sound with the leather of her purse. But the phone was dead: she was surrounded by several thousand tons of steel shelves and dinosaur bones, not to mention the Museum overhead. At least it probably meant the radios of the cops would be equally useless. If her plan worked, that would prove useful.

"Dr. Kelly!" The voices were coming from her left now, away from the door.

She crept forward between the shelves, strained to catch a glimpse of them, but she could see nothing but the beam of a flashlight stabbing through the dark piles of bone.

There was no more time: she had to get out.

She listened closely to the footsteps of the cops. Good: they seemed to still be together. In their joint eagerness to take credit for the collar, they'd been too stupid to leave one to guard the door.

"All right!" she called. "I give up! Sorry, I guess I just lost my head."

There was a brief flurry of whispers.

"We're coming!" O'Grady shouted. "Don't go anywhere!"

She heard them moving in her direction, more quickly now, the flashlight beam wobbling and weaving as they ran. Watching the direction of the beam, she scooted away, keeping low, angling back toward the front of the storage room, moving as quickly and silently as she could.

"Where are you?" she heard a voice cry, fainter now, several aisles away. "Dr. Kelly?"

"She was over there, O'Grady."

"Damn it, Finester, you know she was much farther—"

In a flash Nora was out the door. She turned, slammed it shut, turned her key in the lock. In another five minutes she was out on Museum Drive.

Panting hard, she slipped her cell phone out of her purse again and dialed.

SEVEN

THE SILVER WRAITH GLIDED NOISELESSLY UP TO THE Seventy-second Street curb. Pendergast slid out and stood for a moment in the shadow of the Dakota, deep in thought, while the car idled.

The interview with his great-aunt had left him with an unfamiliar feeling of dread. Yet it was a dread that had been growing within him since he first heard of the discovery of the charnel pit beneath Catherine Street.

For many years he had kept a silent vigil, scanning the FBI and Interpol services, on the lookout for a specific modus operandi. He'd hoped it would never surface—but always, in the back of his mind, had feared it would.

"Good evening, Mr. Pendergast," the guard said at his approach, stepping out of the sentry box. An envelope lay in his white-gloved hand. The sight of the envelope sent Pendergast's dread soaring.

"Thank you, Johnson," Pendergast replied, without taking the envelope. "Did Sergeant O'Shaughnessy come by, as I mentioned he would?"

"No sir. He hasn't been by all evening."

Pendergast grew more pensive, and there was a long

moment of silence. "I see. Did you take delivery of this envelope?"

"Yes, sir."

"From whom, may I ask?"

"A nice, old-fashioned sort of gent, sir."

"In a derby hat?"

"Precisely, sir."

Pendergast scanned the crisp copperplate on the front of the envelope: *For A. X. L. Pendergast, Esq., D. Phil., The Dakota. Personal and Confidential.* The envelope was handmade from a heavy, old-fashioned laid paper, with a deckle edge. It was precisely the sort of paper made by the Pendergast family's private stationer. Although the envelope was yellow with age, the writing on it was fresh.

Pendergast turned to the guard. "Johnson, may I borrow your gloves?"

The doorman was too well trained to show surprise. Donning the gloves, Pendergast slipped into the halo of light around the sentry box and broke the envelope's seal with the back of his hand. Very gingerly, he bowed it open, looking inside. There was a single sheet of paper, folded once. In the crease lay a single small, grayish fiber. To the untrained eye, it looked like a bit of fishing line. Pendergast recognized it as a human nerve strand, undoubtedly from the cauda equina at the base of the spinal cord.

There was no writing on the folded sheet. He angled it toward the light, but there was nothing else at all, not even a watermark.

At that moment, his cell phone rang.

Putting the envelope carefully aside, Pendergast plucked his phone from his suit pocket and raised it to his ear.

"Yes?" He spoke in a calm, neutral voice.

"It's Nora. Listen, Smithback figured out where Leng lives."

"And?"

"I think he went up there. I think he went into the house."

The Search

ONE

NORA WATCHED THE SILVER WRAITH APPROACH HER AT AN alarming speed, weaving through the Central Park West traffic, red light flashing incongruously on its dashboard. The car screeched to a stop alongside her as the rear door flew open.

"Get in!" called Pendergast.

She jumped inside, the sudden acceleration throwing her back against the white leather of the seat.

Pendergast had lowered the center armrest. He looked straight ahead, his face grimmer than Nora had ever seen it. He seemed to see nothing, notice nothing, as the car tore northward, rocking slightly, bounding over potholes and gaping cracks in the asphalt. To Nora's right, Central Park raced by, the trees a blur.

"I tried reaching Smithback on his cell phone," Nora said. "He isn't answering."

Pendergast did not reply.

"You really believe Leng's still alive?"

"I *know* so."

Nora was silent a moment. Then she had to ask. "Do you think— Do you think he's got Smithback?"

Pendergast did not answer immediately. "The expense voucher Smithback filled out stated he would return the car by five this evening."

By five this evening . . . Nora felt herself consumed by agitation and panic. Already, Smithback was over six hours overdue.

"If he's parked near Leng's house, we might just be able to find him." Pendergast leaned forward, sliding open the glass panel that isolated the rear compartment. "Proctor, when we reach 131st Street, we'll be looking for a silver Ford Taurus, New York license ELI-7734, with rental car decals."

He closed the panel, leaned back against the seat. Another silence fell as the car shot left onto Cathedral Parkway and sped toward the river.

"We would have known Leng's address in forty-eight hours," he said, almost to himself. "We were very close. A little more care, a little more method, was all it would have taken. Now, we don't have forty-eight hours."

"How much time do we have?"

"I'm afraid we don't have any," Pendergast murmured.

TWO

CUSTER WATCHED BRISBANE UNLOCK HIS OFFICE DOOR, open it, then step irritably aside to allow them to enter. Custer stepped through the doorway, the flush of returning confidence adding gravity to his stride. There was no need to hurry; not anymore. He turned, looked around: very clean and modern, lots of chrome and glass. Two large windows looked over Central Park and, beyond, at the twinkling wall of lights that made up Fifth Avenue. His eyes fell to the desk that dominated the center of the room. Antique inkwell, silver clock, expensive knickknacks. And a glass box full of gemstones. Cushy, cushy.

"Nice office," he said.

Shrugging the compliment aside, Brisbane draped his tuxedo jacket over his chair, then sat down behind the desk. "I don't have a lot of time," he said truculently. "It's eleven o'clock. I expect you to say what you have to say, then have your men vacate the premises until we can determine a mutually agreeable course of action."

"Of course, of course." Custer moved about the office, hefting a paperweight here, admiring a picture there. He could see Brisbane growing increasingly irritated. Good. Let the man stew. Eventually, he'd say something.

"Shall we get on with it, Captain?" Brisbane pointedly gestured for Custer to take a seat.

Just as pointedly, Custer continued circling the large office. Except for the knickknacks and the case of gems on the desk and the paintings on the walls, the office looked bare, save for one wall that contained shelving and a closet.

"Mr. Brisbane, I understand you're the Museum's general counsel?"

"That's right."

"An important position."

"As a matter of fact, it is."

Custer moved toward the shelves, examined a mother-of-pearl fountain pen displayed on one of them. "I understand your feelings of invasion here, Mr. Brisbane."

"That's reassuring."

"To a certain extent, you feel it's your place. You feel protective of the Museum."

"I do."

Custer nodded, his gaze moving along the shelf to an antique Chinese snuffbox set with stones. He picked it up. "Naturally, you don't like a bunch of policemen barging in here."

"Frankly, I don't. I've told you as much several times already. That's a very valuable snuffbox, Captain."

Custer returned it, picked up something else. "I imagine this whole thing's been rather hard on you. First, there was the discovery of the skeletons left by that nineteenth-century serial killer. Then there was that letter discovered in the Museum's collections. Very unpleasant."

"The adverse publicity could have easily harmed the Museum."

"Then there was that curator—?"

"Nora Kelly."

Custer noted a new tone creeping into Brisbane's voice: dislike, disapproval, perhaps a sense of injury.

"The same one who found the skeletons—and the hidden letter, correct? You didn't like her working on this case. Worried about adverse publicity, I suppose."

"I thought she should be doing her research. That's what she was being paid to do."

"You didn't want her helping the police?"

"Naturally, I wanted her to do what she could to help the police. I just didn't want her neglecting her museum duties."

Custer nodded sagely. "Of course. And then she was chased in the Archives, almost killed. By the Surgeon." He moved to a nearby bookshelf. The only books it contained were half a dozen fat legal tomes. Even their bindings managed to look stultifyingly dull. He tapped his finger on a spine. "You're a lawyer?"

"*General counsel* usually means *lawyer.*"

This bounced off Custer without leaving a dent. "I see. Been here how long?"

"A little over two years."

"Like it?"

"It's a very interesting place to work. Now look, I thought we were going to talk about getting your men out of here."

"Soon." Custer turned. "Visit the Archives much?"

"Not so much. More, lately, of course, with all the activity."

"I see. Interesting place, the Archives." He turned briefly to see the effect of this observation on Brisbane. *The eyes. Watch the eyes.*

"I suppose some find it so."

"But not you."

"Boxes of paper and moldy specimens don't interest me."

"And yet you visited there"—Custer consulted his notebook—"let's see, no less than eight times in the last ten days."

"I doubt it was that often. On Museum business, in any case."

"In any case." He looked shrewdly back at Brisbane. "The Archives. Where the body of Puck was found. Where Nora Kelly was chased."

"You mentioned her already."

"And then there's Smithback, that annoying reporter?"

"Annoying is an understatement."

"Didn't want him around, did you? Well, who would?"

"My thinking exactly. You've heard, of course, how he impersonated a security officer? Stole Museum files?"

"I've heard, I've heard. Fact is, we're looking for the man, but he seems to have disappeared. You wouldn't know where he was, by any chance, would you?" He added a faint emphasis to this last phrase.

"Of course not."

"Of course not." Custer returned his attention to the gems. He stroked the glass case with a fat finger. "And then there's that FBI agent, Pendergast. The one who was attacked. Also very annoying."

Brisbane remained silent.

"Didn't much like him around either—eh, Mr. Brisbane?"

"We had enough policemen crawling over the place. Why compound it with the FBI? And speaking of policemen crawling around—"

"It's just that I find it very curious, Mr. Brisbane . . ." Custer let the sentence trail off.

"What do you find curious, Captain?"

There was a commotion in the hallway outside, then the

door opened abruptly. A police sergeant entered, dusty, wide-eyed, sweating.

"Captain!" he gasped. "We were interviewing this woman just now, a curator, and she locked—"

Custer looked at the man—O'Grady, his name was—reprovingly. "Not now, Sergeant. Can't you see I'm conducting a conversation here?"

"But—"

"You *heard* the captain," Noyes interjected, propelling the protesting sergeant toward the door.

Custer waited until the door closed again, then turned back to Brisbane. "I find it curious how very *interested* you've been in this case," he said.

"It's my job."

"I know that. You're a very dedicated man. I've also noticed your dedication in human resources matters. Hiring, firing . . ."

"That's correct."

"Reinhart Puck, for example."

"What about him?"

Custer consulted his notebook again. "Why exactly *did* you try to fire Mr. Puck, just two days before his murder?"

Brisbane started to say something, then hesitated. A new thought seemed to have occurred to him.

"Strange timing there, wouldn't you agree, Mr. Brisbane?"

The man smiled thinly. "Captain, I felt the position was extraneous. The Museum is having financial difficulties. And Mr. Puck had been . . . well, he had not been cooperative. Of course, it had nothing to do with the murder."

"But they wouldn't let you fire him, would they?"

"He'd been with the Museum over twenty-five years. They felt it might affect morale."

"Must've made you angry, being shot down like that."

Brisbane's smile froze in place. "Captain, I hope you're not suggesting *I* had anything to do with the murder."

Custer raised his eyebrows in mock astonishment. "Am I?"

"Since I assume you're asking a rhetorical question, I won't bother to answer it."

Custer smiled. He didn't know what a rhetorical question was, but he could see that his questions were finding their mark. He gave the gem case another stroke, then glanced around. He'd covered the office; all that remained was the closet. He strolled over, put his hand on the handle, paused.

"But it *did* make you angry? Being contradicted like that, I mean."

"No one is pleased to be countermanded," Brisbane replied icily. "The man was an anachronism, his work habits clearly inefficient. Look at that typewriter he insisted on using for all his correspondence."

"Yes. The typewriter. The one the murderer used to write one—make that two—notes. You knew about that typewriter, I take it?"

"Everybody did. The man was infamous for refusing to allow a computer terminal on his desk, refusing to use e-mail."

"I see." Custer nodded, opened the closet.

As if on cue, an old-fashioned black derby hat fell out, bounced across the floor, and rolled in circles until it finally came to rest at Custer's feet.

Custer looked down at it in astonishment. It couldn't have happened more perfectly if this had been an Agatha Christie murder mystery. This kind of thing just didn't happen in real policework. He could hardly believe it.

He looked up at Brisbane, his eyebrows arching quizzically.

Brisbane looked first confounded, then flustered, then angry.

"It was for a costume party at the Museum," the lawyer said. "You can check for yourself. Everyone saw me in it. I've had it for years."

Custer poked his head into the closet, rummaged around, and removed a black umbrella, tightly furled. He brought it out, stood it up on its point, then released it. The umbrella toppled over beside the hat. He looked up again at Brisbane. The seconds ticked on.

"This is absurd!" exploded Brisbane.

"I haven't said anything," said Custer. He looked at Noyes. "Did *you* say anything?"

"No, sir, I didn't say anything."

"So what exactly, Mr. Brisbane, is absurd?"

"What you're thinking—" The man could hardly get out the words. "That I'm . . . that, you know . . . Oh, this is perfectly *ridiculous!*"

Custer placed his hands behind his back. He came forward slowly, one step after another, until he reached the desk. And then, very deliberately, he leaned over it.

"What *am* I thinking, Mr. Brisbane?" he asked quietly.

THREE

THE ROLLS ROCKETED UP RIVERSIDE, ITS DRIVER WEAVING expertly through the lines of traffic, threading the big vehicle through impossibly narrow gaps, sometimes forcing opposing cars onto the curb. It was after eleven P.M., and the traffic was beginning to thin out. But the curbs of Riverside and the side streets that led away from it remained completely jammed with parked cars.

The car swerved onto 131st Street, slowing abruptly. And almost immediately—no more than half a dozen cars in from Riverside—Nora spotted it: a silver Ford Taurus, New York plate ELI-7734.

Pendergast got out, walked over to the parked car, leaned toward the dashboard to verify the VIN. Then he moved around to the passenger door and broke the glass with an almost invisible jab. The alarm shrieked in protest while he searched the glove compartment and the rest of the interior. In a moment he returned.

"The car's empty," he told Nora. "He must have taken the address with him. We'll have to hope Leng's house is close by."

Telling Proctor to park at Grant's Tomb and wait for their

call, Pendergast led the way down 131st in long, sweeping strides. Within moments they reached the Drive itself. Riverside Park stretched away across the street, its trees like gaunt sentinels at the edge of a vast, unknown tract of darkness. Beyond the park was the Hudson, glimmering in the vague moonlight.

Nora looked left and right, at the countless blocks of decrepit apartment buildings, old abandoned mansions, and squalid welfare hotels that stretched in both directions. "How are we going to find it?" she asked.

"It will have certain characteristics," Pendergast replied. "It will be a private house, at least a hundred years old, not broken into apartments. It will probably look abandoned, but it will be very secure. We'll head south first."

But before proceeding, he stopped and placed a hand on her shoulder. "Normally, I'd never allow a civilian along on a police action."

"But that's my boyfriend caught—"

Pendergast raised his hand. "We have no time for discussion. I have already considered carefully what it is we face. I'm going to be as blunt as possible. If we do find Leng's house, the chances of my succeeding without assistance are very small."

"Good. I wouldn't let you leave me behind, anyway."

"I know that. I also know that, given Leng's cunning, two people have a better chance of success than a large—and loud—official response. Even if we could get such a response in time. But I must tell you, Dr. Kelly, I am bringing you into a situation where there are an almost infinite number of unknown variables. In short, it is a situation in which it is very possible one or both of us may be killed."

"I'm willing to take that risk."

"One final comment, then. In my opinion, Smithback is

already dead, or will be by the time we find the house, get inside, and secure Leng. This rescue operation is already, therefore, a probable failure."

Nora nodded, unable to reply.

Without another word, Pendergast turned and began to walk south.

They passed several old houses clearly broken into apartments, then a welfare hotel, the resident alcoholics watching them apathetically from the steps. Next came a long row of sordid tenements.

And then, at Tiemann Place, Pendergast paused before an abandoned building. It was a small townhouse, its windows boarded over, the buzzer missing. He stared up at it briefly, then went quickly around to the side, peered over a broken railing, returned.

"What do you think?" Nora whispered.

"I think we go in."

Two heavy pieces of plywood, chained shut, covered the opening where the door had been. Pendergast grasped the lock on the chain. A white hand slid into his suit jacket and emerged, holding a small device with toothpick-like metal attachments projecting from one end. It gleamed in the reflected light of the street lamp.

"What's that?" Nora asked.

"Electronic lockpick," Pendergast replied, fitting it to the padlock. The latch sprung open in his long white hands. He pulled the chain away from the plywood and ducked inside, Nora following.

A noisome stench welled out of the darkness. Pendergast pulled out his flashlight and shined the beam over a blizzard of decay: rotting garbage, dead rats, exposed lath, needles and crack vials, standing puddles of rank water. Without a word he turned and exited, Nora following.

They worked their way down as far as 120th Street. Here, the neighborhood improved and most of the buildings were occupied.

"There's no point in going farther," Pendergast said tersely. "We'll head north instead."

They hurried back to 131st Street—the point where their search had begun—and continued north. This proved much slower going. The neighborhood deteriorated until it seemed as if most of the buildings were abandoned. Pendergast dismissed many out of hand, but he broke into one, then another, then a third, while Nora watched the street.

At 136th Street they stopped before yet another ruined house. Pendergast looked toward it, scrutinizing the facade, then turned his eyes northward, silent and withdrawn. He was pale; the activity had clearly taxed his weakened frame.

It was as if the entire Drive, once lined with elegant townhouses, was now one long, desolate ruin. It seemed to Nora that Leng could be in any one of those houses.

Pendergast dropped his eyes toward the ground. "It appears," he said in a low voice, "that Mr. Smithback had difficulty finding parking."

Nora nodded, feeling a rising despair. The Surgeon now had Smithback at least six hours, perhaps several more. She would not follow that train of thought to its logical conclusion.

FOUR

CUSTER ALLOWED BRISBANE TO STEW FOR A MINUTE, THEN two. And then he smiled—almost conspiratorially—at the lawyer. "Mind if I . . .?" he began, nodding toward the bizarre chrome-and-glass chair before Brisbane's desk.

Brisbane nodded. "Of course."

Custer sank down, trying to maneuver his bulk into the most comfortable position the chair would allow. Then he smiled again. "Now, you were about to say something?" He hiked a pant leg, tried to throw it over the other, but the weird angle of the chair knocked it back against the floor. Unruffled, he cocked his head, raising an eyebrow quizzically across the desk.

Brisbane's composure had returned. "Nothing. I just thought, with the hat . . ."

"What?"

"Nothing."

"In that case, tell me about the Museum's costume party."

"The Museum often throws fund-raisers. Hall openings, parties for big donors, that sort of thing. Once in a while, it's a costume ball. I always wear the same thing. I dress like an

English banker on his way to the City. Derby hat, pinstriped pants, cutaway."

"I see." Custer glanced at the umbrella. "And the umbrella?"

"Everybody owns a black umbrella."

A veil had dropped over the man's emotions. Lawyer's training, no doubt.

"How long have you owned the hat?"

"I already told you."

"And where did you buy it?"

"Let's see . . . at an old antique shop in the Village. Or perhaps TriBeCa. Lispinard Street, I believe."

"How much did it cost?"

"I don't remember. Thirty or forty dollars." For a moment, Brisbane's composure slipped ever so slightly. "Look, why are you so interested in that hat? A lot of people own derby hats."

Watch the eyes. And the eyes looked panicked. The eyes looked guilty.

"Really?" Custer replied in an even voice. "A lot of people? The only person I know who owns a derby hat in New York City is the killer."

This was the first mention of the word "killer," and Custer gave it a slight, but noticeable, emphasis. Really, he was playing this beautifully, like a master angler bringing in a huge trout. He wished this was being captured on video. The chief would want to see it, perhaps make it available as a training film for aspiring detectives. "Let's get back to the umbrella."

"I bought it . . . I can't remember. I'm always buying and losing umbrellas." Brisbane shrugged casually, but his shoulders were stiff.

"And the rest of your costume?"

"In the closet. Go ahead, take a look."

Custer had no doubt the rest of the costume would match the description of a black, old-fashioned coat. He ignored the attempted distraction. "Where did you buy it?"

"I think I found the pants and coat at that used formalwear shop near Bloomingdale's. I just can't think of the name."

"No doubt." Custer glanced searchingly at Brisbane. "Odd choice for a costume party, don't you think? English banker, I mean."

"I dislike looking ridiculous. I've worn that costume half a dozen times to Museum parties, you can check with anyone. I put that costume to good use."

"Oh, I have no doubt you put it to good use. Good use indeed." Custer glanced over at Noyes. The man was excited, a kind of hungry, almost slavering look on his face. He, at least, realized what was coming.

"Where were you, Mr. Brisbane, on October 12, between eleven o'clock in the evening and four o'clock the following morning?" This was the time bracket the coroner had determined during which Puck had been killed.

Brisbane seemed to think. "Let's see . . . It's hard to remember." He laughed again.

Custer laughed, too.

"I can't remember what I did that night. Not precisely. After twelve or one, I would have been in bed, of course. But before then . . . Yes, I remember now. I was at home that night. Catching up on my reading."

"And you live alone, Mr. Brisbane?"

"Yes."

"So you have no one who can vouch for you being at home? A landlady, perhaps? Girlfriend? *Boy*friend?"

Brisbane frowned. "No. No, nothing like that. So, if it's all the same to you—"

"One moment, Mr. Brisbane. And where did you say you live?"

"I didn't say. Ninth Street, near University Place."

"Hmmm. No more than a dozen blocks from Tompkins Square Park. Where the second murder took place."

"That's a very interesting coincidence, no doubt."

"It is." Custer glanced out the windows, where Central Park lay beneath a mantle of darkness. "And no doubt it's a coincidence that the *first* murder took place right out there, in the Ramble."

Brisbane's frown deepened. "Really, Detective, I think we've reached the point where questions end and speculation begins." He pushed back his chair, prepared to stand up. "And now, if you don't mind, I'd like to get on with the business of clearing your men out of this Museum."

Custer made a suppressing motion with one hand, glanced again at Noyes. *Get ready.* "There's just one other thing. The *third* murder." He slid a piece of paper out of his notebook with a nonchalant motion. "Do you know an Oscar Gibbs?"

"Yes, I believe so. Mr. Puck's assistant."

"Exactly. According to the testimony of Mr. Gibbs, on the afternoon of October 12, you and Mr. Puck had a little, ah, *discussion* in the Archives. This was after you found out that Human Resources had not supported your recommendation to fire Puck."

Brisbane colored slightly. "I wouldn't believe everything you hear."

Custer smiled. "I don't, Mr. Brisbane. Believe me, I don't." He followed this with a long, delicious pause. "Now, this Mr. Oscar Gibbs said that you and Puck were yelling at each other. Or rather, you were yelling at Puck. Care to tell me, in *your* words, what that was about?"

"I was reprimanding Mr. Puck."

"What for?"

"Neglecting my instructions."

"Which were?"

"To stick to his job."

"To *stick* to his job. How had he been deviating from his job?"

"He was doing outside work, helping Nora Kelly with her external projects, when I had specifically—"

It was time. Custer pounced.

"According to Mr. Oscar Gibbs, you were (and I will read): *screaming and yelling and threatening to bury Mr. Puck. He* (that's you, Mr. Brisbane) *said he wasn't through by a long shot.*" Custer lowered the paper, glanced at Brisbane. "That's the word you used: '*bury.*'"

"It's a common figure of speech."

"And then, not twenty-four hours later, Puck's body was found, gored on a dinosaur in the Archives. After having been butchered, most likely in those very same Archives. An operation like that takes time, Mr. Brisbane. Clearly, it was done by somebody who knew the Museum's ways very well. Someone with a security clearance. Someone who could move around the Museum without exciting notice. An insider, if you will. And then, Nora Kelly gets a phony note, typed on Puck's typewriter, asking her to come down—and she herself is attacked, pursued with deadly intent. *Nora Kelly.* The other thorn in your side. The third thorn, the FBI agent, was in the hospital at this point, having been attacked by someone *wearing a derby hat.*"

Brisbane stared at him in disbelief.

"Why didn't you want Puck to help Nora Kelly in her—what did you call them—*external* projects?"

This was answered by silence.

"What were you afraid she would find? *They* would find?"

Brisbane's mouth worked briefly. "I . . . I . . ."

Now Custer slipped in the knife. "Why the copycat angle, Mr. Brisbane? Was it something you found in the Archives? Is *that* what prompted you to do it? Was Puck getting too close to learning something?"

At this, Brisbane found his voice at last. He shot to his feet. "Now, just a minute—"

Custer turned. "Officer Noyes?"

"Yes?" Noyes responded eagerly.

"Cuff him."

"No," Brisbane gasped. "You fool, you're making a terrible mistake—"

Custer worked his way out of the chair—it was not as smooth a motion as he would have wished—and began abruptly booming out the Miranda rights: "You have the right to remain silent—"

"This is an outrage—"

"—you have the right to an attorney—"

"I will not accept this!"

"—you have the right—"

He thundered it out to the bitter end, overriding Brisbane's protestations. He watched as the gleeful Noyes slapped the cuffs on the man. It was the most satisfying collar Custer could ever remember. It was, in fact, the single greatest job of police work he had done in his life. This was the stuff of legend. For many years to come, they'd be telling the story of how Captain Custer put the cuffs on the Surgeon.

FIVE

PENDERGAST SET OFF UP RIVERSIDE ONCE AGAIN, BLACK suit coat open and flapping behind him in the Manhattan night. Nora hurried after. Her thoughts returned to Smithback, imprisoned in one of these gaunt buildings. She tried to force the image from her mind, but it kept returning, again and again. She was almost physically sick with worry about what might be happening—what might have *already* happened.

She wondered how she could have been so angry with him. It's true that much of the time he was impossible—a schemer, impulsive, always looking for an angle, always getting himself into trouble. And yet many of those same negative qualities were his most endearing. She thought back to how he'd dressed up as a bum to help her retrieve the old dress from the excavation; how he'd come to warn her after Pendergast was stabbed. When push came to shove, he was there. She had been awfully hard on him. But it was too late to be sorry. She suppressed a sob of bitter regret.

They moved past guttered mansions and once elegant townhouses, now festering crack dens and shooting galleries for junkies. Pendergast gave each building a searching look, always turning away with a little shake of his head.

Nora's thoughts flitted briefly to Leng himself. It seemed impossible that he could still be alive, concealed within one of these crumbling dwellings. She glanced up the Drive again. She had to concentrate, try to pick his house out from the others. Wherever he lived, it would be comfortable. A man who had lived over a hundred and fifty years would be excessively concerned with comfort. But it would no doubt give the surface impression of being abandoned. And it would be well-nigh impregnable—Leng wouldn't want any unexpected visitors. This was the perfect neighborhood for such a place: abandoned, yet once elegant; externally shabby, yet livable inside; boarded up; very private.

The trouble was, so many of the buildings met those criteria.

Then, near the corner of 138th Street, Pendergast stopped dead. He turned, slowly, to face yet another abandoned building. It was a large, decayed mansion, a hulking shadow of bygone glory, set back from the street by a small service drive. Like many others, the first floor had been securely boarded up with tin. It looked just like a dozen other buildings they had passed. And yet Pendergast was staring at it with an expression of intentness Nora had not seen before.

Silently, he turned the corner of 138th Street. Nora followed, watching him. The FBI agent moved slowly, eyes mostly on the ground, with just occasional darted glances up at the building. They continued down the block until they reached the corner of Broadway. The moment they turned the corner, Pendergast spoke.

"That's it."

"How do you know?"

"The crest carved on the escutcheon over the door. Three apothecary balls over a sprig of hemlock." He waved his hand. "Forgive me if I reserve explanations for later. Follow my lead. And be very, very careful."

He continued around the block until they reached the corner of Riverside Drive and 137th. Nora looked at the building with a mixture of curiosity, apprehension, and outright fear. It was a large, four-story, brick-and-stone structure that occupied the entire short block. Its frontage was enclosed in a wrought iron fence, ivy covering the rusty pointed rails. The garden within was long gone, taken over by weeds, bushes, and garbage. A carriage drive circled the rear of the house, exiting on 138th Street. Though the lower windows were securely boarded over, the upper courses remained unblocked, although at least one window on the second story was broken. She stared up at the crest Pendergast had mentioned. An inscription in Greek ran around its edge.

A gust of wind rustled the bare limbs in the yard; the reflected moon, the scudding clouds, flickered in the glass panes of the upper stories. The place looked haunted.

Pendergast ducked into the carriage drive, Nora following close behind. The agent kicked aside some garbage with his shoe and, after a quick look around, stepped up to a solid oak door set into deep shadow beneath the porte-cochère. It seemed to Nora as if Pendergast merely caressed the lock; and then the door opened silently on well-oiled hinges.

They stepped quickly inside. Pendergast eased the door closed, and Nora heard the sound of a lock clicking. A moment of intense darkness while they stood still, listening for any sounds from within. The old house was silent. After a minute, the yellow line of Pendergast's hooded flashlight appeared, scanning the room around them.

They were standing in a small entryway. The floor was polished marble, and the walls were papered in heavy velvet fabric. Dust covered everything. Pendergast stood still, directing his light at a series of footprints—some shod, some stockinged—that had disturbed the dust on the floor. He looked at them for so long, studying them as an art student studies an old master, that Nora felt impatience begin to overwhelm her. At last he led the way, slowly, through the room and down a short passage leading into a large, long hall. It was paneled in a very rich, dense wood, and the low ceiling was intricately worked, a blend of the gothic and austere.

This hall was full of an odd assortment of displays Nora was unable to comprehend: weird tables, cabinets, large boxes, iron cages, strange apparatus.

"A magician's warehouse," Pendergast murmured in answer to her unspoken question.

They passed through the room, beneath an archway, and into a grand reception hall. Once again, Pendergast stopped to study several lines of footprints that crossed and recrossed the parquet floor.

"Barefoot, now," she heard him say to himself. "And this time, he was running."

He quickly probed the immense space with his beam. Nora saw an astonishing range of objects: mounted skeletons, fossils, glass-fronted cabinets full of wondrous and terrible artifacts, gems, skulls, meteorites, iridescent beetles. The flashlight played briefly over all. The scent of cobwebs, leather, and old buckram hung heavy in the thick air, veiling a fainter—and much less pleasant—smell.

"What is this place?" Nora asked.

"Leng's cabinet of curiosities." A two-toned pistol had appeared in Pendergast's left hand. The stench was worse now; sickly sweet, oily, that filled the air like a wet fog, clinging to her hair, limbs, clothes.

He moved forward, warily, his light playing off the various objects in the room. Some of the objects were uncovered, but most were draped. The walls were lined with glass cases, and Pendergast moved toward them, his flashlight licking from one to the next. The glass sparked and shimmered as the beam hit it; dark shadows, thrown from the objects within, reared forward as if living things.

Suddenly, the beam stopped dead. Nora watched as Pendergast's pale face lost what little color it normally had. For a moment, he simply stared, motionless, not even seeming to draw breath. Then, very slowly, he approached the case. The beam of the flashlight trembled a bit as he moved. Nora followed, wondering what had had such a galvanic effect on the agent.

The glass case was not like the rest. It did not contain a skeleton, stuffed trophy, or carven image. Instead, behind the glass stood the figure of a dead man, legs and arms strapped upright between crude iron bars and cuffs, mounted as if for museum display. The man was dressed in severe black, with a nineteenth-century frock coat and striped pants.

"Who—?" Nora managed to say.

But Pendergast was transfixed, hearing nothing, his face rigid. All his attention was concentrated on the mounted man. The light played mercilessly about the corpse. It lingered for a long time on one particular detail—a pallid hand, the flesh shrunken and shriveled, a single knucklebone poking from a tear in the rotten flesh.

Nora stared at the exposed knuckle, red and ivory against the parchment skin. With a nauseous lurch in the pit of her stomach, she realized that the hand was missing all its fingernails; that, in fact, nothing remained of the fingertips but bloody stumps, punctuated by protruding bones.

Then—slowly, inexorably—the light began traveling up the front of the corpse. The beam rose past the buttons of the coat, up the starched shirtfront, before at last stopping on the face.

It was mummified, shrunken, wizened. And yet it was surprisingly well preserved, all the features modeled as finely as if carved from stone. The lips, which had dried and shriveled, were drawn back in a rictus of merriment, exposing two beautiful rows of white teeth. Only the eyes were gone: empty sockets like bottomless pools no light could illuminate.

There was a hollow, muffled sound of rustling coming from inside the skull.

The journey through the house had already numbed Nora with horror. But now her mind went blank with an even worse shock: the shock of recognition.

She automatically turned, speechless, to Pendergast. His frame remained rigid, his eyes wide and staring. Whatever it was he had expected to find, it was not this.

She shifted her horrified gaze back at the corpse. Even in death, there could be no question. The corpse had the same marble-colored skin, the same refined features, the same thin lips and aquiline nose, the same high smooth forehead and delicate chin, the same fine pale hair—as Pendergast himself.

SIX

CUSTER OBSERVED THE PERP—HE'D ALREADY BEGUN TO call him that—with deep satisfaction. The man stood in his office, hands cuffed behind him, black tie askew and white shirt rumpled, hair disheveled, dark circles of sweat beneath his armpits. How are the mighty fallen, indeed. He'd held out a long time, kept up that arrogant, impatient facade. But now, the eyes were red, the lips trembling. He hadn't believed it was really going to happen to him. *It was the cuffs that did it,* Custer thought knowingly to himself. He had seen it happen many times before, to men a lot tougher than Brisbane. Something about the cool clasp of the manacles around your wrists, the realization that you were under arrest, powerless—*in custody*—was more than some people could take.

The true, the pure, police work was over—now it was just a matter of collecting all the little evidentiary details, work for the lower echelons to complete. Custer himself could take leave of the scene.

He glanced at Noyes and saw admiration shining in the small hound face. Then he turned back to the perp.

"Well, Brisbane," he said. "It all falls into place, doesn't it?"

Brisbane looked at him with uncomprehending eyes.

"Murderers always think they're smarter than everyone else. Especially the police. But when you get down to it, Brisbane, you really didn't play it smart at all. Keeping the disguise right here in your office, for example. And then there was the matter of all those witnesses. Trying to hide evidence, lying to me about how often you were in the Archives. Killing victims so close to your own place of work, your place of residence. The list goes on, doesn't it?"

The door opened and a uniformed officer slipped a fax into Custer's hand.

"And here's another little fact just in. Yes, the little facts can be *so* inconvenient." He read over the fax. "Ah. And now we know where you got your medical training, Brisbane: you were pre-med at Yale." He handed the fax to Noyes. "Switched to geology your junior year. Then to law." Custer shook his head again, wonderingly, at the bottomless stupidity of criminals.

Brisbane finally managed to speak. "I'm no murderer! Why would I kill those people?"

Custer shrugged philosophically. "The very question I asked you. But then, why do any serial killers kill? Why did Jack the Ripper kill? Why Jeffrey Dahmer? That's a question for the psychiatrists to answer. Or maybe for God."

On this note, Custer turned back to Noyes. "Set up a press conference for midnight. One Police Plaza. No, hold on— let's make it on the front steps of the Museum. Call the commissioner, call the press. And most importantly, call the mayor, on his private line at Gracie Mansion. This is one call he'll be happy to get out of bed for. Tell them we collared the Surgeon."

"Yes, sir!" said Noyes, turning to go.

"My God, the publicity . . ." Brisbane's voice was high, strangled. "Captain, I'll have your badge for this . . ." He choked up with fear and rage, unable to continue.

But Custer wasn't listening. He'd had another masterstroke.

"Just a minute!" he called to Noyes. "Make sure the mayor knows that he'll be the star of our show. We'll *let him* make the announcement."

As the door closed, Custer turned his thoughts to the mayor. The election was a week away. He would need the boost. Letting him make the announcement was a clever move; very clever. Rumor had it that the job of commissioner would become vacant after reelection. And, after all, it was never too early to hope.

SEVEN

AGAIN, NORA LOOKED AT PENDERGAST. AND AGAIN SHE was unnerved by the depth of his shock. His eyes seemed glued to the face of the corpse: the parchment skin, the delicate, aristocratic features, the hair so blond it could have been white.

"The face. It looks just like—" Nora struggled to understand, to articulate her thoughts.

Pendergast did not respond.

"It looks just like you," Nora finally managed.

"Yes," came the whispered response. "Very much like me."

"But who is it—?"

"Enoch Leng."

Something in the way he said this caused Nora's skin to crawl.

"*Leng?* But how can that be? I thought you said he was alive."

With a visible effort Pendergast wrenched his eyes from the glass case and turned them on her. In them, she read many things: horror, pain, dread. His face remained colorless in the dim light.

"He was. Until recently. Someone appears to have killed Leng. Tortured him to death. And put him in that case. It seems we are now dealing with that *other someone*."

"I still don't—"

Pendergast held up one hand. "I cannot speak of it now," was all he said.

He turned from the figure, slowly, almost painfully, his light stabbing farther into the gloom.

Nora inhaled the antique, dust-laden air. Everything was so strange, so terrible and unexpected; the kind of weirdness that happened only in a nightmare. She tried to calm her pounding heart.

"Now he is unconscious, being dragged," whispered Pendergast. His eyes were once again on the floor, but his voice and manner remained dreadfully changed.

With the flashlight as a guide, they followed the marks across the reception hall to a set of closed doors. Pendergast opened them to reveal a carpeted, well-appointed space: a two-story library, filled with leather-bound books. The beam probed farther, slicing through drifting clouds of dust. In addition to books, Nora saw that, again, many of the shelves were lined with specimens, all carefully labeled. There were also numerous freestanding specimens in the room, draped in rotting duck canvas. A variety of wing chairs and sofas were positioned around the library, the leather dry and split, the stuffing unraveling.

The beam of the flashlight licked over the walls. A salver sat on a nearby table, holding a crystal decanter of what had once been port or sherry: a brown crust lined its bottom. Next to the tray sat a small, empty glass. An unsmoked cigar, shriveled and furred with mold, lay alongside it. A fireplace carved of gray marble was set into one of the walls, a fire laid but not lit. Before it was a tattered zebra skin, well chewed by mice. A sideboard nearby held more crystal decanters, each with a brown or black substance dried within. A hominid skull—Nora recognized it as Australopithecine— sat on a side table with a candle set into it. An open book lay nearby.

Pendergast's light lingered on the open book. Nora could see it was an ancient medical treatise, written in Latin. The page showed engravings of a cadaver in various stages of dissection. Of all the objects in the library, only this looked fresh, as if it had been handled recently. Everything else was layered with dust.

Once again, Pendergast turned his attention to the floor, where Nora could clearly see marks in the moth-eaten, rotting carpet. The marks appeared to end at a wall of books.

Now, Pendergast approached the wall. He ran his light over their spines, peering intently at the titles. Every few moments he would stop, remove a book, glance at it, shove it back. Suddenly—as Pendergast removed a particularly massive tome from a shelf—Nora heard a loud metallic click. Two large rows of adjoining bookshelves sprang open. Pendergast drew them carefully back, exposing a folding brass gate. Behind the closed gate lay a door of solid maple. It took Nora a moment to realize what it was.

"An old elevator," she whispered.

Pendergast nodded. "Yes. The old service elevator to the basement. There was something exactly like this in—"

He went abruptly silent. As the sound of his voice faded away, Nora heard what she thought was a noise coming from within the closed elevator. A shallow breath, perhaps, hardly more than a moan.

Suddenly, a terrible thought burst over Nora. At the same time, Pendergast stiffened visibly.

She let out an involuntary gasp. "That's not—" She couldn't bring herself to say Smithback's name.

"We must hurry."

Pendergast carefully examined the brass gate with the beam. He reached forward, gingerly tried the handle. It did not move. He knelt before the door and, with his head close to the latching mechanism, examined it. Nora saw him remove a flat, flexible piece of metal from his suit and slide it into the mechanism. There was a faint click. He worked the shim back and forth, teasing and probing at the latch, until there was a second click. Then he stood up and, with infinite caution, drew back the brass gate. It folded to one side easily, almost noiselessly. Again, Pendergast approached, crouching before the handle of the maple door, regarding it intently.

There was another sound: again a faint, agonized attempt to breathe. Her heart filled with dread.

A sudden rasping noise filled the study. Pendergast jumped back abruptly as the door shot open of its own accord.

Nora stood transfixed with horror. A figure appeared in the back of the small compartment. For a moment, it remained motionless. And then, with the sound of rotten fabric tearing away, it slowly came toppling out toward them. For a terrible moment, Nora thought it would fall upon Pendergast. But then the figure jerked abruptly to a stop, held by a rope around its neck, leaning toward them at a grotesque angle, arms swinging.

"It's O'Shaughnessy," said Pendergast.

"O'Shaughnessy!"

"Yes. And he's still alive." He took a step forward and grabbed the body, wrestling it upright, freeing the neck from the rope. Nora came quickly to his side and helped him lower the sergeant to the floor. As she did so, she saw a huge, gaping hole in the man's back. O'Shaughnessy coughed once, head lolling.

There was a sudden jolt; a protesting squeal of gears and machinery; and then, abruptly, the bottom dropped out of their world.

EIGHT

CUSTER LED THE MAKESHIFT PROCESSION DOWN THE LONG echoing halls, toward the Great Rotunda and the front steps of the Museum that lay beyond. He'd allowed Noyes a good half hour to give the press a heads-up, and while he was waiting he'd worked out the precedence down to the last detail. He came first, of course, followed by two uniformed cops with the perp between them, and then a phalanx of some twenty lieutenants and detectives. Trailing them, in turn, was a ragged, dismayed, disorganized knot of museum staffers. This included the head of public relations; Manetti the security director; a gaggle of aides. They were all in a frenzy, clearly out of their depth. If they'd been smart, if they'd assisted rather than tried to impede good police work and due process, maybe this circus could have been avoided. But now, he was going to make it hard on them. He was going to hold the press conference in their own front yard, right on those nice wide steps, with the vast spooky facade of the Museum as backdrop—perfect for the early morning news. The cameras would eat it up. And now, as the group crossed the Rotunda, the echoes of their footsteps mingling with the murmuring of voices, Custer held his head erect, sucked in his gut. He wanted to make sure the moment would be well recorded for posterity.

The Museum's grand bronze doors opened, and beyond lay Museum Drive and a seething mass of press. Despite the advance groundwork, he was still amazed by how many had gathered, like flies to shit. Immediately, a barrage of flashes went off, followed by the sharp, steady brilliance of the television camera lights. A wave of shouted questions broke over him, individual voices indistinguishable in the general roar. The steps themselves had been cordoned off by police ropes, but as Custer emerged with the perp in tow the waiting crowd surged forward as one. There was a moment of intense excitement, frantic shouting and shoving, before the cops regained control, pushing the press back behind the police cordon.

The perp hadn't said a word for the last twenty minutes, apparently shocked into a stupor. He was so out of it he hadn't even bothered to conceal his face as the doors of the Rotunda opened onto the night air. Now, as the battery of lights hit his face—as he saw the sea of faces, the cameras and outstretched recorders—he ducked his head away from the crowd, cringing away from the burst of flash units, and had to be propelled bodily along, half dragged, half carried, toward the waiting squad car. At the car, as Custer had instructed, the two cops handed the perp over to him. *He* would be the one to thrust the man into the back seat. This was the photo, Custer knew, that would be splashed across the front page of every paper in town the next morning.

But getting handed the perp was like being tossed a 175-pound sack of shit, and he almost dropped the man trying to maneuver him in the back seat. Success was achieved at last to a swelling fusillade of flash attachments; the squad car turned on its lights and siren; and nosed forward.

Custer watched it ease its way through the crowd, then turned to face the press himself. He raised his hands like Moses, waiting for silence to fall. He had no intention of stealing the mayor's thunder—the pictures of him bundling the cuffed perp into the vehicle would tell everyone who had made the collar—but he had to say a little something to keep the crowd contained.

"The mayor is on his way," he called out in a clear, commanding voice. "He will arrive in a few minutes, and he will have an important announcement to make. Until then, there will be no further comments whatsoever."

"How'd you get him?" a lone voice shouted, and then there was a sudden roar of questions; frantic shouting; waving; boomed mikes swinging out in his direction. But Custer magisterially turned his back on it all. The election was less than a week away. Let the mayor make the announcement and take the glory. Custer would reap his own reward, later.

NINE

THE FIRST THING THAT RETURNED WAS THE PAIN. NORA came swimming back into consciousness, slowly, agonizingly. She moaned, swallowed, tried to move. Her side felt lacerated. She blinked, blinked again, then realized she was surrounded by utter darkness. She felt blood on her face, but when she tried to touch it her arm refused to move. She tried again and realized that both her arms and legs were chained.

She felt confused, as if caught in a dream from which she could not awake. What was going on here? Where was she?

A voice came from the darkness, low and weak. "Dr. Kelly?"

At the sound of her own name, the dream-like confusion began to recede. As clarity grew, Nora felt a sudden shock of fear.

"It's Pendergast," the voice murmured. "Are you all right?"

"I don't know. A few bruised ribs, maybe. And you?"

"More or less."

"What happened?"

There was a silence. Then Pendergast spoke again. "I am

very, very sorry. I should have expected the trap. How brutal, using Sergeant O'Shaughnessy to bait us like that. Unutterably brutal."

"Is O'Shaughnessy—?"

"He was dying when we found him. He cannot have survived."

"God, how awful," Nora sobbed. "How horrible."

"He was a good man, a loyal man. I am beyond words."

There was a long silence. So great was Nora's fear that it seemed to choke off even her grief and horror at what had happened to O'Shaughnessy. She had begun to realize the same was in store for them—as it may have already been for Smithback.

Pendergast's weak voice broke the silence. "I've been unable to maintain proper intellectual distance in this case," he said. "I've simply been too close to it, from the very beginning. My every move has been flawed—"

Abruptly, Pendergast fell silent. A few moments later, Nora heard a noise, and a small rectangle of light slid into view high up in the wall before her. It cast just enough light for her to see the outline of their prison: a small, damp stone cellar.

A pair of wet lips hovered within the rectangle.

"Please do not discompose yourself," a voice crooned in a deep, rich accent curiously like Pendergast's own. "All this will be over soon. Struggle is unnecessary. Forgive me for not playing the host at the present moment, but I have some pressing business to take care of. Afterward, I assure you, I will give you the benefit of my *undivided* attention."

The rectangle scraped shut.

For a minute, perhaps two, Nora remained in the darkness, hardly able to breathe in her terror. She struggled to retake possession of her mind.

"Agent Pendergast?" she whispered.

There was no answer.

And then the watchful darkness was rent asunder by a distant, muffled scream—strangled, garbled, choking.

Instantly, Nora knew—beyond the shadow of a doubt—that the voice was Smithback's.

"Oh my God!" she screamed. "Agent Pendergast, did you hear that?"

Still Pendergast did not answer.

"Pendergast!"

The darkness continued to yield nothing but silence.

In the Dark

ONE

PENDERGAST CLOSED HIS EYES AGAINST THE DARKNESS.
Gradually, the chessboard appeared, materializing out of a
vague haze. The ivory and ebony chess pieces, smoothed by
countless years of handling, stood quietly, waiting for the
game to begin. The chill of the damp stone, the rough grasp
of the manacles, the pain in his ribs, Nora's frightened voice,
the occasional distant cry, all fell away one by one, leaving
only an enfolding darkness, the board standing quietly in a
pool of yellow light. And still Pendergast waited, breathing
deeply, his heartbeat slowing. Finally, he reached forward,
touched a cool chess piece, and advanced his king's pawn
forward two spaces. Black countered. The game began,
slowly at first, then faster, and faster, until the pieces flew
across the board. Stalemate. Another game, and still another,
with the same results. And then, rather abruptly, came
darkness—utter darkness.

When at last he was ready, Pendergast once again opened
his eyes.

He was standing in the wide upstairs hallway of the
Maison de la Rochenoire, the great old New Orleans house
on Dauphine Street in which he had grown up. Originally a

monastery erected by an obscure Carmelite order, the rambling pile had been purchased by Pendergast's distant grandfather many times removed in the eighteenth century, and renovated into an eccentric labyrinth of vaulted rooms and shadowy corridors.

Although the Maison de la Rochenoire had been burned down by a mob shortly after Pendergast left for boarding school in England, he continued to return to it frequently. Within his mind, the structure had become more than a house. It had become a memory palace, a storehouse of knowledge and lore, the place for his most intense and difficult meditations. All of his own experiences and observations, all of the many Pendergast family secrets, were housed within. Only here, safe in the mansion's Gothic bosom, could he meditate without fear of interruption.

And there was a great deal to meditate upon. For one of the few times in his life, he had known failure. If there was a solution to this problem, it would lie somewhere within these walls—somewhere within his own mind. Searching for the solution would mean a physical search of his memory palace.

He strolled pensively down the broad, tapestried corridor, the rose-colored walls broken at regular intervals by marble niches. Each niche contained an exquisite miniature leather-bound book. Some of these had actually existed in the old house. Others were pure memory constructs—chronicles of past events, facts, figures, chemical formulae, complex mathematical or metaphysical proofs—all stored by Pendergast in the house as a physical object of memory, for use at some unknown future date.

Now, he stood before the heavy oaken door of his own room. Normally he would unlock the door and linger within, surrounded by the familiar objects, the comforting iconography, of his childhood. But today he continued on, pausing only to pass his fingers lightly over the brass knob of the door. His business lay elsewhere, below, with things older and infinitely stranger.

He had mentioned to Nora his inability to maintain proper intellectual distance in the case, and this was undeniably true. This was what had led him, and her—and, to his deepest sorrow, Patrick O'Shaughnessy—into the present misfortune. What he had not revealed to Nora was the profound shock he felt when he saw the face of the dead man. It was, as he now knew, Enoch Leng—or, more accurately, his own great-grand-uncle, Antoine Leng Pendergast.

For Great-Grand-Uncle Antoine had succeeded in his youthful dream of extending his life.

The last remnants of the ancient Pendergast family— those who were *compos mentis*—assumed that Antoine had died many years ago, probably in New York, where he had vanished in the mid ninteenth century. A significant portion of the Pendergast family fortune had vanished with him, much to the chagrin of his collateral descendants.

But several years before, while working on the case of the Subway Massacre, Pendergast—thanks to Wren, his library acquaintance—had stumbled by chance upon some old newspaper articles. These articles described a sudden rash of disappearances: disappearances that followed not long after the date Antoine was supposed to have arrived in New York. A corpse had been discovered, floating in the East River, with the marks of a diabolical kind of surgery. It was a street waif, and the crime was never solved. But certain uncomfortable details caused Pendergast to believe it to be the work of Antoine, and to feel the man was attempting to achieve his youthful dream of immortality. A perusal of later newspapers brought a half-dozen similar crimes to light, stretching as far forward as 1930.

The question, Pendergast realized, became: had Leng succeeded? Or had he died in 1930?

Death seemed by far the most likely result. And yet, Pendergast had remained uneasy. Antoine Leng Pendergast was a man of transcendental genius, combined with transcendental madness.

So Pendergast waited and watched. As the last of his line, he'd felt it his responsibility to keep vigil against the unlikely chance that, someday, evidence of his ancestor's continued existence would resurface. When he heard of the discovery on Catherine Street, he immediately suspected what had happened there, and who was responsible. And when the murder of Doreen Hollander was discovered, he knew that what he most dreaded had come to pass: Antoine Pendergast had succeeded in his quest.

But now, Antoine was dead.

There could be no doubt that the mummified corpse in the glass case was that of Antoine Pendergast, who had taken, in his journey northward, the name Enoch Leng. Pendergast had come to the house on Riverside Drive expecting to confront his own ancestor. Instead, he had found his great-grand-uncle tortured and murdered. Someone, somehow, had taken his place.

Who had killed the man who called himself Enoch Leng? Who now held them prisoner? The corpse of his ancestor was *only recently dead*—the state of the corpse suggested that death had occurred within the last two months—pegging the murder of Enoch Leng *before* the discovery of the charnel on Catherine Street.

The timing was very, very interesting.

And then there was that other problem—a very quiet, but

persistent feeling that there was a connection still to be made here—that had been troubling Pendergast almost since he first set foot within Leng's house.

Now, inside the memory crossing, he continued down the hall. The next door—the door that had once been his brother's—had been sealed by Pendergast himself, never to be opened again. He quickly moved on.

The hallway ended in a grand, sweeping staircase leading down to a great hall. A heavy cut-glass chandelier hovered over the marble floor, mounting on a gilt chain to a domed trompe l'oeil ceiling. Pendergast descended the stairs, deep in thought. To one side, a set of tall doors opened into a two-story library; to the other, a long hall retreated back into shadow. Pendergast entered this hall first. Originally, this room had been the monastery's refectory. In his mind, he had furnished it with a variety of family heirlooms: heavy rosewood chiffoniers, oversized landscapes by Bierstadt and Cole. There were other, more unusual heirlooms here, as well: sets of Tarot cards, crystal balls, a spirit-medium apparatus, chains and cuffs, stage props for illusionists and magicians. Other objects lay in the corners, shrouded, their outlines sunken too deeply into shadow to discern.

As he looked around, his mind once again felt the ripples of a disturbance, of a connection not yet made. It was here, it was all around him; it only awaited his recognition. And yet it hovered tantalizingly out of grasp.

This room could tell him no more. Exiting, he recrossed the echoing hall and entered the library. He looked around a moment, savoring the books, real and imaginary, row upon comforting row, that rose to the molded ceiling far above. Then he stepped toward one of the shelves on the nearest wall. He glanced along the rows, found the book he wanted, pulled it from the shelf. With a low, almost noiseless click, the shelf swung away from the wall.

. . . And then, abruptly, Pendergast found himself back in Leng's house on Riverside Drive, standing in the grand foyer, surrounded by Leng's astonishing collections.

He hesitated, momentarily stilled by surprise. Such a shift, such a morphing of location, had never happened in a memory crossing before.

But as he waited, looking around at the shrouded skeletons and shelves covered with treasures, the reason became clear. When he and Nora first passed through the rooms of Leng's house—the grand foyer; the long, low-ceilinged exhibit hall; the two-storied library—Pendergast had found himself experiencing an unexpected, uncomfortable feeling of *familiarity*. Now he knew why: in his house on Riverside Drive, *Leng had re-created, in his own dark and twisted way, the old Pendergast mansion on Dauphine Street.*

He had finally made the crucial connection. Or had he?

Great-Uncle Antoine? Aunt Cornelia had said. *He went north, to New York City. Became a Yankee.* And so he had. But, like all members of the Pendergast family, he had been unable to escape his legacy. And here in New York, he had re-created his own Maison de la Rochenoire—an idealized mansion, where he could amass his collections and carry on his experiments, undisturbed by prying relations. It was not unlike, Pendergast realized, the way he himself had re-created the Maison de la Rochenoire in his own mind, as a memory palace.

This much, at least, was now clear. But his mind remained troubled. Something else was eluding him: a realization hovering at the very edge of awareness. Leng had a lifetime, several lifetimes, in which to complete his own cabinet of curiosities. Here it was, all around him, possibly the finest natural history collection ever assembled. And yet, as Pendergast looked around, he realized that the collection was incomplete. One section was missing. Not just any section, in fact, but the *central* collection: the one thing that had fascinated the young Antoine Leng Pendergast most. Pendergast felt a growing astonishment. Antoine—as Leng—had had a century and a half to complete this ultimate cabinet of curiosities. Why was it not here?

Pendergast knew it existed. It *must* exist. Here, in this house. It was just a question of where . . .

A sound from the outside world—a strangely muffled scream—suddenly intruded into Pendergast's memory crossing. Quickly, he withdrew again, plunging as deeply as he could into the protective darkness and fog of his own mental construct, trying to recover the necessary purity of concentration.

Time passed. And then, in his mind, he found himself once again back in the old house on Dauphine Street, standing in the library.

He waited a moment, reacclimating himself to the surroundings, giving his new suspicions and questions time to mature. In his mind's eye he recorded them on parchment and bound them between gilt covers, placing the book on one of the shelves beside a long row of similar books—all books of questions. Then he turned his attention to the bookcase that had swung open. It revealed an elevator.

He stepped into the elevator at the same, thoughtful pace, and descended.

The cellar of the former monastery on Dauphine Street was damp, the walls thick with efflorescence. The mansion's cellars consisted of vast stone passageways crusted with lime, verdigris, and the soot from tallow candles. Pendergast threaded his way through the maze, arriving at last at a cul-de-sac formed by a small, vaulted room. It was empty, devoid of ornament, save for a single carving that hung over a bricked-up arch in one of the walls. The carving was of a shield, containing a lidless eye over two moons: one crescent, the other full. Below was a lion, couchant. It was the Pendergast family crest: the same crest that Leng had perverted into his own escutcheon, carved onto the facade of the mansion on Riverside Drive.

Pendergast approached this wall, stood beneath the crest for a moment, gazing at it. Then, placing both hands upon the cold stone, he applied a sharp forward pressure. The wall instantly swung away, revealing a circular staircase, sloping down and away at a sharp angle into the subbasement.

Pendergast stood at the top of the stairs, feeling the steady stream of chill air that wafted like a ghostly exhalation from the depths below. He remembered the day, many years ago, when he had first been inducted into the family secrets: the hidden panel in the library, the stone chambers beneath, the room with the crest. And finally this, the greatest secret of all.

In the real house on Dauphine Street, the stairs had been dark, approachable only with a lantern. But in Pendergast's mind, a faint greenish light now issued up from far below. He began to descend.

The stairs led downward in a spiral. At last, Pendergast emerged into a short tunnel that opened into a vaulted space. The floor was earthen. Long ranks of carefully mortised bricks rose to a groined ceiling. Rows of torches flamed on the walls, and chunks of frankincense smoked in copper braziers, overlaying a much stronger smell of old earth, wet stone, and the dead.

A brick pathway ran down the center of the room, flanked on both sides by stone tombs and crypts. Some were marble, others granite. A few were heavily decorated, carved into fantastic minarets and arabesques; others were squat, black, monolithic. Pendergast started down the path, glancing at the bronze doors set into the facades, the familiar names graven onto the face plates of tarnished brass.

What the old monks had used this subterranean vault for, Pendergast never learned. But almost two hundred years before, this place had become the Pendergast family necropolis. Here, over a dozen generations on both sides of the family—the fallen line of French aristocrats, the mysterious denizens of the deep bayou—had been buried or, more frequently, reburied. Pendergast walked on, hands behind his back, staring at the carved names. Here was Henri Prendregast de Mousqueton, a seventeenth-century mountebank who pulled teeth, performed magic and comedy, and practiced quack medicine. And here, encased in a mausoleum bedecked with quartz minarets, was Eduard Pendregast, a well-known Harley Street doctor in eighteenth-century London. And here, Comstock Pendergast, famed mesmerist, magician, and mentor of Harry Houdini.

Pendergast strolled farther, passing artists and murderers, vaudeville performers and violin prodigies. At last he stopped beside a mausoleum grander than those around it: a ponderous conflation of white marble, carved into an exact replica of the Pendergast mansion itself. This was the tomb of Hezekiah Pendergast, his own great-great-grandfather.

Pendergast let his eye roam over the familiar turrets and finials, the gabled roof and mullioned windows. When Hezekiah Pendergast arrived on the scene, the Pendergast family fortune was almost gone. Hezekiah was released into the world penniless, but with big ambitions. Originally a snake-oil salesman allied with traveling medicine shows, he soon became known as a hippocratic sage, a man whose patent medicine could cure almost any disease. On the big bill, he appeared between Al-Ghazi, the contortionist, and Harry N. Parr, Canine Instructor. The medicine he peddled during these shows sold briskly, even at five dollars the bottle. Hezekiah soon established his own traveling medicine show, and with shrewd marketing, Hezekiah's Compound Elixir and Glandular Restorative quickly became the first widely marketed patent medicine in America. Hezekiah Pendergast grew rich beyond the fondest visions of avarice.

Pendergast's eyes swept downward, to the deep layers of shadow that surrounded the tomb. Ugly rumors began to surface about Hezekiah's Compound Elixir within a year of its introduction: tales of madness, deformed births, wasting deaths. And yet sales grew. Doctors protested the elixir, calling it violently addictive and harmful to the brain. And still sales grew. Hezekiah Pendergast introduced a highly successful formula for babies, "Warranted to Make Your Child Peaceful." In the end, a reporter for *Collier's* magazine, together with a government chemist, finally exposed the elixir as an addictively lethal blend of chloroform, cocaine hydrochloride, acetanilid, and botanicals. Production was forced to cease—but not before Hezekiah's own wife had succumbed to the addiction and died. Carlotta Leng Pendergast.

Antoine's mother.

Pendergast turned away from the tomb. Then he stopped, glancing back. A smaller, simpler mausoleum of gray granite lay beside the greater one. The engraved plaque on its face read, simply, *Carlotta*.

He paused, recalling the words of his great-aunt: *And then he began spending a lot of time down . . . down there. Do you know where I mean?* Pendergast had heard the stories about how the necropolis became Antoine's favorite place after his mother's death. He'd spent his days here, year in and year out, in the shadow of her tomb, practicing the magic tricks his father and grandfather had taught him, performing experiments on small animals—and especially working with chemicals, developing nostrums and poisons. What else was it Aunt Cornelia had said? *They say he always felt more comfortable with the dead than with the living.*

Pendergast had heard rumors even Aunt Cornelia had been unwilling to hint at: rumors worse than the bad business with Marie LeClaire; rumors of certain hideous things found in the deep shadows of the tombs; rumors of the real reason behind Antoine's permanent banishment from the house on Dauphine Street. But it wasn't just the prolongation of life that had fixed Antoine's attention. No, there had always been something else, something behind the prolongation of life, some project that he had kept the deepest of secrets . . .

Pendergast stared at the nameplate as a sudden revelation swept over him. *These underground vaults* had been Antoine's workplace as a child. This is where he had played and studied, collected his appalling childhood trophies. *This* was where he had experimented with his chemicals; and it was here, in the cool, dark underground, *where he had stored his vast collection of compounds, botanicals, chemicals, and poisons.* Here, the temperature and humidity never changed: the conditions would be perfect.

More quickly now, Pendergast turned away, walking back down the pathway and passing beneath the tunnel, beginning the long climb back toward consciousness. For he knew, at last, where in the house on Riverside Drive the missing collection of Antoine Pendergast—of Enoch Leng—would be found.

TWO

Nora heard the faint rattle of a chain, then a faint, whispered exhalation of breath from out of the nearby darkness. She licked dry lips, worked her mouth in an attempt to speak. "Pendergast?"

"I'm here," came the weak voice.

"I thought you were dead!" Her body spasmed in an involuntary sob. "Are you all right?"

"I'm sorry I had to leave you. How much time has passed?"

"My God, are you deaf? That madman's doing something terrible to Bill!"

"Dr. Kelly—"

Nora lunged against her chains. She felt wild with terror and grief, a frenzy that seemed to physically possess her body. *"Get me out of here!"*

"Dr. Kelly." Pendergast's voice was neutral. "Be calm. There is something we can do. But you must be calm."

Nora stopped struggling and sank back, trying to control herself.

"Lean against the wall. Close your eyes. Take deep, regular breaths." The voice was slow, hypnotic.

Nora closed her eyes, trying to push away the crowding terror, trying to regulate her breathing.

There was a long silence. And then Pendergast spoke again. "All right?"

"I don't know."

"Keep breathing. Slowly. Now?"

"Better. What happened to you? You really frightened me, I was sure—"

"There's no time to explain. You must trust me. And now, I'm going to remove these chains."

Nora felt a twinge of disbelief. There was a clanking and rattling, followed by a sudden silence.

She strained against her chains, listening intently. What was he doing? Had he lost his senses?

And then, abruptly, she felt someone take hold of her elbow, and simultaneously a hand slipped over her mouth. "I'm free," Pendergast's voice whispered in her ear. "Soon you will be, too."

Nora felt stuporous with disbelief. She began to tremble.

"Relax your limbs. Relax them *completely.*"

It was as if he brushed her arms and legs ever so lightly. She felt the cuffs and chains simply fall away. It seemed magical.

"How did—?"

"Later. What kind of shoes are you wearing?"

"Why?"

"Just answer the question."

"Let me think. Bally. Black. Flat heels."

"I'm going to borrow one."

She felt Pendergast's narrow hands remove the shoe. There was a faint noise, a kind of metallic scraping sound, and then the shoe was slipped back onto her foot. Then she heard a low tapping, as if the iron cuffs were being struck together.

"What are you doing?"

"Be very quiet."

Despite her best efforts, she felt the terror begin to rise again, overwhelming her mind. There hadn't been any sounds from outside for several minutes. She stifled another sob. "Bill—"

Pendergast's cool, dry hand slipped over hers. "Whatever has happened, has happened. Now, I want you to listen to me very carefully. Respond yes by squeezing my hand. Do not speak further."

Nora squeezed his hand.

"I need you to be strong. I must tell you that I believe Smithback is now dead. But there are two other lives here, yours and mine, that need to be saved. And we *must* stop this man, whoever he is, or many more will die. Do you understand?"

Nora squeezed. Hearing her worst fears stated so baldly seemed almost to help, a little.

"I've made a small tool out of a piece of metal from the sole of your shoe. We will escape from this cell in a moment—the lock is no doubt quite primitive. But you must be ready to do exactly as I tell you."

She squeezed.

"You need to know something first. I understand now, at least in part, what Enoch Leng was doing. He wasn't prolonging his life as an end in itself. He was prolonging his life *as a means to an end.* He was working on a project that was even bigger than extended life—a project he realized would take several lifetimes to complete. That is why he went to the trouble of prolonging his life: so that he could accomplish this other thing."

"What could be bigger than extended life?" Nora managed to say.

"Hush. I don't know. But it is making me very, very afraid."

There was a silence. Nora could hear Pendergast's quiet breathing. Then he spoke again. "Whatever that project is, it is here, hidden *in this house.*"

There was another, briefer silence.

"Listen very carefully. I am going to open the door of this cell. I will then go to Leng's operating room and confront the man who has taken his place. You will remain hidden here for ten minutes—no more, and no less—and then you will go to the operating room yourself. As I say, I believe Smithback to be dead, but we need to make sure. By that time the impostor and I will be gone. Do *not* pursue us. No matter what you hear, do not try to help. Do not come to my aid. My confrontation with this man will be decisive. One of us will not survive it. The other one will return. Let us hope that person is me. Do you understand so far?"

Another squeeze.

"If Smithback is still alive, do what you can. If he's beyond help, you are to get out of the basement and the house as quickly as possible. Find your way upstairs and escape from a second-story window—I think you will find all the exits on the first floor to be impenetrable."

Nora waited, listening.

"There is a chance that my plan will fail, and that you will find me dead on the floor of the operating room. In that case, all I can say is you must run for your life, fight for your life—and, if necessary, *take* your life. The alternative is too terrible. Can you do that?"

Nora choked back a sob. Then she squeezed his hand once again.

THREE

THE MAN EXAMINED THE INCISION THAT RAN ALONG THE resource's lower spine from L2 to the sacrum. It was a very fine piece of work, the kind he had been so well appreciated for in medical school—back before the unpleasantness began.

The newspapers had nicknamed him the Surgeon. He liked the name. And as he gazed down, he found it particularly appropriate. He'd defined the anatomy perfectly. First, a long vertical incision from the reference point along the spinal process, a single steady stroke through the skin. Next, he had extended the incision down into the subcutaneous tissue, carrying it as far as the fascia, clamping, dividing, and ligating the larger vessels with 3-0 vicryl. He'd opened the fascia, then used a periosteal elevator to strip the muscle from the spinous processes and laminae. He'd been enjoying the work so much that he had taken more time at it than intended. The paralyzing effects of the succinyl choline had faded, and there had been rather a lot of struggling and noise at this point, yet his tie work remained as fastidious as a seamstress's. As he cleared the soft tissue with a curette, the spinal column gradually revealed itself, grayish white against the bright red of the surrounding flesh.

The Surgeon plucked another self-retaining retractor from the instrument bin, then stood back to examine the incision. He was pleased: it was a textbook job, tight at the corners and spreading out slightly toward the middle. He could see everything: the nerves, the vessels, all the marvelous inner architecture. Beyond the lamina and ligamentum flavum, he could make out the transparent dura of the spinal cord. Within, bluish spinal fluid pulsed in time to the respiration of the resource. His pulse quickened as he watched the fluid bathe the cauda equina. It was undoubtedly his finest incision to date.

Surgery, he reflected, was more an art form than a science, requiring patience, creativity, intuition, and a steady hand. There was very little ratiocination involved; very little intellect came into play. It was an activity at once physical and creative, like painting or sculpture. He would have been a good artist—had he chosen that route. But of course, there would be time; there would be time . . .

He thought back once again to medical school. Now that the anatomy had been defined, the next step would normally be to define the pathology, then correct that pathology. But, of course, this was the point at which his work departed from the course of a normal operation and became something closer to an autopsy.

He looked back toward the nearby stand, making sure that everything he needed for the excision—the chisels, diamond burr drill, bone wax—was ready. Then he looked at the surrounding monitors. Although, most regrettably, the resource had slipped into unconsciousness, the vitals were still strong. New strides could not be taken, but the extraction and preparation should be successful nonetheless.

Turning toward the Versed drip inserted into the saline bag hung from the gurney, he turned the plastic stopcock to stop the flow: tranquilization, like the intubation, was no longer necessary. The trick now would be to keep the resource alive as far into the surgery as possible. There was still much to do, starting with the bony dissection: the removal of the lamina with a Kerrison rongeur. The goal at this point was to have the vitals still detectable when the operation was complete, with the *cauda equina* removed and lying intact in the special chilled cradle he had designed to receive it. He had reached that goal only twice before—with the slender young woman and the policeman—but this time he felt a swell of confidence in himself and his skills. He knew that he would achieve it again.

So far, everything had gone according to plan. The great detective, Pendergast, whom he had so feared, had proven less than formidable. Using one of the many traps in this strange old house against the agent had proven ridiculously easy. The others were minor irritants only. He had removed them all, swept them aside with so little effort it was almost risible. In fact it *was* risible, how pathetic they all were. The colossal stupidity of the police, the moronic Museum officials: how delightful it had all been, how very diverting. There was a certain justice in the situation, a justice that only he could appreciate.

And now he had almost achieved his goal. Almost. After these three had been processed, he felt sure he would be there. And how ironic it was that it would be these three, of all people, who helped him reach it . . .

He smiled slightly as he bent down to set another self-retaining retractor into place. And that was when he saw a small movement at the extreme edge of his peripheral vision.

He turned. It was the FBI agent, Pendergast, casually

leaning against a wall just inside the archway leading into the operating room.

The man straightened, controlling the highly unpleasant surprise that rose within him. But Pendergast's hands were empty; he was, of course, unarmed. With one swift, economical movement, the Surgeon took up Pendergast's own gun—the two-tone Colt 1911, lying on the instrument table—pushed down on the safety with his thumb, and pointed the weapon at the agent.

Pendergast continued to lean against the wall. For the briefest of moments, as the two exchanged glances, something like astonishment registered in the pale cat's eyes. Then Pendergast spoke.

"So it's *you* who tortured and killed Enoch Leng. I wondered who the impostor was. I am surprised. I do not like surprises, but there it is."

The man aimed the gun carefully.

"You're already holding my weapon," said Pendergast, showing his hands. "I'm unarmed." He continued leaning casually against the wall.

The man tightened his finger on the trigger. He felt a second unpleasant sensation: internal conflict. Pendergast was a very dangerous man. It would no doubt be best to pull the trigger now and have done with it. But by shooting now, he would ruin a specimen. Besides, he needed to know how Pendergast had escaped. And then, there was the girl to consider . . .

"But it begins to make sense," Pendergast resumed. "Yes, I see it now. You're building that skyscraper on Catherine Street. You didn't just discover those bodies by accident. No—you were *looking* for those bodies, weren't you? You already knew that Leng had buried them there, 130 years ago. And how did you learn about them? Ah, it all falls into place: your interest in the Museum, your visits to the Archives. *You* were the one who examined the Shottum material before Dr. Kelly. No wonder it was all in such disarray—you'd already removed anything you felt useful. But you didn't know about Tinbury McFadden, or the elephant's-foot box. Instead, you first learned about Leng and his work, about his lab notebooks and journals, from Shottum's personal papers. But when you ultimately tracked down Leng, and found him alive, he wasn't as talkative as you would have liked. He didn't give you the formula. Even under torture, did he? So you had to fall back on what Leng had left behind: his victims, his lab, perhaps his journals, buried beneath Shottum's Cabinet. And the only way to get to those was to buy the land, tear down the brownstones above, and dig a foundation for a new building." Pendergast nodded, almost to himself. "Dr. Kelly mentioned missing pages in the Archives logbook; pages removed with a razor. Those pages were the ones with your name on them, correct? And the only one who knew you had been a frequent visitor to the Archives was Puck. So he had to die. Along with those who were already on your own trail: Dr. Kelly, Sergeant O'Shaughnessy, myself. Because the closer we came to finding Leng, the closer we came to finding *you*."

A pained expression came over the agent's face. "How could I have been so obtuse not to see it? It should have become clear when I first saw Leng's corpse. When I realized Leng had been tortured to death *before* the Catherine Street bodies were found."

Fairhaven did not smile. The chain of deduction was astonishingly accurate. *Just kill him*, a voice in his head said.

"What is it the Arab sages call death?" Pendergast went on. *"The destroyer of all earthly pleasures*. And how true it is: old age, sickness, and at last death comes to us all. Some console themselves with religion, others through denial, others through philosophy or mere stoicism. But to you, who had always been able to buy everything, death must have seemed a dreadful injustice."

The image of his older brother, Arthur, came unbidden to the Surgeon's mind: dying of progeria, his young face withered with senile keratoses, his limbs twisted, his skin cracked with hideously premature age. The fact that the disease was so rare, its causes so unknown, had been no comfort. Pendergast didn't know everything. Nor would he.

He forced the image from his mind. *Just kill the man.* But somehow his hand would not act—not yet, not until he had heard more.

Pendergast nodded toward the still form on the table. "You're never going to get there that way, Mr. Fairhaven. Leng's skills were infinitely more refined than yours. You will never succeed."

Not true, Fairhaven thought to himself. *I have already succeeded. I am Leng as he should have been. Only through me can Leng's work attain its truest perfection . . .*

"I know," Pendergast said. "You're thinking I'm wrong. You believe you have succeeded. But you *have not* succeeded, and you never will. Ask yourself: Do you feel any different? Do you feel any revivification of the limbs, any quickening of the life essence? If you're honest with yourself, you can still feel the terrible weight of time pressing on you; that awful, relentless, bodily corruption that is happening constantly to us all." He smiled thinly, wearily, as if he knew the feeling all too well. "You see, you've made one fatal mistake."

The Surgeon said nothing.

"The truth is," Pendergast said, "you don't know the first

thing about Leng, or his *real* work. Work for which life extension was just a means to an end."

Years of self-discipline, of high-level corporate brinksmanship, had taught Fairhaven never to reveal anything: not in the facial expression, not in the questions asked. Yet the sudden stab of surprise he felt, followed immediately by disbelief, was hard to conceal. What real work? What was Pendergast talking about?

He would not ask. Silence was always the best mode of questioning. If you remained silent, they always talked out the answer in the end. It was human nature.

But this time it was Pendergast who remained silent. He simply stood there, leaning almost insolently against the doorframe, glancing around at the walls of the chamber. The silence stretched on, and the man began to think of his resource, lying there on the gurney. Gun on Pendergast, he glanced briefly at the vitals. Good, but starting to flag. If he didn't get back to work soon, the specimen would be spoiled.

Kill him, the voice said again.

"What real work?" Fairhaven asked.

Still, Pendergast remained silent.

The merest spasm of doubt passed through Fairhaven, quickly suppressed. What was the man's game? He was wasting his time, and there was no doubt a reason why he was wasting his time, which meant it was best just to kill him now. At least he knew the girl could not escape from the basement. He would deal with her in good time. Fairhaven's finger tightened on the trigger.

At last, Pendergast spoke. "Leng didn't tell you anything in the end, did he? You tortured him to no avail, because you're still thrashing about, wasting all these people. But I *do* know about Leng. I know him very well indeed. Perhaps you noticed the resemblance?"

"What?" Again Fairhaven was taken off guard.

"Leng was my great-grand-uncle."

It hit Fairhaven then. His grip on the weapon loosened. He remembered Leng's delicate white face, his white hair, and his very pale blue eyes—eyes that regarded him without begging, without pleading, without beseeching, no matter how hideous it had become for him. Pendergast's eyes were the same. But Leng had died anyway, and so would he.

So would he, the voice echoed, more insistently. *His information is not as important as his death. This resource is not worth the risk. Kill him.*

The man reapplied pressure to the trigger. At this distance, he could not miss.

"It's hidden here in the house, you know. Leng's ultimate project. But you've never found it. All along you've been looking for the wrong thing. And as a result, you will die a long, slow, wasting death of old age. Just like the rest of us. You cannot succeed."

Squeeze the trigger, the voice in his head insisted.

But there was something in the agent's tone. He knew something, something important. He wasn't just talking. Fairhaven had dealt with bluffers before, and this man was not bluffing.

"Say what you have to say now," said Fairhaven. "Or you will die instantly."

"Come with me. I'll show you."

"Show me what?"

"I'll show you what Leng was *really* working on. It's in the house. Here, right under your nose."

The voice in his head was no longer little; it was practically shouting. *Do not allow him to continue talking, no matter how important his information may be.* And Fairhaven finally heeded the wisdom of that advice.

Pendergast was leaning against the wall, off balance, his hands clearly in view. It would be impossible for the man, in the time it took to squeeze off one shot, to reach inside his suit and pull out a backup weapon. Besides, he *had* no such weapon; Fairhaven had searched him thoroughly. He took a fresh bead on Pendergast, then held his breath, increasing the pressure on the trigger. There was a sudden roar and the gun kicked in his hand. And he knew instantly: it had been a true shot.

FOUR

THE CELL DOOR STOOD OPEN, ALLOWING A FAINT LIGHT TO filter in from the passageway beyond. Nora waited, shrinking back into the pool of darkness behind the cell door. Ten minutes. Pendergast had said ten minutes. In the dark, with her heart pounding like a sledgehammer, every minute seemed an hour, and it was almost impossible to tell the passage of time. She forced herself to count each second. *A thousand one, a thousand two . . .* Each count made her think of Smithback, and what might be happening to him. Or *had* happened to him.

Pendergast had told her he thought Smithback was dead. He had said this to spare her the shock of discovering it for herself. *Bill is dead. Bill is dead.* She tried to absorb it, but found her mind would not accept the fact. It felt unreal. Everything felt unreal. *A thousand thirty. A thousand thirty-one.* The seconds rolled on.

At six minutes and twenty-five seconds, the sound of a gunshot came, deafening in the confined spaces of the cellar.

Her whole body kicked in fear. It was all she could do not to scream. She crouched, waiting for the absurd skipping of her heart to slow. The terrible sound echoed and re-echoed, rumbling and rolling through the basement corridors. Finally, silence—dead silence—returned.

She felt her breath coming in gasps. Now it was doubly hard to count. Pendergast had said to wait ten minutes. Had another minute passed since the shot? She decided to resume the count again at seven minutes, hoping the monotonous, repetitive activity would calm her nerves. It did not.

And then she heard the sound of rapid footsteps ringing against stone. They had an unusual, syncopated cadence, as if someone was descending a staircase. The footfalls quickly grew fainter. Silence returned once again.

At ten minutes, she stopped counting. Time to move.

For a moment, her body refused to respond. It seemed frozen with dread.

What if the man was still out there? What if she found Smithback dead? What if Pendergast was dead, too? Would she be able to run, to resist, to die, rather than be caught herself and face a fate far worse?

Speculation was useless. She would simply follow Pendergast's orders.

With an immense effort of will, she rose from her crouch, then stepped out of the darkness, easing her way around the open door. The corridor beyond the cell was long and damp, with irregular stone floor and walls, streaked with lime. At the far end was a door that opened into a bright room: the lone source of light, it seemed, in the entire basement. It was in that direction Pendergast had gone; that direction from which the shot had come; that direction from which she'd heard the sound of running feet.

She took a hesitant step forward, and then another, walking on trembling legs toward the brilliant rectangle of light.

FIVE

THE SURGEON COULD HARDLY BELIEVE HIS EYES. WHERE Pendergast should have been lying dead in a pool of blood, there was nothing. The man had vanished.

He looked around wildly. It was inconceivable, a physical impossibility . . . And then he noticed that the section of wall Pendergast had been leaning against was now a door, swiveled parallel to the stone face that surrounded it. A door he never knew existed, despite his diligent searches of the house.

The Surgeon waited, stilling his mind with a great effort of will. Deliberation in all things, he had found, was absolutely necessary for success. It had brought him this far, and with it he would prevail now.

He stepped forward, Pendergast's gun at the ready. On the far side of the opening, a stone staircase led downward into blackness. The FBI agent obviously wanted him to follow, to descend the staircase whose end was hidden around the dark curve of the stone wall. It could easily be a trap. In fact, it could *only* be a trap.

But the Surgeon realized he had no choice. He had to stop Pendergast. And he had to find out what lay below. He had a gun, and Pendergast was unarmed, perhaps even wounded by the shot. He paused, briefly, to examine the pistol. The Surgeon knew something about weapons, and he recognized this as a Les Baer custom, .45 Government Model. He turned it over in his hands. With the tritium night sights and laser grips, easily a three-thousand-dollar handgun. Pendergast had good taste. Ironic that such a fine weapon would now be used against its owner.

He stepped back from the false wall. Keeping a watchful eye on the stairway, he retrieved a powerful flashlight from a nearby drawer, then darted a regretful glance toward his specimen. The vital signs were beginning to drop now; the operation was clearly spoiled.

He returned to the staircase and shone the flashlight down into the gloom. The imprint of Pendergast's footsteps was clearly visible in the dust that coated the steps. And there was something else, something besides the footsteps: a drop of blood. And another.

So he *had* hit Pendergast. Nevertheless, he would have to redouble his caution. Wounded humans, like wounded animals, were always the most dangerous.

He paused at the first step, wondering if he should go after the woman first. Was she still chained to the wall? Or had Pendergast managed to free her, as well? Either way, she posed little danger. The house was a fortress, the basement securely locked. She would be unable to escape. Pendergast remained the more pressing problem. Once he was dead, the remaining resource could be tracked down and forced to take the place of Smithback. He'd made the mistake of listening to Pendergast once. When he found him, he wouldn't make that mistake again. The man would be dead before he even opened his mouth.

The staircase spiraled down, down, corkscrewing

endlessly into the earth. The Surgeon descended slowly, treating each curve as a blind corner behind which Pendergast might be lying in wait. At last he reached the bottom. The stairs debouched into a dark, murky room, heavy with the smell of mildew, damp earth, and—what? Ammonia, salts, benzene, the faint smell of chemicals. There was a flurry of footprints, more drops of blood. Pendergast had stopped here. The Surgeon shone his light on the nearest wall: a row of old brass lanterns, hanging from wooden pegs. One of the pegs was empty.

He took a step to one side, then—using the stone pillar of the staircase as cover—lifted his heavy flashlight and shone it into the gloom.

An astonishing sight met his eye. A wall of jewels seemed to wink back at him: a thousand, ten thousand glittering reflections in myriad colors, like the reflective surface of a fly's eye under intense magnification. Suppressing his surprise, he moved forward cautiously, gun at the ready.

He found himself in a narrow stone chamber, pillars rising toward a low, arched ceiling. The walls were lined with countless glass bottles of identical shape and size. They were stored on oaken shelving that rose from floor to ceiling, row upon row upon row, crowded densely together, shut up behind rippled glass. He had never seen so many bottles in his life. It looked, in fact, like a museum of liquids.

His breath came faster. Here it was: Leng's final laboratory. No doubt *this* was the place where he had perfected the arcanum, his formula for life prolongation. This place must hold the secret for which he had unsuccessfully tortured Leng. He remembered his feeling of disappointment, almost despair, when he'd discovered that Leng's heart had stopped beating—when he realized he had pushed a little too hard. No matter now: the formula was right here, under his nose, just as Pendergast had said.

But then he remembered what else Pendergast had said: something about Leng working on something completely different. That was absurd, clearly a red herring. What could be bigger than the prolongation of the human life span? What else could this huge collection of chemicals be for, if not that?

He shook these speculations from his mind. Once Pendergast was dealt with and the girl harvested, there would be plenty of time for exploration.

He raked the ground with his light. There was more blood, along with a ragged set of footprints that headed straight through the corridor of bottles. He had to be careful, exceedingly careful. The last thing he wanted to do was begin shooting up these rows of precious liquids, destroying the very treasure he had strived so hard to find. He raised his arm, aimed the handgun, applied pressure to the grip. A small red dot appeared on the far wall. *Excellent.* Although the laser would not be sighted in precisely, it would nevertheless leave little margin for error.

Releasing his pressure on the laser grip, the Surgeon moved cautiously through the vast apothecary. Each bottle, he could see now, had been meticulously labeled in a spidery script, with both a name and a chemical formula. At the far end, he ducked beneath a low archway into an identical narrow room. The bottles in the next room were full of solid chemicals—chunks of minerals, glittering crystals, ground powders, metal shavings.

It seemed that the arcanum, the formula, was far more

complicated than he had envisioned. Why else would Leng need all these chemicals?

He continued following Pendergast's trail. The footsteps were no longer a single-minded beeline past the endless rows of glass. Instead, the Surgeon began to notice quick detours in the footsteps toward a particular cabinet or other, almost as if the man was looking for something.

In another moment he had reached a Romanesque vault at the end of the forest of cabinets. A hanging tapestry with a fringe of gold brocade covered the archway beyond. He edged nearer, keeping his body once again behind a pillar, and parted the curtain with the gun barrel while shining his torch through the gap. Another room met his eye: larger, broader, filled with oaken cases fronted by glass. Pendergast's trail led right into the thick of them.

The Surgeon crept forward with infinite care. Again, Pendergast's tracks seemed to explore the collection, stopping at occasional cases. His tracks had begun to take on an irregular, weaving pattern. It was the spoor of a gravely wounded animal. The blood was not diminishing. If anything, the bleeding was getting worse. Almost certainly that meant a shot to the gut. There was no need to hurry, to force a confrontation. The longer he waited, the weaker Pendergast would become.

He reached a spot where a larger pool of blood shone in the beam of his flashlight. Clearly, Pendergast had stopped here. He had been looking at something, and the Surgeon peered into the case to see what it was. It wasn't more chemicals, as he had assumed. Instead, the case was filled with thousands of mounted insects, all exactly alike. It was an odd-looking bug with sharp horns on its iridescent head. He moved to the next case. Strange: this contained bottles housing only insect parts. Here were bottles filled with gossamer dragonfly wings, while over there were others with what looked like curled-up abdomens of honeybees. Yet others held innumerable tiny, dried-up white spiders. He moved to the next case. It contained desiccated salamanders and wrinkled frogs in a multitude of bright colors; a row of jars containing a variety of scorpion tails; other jars full of numberless evil-looking wasps. In the next case were jars holding small dried fish, snails, and other insects the Surgeon had never seen before. It was like some vast witch's cabinet for brewing potions and concocting spells.

It was quite strange that Leng had felt the need for such a vast collection of potions and chemicals. Perhaps, like Isaac Newton, he had ended up wasting his life in alchemical experiments. The "ultimate project" Pendergast mentioned might not be a red herring, after all. It could very well have been some useless attempt to turn lead into gold, or similar fool's challenge.

Pendergast's trail led out of the cabinets and through another arched doorway. The Surgeon followed, gun at the ready. Beyond lay what looked like a series of smaller rooms—closer to individual stone crypts or vaults, actually—each containing a collection of some kind. Pendergast's trail weaved back and forth between them. More oaken cabinets, filled with what looked like bark and leaves and dried flowers. He stopped a moment, staring around curiously.

Then he reminded himself that Pendergast was the pressing issue. Judging from the weaving tracks, the man was now having trouble walking.

Of course, knowing Pendergast, it could be a ruse. A new suspicion arose within him, and the Surgeon crouched beside the nearest scattering of crimson droplets, touching his fingers to one, rubbing them together. Then he tasted it. No doubt about it: human blood, and still warm. There could be no way of faking that. Pendergast was definitely wounded. Gravely wounded.

He stood up, raised the gun again, and moved stealthily forward, his flashlight probing the velvety darkness ahead.

SIX

NORA STEPPED WARILY THROUGH THE DOORWAY. AFTER THE darkness of the cell, the light was so bright that she shrank back into shadow, temporarily blinded. Then she came forward again.

As her eyes adjusted, objects began to take form. Metal tables, covered with gleaming instruments. An empty gurney. An open door, leading onto a descending staircase of rough-hewn stone. And a figure, strapped facedown onto a stainless steel operating table. Except the table was different from others she had seen. Gutters ran down its sides into a collecting chamber, full now with blood and fluid. It was the kind of table used for an autopsy, not an operation.

The head and torso of the figure, as well as the waist and legs, were covered by pale green sheets. Only the lower back remained exposed. As Nora came forward, she could see a ghastly wound: a red gash almost two feet long. Metal retractors had been set, spreading the edges of the wound apart. She could see the exposed spinal column, pale gray amidst the pinks and reds of exposed flesh. The wound had bled freely, red coagulating tributaries that had flowed down either side of the vertical cut, across the table, and into the metal gutters.

Nora knew, even without drawing back the sheet, that the body was Smithback's. She suppressed a cry.

She tried to steady herself, remembering what Pendergast had said. There were things that needed to be done. And the first was to verify that Smithback was dead.

She took a step forward, glancing quickly around the operating theater. An IV rack stood beside the table, its clear narrow tube snaking down and disappearing beneath the green sheets. Nearby was a large metal box on wheels, its panel festooned with tubes and dials—probably a ventilator. Several bloody scalpels sat in a metal basin. On a nearby surgical tray were forceps, sterile sponges, a squirt bottle of Betadine solution. Other instruments lay in a scatter on the gurney, where they had apparently been dropped when the surgery was interrupted.

She glanced at the head of the table, at the rack of machines monitoring the vital signs. She recognized an EKG screen, a ghostly line of green tracing a course from left to right. Tracing a heartbeat. *My God,* she thought suddenly, *is it possible Bill's still alive?*

Nora took a rapid step forward, reached over the gaping incision, and lifted the sheet away from his shoulders. Smithback's features came into view: the familiar tousled hair with the unrepentant cowlick, the skinny arms and shoulders, the curl of hair at the nape of his neck. She reached forward and touched his neck, felt the faint pulse of the carotid artery.

He *was* alive. But barely.

Had he been drugged? What should she do? How could she save him?

She realized she was hyperventilating, and struggled to

slow both her breathing and her thoughts. She scanned the machines, thinking back to the pre-med classes she'd taken in college; to the courses in gross anatomy, biological and forensic anthropology in graduate school; her brief experience as a hospital candy striper.

She quickly moved on to the next machine, trying to frame the overall situation. The machine was clearly a blood pressure monitor. She glanced at the systolic and diastolic readouts: 91 over 60. At least he had pressure as well as pulse. But it seemed low, too low. Beside it was another machine, connected to a line leading to a clip on Smithback's index finger. Nora's uncle had worn one of these when he'd been in the hospital a year before, suffering from congestive heart failure: it was a pulse-oximeter. It shone a light upon the fingernail, and measured the oxygen saturation of the blood. The readout was 80. Could that be right? She seemed to recall that anything less than 95 was cause for concern.

Nora looked back now at the EKG machine, at the pulse readout in its lower right corner. It stood at 125.

Abruptly, the blood pressure meter began bleating a warning.

She knelt toward Smithback, listening to his breathing. It was rapid and shallow, barely audible.

She straightened, gazing around at the machines with a moan of despair. God, she had to do *something*. She couldn't move him; that would mean certain death. Whatever she did, she would have to do it here and now. If she couldn't help him, Smithback would die.

She fought to control her panic, struggled with her memory. What did this all mean: low blood pressure; abnormally fast heart rate; low blood oxygen?

Exsanguination. She looked at the appalling pool of blood

in the collecting basin at the bottom of the table. Smithback was suffering from massive blood loss.

How did the body react in such cases? She thought back to the distant lectures she'd only half paid attention to. First, by tachycardia, as the heart beat faster in an attempt to profuse the tissues with oxygen. Next, by—what was the damn term?—vasospasm. She quickly stretched out a hand, felt Smithback's fingers. As she expected, they were ice cold, the skin mottled. The body had shut down blood to the extremities to maximize oxygen in the critical areas.

The blood pressure would be the last to go. And Smithback's was already dropping. After that . . .

She did not want to think about what would happen after that.

A wave of sickness passed over her. This was insane. She wasn't a doctor. Anything she did could easily make things worse.

She took a deep breath, staring at the raw wound, forcing herself to concentrate. Even if she knew how, closing and suturing the incision would not help: the blood loss was already too great. There was no plasma around for a blood transfusion, and had there been any, administering a transfusion was beyond her abilities.

But she knew that patients who had lost a lot of blood could be rehydrated with crystalloids or a saline solution.

She looked again at the IV rack beside the table. A thousand-cc bag of saline solution hung from it, tube drooping down from the metal stand and into the vein in Smithback's wrist. The stopcock had been shut off. A hypodermic syringe, half empty, dangled near the bottom, its needle inserted into the tube. She realized what it was: a local monitored anaesthetic, probably Versed, given as a drip because Versed doesn't last much more than five minutes. It would keep the victim conscious, but reduce any resistance, perhaps. Why hadn't the Surgeon used general, or spinal, anesthesia for the procedure?

It didn't matter. The point was to replace Smithback's fluids as quickly as possible, get his blood pressure up—and here were the means to do it.

She plucked the hypodermic from the IV tube and threw it across the room. Then, reaching for the stopcock at the base of the liter bag of saline, she turned it clockwise as far as it would go.

It isn't enough, she thought as she watched the solution drip rapidly through the tube. *It's not enough to replace the fluid volume. Oh, Jesus, what else can I do?*

But there seemed to be nothing else she could do.

She stepped back, helplessly, eyes darting once again to the machines. Smithback's pulse had risen to 140. Even more alarmingly, his blood pressure had dropped to 80 over 45.

She leaned toward the gurney, took Smithback's cold, still hand in hers.

"Damn you, Bill," she whispered, pressing his hand. "You've got to make it. You've *got* to."

She waited, motionless beneath the lights, her eyes fixed on the monitors.

SEVEN

In the stone chambers deep beneath 891 Riverside, the air smelled of dust, ancient fungus, and ammonia. Pendergast moved painfully through the darkness, lifting the hood from the lantern infrequently, as much to inspect Leng's cabinet as to get his bearings. He paused, breathing hard, at the center of a room full of glass jars and specimen trays. He listened intently. His hyperacute ears picked up the sound of Fairhaven's stealthy footsteps. They were at most one, perhaps two chambers away. There was so little time. He was gravely wounded, without a weapon, bleeding heavily. If he was to find any way to level the playing field, it would have to come from the cabinet itself. The only way to defeat Fairhaven was to understand Leng's ultimate project—to understand *why* Leng had been prolonging his life.

He uncovered the lantern again and examined the cabinet in front of him. The jars contained dried insects, shimmering with iridescence in the beam of light. The jar was labeled *Pseudopena velenatus,* which Pendergast recognized as the false featherwing beetle from the Mato Grosso swamps, a mildly poisonous insect natives used for medicine. In the row below, another series of jars contained the dried-up corpses of deadly Ugandan bog spiders in brilliant purples and yellows. Pendergast moved down the case, uncloaked the lantern again. Here were bottle after bottle of dried lizards: the harmless albino cave gekko from Costa Rica, a bottle full of dried saliva glands from the Gila monster of the Sonoran Desert, two jars full of the shriveled corpses of the tiny red-bellied lizard of Australia. Farther along were numberless cockroaches, from the giant Madagascar hissing cockroaches to beautiful green Cuban roaches, winking in their jars like tiny emerald leaves.

Pendergast realized these creatures had not been collected for taxonomic or classification purposes. One did not need a thousand bog spiders in order to do taxonomic studies—and drying insects was a poor way to preserve their biological details. And they were arranged in these cabinets in no conceivable taxonomic order.

There was only one answer: these insects had been collected because of the complex *chemical* compounds they contained. This was a collection of biologically active compounds, pure and simple. It was, in fact, a continuation of the inorganic chemical cabinets he had observed in the preceding rooms.

Pendergast now felt even more certain that this grand, subterranean cabinet of curiosities—this stupendous collection of chemicals—was directly related to Leng's real work. The collections here perfectly filled the hole he'd noticed in the collections displayed in the house above. This was Antoine Leng Pendergast's ultimate cabinet of curiosities.

In contrast to those other collections, however, this was clearly a *working* cabinet: many of the jars were only partially full, and some almost empty. Whatever Leng had been doing had required an enormous variety of chemical compounds. But what *had* he been doing? What was this grand project?

Pendergast covered the lantern again, trying to will the pain away long enough to think. According to his great-aunt, just before heading north to New York, Leng had talked of saving the human race. He remembered the word his great-aunt had used: *healing.* Leng would heal the world. This vast cabinet of chemicals and compounds was central to that project. It was something Leng believed would benefit humanity.

Pendergast felt a sudden spasm of pain that threatened to bend him double. With a supreme effort of will, he recovered. He *had* to keep going, to keep looking for the answer.

He moved out of the forest of cabinets, through an archway of hanging tapestries, into the next room. As he moved, he was racked by a second intense spasm of pain. He stopped, waiting for it to pass.

The trick he'd intended to play on Fairhaven—ducking through the secret panel without being shot—had required exquisite timing. During their encounter, Pendergast had watched Fairhaven's face intently. Almost without exception, people betrayed by their expression the moment they decided to kill, to pull the trigger, to end the life of another. But Fairhaven had given no such signal. He had pulled the trigger with a coolness that had taken Pendergast by surprise. The man had used Pendergast's own custom Colt. It was regarded as one of the most dependable and accurate .45 semiautomatics available, and Fairhaven clearly knew how to use it. If it hadn't been for the man's pause in breathing just before squeezing off the shot, Pendergast would have taken the bullet dead center and been killed instantly.

Instead, he had taken the bullet in his side. It had passed just below the left rib cage and penetrated into the peritoneal cavity. In as detached a way as possible, Pendergast once again considered the precise form and nature of the pain. The bullet had, at the very least, ruptured his spleen and perhaps perforated the splenetic flexure of the colon. It had missed the abdominal aorta—he would have bled to death otherwise—but it must have nicked either the left colic vein or some tributaries of the portal vein, because the blood loss was still grave. The law enforcement Black Talon slug had done extensive damage: the wound would prove fatal if not treated within a few hours. Worse, it was severely debilitating him, slowing him down. The pain was excruciating, but for the most part he could manage pain. He could not, however, manage the growing numbness that was enfeebling his limbs. His body, bruised from the recent fall and still not fully recovered from the knife wound, had no reserves to fall back on. He was fading fast.

Once again, motionless in the dark, Pendergast reviewed how his plans had miscarried; how he had miscalculated. From the beginning, he had known this would be the most difficult case of his career. But what he had not anticipated were his own psychological shortcomings. He had cared too much; the case had become too important to him. It had colored his judgment, crippled his objectivity. And now for the first time he realized that there was a possibility—indeed, a high probability—of failure. And failure meant not only his own death—which was inconsequential—but also the deaths of Nora, Smithback, and many other innocent people in the future.

Pendergast paused to explore the wound with his hand. The bleeding was growing worse. He slipped off his jacket and tied it as tightly as he could around his lower torso. Then he uncloaked the lantern and, once again, held it briefly aloft.

He was in a smaller room now, and he was surprised at

what he found. Instead of more chemical compounds, the tiny space was crowded with cases of birds, stuffed with cotton. *Migrating* birds. All arranged taxonomically. A superb collection, even including a suite of now-extinct passenger pigeons. But how did this collection fit with the rest? Pendergast felt staggered. He knew, deep down, that all this fit together, was part of some great plan. But what plan?

He stumbled on, jostling his wound as little as possible, into the next room. He lifted his light once again, and this time froze in utter astonishment.

Here was a collection entirely different from the others. The lantern revealed a bizarre aggregation of clothing and accessories, arrayed on dressmaker's dummies and in cases along both walls: rings, collars, hats, fountain pens, umbrellas, dresses, gloves, shoes, watches, necklaces, cravats—all carefully preserved and arranged as if in a museum, but this time with no apparent systemization. It seemed very unlike Leng, this haphazard collection from the past two thousand years, from all over the world. What did a nineteenth-century Parisian man's white kid glove have to do with a medieval gorget? And what did a pair of ancient Roman earrings have to do with an English umbrella, or to the Rolex watch sitting next to it, or to the flapper-era high-heeled shoes beside that? Pendergast moved painfully forward. Against the far wall, in another case, were door handles of all kinds—none holding the slightest aesthetic or artistic interest—beside a row of eighteenth-century men's powdered wigs.

Pendergast hid the lantern, pondering. It was an utterly bizarre collection of commonplace objects, none of them particularly distinguished, arranged without regard to period or category. Yet here they were, preserved in cases as if they were the most precious objects in the world.

As he stood in the dark, listening to the drip of his blood against the stone floor, Pendergast wondered for the first time if Leng had not, in the end, gone mad. This certainly seemed the last collection of a madman. Perhaps, as he prolonged his life, the brain had deteriorated even while the body had not. This grotesque collection made no sense.

Pendergast shook his head. Once again, he was reacting emotionally, allowing his judgment to be affected by feelings of familial guilt. Leng had not gone mad. No madman could have assembled the collections he had just passed through, perhaps the greatest collection of chemicals, inorganic and organic, the world had ever seen. The tawdry objects in this room *were* related. There was a systematic arrangement here, if only he could see it. The key to Leng's project was here. He *had* to understand what Leng was doing, and why. Otherwise . . .

Then he heard the scrape of a foot on stone, saw the beam of Fairhaven's flashlight lance over him. Suddenly, the small red dot of a laser appeared on the front of his shirt. He threw himself sideways just as the crash of the gun sounded in the confined space.

He felt the bullet strike his right elbow, a sledgehammer blow that knocked him off his feet. He lay on the ground for a moment, as the laser licked through the dusty air. Then he rolled to his feet and limped forward, ducking from case to case as he crossed the room.

He had allowed himself to become distracted by the strange collection; he had neglected to listen for Fairhaven's approach. Once again, he had failed. With this thought came the realization that, for the first time, he was about to lose.

He took another step forward, cradling his shattered elbow. The bullet seemed to have passed above the medial supracondlar ridge and exited near the coronoid process of the ulna. It would aggravate the blood loss, render him incapable of resistance. He *must* get to the next room. Each room had its own clues, and perhaps the next would reveal Leng's secret. But as he moved a wave of dizziness hit him, followed by a stab of nausea. He swayed, steadied himself.

Using the reflected light of Fairhaven's searching beam, he ducked beneath an archway into the next room. The exertion of the fall, the shock of the second bullet, had drained the last of his energy, and the heavy curtain of unconsciousness drew ever closer. He leaned back against the inside wall, breathing hard, eyes wide against the darkness.

The flashlight beam stabbed abruptly through the archway, then flicked away again. In its brief illumination, Pendergast saw the glitter of glass; rows of beakers and retorts; columnar distillation setups rising like city spires above long worktables.

He had penetrated Enoch Leng's secret lab.

EIGHT

NORA STOOD OVER THE METAL TABLE, HER GAZE MOVING
from the monitoring machines to Smithback's pallid form,
then back again. She had removed the retractors, cleaned and
dressed the wound as best she could. The bleeding had finally
stopped. But the damage was already done. The blood
pressure machine continued to sound its dire warning. She
glanced toward the saline bag: it was almost empty, but the
catheter was small, and even at maximum volume it would
be difficult to replenish lost fluids quickly enough.

She turned abruptly as the sound of a second shot echoed
up from the dark staircase. It sounded faint, muffled, as if
coming from deep underground.

For a moment she stood motionless, lanced by fear. What
had happened? Had Pendergast shot—or been shot?

Then she turned back toward Smithback's inert form.
Only one man was going to come up that staircase:
Pendergast, or the other. When the time came, she'd deal
with it. Right now, her responsibility lay with Smithback.
And she wasn't going to leave him.

She glanced back at the vitals: blood pressure down to 70
over 35; the heart rate slowing too, now, down to 80 beats per

minute. At first, this latter development sent relief coursing through her. But then another thought struck, and she raised her palm to Smithback's forehead. It was growing as cold as his limbs had been.

Bradycardia, she thought, as panic replaced the transitory feeling of relief. When blood loss is persistent, and there are no more areas for the body to shut down, the patient decompensates. The critical areas start to go. The heart slows. And then stops for good.

Hand still on Smithback's forehead, Nora turned her frantic gaze back to the EKG. It looked strangely diminished, the spikes smaller, the frequency slower. The pulse was now 50 beats per minute.

She dropped her hands to Smithback's shoulders, shook him roughly. "Bill!" she cried. "Bill, damn it, come on! *Please!*"

The peeping of the EKG grew erratic. Slowed.

There was nothing more she could do.

She stared at the monitors for a moment, a horrible feeling of powerlessness stealing over her. And then she closed her eyes and let her head sink onto Smithback's shoulder: bare, motionless, cold as a marble tomb.

NINE

PENDERGAST STUMBLED PAST THE LONG TABLES OF THE OLD laboratory. Another spasm of pain wracked his gut and he paused momentarily, mentally willing it to pass. Despite the severity of his wounds, he had so far managed to keep one corner of his mind clear, sharp, free of distraction. He tried to focus on that corner through the thickening fog of pain; tried to observe and understand what lay around him.

Titration and distillation apparatuses, beakers and retorts, burners; a vast thicket of glassware and metal. And yet, despite the extent of the equipment, there seemed to be few clues to the project Leng had been working on. Chemistry was chemistry, and you used the same tools and equipment, regardless of what chemicals you were synthesizing or isolating. There were a larger number of hoods and vintage glove boxes than Pendergast expected, implying that Leng had been handling poisons or radioactive substances in his laboratory. But even this merely corroborated what he had already surmised.

The only surprise had been the state of the laboratory. There was no mass spectrometer, no X-ray diffraction equipment, no electrophoresis apparatus, and certainly no

DNA sequencer. No computers, nothing that seemed to contain any integrated circuits. There was nothing to reflect the revolution in biochemistry technology that had occurred since the 1960s. Judging by the age of the equipment and its neglected condition, it looked, in fact, as if all work in the lab had ceased around fifty years before.

But that made no sense. Leng would certainly have availed himself of the latest scientific developments, the most modern equipment, to help him in his quest. And, until very recently, the man had been alive.

Could Leng have finished his project? If so, where was it? *What* was it? Was it somewhere in this vast basement? Or had he given up?

The flicker of Fairhaven's light was licking closer now, and Pendergast ceased speculating and forced himself onward. There was a door in the far wall, and he dragged himself toward it through an overwhelming wash of pain. If this was Leng's laboratory, there would be no more than one, perhaps two, final workrooms beyond. He felt an almost overpowering wave of dizziness. He had reached the point where he could barely walk. The endgame had arrived.

And still he didn't know.

Pendergast pushed the door ajar, took five steps into the next room. He uncloaked the lantern and tried to raise it to get his bearings, examine the room's contents, make one final attempt at resolving the mystery.

And then his legs buckled beneath him.

As he fell, the lantern crashed to the floor, rolling away, its light flickering crazily across the walls. And along the walls, a hundred edges of sharpened steel reflected the light back toward him.

TEN

THE SURGEON SHONE THE LIGHT HUNGRILY AROUND THE chamber as the echoes of the second shot died away. The beam illuminated moth-eaten clothing, ancient wooden display cases, motes of disturbed dust hanging in the air. He was certain he had hit Pendergast again.

The first shot, the gut shot, had been the more severe. It would be painful, debilitating, a wound that would grow steadily worse. The last kind of wound you wanted when you were trying to escape. The second shot had hit a limb—an arm, no doubt, given that the FBI agent could still walk. Exceedingly painful, and with luck it might have nicked the basilic vein, adding to Pendergast's loss of blood.

He stopped where Pendergast had fallen. There was a small spray of blood against a nearby cabinet, and a heavier smear where the agent had obviously rolled across the ground. He stepped back, glancing around with a feeling of contempt. It was another of Leng's absurd collections. The man had been a neurotic collector, and the basement was of a piece with the rest of the house. There would be no arcanum here, no philosopher's stone. Pendergast had obviously been trying to throw him off balance with that talk of Leng's ultimate purpose. What purpose could be more grand than the prolongation of the human life span? And if this ridiculous collection of umbrellas and walking sticks and wigs was an example of Leng's ultimate project, then it merely corroborated how unfit he was for his own discovery. Perhaps with the long, cloistered years had come madness. Although Leng had seemed quite sane when he'd first confronted him, six months before—as much as one could tell anything from such a silent, ascetic fellow—appearances meant nothing. One never knew what went on inside a man's head. But in the end, it made no difference. Clearly, the discovery was destined for *him*. Leng was only a vessel to bring this stupendous advancement across the years. Like John the Baptist, he had merely paved the way. The elixir was Fairhaven's destiny. God had placed it in his path. He would be Leng, as Leng should have been—perhaps *would* have been, had it not been for his weaknesses, his fatal flaws.

Once he had achieved success, he, Fairhaven, would not hole up like a recluse in this house to let the years roll endlessly by. Once the transformation was complete—once he had perfected the elixir, absorbed all Leng had to give into himself—he would emerge, like a butterfly from a pupa. He would put his long life to wonderful use: travel, love, learning, pleasure, exotic experiences. Money would never be a problem.

The Surgeon forced himself to put aside these reflections and once again take up Pendergast's irregular path. The footprints were growing smudged at the heels: the man was dragging his feet along the ground. Of course, Pendergast could be faking the gravity of his wound, but Fairhaven sensed he wasn't. One couldn't fake that heavy loss of blood. And the man couldn't fake that he had been hit—not once, but twice.

Following the trail of blood, he crept through the archway in the far wall and entered the next room. His flashlight revealed what looked like an ancient laboratory: long tables set up with all manner of strange glassware, racked into fantastic shapes, tubes and coils and retorts mounting almost to the ceiling of undressed rock. It was old and dusty, the test tubes caked with rust-colored deposits. Leng clearly hadn't used the place in years. On the nearest table, one of the racks had rusted through, causing glassware to fall and shatter into pieces on the dark woodwork.

Pendergast's ragged steps went straight through this lab, without stopping, to a door on the far side. Fairhaven followed more quickly now, gun raised, steady pressure on the trigger. *It's time,* he thought to himself as he approached the door. *Time to finish this.*

And as he moved eagerly ahead into the next room, Pendergast's weapon pointing the way, he was unaware of the small pair of eyes that watched him from the darkness behind a wall tapestry: eyes that, somehow, managed to appear both young and very old at the same time.

ELEVEN

As HE ENTERED THE ROOM, FAIRHAVEN IMMEDIATELY SAW Pendergast: on his knees, head drooping, in a widening pool of blood. There was to be no more hiding, no more evading, no more clever dissembling.

The man reminded Fairhaven of the way an animal died when gut-shot. It didn't instantly keel over dead. Instead, it happened in stages. First, the animal stood there, shocked, trembling slightly. Then it slowly kneeled, holding the position for a minute or more, as if praying. Then its rear legs collapsed into a sitting position. And there it might remain for several minutes before suddenly rolling onto its side. The slow-motion ballet always ended with a spasm, that violent jerk of the legs at the moment of death.

Pendergast was in the second stage. He could survive as much as a few more hours—helpless as a baby, of course. But he wasn't going to live that long. The chase had been diverting, but pressing business remained upstairs. Smithback was spoiled by now, but the girl was waiting.

The Surgeon approached Pendergast, gun hand extended, allowing himself to briefly savor the triumph. The clever, the diabolically cunning Special Agent Pendergast lay before him: stuporous, unresisting. Then he stepped back to give himself room for the final shot and, without much curiosity, raised his light to illuminate the room. He wouldn't want to spoil anything with his bullet, on the remote chance this room contained anything useful.

He was amazed at what he saw. Yet another bizarre collection of Leng's. Only this one was different. This was all weapons and armor. Swords, daggers, crossbows and bolts, harquebuses, lances, arrows, maces were mixed higgledy-piggledy with more modern guns, rifles, blackjacks, grenades, and rocket launchers. There were also medieval suits of armor, iron helmets, chain-mail, Crimean, Spanish-American, and World War I army helmets; early bulletproof vests and stacks of ammunition—a veritable arsenal, dating from Roman times to the early twentieth century.

The Surgeon shook his head. The irony was incredible. If Pendergast had been able to get here a few minutes earlier, in better condition, he could have armed himself with enough firepower to fight off a battalion. The contest might have gone very differently. But as it was, he'd spent too much time browsing the earlier collections. He'd arrived here a little too late. Now he lay there in his own blood, half dead, lantern near his feet. Fairhaven barked a laugh, his voice ringing off the vaults, and raised the gun.

The sound of laughter seemed to rouse the agent, who looked up at him, eyes glassy. "All I ask is that you make it quick," he said.

Don't let him speak, the voice said. *Just kill him.*

Fairhaven aimed the gun, placing Pendergast's head squarely before the center dot of the tritium sights. A solid hit with a hollow-point bullet would effectively decapitate the FBI agent. It would be about as quick as you could get. His finger tightened on the trigger.

And then something occurred to him.

Quick was a lot more than Pendergast deserved. The man had caused him a lot of grief. Pendergast had dogged his trail; ruined his latest specimen; brought him anxiety and suffering at the very moment of triumph.

As he stood over the agent, he felt a hatred rise within him; the hatred he had felt for the other one, Leng, who had looked so similar. The hatred he had felt for the trustees and professors of his medical school, who had refused to share his vision. Hatred for the pettiness and small-mindedness that kept people like him from achieving their true greatness.

So Pendergast wanted it quick? Not with this arsenal at his disposal.

He walked over to Pendergast and once again searched the unresisting man carefully, recoiling a little from the warm sticky blood that soaked his side. Nothing. The man had not been able to slip a weapon from the surrounding walls. In fact, he could see that Pendergast's faltering footsteps led directly to the center of the room, where he had collapsed. But it would do to be careful. Pendergast, even in this pathetic state, was dangerous. If he tried to talk, it would be best to just shoot him. Words, in the mouth of this man, were subtle and pernicious.

He looked around again, more carefully this time. There was every weapon imaginable on the walls. He had read histories of some of them, studied others in museums. The choice would prove amusing.

The word *fun* came to mind.

Always keeping Pendergast in his field of vision, Fairhaven shone his light around, finally selecting a bejeweled sword. He plucked it from the wall, hefted it, turned it around in the beam of the flashlight. It would have served his purpose, except it was rather heavy, and the blade was so rusty it looked as if it wouldn't cut butter. Besides, the handle was sticky and unpleasant. He hung it back up on the shelf, wiping his hands on his surgical cloth.

Pendergast was still sitting, watching him with pale, cloudy eyes. Fairhaven grinned. "Got any preferences?"

There was no reply, but Fairhaven could see a look of profound distress cross the agent's face.

"That's right, Agent Pendergast. 'Quick' is no longer in the cards."

A slight, terrified widening of the eyes was Pendergast's only response. It was enough. The Surgeon felt a swell of satisfaction.

He moved along the collections, picked up a dagger with a handle of gold and silver, turned it over, laid it down. Next to it was a helmet shaped like a man's head, with spikes inside that you could screw closed, driving the spikes bit by bit through the skull. Too primitive, too messy. Hanging on the wall nearby was an oversized leather funnel. He'd heard of this: the torturer would jam it into the victim's mouth, then pour water down the victim's throat until the poor wretch either drowned or exploded. Exotic, but too time-consuming. Nearby was a large wheel on which people could be broken—too much trouble. A cat-o'-nine tails, studded with iron hooks. He hefted it, lashed it overhead, laid it back down, again wiping his hands. The stuff was filthy. All this junk had probably been hanging around in Leng's dingy subbasement for more than a century.

There had to be something here that would be suitable for his needs. And then his eye fell on an executioner's axe.

"What do you know?" said Fairhaven, his smile broadening. "Perhaps you'll get your wish, after all."

He plucked the axe from its mounting hooks and gave it

a few swings. The wooden shaft was almost five feet long, fitted with several rows of dull brass nails. It was heavy, but well balanced and sharp as a razor. It made a whistling noise as it cut through the air. Sitting below the axe was the second part of the executioner's outfit: a tree stump, well worn and covered with a dark patina. A semicircle had been hollowed from it, clearly intended to receive the neck. It had been well used, as many chop marks attested. He set down the axe, rolled the block over to Pendergast, tipped it flat, positioned the block in front of the agent.

Suddenly, Pendergast resisted, struggling feebly, and the Surgeon gave him a brutal kick in the side. Pendergast went rigid with pain, then abruptly fell limp. The Surgeon had a brief, unpleasant sensation of déjà vu, remembering how he had pushed Leng just a little too hard and ended up with a corpse. But no: Pendergast was still conscious. His eyes, though clouded with pain, remained open. He would be present and conscious when the axe fell. He knew what was coming. That was important to the Surgeon: very important.

And now another thought occurred to him. He recalled how, when Anne Boleyn was to be put to death, she'd sent for a French executioner, skilled in the art of decapitating with a sword. It was a cleaner, quicker, surer death than an axe. She had knelt, head erect, with no unseemly block. And she had tipped the man well.

The Surgeon hefted the axe in his hands. It seemed heavy, heavier than it had before. But surely he could swing it true. It would be an interesting challenge to do without the block.

He shoved the block away with his foot. Pendergast was already kneeling as if he had arranged himself in position, hands limp at his sides, head drooping, helpless and resigned.

"Your struggles cost you that quick death you asked for," he said. "But I'm sure we'll have it off in—oh—no more than two or three strokes. Either way, you're about to experience something I've always wondered about. After the head goes rolling off, how long does the body remain conscious? Do you see the world spinning around as your head falls into the basket of sawdust? When the executioner raised the heads in Tower Yard, crying out 'Behold the head of a traitor!,' the eyes and lips continued to move. Did they actually *see* their own headless corpse?"

He gave the axe a practice swing. Why was it so heavy? And yet he was enjoying drawing out this moment. "Did you know that Charlotte Corday, who was guillotined for assassinating Marat during the French Revolution, blushed after the assistant executioner slapped her severed head before the assembled crowd? Or how about the pirate captain who was caught and sentenced to death? They lined up his men in a row. And they told him that after he was beheaded, whichever men he managed to walk past would be reprieved. So they cut off his head as he stood, and wouldn't you know it, but that headless captain began to walk along the row of men, one step at a time. The executioner was so upset that he wouldn't have any more victims that he stuck out his foot and tripped the captain."

With this the Surgeon roared with laughter. Pendergast did not join in.

"Ah well," Fairhaven said. "I guess I'll never know how long consciousness lasts after one has lost one's head. But *you* will. Shortly."

He raised the axe over his right shoulder, like a bat, and took careful aim.

"Give my regards to your great-grand-uncle," he said, as he tensed his muscles to deliver the stroke.

TWELVE

NORA PILLOWED HER HEAD ON SMITHBACK'S SHOULDER, tears seeping through her closed eyelids. She felt weak with despair. She had done all she could—and yet, all she could was not enough.

And then, through the fog of grief, she realized something: the beeping of the EKG had steadied.

She quickly raised her head, glanced at the monitors. Blood pressure had stabilized, and the pulse had risen slightly, to 60 beats per minute.

She stood in the chill room, trembling. In the end, the saline solution had made the crucial difference. *Thank you. Thank you.*

Smithback was still alive. But he was far from out of the woods. If she didn't further replenish his fluid volume, he'd slip into shock.

The saline bag was empty. She glanced around the room, spotted a small refrigerator, opened it. Inside were half a dozen liter bags of similar solution, feeder lines wrapped around them. She pulled one out, detached the old line from the catheter, removed the empty bag from the IV rack and tossed it aside, then hung the new bag and attached its line.

She watched the fluid dribble rapidly down the clear tube. Throughout, Smithback's vital signs remained weak but stable. With any luck, he'd make it—if she could get him out of here and to a hospital.

She examined the gurney. It was on wheels, but detachable. There were straps. If she could find a way out of the basement, she just might be able to drag the gurney up a flight of stairs. It was worth a try.

She searched through the nearby cabinets, pulled out half a dozen green surgical sheets, and covered Smithback with them. She plucked a medical light from one of the cabinets, slipped it into her pocket. She gave another glance at the monitors at the head of the operating table, another look into the dark opening that led down into darkness. It was from there that the sound of the second shot had come. But the way out of the house lay up, not down. She hated to leave Smithback, if only for a moment, but it was vital he get real medical attention as soon as possible.

She pulled the flashlight from her pocket and, crossing the room, stepped through the doorway into the stone corridor beyond.

It was the work of five minutes to explore the basement, a warren of narrow passages and small damp rooms, all of the same undressed stone. The passages were low and dark, and she lost her way more than once. She found the crashed elevator—and, tragically, the corpse of O'Shaughnessy—but the elevator was inoperable, and there was no way up the shaft. Ultimately, she found a massive iron door, banded and riveted, which clearly led upstairs. It was locked. *Pendergast,* she thought, *might be able to pick the lock—but then Pendergast wasn't here.*

At last she returned to the operating room, chilled and

despondent. If there was another way out of the basement, it was too well hidden for her to find. They were locked in.

She approached the unconscious Smithback and caressed his brown hair. Once again, her eye fell on the opening in the wall that gave onto a descending staircase. It was pitch black, silent. She realized it had been silent for what seemed a long time, ever since the second shot. *What could have happened?* she wondered. *Could Pendergast . . .*

"Nora?"

Smithback's voice was barely a whisper. She glanced down quickly. His eyes were open, his pale face tight with pain.

"Bill!" she cried, grabbing his hands. "Thank God."

"This is getting old," he murmured.

At first, she thought he was delirious. "What?"

"Getting hurt, waking up to find you ministering to me. The same thing happened in Utah, remember? Once was enough." He tried to smile, but his face contorted in agony.

"Bill, don't talk," she said, stroking his cheek. "You're going to be okay. We're going to get you out of here. I'll find a—"

But—mercifully—he had already slipped back into unconsciousness.

She glanced at the vitals and felt a huge rush of relief. They had improved—slightly. The saline bag continued to deliver critical fluid.

And then she heard the scream.

It came up from the dark stairs, faint and muffled. Nevertheless it was the most frightening, bone-chilling sound she had ever heard. It started at a high, tearing pitch: shrill, inhuman. It remained at a piercing high for what seemed at least a minute, then began wavering, ululating, before dropping into a gasping, slobbering growl. And then there was the distant clang of metal against stone.

And then, silence once again.

She stared at the opening in the wall, mind racing through the possibilities. What had happened? Was Pendergast dead? His opponent? Were they *both* dead?

If Pendergast was hurt, she had to help him. He'd be able to pick the lock on the iron door, or find some other way for them to get Smithback out of this hell-hole. On the other hand—if the Surgeon was still alive, and Pendergast dead— she'd have to face him sooner or later anyway. It might as well be sooner: and on her own terms. She was damned if she was going to wait up here, a sitting duck, for the Surgeon to return and pick her off—and then finish the job on Smithback.

She plucked a large-bladed scalpel from the surgical stand. Then—holding the light in one hand and the scalpel in the other—she approached the doorway that led down into the subbasement.

The narrow stone panel, swung to one side, had been perfectly disguised to look part of the wall. Beyond was a pool of blackness. Shining the beam ahead of her, she began descending, slowly and silently.

Reaching the last turn at the bottom, she turned off the light and waited, heart beating rapidly, wondering what to do. If she shone her light around, it might betray her presence, give the Surgeon—if he was waiting out there in the darkness—a perfect target. But with the light off, she simply could not proceed.

The light was a risk she'd have to take. She snapped it back on, stepped out of the stairwell, then gasped involuntarily.

She was in a long, narrow room, crowded floor to ceiling

with bottles. Her powerful beam, lancing through the endless rows, cast myriad glittering colors about the room, making her feel as if she was somehow inside a window of stained glass.

More collections. What could all this mean?

But there was no time to pause, no time to wonder. Two sets of footprints led on into the darkness ahead. And there was blood on the dusty floor.

She moved through the room as quickly as she could, beneath an archway and into another room filled with more bottles. The trail of footsteps continued on. At the end of this room was another archway, covered by a fringed tapestry.

She turned off her light and advanced toward it. There she waited, in the pitch black, listening. There was no sound. With infinite care, she drew back the tapestry and peered into the darkness. She could see nothing. The room beyond seemed empty, but there was no way to be sure: she would simply have to take a chance. She took a deep breath, switched on her light.

The beam illuminated a larger room, filled with wooden display cases. She hurried ahead, sidestepping from case to case, to an archway in the far wall that led on into a series of smaller vaults. She ducked into the nearest and turned off her light again, listening for any sound that might indicate that her presence had been noticed. Nothing. Turning on the light again, she moved forward, into a room whose cases were filled with frogs and lizards, snakes and roaches, spiders of infinite shapes and colors. *Was there no end to Leng's cabinet?*

At the far end of the room, before another low archway that led into further darkness, she again crouched, turning off her light to listen for any noises that might be coming from the room beyond.

It was then she heard the sound.

It came to her faintly, echoing and distorted by its passage through intervening stone. Remote as it was, it instantly chilled her blood: a low, gibbering moan, rising and falling in a fiendish cadence.

She waited a moment, flesh crawling. For a moment, her muscles tensed for an involuntary retreat. But then, with a supreme effort, she steeled herself. Whatever lay beyond, she would have to confront it sooner or later. Pendergast might need her help.

She gathered up her courage, switched on her light, and sprinted forward. She ran past more rooms full of glass-fronted cases; through a chamber that seemed to contain old clothing; and then into an ancient laboratory, full of tubes and coils, dust-heavy machines festooned with dials and rusted switches. Here, between the lab tables, she pulled up abruptly, pausing to listen again.

There was another sound, much closer now, perhaps as close as the next room. It was the sound of something walking—*shambling*—toward her.

Almost without thinking, she threw herself beneath the nearest table, switching off her light.

Another sound came, hideously alien and yet unmistakably human. It started as a low chatter, a tattoo of rattling teeth, punctuated with a few gasps as if for breath. Then came a high keening, at the highest edge of audibility. Abruptly, the noise stopped. And then Nora heard, in the silence, the footsteps approach once again.

She remained hidden behind the table, immobilized by fear, as the shuffling drew closer in the pitch black. All of a sudden, the darkness was ripped apart by a terrible shriek. This was immediately followed by a coughing, retching sound and the splatter of fluid on stone. The echoes of the shriek died out slowly, ringing on through the stone chambers behind her.

Nora struggled to calm her pounding heart. Despite the unearthly sound, the thing that was approaching her was human. It *had* to be, she *had* to remember that. And if it was human, who could it be but Pendergast or the Surgeon? Nora felt it *had* to be the Surgeon. Perhaps he had been wounded by Pendergast. Or perhaps he was utterly insane.

She had one advantage: he didn't seem to know she was there. She could ambush him, kill him with the scalpel. If she could summon the courage.

She crouched behind the lab table, scalpel in one trembling hand and light in the other, waiting in the enfolding dark. The shambling seemed to have stopped. A minute, an eternity, of silence ticked by. Then she heard the unsteady footsteps resume. He was now in the room with her.

The footsteps were irregular, punctuated by frequent pauses. Another minute went by in which there was no movement; then, half a dozen jerky footsteps. And now she could hear breathing. Except it wasn't normal breathing, but a gasping, sucking sound, as if air were being drawn down through a wet hole.

There was a sudden explosion of noise as the person stumbled into a huge apparatus, bringing it to the ground with a massive crash of glass. The sound echoed and reechoed through the stone vaults.

Maintain, Nora said to herself. *Maintain.* If it's the Surgeon, Pendergast must have wounded him badly. But then, where was Pendergast? Why wasn't he pursuing?

The noises seemed to be less than twenty feet away now. She heard a scrabbling, a muttering and panting, and the tinkling of something shedding broken glass: he was getting up from his fall. There was a shuffling thump, and another.

Still he was coming, moving with excruciating slowness. And all the time came that *breathing:* stertorous, with a wet gurgle like air drawn through a leaky snorkel. Nothing Nora had ever heard in her life was quite so unnerving as the sound of that breathing.

Ten feet. Nora gripped the scalpel tighter as adrenaline coursed through her. She would turn on her light and lunge forward. Surprise would give her the advantage, especially if he was wounded.

There was a loud wet snoring sound, another heavy footfall; a gasp, the spastic stamp of a foot; silence; then the dragging of a limb. He was almost upon her. She crouched, tensing all her muscles, ready to blind the man with her light and strike a fatal blow.

Another step, another snuffle: and she acted. She switched on the light—but, instead of leaping with her scalpel, she froze, arm raised, knife edge glittering in the beam of light.

And then she screamed.

THIRTEEN

CUSTER STOOD ATOP THE GREAT FLIGHT OF STEPS RISING above Museum Drive, looking out over the sea of press with an indescribable feeling of satisfaction. To his left was the mayor of the City of New York, just arriving with a gaggle of aides; to his right, the commissioner of police. Just behind stood his two top detectives and his man, Noyes. It was an extraordinary assemblage. There were so many onlookers, they'd been forced to close Central Park West to traffic. Press helicopters hovered above them, cameras dangling, brilliant spotlights swiveling back and forth. The capture of the Surgeon, aka Roger C. Brisbane III—the Museum's respected general counsel and first vice president—had riveted the media's attention. The copycat killer who had terrorized the city hadn't been some crazy homeless man, living in Central Park on a piece of cardboard. It had instead been one of the pillars of Manhattan society, the smiling, cordial fixture at so many glittering fund-raisers and openings. Here was a man whose face and impeccably tailored figure were often seen in the society pages of *Avenue* and *Vanity Fair.* And now he stood revealed as one of New

York's most notorious serial killers. What a story. And he, Custer, had cracked the case single-handedly.

The mayor was conferring sotto voce with the commissioner and the Museum's director, Collopy, who had at last been tracked down to his own West End residence. Custer's gaze lingered on Collopy. The man had the gaunt, pinched look of a fire-and-brimstone preacher, and he wore clothes straight out of an old Bela Lugosi movie. The police had finally broken down his front door, suspecting foul play when they observed figures moving against the drawn shades. The scuttlebutt was that the police found him in a pink lace teddy, tied to his bed, with his wife and a second female dressed in dominatrix uniforms. Staring at the man, Custer refused to believe such a rumor. True, the man's somber clothes looked just a tad disheveled. Still, it was impossible to believe such a pillar of propriety could ever have donned a teddy. Wasn't it?

Now, Custer saw Mayor Montefiori's eyes dart toward him. They were talking about *him*. Although he maintained his stolid expression, arranging his face into a mask of duty and obedience, he was unable to prevent a flush of pleasure from suffusing his limbs.

Commissioner Rocker broke away from the mayor and Collopy and came over. To Custer's surprise, he did not look altogether happy.

"Captain."

"Yes, sir."

The commissioner stood there a moment, indecisive, face full of anxiety. Finally he leaned closer. "Are you sure?"

"Sure, sir?"

"Sure that it's Brisbane."

Custer felt a twinge of doubt, but quickly stepped down on it. The evidence was overwhelming.

"Yes, sir."

"Did he confess?"

"No, not confess—exactly—but he made a number of self-incriminating statements. I expect he'll confess when he's formally questioned. They always do. Serial killers, I mean. And we found incriminating evidence in his Museum office—"

"No mistake about it? Mr. Brisbane is a very prominent person."

"No mistake about it, sir."

Rocker scrutinized his face a moment longer. Custer stirred uneasily. He had been expecting congratulations, not the third degree.

Then the commissioner leaned still closer and lowered his voice to a slow, deliberate whisper. "Custer, all I can say is, *you'd better be right.*"

"I am right, sir."

The commissioner nodded, a look of guarded relief, still mixed with anxiety, settling on his face.

Now Custer stepped respectfully into the background, letting the mayor, his aides, Collopy, and the commissioner arrange themselves before the throngs of press. A feeling like electricity, an anticipatory tingling, filled the air.

The mayor raised his hand, and a hush fell on the crowd. Custer realized the man wasn't even permitting his aides to introduce him. He was going to handle this personally. With the election so near, he wasn't going to let even a crumb of glory escape.

"Ladies and gentlemen of the press," the mayor began. "We have made an arrest in the case of the serial killer popularly known as the Surgeon. The suspect taken into custody has been identified as Roger C. Brisbane III, first vice president and general counsel of the New York Museum of Natural History."

There was a collective gasp. Although everyone in the crowd already knew this, hearing it from the mayor made it official.

"Although it's important to state that Mr. Brisbane must naturally be presumed innocent at this time, the evidence against him is substantial."

There was a brief hush.

"As mayor, I made this case a top priority. All available resources were brought to bear. I therefore want to thank, first of all, the fine officers of the NYPD, Commissioner Rocker, and the men and women of the homicide division, for their tireless work on this difficult case. And I would especially like to single out Captain Sherwood Custer. As I understand it, Captain Custer not only headed the investigation, but personally solved the case. I am shocked, as many of you must be, at the most unusual twist this tragic case has taken. Many of us know Mr. Brisbane personally. Nevertheless, the commissioner has assured me in no uncertain terms that they have the right man, and I am satisfied to rely on his assurances."

He paused.

"Dr. Collopy of the Museum would like to say a few words."

Hearing this, Custer tensed. The director would no doubt put up a dogged defense of his own right-hand man; he'd question Custer's police work and investigative technique, make him look bad.

Collopy stood before the microphone, rigid and correct, his arms clasped behind his back. He spoke in cool, stately, and measured tones.

"First, I wish to add my thanks to the fine men and women of the New York Police Department, the commissioner, and the mayor, for their tireless work on this tragic case. This is a sad day for the Museum, and for me personally. I wish to extend my deepest apologies to the City of New York and to the families of the victims for the heinous actions of our trusted employee."

Custer listened with growing relief. Here, Brisbane's own boss was practically throwing him to the wolves. So much the better. And he felt a twinge of resentment at Commissioner Rocker's excessive concern about Brisbane, which, it seemed, even his own boss didn't share.

Collopy stepped back, and the mayor returned to the microphone. "I will now take questions," he said.

There was a roar, a rippling flurry of hands through the crowd. The mayor's spokesperson, Mary Hill, stepped forward to manage the questioning.

Custer looked toward the crowd. The unpleasant memory of Smithback's hangdog visage flitted across his mind, and he was glad not to see it among the sea of faces.

Mary Hill had called on someone, and Custer heard the shouted question. "Why did he do it? Was he really trying to prolong his life?"

The mayor shook his head. "I cannot speculate on motive at this time."

"This is a question for Captain Custer!" a voice shouted. "How did you know it was Brisbane? What was the smoking gun?"

Custer stepped forward, once again gathering his face into a mask of stolidity. "A derby hat, umbrella, and black suit," he said, significantly, and paused. "The so-called Surgeon, when he went out to stalk his victims, was seen to wear just such an outfit. I discovered the disguise myself in Mr. Brisbane's office."

"Did you find the murder weapon?"

"We are continuing to search the office, and we have

dispatched teams to search Mr. Brisbane's apartment and summer house on Long Island. The Long Island search," he added significantly, "will include cadaver-trained tracking dogs."

"What was the role of the FBI in this case?" a television reporter shouted.

"Nothing," the commissioner answered hastily. "There was no role. All the work was done by local law enforcement. An FBI agent did take an unofficial interest early on, but those leads led nowhere and as far as we know he has abandoned the case."

"Another question for Captain Custer, please! How does it feel, sir, to have cracked the biggest case since Son of Sam?"

It was that prepped-out weenie, Bryce Harriman. It was the question he had longed for someone to ask. Once again, the man had ridden to his rescue. It was beautiful how these things worked out.

Custer summoned up his most impassive monotone: "I was just doing my duty as a police officer. Nothing less, and nothing more."

Then he stood back and basked, poker-faced, in the endless flare of flashbulbs that ensued.

FOURTEEN

THE IMAGE THAT BURST INTO THE BEAM OF NORA'S LIGHT was so unexpected, so horrifying, that she instinctively scrambled backward, dropped the scalpel, and ran. Her only conscious desire was to put some distance between herself and the awful sight.

But at the door she stopped. The man—she had to think of him as that—was not following her. In fact, he seemed to be shuffling along as before, zombie-like, unaware of her presence. With a shaking hand she trained the light back on him.

The man's clothes hung from his frame in tatters, skin raked and scored and bleeding as if by frenzied scratching. The scalp was torn, skin hanging away in flaps from where it had apparently been ripped from the skull. Tufts of bloody hair remained clutched rigidly between the fingers of the right hand: a hand whose epithelial layers were sloughing away in parchment-like curls of tissue. The lips had swollen to a grotesque size, liver-colored bananas covered with whitish weals. A tongue, cracked and blackened, forced its way between them. A wet gargling came from deep inside the throat, and each effort to suck in or expel air caused the tongue to quiver. Through the gaps in the ragged shirt, Nora could see angry-looking chancres on the chest and abdomen, weeping clear fluid. Below the armpits were thick colonies of pustules like small red berries, some of which she saw— with a sickening sense of fast-motion photography—were swelling rapidly; even as she watched, one burst with a sickening pop, while more blistered and swelled to take its place.

But what horrified Nora most were the eyes. One was twice normal size, blood-engorged, protruding freakishly from the orbital socket. It jittered and darted about, roving wildly but seeing nothing. The other, in contrast, was dark and shriveled, motionless, sunken deep beneath the brow.

A fresh shudder of revulsion went through Nora. It must be some pathetic victim of the Surgeon. But what had happened to him? What dreadful torture had he undergone?

As she watched, spellbound with horror, the figure paused, and seemed to look at her for the first time. The head tilted up and the jittery eye paused and appeared to fix on her. She tensed, ready for flight. But the moment passed. The figure underwent a violent trembling from head to toe; then the head dropped down, and it once more resumed its quivering walk to nowhere.

She turned the light away from the obscene spectacle, feeling sick. Worse even than the loathsome sight was her sudden recognition. It had come to her in a flash, when the bloated eye had fixed on hers: *she knew this man.* As grotesquely malformed as it now was, she remembered seeing that distinctive face before, so powerful, so self-confident, emerging from the back of a limousine outside the Catherine Street digsite.

The shock nearly took her breath away. She looked with

horror at the figure's retreating back. What had the Surgeon done to him? Was there anything she could do to help?

Even as the thought came to her, she realized the man was far beyond help. She lowered the flashlight from the grotesque form as it shuffled slowly, aimlessly away from her, back toward a room beyond the lab.

She thrust the light forward. And then, in the edge of the flashlight's beam, she made out Pendergast.

He was in the next room, lying on his side, blood pooling on the ground below him. He looked dead. Nearby, a large, rusted axe lay on the floor. Beyond it was an upended executioner's block.

Suppressing a cry, she ran through the connecting archway and knelt before him. To her surprise, the FBI agent opened his eyes.

"What happened?" she cried. "Are you all right?"

Pendergast smiled weakly. "Never better, Dr. Kelly."

She flashed her light at the pool of blood, at the crimson stain that covered his shirtfront. "You've been hurt!"

Pendergast looked at her, his pale eyes cloudy. "Yes. I'm afraid I'll need your help."

"But what happened? Where's the Surgeon?"

Pendergast's eyes seem to clear a little. "Didn't you see him, ah, walk past?"

"What? The man covered with sores? Fairhaven? *He's the killer?"*

Pendergast nodded.

"Jesus! What happened to him?"

"Poisoned."

"How?"

"He picked up several of the objects in this room. Take care not to follow his example. Everything you see here is an experimental poison-delivery system. When he handled the various weapons, Fairhaven absorbed quite a cocktail of poisons through his skin: neurotoxins and other fast-acting systemics, no doubt."

He grasped her hand with his own, slippery with blood. "Smithback?"

"Alive."

"Thank God for that."

"Fairhaven had started to operate."

"I know. Is he stable?"

"Yes, but I don't know for how long. We've got to get him—and you—to a hospital right away."

Pendergast nodded. "There's an acquaintance of mine, a doctor, who can arrange everything."

"How are we going to get out of here?"

Pendergast's gun lay on the ground nearby, and he reached for it, grimacing a little. "Help me up, please. I need to get back to the operating room, to check on Smithback and stop my own bleeding."

She helped the agent to his feet. Pendergast stumbled a little, leaning heavily on her arm. "Shine your light on our friend a moment, if you please," he said.

The Fairhaven-thing was shuffling along one wall of the room. He ran into a large wooden cabinet, stopped, backed up, came forward again, as if unable to negotiate the obstacle. Pendergast gazed at the thing for a moment, then turned away.

"He's no longer a threat," he murmured. "Let's get back upstairs, as quickly as possible."

They retraced their steps back through the chambers of the subbasement, Pendergast stopping periodically to rest. Slowly, painfully, they mounted the stairs.

In the operating room, Smithback lay on the table, still unconscious. Nora scanned the monitors quickly: the vitals remained weak, but steady. The liter bag of saline was almost empty, and she replaced it with a third. Pendergast bent over the journalist, drew back the covers, and examined him. After a few moments, he stepped back.

"He'll survive," he said simply.

Nora felt a huge sense of relief.

"Now I'm going to need some help. Help me get my jacket and shirt off."

Nora untied the jacket around Pendergast's midsection, then helped him remove his shirt, exposing a ragged hole in his abdomen, thickly encrusted in blood. More blood was dripping from his shattered elbow.

"Roll that tray of surgical instruments this way," he said, gesturing with his good hand.

Nora rolled the tray over. She could not help but notice that his torso, although slender, was powerfully muscled.

"Grab those clamps over there, too, please." Pendergast swabbed the blood away from the abdominal wound, then irrigated it with Betadine.

"Don't you want something for the pain? I know there's some—"

"No time." Pendergast dropped the bloody gauze to the floor and angled the overhead light toward the wound in his abdomen. "I have to tie off these bleeders before I grow any weaker."

Nora watched him inspect the wound.

"Shine that light a little lower, would you? There, that's good. Now, if you'd hand me that clamp?"

Although Nora had a strong stomach, watching Pendergast probe his own abdomen made her feel distinctly queasy. After a moment he laid down the clamp, took up a scalpel, and made a short cut perpendicular to the wound.

"You're not going to operate on yourself, are you?"

Pendergast shook his head. "Just a quick-and-dirty effort to stop the bleeding. But I've got to reach this colic vein, which, with all my exertion, has unfortunately retracted." He made another little cut, and then probed into the wound with a large, tweezer-like instrument.

Nora winced, tried to think of something else. "How are we going to get out of here?" she asked again.

"Through the basement tunnels. My research on this area turned up the fact that a river brigand once lived along this stretch of Riverside. Based on the extent of the cellars below us, I feel certain now that this was his residence. Did you notice the superb view of the Hudson the house commanded?"

"No," Nora replied, swallowing. "Can't say I did."

"That's understandable, considering the North River Water Pollution Control Plant now blocks much of the view," Pendergast said as he fished a large vein out of the wound with the clamp. "But a hundred and fifty years ago, this house would have had a sweeping view of the lower Hudson. River pirates were fairly common in the early nineteenth century. They would slip out onto the river after dark to hijack moored ships or capture passengers for ransom." He paused while he examined the end of the vein. "Leng must have known this. A large subbasement was the first thing he wanted in a house. I believe we will find a way down to the river, via the subbasement. Hand me that absorbable suture, if you please? No, the larger one, the 4-0. Thank you."

Nora looked on, wincing inwardly, as Pendergast ligated the vein.

"Good," he said a few moments later, as he released the clamp and put the suture aside. "That vein was causing most of the bleeding. I can do nothing about my spleen, which has obviously been perforated, so I'll merely cauterize the smaller bleeders and close the wound. Would you hand me the electrocauterer, please? Yes, that's it."

Nora handed the device—a narrow blue pencil at the end of a wire, two buttons marked *cut* and *cauterize* on its side—to the FBI agent. Once again, he bent over his wound. There was a sharp crackling sound as he cauterized a vein. This was followed by another crackling noise—much longer this time—and a thin wisp of smoke rose into the air. Nora averted her eyes.

"What was Leng's ultimate project?" she asked.

Pendergast did not respond immediately. "Enoch Leng wanted to heal the human race," he said at last, still bent over the wound. "He wanted to save it."

For a moment, Nora wasn't sure she had heard correctly. "*Save* the human race? But he was killing people. Scores of people."

"So he was." Another crackling noise.

"Save it how?"

"By *eliminating* it."

Nora looked back at him.

"That was Leng's grand project: to rid the earth of humanity, to save mankind from itself, from its own unfitness. He was searching for the ultimate poison—hence those rooms full of chemicals, plants, poisonous insects and reptiles. Of course, I had plenty of tangential evidence before: the poisonous materials on the glass fragments you unearthed from Leng's old laboratory, for example. Or the Greek inscription on the escutcheon outside the house. Did you notice it?"

Nora nodded her head numbly.

"It's the final words of Socrates, spoken as he took the fatal poison. ὦ Κρίτων, τῷ Ἀσκληπιῷ ὀφείλομεν ἀλεκτρυόνα. ἀλλὰ ἀπόδοτε καὶ μὴ ἀμελήσητε. 'Crito, I owe a cock to Asclepius;

will you remember to pay the debt?' Yet another thing I should have realized sooner." He cauterized another vein. "But it wasn't until I saw the room full of weapons that I made the connection and realized the scope of his plans. Because creating the ultimate poison alone wasn't enough—he would also have to create a *delivery system*, a way to make it reach across the globe. That's when the more vexing, inexplicable parts of the cabinet—the clothing, weapons, migratory birds, windborne spores, and the rest—made sense to me. Among other things, while researching this delivery system, he had collected all manner of poisoned objects: clothing, weapons, accessories. And much of it was poisoned by himself—redundant experiments with all manner of poisons."

"My God," Nora said. "What a crazy scheme."

"It was an ambitious scheme, certainly. One he realized would take several lifetimes to complete. That was why he developed his, ah, method of life extension."

Pendergast put the electrocauterer carefully to one side. "I've seen no evidence here of any supplies for closing incisions," he said. "Clearly, Fairhaven had no need of them. If you'll hand me that gauze and the medical tape, I'll butterfly the wound until it can be properly attended to. Again, I'll need your assistance."

Nora handed him the requested items, then helped him close. "Did he succeed in finding the ultimate poison?" she asked.

"No. Based on the state of his laboratory, I would say he gave up around 1950."

"Why?"

"I don't know," Pendergast said as he taped gauze over the exit wound. The troubled look she'd noticed earlier returned. "It's very curious. It's a great mystery to me."

Dressing completed, Pendergast straightened up.

Following his instructions, Nora helped him make a sling for his injured arm using torn surgical sheets, then helped him into his shirt.

Pendergast turned once again to Smithback, examining his unconscious form, studying the monitors at the head of the table. He felt Smithback's pulse, examined the dressing Nora had made. After rummaging through the cabinet he brought out a syringe, and injected it into the saline tube.

"That should keep him comfortable until you can get out of here and alert my doctor," he said.

"Me?" Nora said.

"My dear Dr. Kelly, somebody has to keep watch over Smithback. We daren't move him ourselves. With my arm in a sling and a gunshot wound in my abdomen, I fear I'm in no condition to go anywhere, let alone row."

"I don't understand."

"You will, shortly. And now, please assist me back down these stairs."

With a final look at Smithback, Nora helped Pendergast back down the staircase and through the series of stone chambers, past the endless collections. Knowing their purpose made them seem even more dreadful.

At the laboratory, Nora slowed. She angled her light into the weapons room beyond, and saw Fairhaven, still motionless, sitting in the corner. Pendergast regarded him a moment, then moved to the heavy door in the far wall and eased it open. Beyond it lay another descending staircase, much cruder, seemingly fashioned out of a natural cavity in the earth.

"Where does this go?" Nora asked as she approached.

"Unless I'm mistaken, to the river."

They descended the staircase, the perfume of mold and heavy humidity rising to greet them. At the bottom, Nora's light revealed a stone quay, lapped by water, with a watery tunnel leading off into darkness. An ancient wooden boat lay upturned on the quay.

"The river pirate's lair," Pendergast said as Nora shone the light around. "This was how he snuck out to the Hudson to attack shipping. If the boat's still seaworthy, you can take it out into the river."

Nora angled the light toward the skiff.

"Can you row?" Pendergast inquired.

"I'm an expert."

"Good. I believe you'll find an abandoned marina a few blocks south of here. Get to a phone as quickly as possible, call 645-7884; that's the number of my chauffeur, Proctor. Explain to him what's happened. He'll come get you and arrange everything, including the doctor for Smithback and myself."

Nora turned over the rowboat and slid it into the water. It was old, loose-jointed, and leaky, but it appeared to be seaworthy.

"You'll take care of Bill while I'm gone?" she said.

Pendergast nodded, the reflected water rippling across his pale face.

She stepped gingerly into the boat.

Pendergast stepped forward. "Dr. Kelly," he said in a low voice. "There is something more I must tell you."

She looked up from the boat.

"The authorities *must not know about what is in this house.* Somewhere within these walls, I'm convinced, is the formula for the prolongation of human life. Do you understand?"

"I understand," Nora replied after a moment. She stared at him as the full import of what he was saying began to sink in. The secret to prolonged life: it still seemed incredible. Unbelievable.

"I must also admit to a more personal reason for secrecy. I do not wish to bring more infamy down on the Pendergast name."

"Leng was your ancestor."

"Yes. My great-grand-uncle."

Nora nodded as she fitted the oarlocks. It was an antique notion of family honor; but then, she already knew that Pendergast was a man out of his time.

"My doctor will evacuate Smithback to a private hospital upstate where they do not ask inconvenient questions. I will, of course, undergo surgery there myself. We need never mention our adventure to the authorities."

"I understand," she repeated.

"People will wonder what happened to Fairhaven. But I doubt very much the police will ever identify him as the Surgeon, or make the connection with 891 Riverside Drive."

"Then the Surgeon's murders will remain unsolved? A mystery?"

"Yes. But unsolved murders are always the most interesting, don't you think? Now, repeat the telephone number for me, please."

"Six four five-seven eight eight four."

"Excellent. Now please hurry, Dr. Kelly."

She pushed away from the quay, then turned back to look at Pendergast once again, her boat bobbing in the shallow water.

"One more question. How in the world did you escape from those chains? It seemed like magic."

In the dim light, she saw Pendergast's lips part in what appeared to be a smile. "It *was* magic."

"I don't understand."

"Magic and the Pendergast family are synonymous. There have been magicians in my lineage for ten generations. We've all dabbled in it. Antoine Leng Pendergast was no exception: in fact, he was one of the most talented in the family. Surely you noticed the stage apparatus in the refectory? Not to mention the false walls, secret panels, trapdoors? Without knowing it, Fairhaven bound his victims with Leng's trick cuffs. I recognized them right away: the American Guiteau handcuffs and Bean Prison leg-irons, fitted with a false rivet that any magician, once manacled, could remove with his fingers or teeth. To a person who knew the secret, they were about as secure as transparent tape."

And Pendergast began laughing softly, almost to himself.

Nora rowed away, the splashing of the oars distorted in the low, rocky cavern. In a few moments she came to a weed-choked opening between two rocks, just large enough to admit the boat. She pushed through and was suddenly on the broad expanse of the Hudson, the vast bulk of the North River plant rising above her, the great glittering arc of the George Washington Bridge looming farther to the north. Nora took a deep breath of the cool, fresh air. She could hardly believe they were still alive.

She glanced back at the opening through which she had just come. It looked like a tangle of weeds and some boulders leaning together—nothing more.

As she bent to the oars, the abandoned marina just coming into view against the distant gleaming towers of Midtown Manhattan, she thought she could still make out—borne on the midnight wind—the faint sound of Pendergast's laughter.

epilogue:
Arcanum

FALL HAD TURNED TO WINTER: ONE OF THOSE CRISP, SUNNY days of early December before the first snowfall, when the world seemed almost crystalline in its perfection. As Nora Kelly walked up Riverside Drive, holding hands with Bill Smithback, she looked out over the Hudson. Already, cakes of ice were drifting down from the upper reaches. The New Jersey Palisades were etched in stark sunlight, and the George Washington Bridge seemed to float above the river, silvery and weightless.

Nora and Smithback had found an apartment on West End Avenue in the Nineties. When Pendergast had contacted them and asked them to meet him at 891 Riverside Drive, they had decided to walk the two miles, taking advantage of the beautiful day.

For the first time since the hideous discovery on Catherine Street, Nora had felt a certain peace return to her life. Her work at the Museum was progressing well. All the carbon-14 dates on her Utah specimens had come back, and they were a gratifying confirmation of her theory regarding the Anasazi-Aztec connection. There had been a terrific housecleaning at the Museum, with a whole new administration put in place—

except Collopy, who had somehow come through it all with his reputation and prestige intact, if not enhanced. In fact, Collopy had offered Nora an important administrative post—which she had politely declined. The unfortunate Roger Brisbane had been released: the arrest warrant voided a day before the election, after Brisbane's lawyer provided airtight alibis for the time periods of all three copycat murders, and an angry judge pointed out there was no physical evidence linking the man to any crime. Now, Brisbane was suing the city for wrongful arrest. The papers were screaming that the Surgeon was still at large. The mayor had lost his reelection bid. Captain Custer had been busted all the way down to street cop.

There had been a flurry of newspaper stories about the sudden disappearance of Anthony Fairhaven, but the speculation had ended with an IRS raid on his company. After that, everyone assumed tax problems were the reason for his disappearance. Word was Fairhaven had been last spotted on a beach somewhere in the Netherlands Antilles, drinking daiquiris and reading the *Wall Street Journal.*

Smithback had spent two weeks at the Feversham Clinic, north of Cold Spring, where his wound had been sewn and dressed. It had healed surprisingly quickly. Pendergast had also spent several weeks recuperating at Feversham after a series of operations to his elbow and abdomen. Then he had disappeared, and neither Nora nor Smithback had heard from him. Until this mysterious summons.

"I still can't believe we're up here again," Smithback said as they walked northward.

"Come on, Bill. Aren't you curious to see what Pendergast wants?"

"Of course. I just don't see why it couldn't be someplace

else. Someplace comfortable. Like, say, the restaurant at the Carlyle."

"I'm sure we'll learn the reason."

"I'm sure we will. But if he offers me a Leng cocktail out of one of those mason jars, I'm leaving."

Now the old house appeared in the distance, up the Drive. Even in the bright sunlight it seemed somehow dark: sprawling, haunted, framed by bare trees, black upper windows staring westward like empty eye sockets.

As if at a single thought, Nora and Smithback paused.

"You know, just the sight of that old pile still scares the bejesus out of me," Smithback muttered. "I'll tell you, when Fairhaven had me laid out on that operating table, and I felt the knife slice into my—"

"Bill, *please,*" Nora pleaded. Smithback had grown fond of regaling her with gory details.

He drew his arm around her. He was wearing the blue Armani suit, but it hung a little loosely now, his gaunt frame thinner for the ordeal. His face was pale and drawn, but the old humor, the mischievous twinkle, had returned to his eyes.

They continued walking north, crossing 137th Street. There was the carriage entrance, still partially blocked by windblown piles of trash. Smithback stopped again, and Nora watched his eye travel up the facade of the building, toward a broken window on the second floor. For all his display of bravado, the writer's face paled for a moment. Then he stepped forward resolutely, following Nora under the porte-cochère, and they knocked.

A minute passed, then two. And then at last the door creaked open, and Pendergast stood before them. He was wearing heavy rubber gloves, and his elegant black suit was covered in plaster dust. Without a word of greeting he turned away, and they followed him through silent echoing passages toward the library. Portable halogen lamps were arrayed along the hallways, throwing cold white light onto the surfaces of the old house. Even with the light, however, Nora felt a shiver of fear as she retraced the corridors. The foul odor of decay was gone, replaced by a faint chemical wash. The interior was barely recognizable: panels had been taken off walls, drawers stood open, plumbing and gas lines exposed or removed, boards ripped from the floor. It looked as if the house had been torn apart in an unbelievably exhaustive search.

Within the library, all the sheets had been removed from the skeletons and mounted animals. The light was dimmer here, but Nora could see that half the shelves were empty, and the floor covered with carefully piled stacks of books. Pendergast threaded his way through them to the vast fireplace in the far wall, then—at last—turned back toward his two guests.

"Dr. Kelly," he said, nodding to her. "Mr. Smithback. I'm pleased to see you looking well."

"That Dr. Bloom of yours is as much an artist as he is a surgeon," Smithback replied, with strained heartiness. "I hope he takes Blue Cross. I have yet to see the bill."

Pendergast smiled thinly. A brief silence ensued.

"So why are we here, Mr. Pendergast?" Nora asked.

"You two have been through a terrible ordeal," Pendergast replied as he pulled off the heavy gloves. "More than anyone should ever have to endure. I feel in large part responsible."

"Hey, that's what bequests are for," Smithback replied.

"I've learned some things in the last several weeks. Far too many are already past help: Mary Greene, Doreen Hollander, Mandy Eklund, Reinhart Puck, Patrick O'Shaughnessy. But for you two, I thought perhaps hearing the real story—a story nobody else *must ever know*—might help exorcize the demons."

There was another brief pause.

"Go ahead," Smithback said, in an entirely different tone of voice.

Pendergast looked from Nora, to Smithback, then back again.

"From childhood, Fairhaven was obsessed with mortality. His older brother died at age sixteen of Hutchinson-Guilford syndrome."

"Little Arthur," Smithback said.

Pendergast looked at him curiously. "That's correct."

"Hutchinson-Guilford syndrome?" Nora asked. "Never heard of it."

"Also known as progeria. After a normal birth, children begin to age extremely rapidly. Height is stunted. Hair turns gray and then falls out, leaving prominent veins. There are usually no eyebrows or eyelashes, and the eyes grow too large for the skull. The skin turns brown and wrinkled. The long bones become decalcified. Basically, by adolescence the child has the body of an old man. They become susceptible to atherosclerosis, strokes, heart attacks. The last is what killed Arthur Fairhaven, when he was sixteen.

"His brother saw mortality compressed into five or six years of horror. He never got over it. We're all afraid of death, but for Anthony Fairhaven the fear became an obsession. He attended medical school, but after two years was forced to leave for certain unauthorized experiments he'd undertaken; I'm still looking into their exact nature. So by default he went into the family business of real estate. But health remained an obsession with him. He experimented with health foods, diets, vitamins and supplements, German spas, Finnish smoke saunas. Taking hope from the Christian promise of eternal life, he became intensely religious—but when his prayers were slow in being answered he began hedging his bets, supplementing his religious fervor with an equally profound and misplaced fervor for science, medicine, and natural history. He became a huge benefactor to several obscure research institutes, as well as to Columbia Medical School, the Smithsonian, and of course the New York Museum of Natural History. And he founded the Little Arthur Clinic, which in fact has done important work on rare diseases of children.

"We cannot be sure, exactly, when he first learned of Leng. He spent a lot of time digging around in the Museum Archives, following up some line of research or other. At some point, he came across information about Leng in the Museum's Archives. Whatever he found gave him two critical pieces of information: the nature of Leng's experiments, and the location of his first lab. Here was this man who claimed to have succeeded in extending his life. You can imagine how Fairhaven must have reacted. He had to find out what this man had done, and if he had really succeeded. Of course, this is why Puck had to die: he alone knew of Fairhaven's visits to the Archives. He alone knew what Fairhaven had been examining. This wasn't a problem until we found the Shottum letter: but then it became essential to remove Puck. Even a casual mention by Puck of Fairhaven's visits would have linked him directly to Leng. It would have made him suspect number one. By luring you down there, Dr. Kelly, Fairhaven figured he could kill two birds with one stone. You had proven yourself unusually dangerous and effective.

"But I get ahead of myself. After Fairhaven discovered Leng's work, he next wondered if Leng had succeeded—in other words, if Leng was still alive. So he began to track him down. When I myself started to hunt for Leng's whereabouts, I often had the sense someone had walked the trail before me in the not too distant past.

"Ultimately, Fairhaven discovered where Leng had once lived. He came to this house. Imagine his exultation when he found my great-grand-uncle still alive—when he realized that Leng had, in fact, *succeeded* in his attempt to prolong life. Leng had the very secret that Fairhaven so desperately wanted.

"Fairhaven tried to make Leng divulge his secret. As we know, Leng had abandoned his ultimate project. And I now know why. Studying the papers in his laboratory, I realized that Leng's work stopped abruptly around the first of March 1954. I wondered a long time about the significance of that date. And then I understood. That was the date of Castle Bravo."

"Castle Bravo?" Nora echoed.

"The first dry thermonuclear bomb, exploded at Bikini. It 'ran away' to fifteen megatons, and the fireball expanded to four miles in diameter. Leng was convinced that, with the invention of the thermonuclear bomb, the human race was destined to kill itself anyway, and far more efficiently than he ever could. The march of technology had solved his problem for him. So he gave up his search for the ultimate poison. He could grow old and die in peace, knowing it was only a matter of time before his dream of curing the earth of its human plague came true.

"So, by the time Fairhaven found him, Leng had not taken the elixir for many years—since March 1954, in fact. He had grown old. Perhaps he almost wanted to die. At any rate, he refused, even under brutal torture, to reveal his formula. Fairhaven pushed too hard and killed him.

"But there was still another chance for Fairhaven. There

was still Leng's old lab, where crucial information—both in the form of human remains, and especially in the form of Leng's journal—might be found. And Fairhaven knew where the lab was: underneath Shottum's Cabinet. Of course, the lot was now covered by apartment buildings. But Fairhaven was in the perfect position to buy the land and tear down the buildings, all in the name of urban renewal. Construction workers I've spoken to mentioned that Fairhaven was conspicuously present at the site while the foundation was being dug. He was the second man to enter the charnel pit, after the worker who originally found the bones had fled. No doubt he found Leng's notebook in there. Later, he was able to study the effects taken from the tunnel at his leisure. Including the bones—and that, no doubt, is why the marks on both the old corpses and the new were so similar.

"Now, Fairhaven had Leng's notebooks. He began trying to replicate Leng's experiments, hoping to retrace the path Leng had taken. But of course, his attempts were amateurish, with no real understanding of Leng's true work."

As Pendergast's narrative ceased, the old house settled into a profound silence.

"I can't believe it," Smithback said at last. "When I interviewed him, Fairhaven seemed so confident, so calm. So . . . so *sane*."

"Madness wears many disguises," Pendergast replied. "Fairhaven's obsession was deep, too deep and abiding to show itself openly. And one can reach the gates of hell just as easily by short steps as by large. Fairhaven seemed to think that the formula for longevity had always been destined for him. Having taken in Leng's life essence, he now began to believe that he was Leng—Leng *as he should have been*. He took on Leng's persona, his manner of dress. And the copycat killings began. But a different sort of copycat killing than the police ever imagined. Killings, by the way, that had nothing to do with your article, Mr. Smithback."

"Why did he try to kill you?" Smithback asked. "It was such a risk. I never understood that."

"Fairhaven was a man who thought far, far ahead. That was why he was so successful in business—and, of course, one reason why he was so frightened of death. When I succeeded in finding Mary Greene's address, he realized it was only a matter of time before I found Leng's. Whether I believed Leng was alive or dead didn't matter—he *knew* I would come to Leng's house, and then all his efforts would be ruined. It would expose the connection between the modern-day killer known as the Surgeon and the old killer named Leng. It was the same with Nora. She was hot on the trail; she'd been to visit McFadden's daughter; she had the archaeological expertise I lacked. Clearly, it was only a matter of time before we figured out where Leng lived. We couldn't be allowed to proceed."

"And O'Shaughnessy? Why kill him?"

Pendergast bowed his head. "I will never forgive myself for that. I sent O'Shaughnessy on what I believed was a safe errand, investigating New Amsterdam Chemists, where Leng had procured his chemicals many years ago. While there, it seems O'Shaughnessy had the luck to find some old journals, listing chemical purchases in the 1920s. I call it luck, but it turned out to be quite the opposite, I'm afraid. I didn't realize Fairhaven was on high alert, monitoring our every move. When he became aware that O'Shaughnessy not only knew where Leng bought his chemicals, but had managed to retrieve some old sales books—which might be extremely useful, and certainly dangerous in our hands—he had to kill him. Immediately."

"Poor Patrick," said Smithback. "What a terrible way to die."

"Terrible, terrible indeed," Pendergast murmured, the anguish all too clear on his face. "And the responsibility for it lies on my shoulders. It was the least I could do to see him given a proper Catholic burial and to provide his nearest relations with a modest legacy—anonymously, of course. He was a good man, and a fine officer."

Looking up at the rows of leather-bound books, at the worm-eaten tapestries and peeling wallpaper, Nora shivered.

"Oh, God," Smithback murmured at last, shaking his head. "And to think I can't publish any of this." Then he looked over at Pendergast. "So what happened to Fairhaven?"

"That which he feared most, death, came at last. In a nod to Poe, I walled up the poor wretch within a basement alcove. It would not do for his body to surface."

This was followed by a short silence.

"So what are you going to do with this house and all these collections?" Nora asked.

A wan smile played about Pendergast's lips. "Through a tortuous route of inheritance, this house and its contents have ended up in my possession. Someday, perhaps, some of these collections will find their way anonymously into the great museums of the world—but not for a very long time."

"And what's happened to the house? It's torn apart."

"That brings me to one final request I would make of you both."

"And that is—?"

"That you come with me."

They followed Pendergast down winding passageways to the door leading to the porte-cochère. Pendergast opened the door. Outside, Pendergast's Rolls was silently idling, jarring in this forlorn neighborhood.

"Where are we going?" Smithback asked.

"Gates of Heaven Cemetery."

The drive out of Manhattan, into the crisp winter hills of Westchester, took half an hour. During that time, Pendergast said nothing, sitting motionless, wrapped in his own thoughts. At last they passed through the dark metal gates and began climbing the gentle curve of a hill. Beyond lay another hill, and then another: a vast city of the dead, full of monuments and ponderous tombs. In time, the car stopped in a far corner of the cemetery, on a rise dotted with marble.

Pendergast got out, then led them along a manicured path to a fresh row of graves. They were long frozen mounds of earth, laid out in geometrical precision, without tombstones, flowers, or markings of any kind save a spike at each head. Aluminum frames were set into each spike, holding cardboard placards, and on each placard was written a number, streaked with moisture, already mildewed and faded.

They walked along the row of graves until they came to number 12. Pendergast stopped over it and remained there, head bowed, hands clasped as if praying. Beyond, the weak winter sun shone through the twisted branches of the oaks, and the hill fell away into mist.

"Where are we?" Smithback asked, looking around. "Whose graves are these?"

"This is where Fairhaven buried the thirty-six skeletons from Catherine Street. It was a very clever move. It takes a court order to get an exhumation, a long and difficult process. This was the next best thing to cremation, which of course he wasn't allowed to do, by law. He did not want *anyone* to have access to these skeletons."

Pendergast gestured. "This grave, number 12, is the final resting place of Mary Greene. Gone, but no longer forgotten." Pendergast reached into his pocket and removed a tattered piece of paper, folded into a small accordion. It trembled slightly in the breeze. He held it out, over the grave, almost as if it were an offering.

"What is that?" Smithback asked.

"The arcanum."

"The *what?*"

"Leng's formula for extending human life. Perfected. It no longer required the use of human donors. That is why he stopped killing in 1930."

In the sudden silence, Nora and Smithback exchanged glances.

"Leng eventually worked it out. It wasn't possible until the late twenties, when certain synthetic opiates and other biochemical assays became available to him. With this formula, he no longer had need of victims. Leng did not enjoy killing. He was a scientist; the killing was merely a regretful necessity. Unlike Fairhaven, who clearly took pleasure in it."

Smithback stared at the paper in disbelief. "You mean to tell me you're holding the formula for eternal life?"

"There is no such thing as 'eternal life,' Mr. Smithback. Not in this world, at least. This course of treatment would *extend* the human life span, by how much exactly I don't know. At least a hundred years, perhaps longer."

"Where did you find it?"

"It was hidden in the house. As I knew it would be. I knew Leng would not have destroyed it. He would have kept a single copy for himself." The look of internal conflict in

Pendergast's face seemed to grow stronger. "I *had* to find it. To let it fall into other hands would have been . . ." His voice trailed off.

"Have you looked at it?" Nora asked.

Pendergast nodded.

"And?"

"It involves fairly straightforward biochemistry, using chemicals obtainable at any good chemist's. It is an organic synthesis that any reasonably talented chemistry graduate student could perform in a well-equipped laboratory. But there's a trick involved, an original twist, which makes it unlikely it will be independently rediscovered—at least, not in the foreseeable future."

There was a silence. "What are you—what are we—going to do with it?" breathed Smithback.

As if in answer, there was a sharp rasping sound. A small flame now hovered over Pendergast's left hand: a slim gold lighter, burning yellow in the dim light. Without saying a word, he touched the flame to the end of the paper.

"Wait!" cried Smithback, lunging forward. Pendergast, holding the burning paper aloft, adroitly sidestepped his grab.

"What are you doing?" Smithback wheeled around. "For God's sake, give me that—"

The old, accordioned sheet was already half gone, black ash curling, breaking off, dropping to the frozen earth of the grave.

"Stop!" Smithback gasped, stepping forward again. "Think this out! You can't—"

"I *have* thought it out," Pendergast replied. "I've done nothing, these last six weeks of searching, *but* think it out. It was a member of the Pendergast family, to my everlasting shame, who brought this formula to light. So many died for it: so many Mary Greenes that history will never know. I, having uncovered it, must be the one to destroy it. Believe me: this is *the only way*. Nothing created out of such suffering can be allowed to exist."

The flame had crawled up to the final edge; Pendergast opened his fingers, and the unburned corner flared into ash on its way to the turned earth. Gently, Pendergast pressed it into Mary Greene's grave. When he stepped back, nothing remained but a black stain in the brown earth.

A brief, shocked silence followed.

Then Smithback put his head into his hands. "I can't believe it. Did you bring us here just to see that?"

Pendergast nodded.

"Why?"

"Because what I have just done was too important to do alone. It was an action that required witnesses—if only for the sake of history."

As Nora looked at Pendergast, she saw—behind the conflict still evident on his face—a bottomless sorrow, an exhaustion of spirit.

Smithback shook his head miserably. "Do you know what you've done? You've just destroyed the greatest medical advance ever made."

The FBI agent spoke again, his voice low now, almost a whisper. "Can't you see? This formula would have destroyed the world. *Leng already had the answer to his problem right in his hand.* Had he released this into the world, it would have been the end. He only lacked the objectivity to see it."

Smithback did not reply.

Pendergast glanced at the writer for a moment. Then he dropped his gaze to the grave. His shoulders seemed to droop.

Nora had been standing back, watching, listening, without saying a word. Suddenly, she spoke.

"I understand," she said. "I know how difficult that decision must have been. For what it's worth, I think you did the right thing."

As she spoke, Pendergast's eyes remained on the ground. Then, slowly, his gaze rose to meet her own. Perhaps it was her imagination, but the anguish in his face seemed to lessen almost imperceptibly at her words.

"Thank you, Nora," he said quietly.

Now Available in Hardcover

Douglas Preston and Lincoln Child

FEVER DREAM

At the old family manse in Louisiana, Special Agent Pendergast is putting to rest long-ignored reminders of his wife Helen's tragic death, only to make a dreadful discovery. Helen had been mauled by a large and vicious lion while they were big game hunting in Africa. But now Pendergast finds that her rifle—her only protection from the beast—had been deliberately loaded with blanks. Who could have wanted Helen dead . . . and why?

With Lt. Vincent D'Agosta's assistance, Pendergast embarks on a quest for justice. It is a journey that sends him deep into his murdered wife's past, where he is stunned by how much she kept hidden from him. Helen Pendergast had nursed a private obsession with the famed naturalist-painter John James Audubon, and spent years hunting for an infamous, long-lost painting of his known as the Black Frame.

In a night of shocking violence deep in the Louisiana bayou, Pendergast gains some answers to the riddle of his wife's death, but he is left with an even greater mystery: who was the woman he married?

Praise for Preston & Child

"Fans of cerebral action adventure novels know that . . . no one delivers the goods like the veteran writing team of Preston and Child." **—*Publishers Weekly* (Starred)**

"Douglas Preston and Lincoln Child use a well balanced plot, fascinating characters, and downright good writing . . . Aloysius Pendergast measures up to Sherlock Holmes."
—*Sacramento Book Review*

Dear Friend and Reader,

About a dozen times a year we send a short, entertaining note to a select group of our readers. We call it *The Pendergast File*. Each missive includes a surprise or shock: an outlandish bit of Pendergast history, a marvelous giveaway, a contest, hidden clues to buried treasure, upcoming book signings, snide comments about reviewers we dislike, and other amusing tidbits.

In short, *The Pendergast File* is not your ordinary "newsletter."

If you would like to sign up for *The Pendergast File*, please go to our website, **www.preston child.com**, and click on the sign-up button. You can opt out at any time.

With warm regards,

Doug & Linc

P.S.: We will never, under any circumstances, share your e-mail address or information.

More chilling suspense
in a thriller featuring
Special Agent Pendergast!

Please turn this page
for a preview of

STILL LIFE WITH CROWS

Available now in mass market

One

Medicine Creek, Kansas. Early August. Sunset.

The great sea of yellow corn stretches from horizon to horizon under an angry sky. When the wind rises the corn stirs and rustles as if alive, and when the wind dies down the corn falls silent. The heat wave is now in its third week, and dead air hovers over the corn in shimmering curtains.

One road cuts through the corn from north to south; another from east to west. Where the two roads cross lies the town. Sad gray buildings huddle together at the intersection, gradually thinning along both roads into separate houses, then scattered farms, and then nothing. A creek, edged by scraggly trees, wanders in from the northwest, loops lazily around the town, and disappears in the southeast. It is the only curved thing in this landscape of straight lines. To the northeast rises a cluster of mounds surrounded by trees.

A giant slaughterhouse stands south of the town, lost in the corn, its metal sides scoured by years of dust storms. The faint odor of blood and disinfectant drifts in a plume southward from the plant, riding the fitful currents of air. Beyond, just over the horizon, stand three gigantic grain silos, like a tall-masted ship lost at sea.

The temperature is exactly one hundred degrees. Heat lightning flickers silently along the distant northern horizon. The corn is seven feet high, the fat cobs clustered on the stalks. Harvest is two weeks away.

Twilight is falling over the landscape. The orange sky bleeds away into red. A handful of streetlights blink on in the town. A black-and-white police cruiser passes through the main street, heading east into the great nothingness of corn, its headlights stabbing into the rising darkness.

Some three miles ahead of the cruiser, a column of slow-circling turkey vultures rides a thermal above the corn. They wheel down, then rise up again, circling endlessly, uneasily, rising and falling in a regular cadence.

Sheriff Dent Hazen fiddled with the dashboard knobs and cursed at the tepid air that streamed from the vents. He felt the vent with the back of his hand but it wasn't getting any cooler: the AC had finally bit the dust. He muttered another imprecation and cranked down the window, tossing out his cigarette butt. Furnacelike air boiled in, and the cruiser filled with the smell of late-summer Kansas: earth, cornstalks. He could see the circling turkey buzzards rise and dip, rise and dip above the dying smear of sunset along the horizon. *One ugly motherfucker of a bird,* thought Hazen, and he glanced over at the long-barreled Winchester Defender lying on the seat beside him. With any luck, he'd get close enough to assist two or three of them into the next world.

He slowed and glanced once again at the dark birds silhouetted against the sky. *Why the hell aren't any of them landing?* Turning off the main road, he eased the cruiser onto one of the many rutted dirt lanes that cut their way through the thousand square miles of corn surrounding Medicine Creek. He moved forward, keeping a watch on the sky, until the birds were almost directly overhead. This was as close as he was going to get by car. From here, he'd have to walk.

He threw the cruiser into park and, more out of habit than necessity, snapped on the lightbar flashers. He eased his frame out of the cruiser and stood for a moment facing the wall of corn, drawing a rough hand across his stubbled chin. The rows went in the wrong direction and it was going to be a bitch getting through them. Just the thought of shouldering through all those rows made him weary, and for a moment he thought about putting the cruiser in reverse and getting the hell back to town. But it was too late for that now: the neighbor's call had already been logged. Old Wilma Lowry had nothing better to do but look out her window and report the location of dead animals. But this was his last call of the day, and a few extra hours on Friday evening at least guaranteed him a long, lazy, boozy Sunday fishing at Hamilton Lake State Park.

Hazen lit another cigarette, coughed, and scratched himself, looking at the dry ranks of corn. He wondered if it was somebody's cow who'd wandered into the corn and was now dead of bloat and greed. Since when was it a sheriff's responsibility to check on dead livestock? But he already knew the answer: ever since the livestock inspector retired. There was nobody to take his place and no longer a need for one. Every year there were fewer family farms, fewer livestock, fewer people. Most people only kept cows and horses for nostalgic reasons. The whole county was going to hell.

Realizing he'd put off the task long enough, Hazen sighed, hiked up his jangling service belt, slipped his flashlight out of its scabbard, shouldered the shotgun, and pushed his way into the corn.

Despite the lateness of the hour, the sultry air refused to lift. The beam of his light flashed through the cornstalks stretching before him like endless rows of prison bars. His nose filled with the smell of dry stalks, that peculiar rusty smell so familiar it was part of his very being. His feet crunched dry clods of earth, kicking up dust. It had been a wet spring, and until the heat wave kicked in a few weeks back the summer sun had been benevolent. The stalks were as high as Hazen could ever remember, at least a foot or more over his head. Amazing how fast the black earth could turn to dust without rain. Once, as a kid, he'd run into a cornfield to escape his older brother and gotten lost. For two hours. The disorientation he'd felt then came back to him now. Inside the corn rows, the air felt trapped: hot, fetid, itchy.

Hazen took a deep drag on the cigarette and continued forward, knocking the fat cobs aside with irritation. The field belonged to Buswell Agricon of Atlanta, and Sheriff Hazen could not have cared less if they lost a few ears because of his rough passage. Within two weeks Agricon's huge combine harvesters would appear on the horizon, mowing down the corn, each feeding half a dozen streams of kernels into their hoppers. The corn would be trucked to the cluster of huge grain silos just over the northern horizon and from there railed to feed lots from Nebraska to Missouri, to disappear down the throats of mindless castrated cattle, which would in turn be transformed into big fat marbled sirloins for rich assholes in New York and Tokyo. Or maybe this was one of those gasohol fields, where the corn wasn't eaten by man or even beast but burned up in the engines of cars instead. What a world.

Hazen bullied his way through row after row. Already his nose was running. He tossed his cigarette butt away, then realized he should probably have pinched it off first. Hell with it. A thousand acres of the damn corn could burn and Buswell Agricon wouldn't even notice. They should take care of their own fields, pick up their own dead animals. Of course, the executives had probably never set foot in a real cornfield in their lives.

Like almost everyone else in Medicine Creek, Hazen came from a farming family that no longer farmed. They had sold their land to companies like Buswell Agricon. The population of Medicine Creek had been dropping for more than half a century and the great industrial cornfields were now dotted with abandoned houses, their empty window frames staring like dead eyes over the billowy main of crops. But Hazen had stayed. Not that he liked Medicine Creek particularly; what he liked was wearing a uniform and being respected. He liked the town because he knew the town, every last person, every dark corner, every nasty secret. Truth was, he simply couldn't imagine himself anywhere else. He was as much a part of Medicine Creek as Medicine Creek was a part of him.

Hazen stopped suddenly. He swept his beam through the stalks ahead. The air, full of dust, now carried another smell: the perfume of decay. He glanced up. The buzzards were far above now, directly over his head. Another fifty yards and he would be there. The air was still, the silence complete. He unshouldered his shotgun and moved forward more cautiously.

The smell of decay drifted through the rows, sweeter by the moment. Now Hazen could make out a gap in the corn, a clearing directly ahead of him. Odd. The sky had flamed its red farewell and was now dark.

The sheriff raised his gun, eased off the safety with his thumb, and broke through the last corn row into the clearing. For a moment he looked around in wild incomprehension. And then, rather suddenly, he realized what it was he was looking at.

The gun went off when it hit the ground and the load of double-ought buckshot blew by Hazen's ear. But the sheriff barely noticed.

PAGE-TURNING THRILLS FROM
DOUGLAS PRESTON and LINCOLN CHILD

RIPTIDE (0-446-60-717-7)

For generations, treasure hunters have tried to unlock the deadly puzzle known as the Water Pit: a labyrinth of shafts and tunnels that honeycombs the heart of a small island off the coast of Maine. Reputed to be the hiding place of pirate treasure, the Water Pit possesses an inexplicable ability to kill those who venture into it, from professionals to innocent explorers. But now one man has made a startling discovery: The Water Pit is actually a carefully designed fortress, conceived for pirates by a renowned seventeenth-century architect who hid his plans in code. Unlocking the code will break the curse of the Water Pit. Or will it?

THUNDERHEAD (0-446-60-837-8)

On an abandoned Santa Fe ranch a young archaeologist finds a letter written sixteen years ago yet, mysteriously, mailed only recently. In it her father, long believed dead, hints at a lost city of gold that will make him famous—and rich. Now Nora Kelly is leading an expedition into a harsh, remote corner of Utah's canyon country. Searching for her father and his discovery, Nora begins to unravel one of archaeology's greatest mysteries . . .

THE ICE LIMIT (0-446-61-023-2)

On a desolate island off the coast of southern Chile, the largest known meteorite has been found, entombed in the earth for millions of years. In New York, a billionaire decides he must have this incredible find for himself, no matter what the cost. But from the beginning, people begin to die. Now a disgraced Chilean navy officer is out to stop the expedition, a brutal Pacific storm is raging toward them, and a frightening truth is beginning to unfold. The men and women of the *Rolvaag* are not taking this ancient, enigmatic object anywhere. It is taking them . . .

VISIT US ONLINE AT

WWW.HACHETTEBOOKGROUP.COM

FEATURES:

**OPENBOOK BROWSE AND
SEARCH EXCERPTS**

•

AUDIOBOOK EXCERPTS AND PODCASTS

•

AUTHOR ARTICLES AND INTERVIEWS

•

**BESTSELLER AND PUBLISHING
GROUP NEWS**

•

SIGN UP FOR E-NEWSLETTERS

•

**AUTHOR APPEARANCES AND TOUR
INFORMATION**

•

SOCIAL MEDIA FEEDS AND WIDGETS

•

DOWNLOAD FREE APPS

Bookmark Hachette Book Group
@ www.HachetteBookGroup.com